SAMARA'S
PERIL

SAMARA'S PERIL

ILYON CHRONICLES – BOOK THREE

JAYE L. KNIGHT

INK
DRAGON
PRESS

Samara's Peril
Ilyon Chronicles – Book 3
Copyright © 2016 by Jaye L. Knight
www.ilyonchronicles.com

Published by Ink Dragon Press

Ilyon Map © 2023 by Jaye L. Knight

Stonehelm Sketch by Mickayla

All Scriptures are taken from the New American Standard Bible, Copyright © 1960, 1962, 1963, 1968, 1971, 1972, 1973, 1975, 1977, 1995 by The Lockman Foundation. Used by permission. www.Lockman.org

To my King and Savior, who always loves and is always there even when things are at their bleakest, and we wrestle with doubt.

Ilyon

N

Samara

Amberin

Stonehelm

Sinnai Mts.

Arcacia

Graylin Valley

Sidian
Ocean

Dunlow

Fort Rhall

Kinnim

Valcre

Landale

Keaton

Ardakin Bay

Mernin
Fort River

Falspar

Troas

Arda

Graer Mts.

Arvael •

• Bel-gard

Andros Ford

Dorland

Wildmor

Krell Mts.

*"For God so loved the world, that He gave
His only begotten Son, that whoever believes in
Him shall not perish, but have eternal life."*
- John 3:16

-Part One-

Discovery

IT WAS A dream. Somehow, even in his semi-conscious state, Jace knew it, but the realness of it gripped him—the fear, the loss, the despair. Like lurking beasts waiting to devour, they stalked him. He tried to run, but how did you run from something that was inside you?

Jace bolted upright with a gasp, his heart battering his ribs. He ground his teeth together and curled his fists in his blanket. He couldn't deny it now—not after five nights in a row. The dreams had returned. Though not as violent as the nightmares he had suffered in the past, they left a growing darkness that weighed down his spirit. He drew in a breath and let it out in a long sigh as he hung his head. Why did they plague him again? He had let go of the uncertainties that fueled the dreams . . . hadn't he?

No.

He had buried them, deep down, but they remained—waiting for moments of weakness when they could climb out and torment him. No matter how hard he struggled to push them back down, sometimes he just wasn't strong enough to accomplish it.

Breathing deeply again, he glanced around the dim shelter. Kaden, Mick, Trev, and Holden lay still and quiet on their cots, but there would be no more sleep for him. Not today. Tyra watched him from the floor, seeming to sense his unease.

Jace slipped from his cot, cold invading his body the moment he was free of his blankets. He dressed quickly. Even in the shelter, his breath left a momentary white puff in the air, the fire in their small hearth dead. He tugged on a warm wool shirt and his coat before he headed to the door and stepped outside.

Dawn greeted him with a frozen world of gray and white, sprinkled here and there by bright green. Three inches of snow blanketed the forest—likely the last of the season. Spring had arrived and, after this final cold snap, the forest would come alive with greenery and wildlife. This promise of new life would be especially welcome after the losses they had suffered late last fall. Jace always craved the arrival of spring after the long winters; however, the last couple of years had brought a new challenge with it.

Tyra bounded off, her nose pressed into the snow, following the trails of rabbits and other rodents that had passed in the night. Jace shoved his hands into his pockets and followed slowly. The forest still lay shrouded in shadows, the rising sun mostly hidden by the lingering clouds. It was fitting weather for such a day, in his opinion, though maybe he shouldn't feel that way.

Several minutes later, boots crunched in the snow behind Jace. He looked over his shoulder. Holden strode up alongside him and stopped. "Couldn't sleep?"

Jace shook his head.

Holden blew out a breath that lingered in front of him. "Today is only my second time."

A rolling sensation in Jace's gut threatened to upturn his stomach. "Me too."

They stood in silence, contemplating. Did everyone else feel such disquiet when this day came? Did Holden's unrest cut as deeply as Jace's did? He wanted to ask, but hesitated to speak.

After a moment, Holden snapped Jace out of his thoughts.

"Want to help me start a fire and some coffee? We're gonna need it this morning."

Jace nodded, and they turned for the wood supply stacked along the edge of camp. Once they had a fire crackling in the pit, they hung two large coffee pots over the flames. For a long time they stood in silence, keeping warm at the edge of the fire. When the coffee was finished, they each poured a cup. The aroma soon drew the other men from their shelters.

They gathered around, but the usual jokes and good humor were absent as everyone spoke in hushed tones. Apparently, Jace wasn't the only one subdued this morning. His discomfort grew, and he backed away from the group. Though most of the men accepted him now—becoming friends even—it didn't fully erase his feelings of being an outsider. Today that isolation pressed in even stronger. He had dreaded this for weeks.

His gaze strayed to the forest beyond the edge of camp. How easy it would be to slip away until it was all over. The urge pulled at him, but something stronger held him there. He couldn't disappoint Rayad or Kyrin. Escape would be cowardly, for that's what it came down to—he was afraid. Afraid of facing the significance of the coming event and the uncertainty that already frayed at the thin thread holding him to his weak faith.

Dropping his gaze to the steaming dark liquid in his cup, he frowned. He knew what he should do. He should pray. Wasn't that what Rayad and Kyrin would tell him? But whenever he tried lately, the right words never seemed to come. Maybe the inability and reluctance to form a simple prayer pointed back to his fear again—fear of the words echoing hollowly in his heart, unheard by anyone but himself.

"Good morning, Jace."

His head snapped up, and he met Kyrin's inquisitive gaze. A sensation stirred inside his chest—a little up-tick of his heart—something that had been happening more and more often in recent months. It was a reaction he could never explain easily or sensibly. He quickly calmed it, forcing it behind all the fears and uncertainties that only reminded him of why he could never allow it to grow into anything more. He echoed Kyrin, but even his voice lacked the strength he intended to convey.

His gaze faltered, and he stared down at his coffee again. She could read him too easily. He could never hide his fear from her. When he finally looked up again, Kyrin still watched him, but her eyes were full of compassion. Some of his embarrassment eased as a gentle smile grew on her face. She was the only person he knew who had that sort of calming effect on him.

This calm helped carry him through the next hour as everyone shared breakfast quietly. However, Jace declined the food. It wouldn't have settled well in his bunched-up stomach, especially when it came time to leave camp. The tension increased, twisting his insides into an uncomfortable knot.

Everyone in camp who claimed belief in Elôm gathered near the stable. There, several of the men each gathered a small lamb that had been born in the last few weeks. The animals came out, each one pristine white like the snow that had fallen. Jace winced at their loud bleating that echoed through camp.

The group turned into the forest. No one spoke a word as they passed through the trees, leaving camp behind. Jace walked with his head down, but he took quick glances around him. Though everyone wore solemn expressions, did any of them feel as unworthy as he did? Perhaps Holden did, but at least he wasn't half ryrik.

A hand rested on his shoulder and broke him from these thoughts. Looking to his right, he found Rayad. The man's eyes held understanding, and he gave Jace's shoulder a squeeze. After all, they had done this together once before. Jace remembered it clearly. He'd had more confidence then, and had found some relief at the end, but he wasn't so sure now.

Things were different . . . things had happened. Things that had shaken his faith and left it weaker than it had once been.

A mile from camp, the group reached a clearing. In the center, a large pyre sat waiting. They stopped, and Jace felt his stomach heave up into his throat. He forced it down as everyone divided into smaller numbers, each group taking a lamb. Jace moved to the side with Rayad's group, along with Kyrin, her family, and Holden. They all turned to Timothy, who stood facing them.

His gaze swept the groups, and he cleared his throat, though his voice was low when he spoke. "Long ago, the Evil One came into Ilyon, deceiving and swaying the people to join together to try to overthrow Elôm's kingdom. Though Elôm ended the uprising, the rebellion changed our world. Evil taints all of us. It's inherent in our nature and stains us all."

Jace swallowed hard through his constricted throat. He stared at the ground, feeling the most stained of everyone. He was a filthy, wretched creature undeserving of any form of mercy.

"It separates us from our King, who is holy and pure, and it violates His perfect and undefiled standard of righteousness," Timothy continued. "Each one of us has sinned against Him, our Lord and Creator, and these sins will continue to creep into our lives until the day of our deaths. We are every bit rebels to our God as those who first turned on Him. As such, we deserve death and separation from Him forever."

A deep ache pulsed through Jace's chest from the hard thumping of his heart. His eyes stung. He deserved that death and separation, but it terrified him. His palms started to sweat despite the cold, and he clenched his fists.

"But . . ." the word hung in the frozen air with a tone of hope, "Elôm loves us and does not want us to perish in our sin. That is why we take part in this sacrifice. It is our blood that should be spilled, but with these lambs, Elôm has provided a

5

substitute. Innocent blood to cover us so that, when we place our trust in Him, our sin is covered and we may be looked upon as innocent. However, they are only lambs and we must continue to offer such sacrifices every year. They are a finite solution, but someday, Elôm will send us a Savior and an ultimate lamb sacrifice that will not just cover our sins, but remove them completely. Until then, we will continue to perform these sacrifices and look ahead to the day that it will no longer be necessary."

Following these words, each group turned their attention to its lamb. Rayad slipped a knife from his belt and tipped the lamb's head back, placing the sharp blade at its throat. Marcus held a shallow basin beneath it.

Jace squirmed. It was only a lamb, but it felt so much graver than that. The blade sliced flesh. Red poured down the lamb's neck, staining the white wool, and collected in a crimson pool in the basin. Jace watched the blood flow, wanting to look away, but unable to. *It should be yours*, his inner voice accused. *You're the one who deserves death.*

His heart gave an irregular beat, and he gasped in the air he had forgotten to breathe, but his lungs had trouble expanding. Guilt wrapped more tightly around his chest. He was so consumed by it that he almost missed Rayad coming around with the blood-filled basin. He looked to his left as Kyrin dipped her hands in, an action to signify the blood covering her sins. When she pulled them out, blood dripped into the snow at her feet—a glaring contrast. Her head was bowed, but Jace caught the moisture in her eyes and the sorrow in her expression; yet a glow of thankfulness joined it.

Rayad came to Jace next. Jace hesitated, the uncertainty coming on strong. Should he really be a part of this? Was such a sacrifice meant for those with ryrik blood? He met Rayad's eyes. In them he found assurance, and it prompted him to action, though it didn't dispel the doubts. He dipped his trembling hands into the basin. The warm blood oozed up around his fingers, coating his skin. When he pulled them out, he stared at the liquid dripping from his fingertips. At once, memories he desired to bury in the past poured into his mind to condemn him. Could a lamb's blood ever truly cover the many layers of shed blood he already had on his hands?

He squeezed his eyes shut and fought to close his mind to the bombardment, unsuccessfully. The accusations of his guilt were too skilled at tearing through his weak defenses, always leaving him exhausted from fighting them and leaving his heart in shreds. The suffocating touch of despair wormed in and left him struggling for a full breath as it tried to drag him back into the lonely black sea he had spent so much of his life floundering in.

Something nudged his arm. His eyes popped open, jolting him out of the increasingly dark thoughts. He looked to his left, right into Kyrin's face staring up at him. Her dusty blue eyes were wide with concern, but also with earnestness to help him in any way she could. He wasn't alone in his fight. Slowly his lungs freed up, and the tension loosened in his clenched jaw.

Now the group joined everyone else at the pyre, where they laid the slain lambs and the rest of the blood. A couple of the men stepped forward with flaming torches and lit the fuel. Standing around the perimeter, they all watched the sacrifices burn, the smoke drifting heavenward.

They stayed until the lambs and most of the wood had burned up before following their tracks back to camp. The return hike was just as quiet, as they still contemplated the sacrifice.

When they arrived at the edge of camp, Jace fell behind the others and veered off by himself, craving time alone. He walked until the sound of camp died away before he stopped and stared into the snowy forest landscape. Then he looked down at his hands. The blood had almost dried. Dropping to one knee, he scooped up a handful of snow and scrubbed it across his skin. The cold substance prickled and numbed his fingers.

He left behind a patch of red in the snow and settled down at the base of a wide oak, where he leaned his head back against the trunk. Though the intense emotions from the sacrifice had subsided, the persistent questions lingered, stemming from one all-important question: Did he really have a soul that belonged to Elôm? Kyrin and Rayad both insisted he did, but could he ever know for sure? He ached for the answer.

Two years ago, he had trusted Elôm fully and completely for the salvation of his soul—of that he was sure—but doubts had followed, leading back to the question of whether or not he even had a soul to save. For a while, he had propped his shaky faith up against Rayad's constant reassurance, but the death of Kalli and Aldor last spring had caused it all to crash down around him. In the last several months, Kyrin and Rayad had helped him begin to rebuild, but only a few stones were back in place, and those constantly wobbled, threatening to topple and force him to begin again.

Jace breathed out a sigh that ended with a groan. He wanted more than anything to have the same faith and assurance as his friends. He truly did. If only he knew for certain that he had a soul, but he didn't expect to know that until the moment his life ended. The fear of that moment clutched at his throat, and he dug his nails into his palms.

"Elôm." The prayer came out of desperation. "I . . ." He swallowed, shaking his head. "I don't know what to do. I don't know if You hear me or . . . if I am saved. Please, show me." His heart ached with the intensity of the plea. "*Please.*"

For a long time he sat, trying to decipher even the smallest stirring of assurance, but it only led to frustration and more doubt. If Elôm were a part of his life, why wouldn't He speak to him the way He seemed to speak to Rayad and Kyrin? Just once. Just to offer an answer.

The distant tread of light footsteps caught his attention. They were quieter than most. A second set of four-footed steps approached more quickly, and he looked up as Tyra bounded up to him. The wolf nosed his face, her tail wagging slowly as she made sure he was all right. She then stared at him, as if asking why he had wandered off without her. He rubbed the black fur around her neck in apology, and his gaze lifted to meet Kyrin. She too searched his face for signs that things were well. He was tempted to try to hide his struggle, but that was nearly impossible with her talent of observation.

Without a word, she nestled down into the snow next to him, using the same tree as a backrest. He glanced at her hands as she pulled the strap of a canteen from her shoulder and uncorked it. They were clean now. He looked at his own. Blood still stained the creases of his knuckles and around his nails. A fitting picture of his doubt.

Before he could go down that road again, Kyrin handed him the canteen. Steam rose from the opening.

"Coffee?"

Jace took it and brought it to his lips. The hot liquid trickled down his throat and into his stomach, warming him. He let out a sigh. He didn't deserve Kyrin's small acts of kindness.

They sat quietly for a minute or two. Jace fiddled with the strap on the canteen, struggling for what to say. Was he even ready to speak of his doubt?

Kyrin stepped in first to break the silence, her voice quieter than usual. "It's always a sobering day. Shortly after Kaden and I turned to Elôm, Sam took us out to the forest outside of Valcré to perform the sacrifice with us. Even though this was my third time, it's still overwhelming."

Jace gave her a small nod, biting down on his own emotions. His first instinct, from the time he was a child, was to hold things in. People often saw such emotions as weakness. Rayad had been the one to help him begin opening up. Now Kyrin did the same.

He glanced at her as she waited patiently for him to speak. His tongue stuck in his mouth, holding fast to old habits, but, at the same time, a deep desire to share rose inside him. He trusted Kyrin more than he trusted anyone besides Rayad, yet it was still difficult to lay bare such painful aspects of his life.

He opened his mouth, but had to clear his throat before any words would form. "I never feel at peace after . . . never feel like my guilt has been covered."

Kyrin breathed out a long breath, and her gaze moved through the trees in contemplation before resting on him. "I don't know if any of us truly do. I still feel guilty too." A raw, almost sad honesty overcame her expression. She shrugged. "Maybe, after your faith has a chance to grow for several years, but not right now."

Jace tried to let her admission comfort him. After all, neither of them had believed in Elôm for more than a couple of years. They couldn't expect to know and understand everything.

Silence came for another minute before Kyrin broke it again.

"Timothy has been showing me all of the verses in the King's Scrolls that talk about the ultimate lamb sacrifice. It would be amazing to be alive to see it and know that our sins are washed away completely."

Her voice carried a longing and a hope that vibrated in Jace's own heart. But what lamb's blood could ever take away everything he had done? He stared at the blood on his hands again, a reminder of the past. He had felt the life leave a body with these hands—had been the cause of it.

"Jace?"

He jerked from his thoughts, but couldn't look at her. "I don't know if all of mine can be washed away."

The words came out in a hoarse whisper as the tears that never fell stung his eyes again. He finally looked at Kyrin when she pushed away from the tree to sit facing him. A determined but compassionate light shone in her eyes.

"I don't believe that."

He gripped the canteen hard. Kyrin knew of the darkness in his past, but he had never discussed it in detail with her before. Only Rayad knew of all the death and suffering he had experienced. What if sharing such horrors with Kyrin led her to believe the same things he believed about himself? He didn't think he could survive her rejection, yet something urged him to speak.

"What about murder?" He watched her reaction, trembling inside.

Her expression sobered. It was a weighty question and one she probably hadn't expected, but, unlike his own conscience, he saw no condemnation.

Her voice was quiet, yet sure. "Yes, even murder."

Jace hung his head. Why couldn't he be so sure? His spirit broken, words tumbled out before he could weigh whether or not he should speak them.

"I was only about fifteen . . ." He lifted his gaze to her, having to blink the moisture away. "Only fifteen the first time I killed a man."

Lines appeared in Kyrin's forehead as her brows drew together, and fear ripped through Jace's stomach. However, he found only growing compassion and concern in her eyes. She said nothing, and he continued before he could lose the nerve to speak.

"I was sold to a man who treated us all like cattle. Living conditions were poor and we were only fed well enough to keep us working. One of the slaves, Dane, would go around every night and demand half the rations from each of the weakest and newest slaves for himself and his men."

Jace licked his lips and drew a shaky breath, still able to see the slave yard in his mind—bleak, dirty, and filled with the reek of unwashed bodies as they had huddled around small fires for warmth.

"The first night . . . I refused to give mine up. Dane beat me up as a warning." Jace rubbed the groove of a small scar on the side of his jaw and winced. "After that, I became his prime target. Over the next couple of months, I grew stronger working in the fields. Then, one night, I refused to give up my food again, but this time it wasn't a one-sided fight . . ."

He let his words trail away, unable to voice the rest, though the scene played through in his mind. That day had changed the course of his entire life, burdening him with the guilt of taking another man's life. It was the first time he had felt the driving rage of his ryrik blood take over. It had finally shown him what he was and why everyone had always held such fear around him. Any chance to claim that his ryrik blood did not define him had died that night as Dane lay dead at his feet, his neck broken.

Jace could not bear to look at Kyrin, unable to face what thoughts might be evident in her eyes. Yet, now that he'd come this far, he had to finish his story.

"After I killed him, I was punished and thrown into confinement. I was there for a day or two . . . I'm not sure, but when they pulled me out, I was sold to Jasper, who made me a gladiator. I faced thirty-eight opponents." He clenched his teeth. "Thirty-eight . . . and nineteen times it was to the death."

Every one of those fights seared his conscience. For the first time in years, a sob rose up in his chest, but it stuck there, refusing to come any further. His voice broke as he said, "I'm only twenty-one years old, and I've already killed more men than Rayad has."

The shame of that admission consumed him and held his head down. He had never started out to share so much. What must Kyrin think of him? He was a monster next to her gentle innocence.

Silence stretched out, punctuated only by the loud, painful thud of his heart in his ears. He couldn't bring himself to raise his eyes.

Her hand closed around his. He recoiled. In that moment, he felt that his touch would sully her, but she wouldn't let go. He finally looked up. Tears glistened on her cheeks and sparkled on her dark lashes. Jace still could not find an ounce of condemnation in her eyes.

She leaned closer, her expression earnest. "Killing someone when they are trying to kill you is self-defense."

Jace shook his head. He couldn't escape guilt that easily. "I could have refused to fight for Jasper. I could have refused to even learn how. And deep down, I had every intention of killing Dane. I wanted to stop him, permanently. *I* am the one who started the fight."

Kyrin breathed out, her attempts to console him deflated, but she went on just as determinedly. "Then you made a mistake. We all make mistakes."

Jace grimaced. Murder was more than a mistake. Mistakes could usually be fixed in some way. Death could not.

"I don't believe you would make that mistake again now," Kyrin continued, trying her best to reassure him. "And in the arena, you had no choice. You were forced into those fights. You weren't in it for glory or for the sport of it. You didn't choose it. You didn't know Elôm at the time, and you did what was only natural—fight for your survival. But you're not that person anymore, and I believe you would make different choices were you to face Dane or even the arenas again now."

Would he? He shuddered at the thought. If he had one fear that rose above all others besides losing those he cared about, it was finding himself back in the arenas. He didn't think he could face the horror again.

Forcing such contemplations away, he shook his head. "I am guilty of murder, Kyrin."

Her mouth opened partially, but he stopped her this time. "Whether it's just Dane or the men in the arenas too. There's no excuse for that."

Her mouth closed. As difficult as it was, he didn't regret what he had said. She needed to know exactly what he was.

Silently she processed it, unspoken thoughts flitting across her expression. After a moment, her soft fingers squeezed his hand. "The one thing you seem to keep overlooking in all of this is the power of Elôm's love. I won't argue over your guilt, but I will argue that His love is greater than that guilt."

Jace stared at her as his doubts and hopes fought over what to do with her words—such a frustratingly familiar battle. He was growing weary of fighting it. Finally, he gave a slow nod and made a request. "Will you pray that Elôm will make it clear, one way or another, whether that's true for me?"

A bright smile blossomed on Kyrin's face, bringing a little light to the conversation. "Of course I will."

Pushing to her feet, she brushed off her coat and tipped her head. "Are you ready to go back? My mother and Lenae have meat pies waiting at the cabin." She lowered her voice and grinned. "If my brothers haven't eaten them all by now."

The lighthearted jest managed to draw a slight smile from Jace, and he let her pull him up. As they followed Tyra back to camp, he hoped that, if his own prayers weren't answered, Kyrin's would be.

"... Kyrin ... *Kyrin*."

She snapped from her thoughts with a jolt. "I'm sorry, Meredith, what is it?" She looked at the little girl, who stood on a stepstool at the table, her dress and arms powdered in flour.

"It's sticking." Meredith wrinkled her nose and held up her dough-covered hands.

"That means you need more flour. Here, let me help you." Kyrin sprinkled more flour on the bread dough and helped her scrape it off her fingers. "There you go." She smiled as the little girl dutifully went back to kneading. "You're doing very well."

Meredith beamed, and Kyrin watched her for a moment before glancing across the table, where her mother and Lenae worked on their own loaves. She caught Lenae's questioning look.

"Something on your mind?" she asked.

Kyrin's mother looked up at this, curiosity in her eyes as well.

Kyrin shrugged, not sure what or how much to say concerning her distraction. "I was thinking about Jace . . ." Their conversation had lingered in her mind during the last couple of days. She'd had to come to terms with it. She knew he had experienced horrible things in his past, but she hadn't expected him to admit to murder. It was a weighty thing to consider. Still, it didn't change her view of him. If anything, her compassion and desire to help him had grown. He may be guilty of murder, but he was no cold-blooded killer. Of that, she was certain.

Her mother and Lenae still watched her, and Kyrin cleared her throat. "I'm worried about him. He's been struggling lately." She kept the specifics to herself. Jace had shared deeply painful confessions, trusting her—*only* her—with the truth. "I don't think he's sleeping well. I suppose it reminds me of when we first met. I don't want him to have to go through that again."

Lenae nodded knowingly. "The sacrifice seems to have affected him quite a bit."

"It was difficult for him."

"Well, give it a few days before you worry overmuch. I'm sure the days leading up to it were stressful. Once the emotions of it wear off, I think he'll be all right."

"I hope so." Kyrin drew her brows together. "It can't be easy, especially with those suspicious looks Mister Hagen gives him all the time."

The old man and his daughter had shown up a few weeks ago, half-starved and frozen, from a village to the south after getting into trouble with the emperor's men for unpaid taxes. The man wasn't quite right. He acted far more like a small child than a grown man, needing his daughter Alice's almost constant care and supervision. She said it had been like this ever since he had suffered a severe blow to the head a few years ago during a ryrik raid on their village. The marauders had carried off his wife, leaving him with a rabid hatred for anything even hinting of ryriks. Anytime he and Jace crossed paths, the man looked ready to grab the first weapon within reach and run him through. No matter how many times Trask tried to reassure him, the man never seemed to grasp it.

"I know it sounds unwelcoming of me, but I can't help looking forward to when they move on," Kyrin admitted. Jace shouldn't have to live under such suspicion. This was his home, after all.

Lenae offered a look of gentle understanding, but the conversation ended with a knock at the door. Wiping her hands, Lenae crossed the room to answer it.

"Good morning, Lenae." Warin's voice came from outside before the big man stepped into the cabin at Lenae's invitation. He smiled at the women and Meredith before his gaze refocused on Lenae. "I was out near the supply shack and found these for you."

He gave her a small handful of delicate white flowers with a splash of pale blue and gold at the center. A bright smile lit her face.

"They must have just opened this morning." He seemed to have trouble deciding what to do with his hands now that he wasn't holding the flowers. "I thought I'd bring them in so you could enjoy them."

Kyrin shared a discreet look with her mother.

Lenae smiled up at Warin. "Thank you. I will enjoy them very much."

"You're welcome." His sparkling eyes lingered a moment before shifting to the table. "What are you working on, Meredith?"

"Bread." The little girl puffed herself up proudly. "I'm doing it all by myself."

"Really?"

Meredith nodded, but then hesitated. "Well, Kyrin is helping me."

"Just a little," Kyrin said with a grin.

"I bet it will be delicious," Warin told Meredith, making her beam again. "Do you think you can bring me a piece when it's done? I love it when it's warm and buttery."

"Sure!"

"I can't wait." Warin's gaze slid back to Lenae. "I'd better be going. I have to give Trask a report on our supplies."

"Thanks again for the violets."

He nodded, smiling, and turned to let himself out. Lenae watched until the door closed before turning to the table. "Meredith, why don't you get one of the small vases from the shelf? We'll put the flowers on the table so we can all enjoy them while we're working."

Meredith hopped off her stool and quickly retrieved a vase. "Here, Mommy."

She handed the porcelain container to Lenae. Kyrin smiled at how quickly the little girl had adopted Lenae as her new mother. The two of them were perfect together.

"Thank you, sweetheart." Lenae filled the vase with water and arranged the flowers.

Glancing once again at her mother, Kyrin cleared her throat lightly. "I didn't know you liked snow violets, Lenae."

"They're my favorite," she responded. "I look forward to them every spring."

"Then it's a lucky thing that Warin found them and thought of you."

"Not really luck. I went for a walk yesterday to look for some. I met up with him and told him."

Kyrin caught her mother's eye again. Clearly they both sensed the same thing.

"What are you two smiling about?"

They looked at Lenae.

"Nothing." Kyrin tried to hide her smile without much success. Her mother didn't do much better.

Lenae gave them a suspicious look, but a smile lurked on her own lips. They said no more about it, but the interaction between Lenae and Warin told Kyrin more than any words would.

A couple of hours later, Kyrin set one of the finished loaves on the table to cool. She had just turned to get another when the door opened again, letting in a string of excited male voices.

"—see that?"

Kaden walked in first, laughing a breathless chuckle fueled by adrenaline, and flashed a grin at Talas.

The crete shook his head. "I thought for sure you were going down!"

Kyrin could tell by their windblown hair that they had just come from flying, likely another training session for their group of dragon riders. They worked with them nearly every day. The laughter and conversation died, however, when Kaden met their mother's probing gaze.

"What's this about going down?"

Kaden's gaze shifted to Kyrin, looking for support. She lifted her brows. If he was being daring and foolhardy, he wasn't going to get any support from her.

His attention returned to their mother. "Ah . . ." A sheepish grin came to his face that Kyrin remembered him using as a child to cover up wrongdoing. "It's nothing . . . I was just practicing a new maneuver and there was a little incident. That's all."

"Right." Their mother nodded at Talas. "If he thought you were going down, that sounds serious."

Kaden looked over his shoulder at Talas, probably hoping he would downplay the whole thing, but the crete merely shrugged, a mischievous twinkle in his bright green eyes. Turning back to his mother, Kaden insisted, "Really, I was fine. Exsis wasn't going to let me fall."

Their mother let out an exasperated sigh. "I just want you to be careful."

"I am, but flying always involves risk, especially if we're going to have to defend ourselves against attack someday. Now," he quickly changed the subject, "do you have any coffee made?"

Lenae gestured to the pot hanging next to the fireplace. "Help yourselves."

"Thanks." Kaden walked over to it, his gaze catching the fresh bread. "When is that for?"

"Later," their mother said. She still didn't look entirely pleased with him.

As he and Talas each poured a cup of coffee, Kyrin joined them. "Speaking of attacks, how is training coming?"

Kaden nodded enthusiastically. "Great. If Daican does come looking for us, we'll have a good dozen extra men to form a defense."

"Good," Kyrin murmured.

Their encounter with the emperor's hybrid dragons—firedrakes—last fall left their camp in jeopardy. Though well-hidden from any ground search, an airborne force could spot them easily. It changed the dynamics of their plans. Trask had set up camp for refugees of the emperor's persecution, but this was no longer an option. Now it served as more of a waystation to prepare and send people east, farther away from Daican's reach.

"With the weather getting warmer, Captain Darq will probably soon send help to lead the people to safety," Talas said. "Then, if we *are* attacked, at least we won't have a lot of civilians in harm's way."

Kaden agreed. "I wonder if Trask will start setting up other camps to house the militia. At least then we won't lose everything if we have to evacuate."

Kyrin glanced at her mother while the men continued discussing these plans. Kaden, Marcus, and Liam would no doubt remain here in camp, but she wasn't sure yet about her mother and younger brothers. Would they move farther east with the other refugees? She wanted them safe, of course, but hated the thought of breaking up their family again. The last few months together had been something she had only ever dreamed of experiencing.

Once the men finished their coffee, they set their cups in the washbasin and headed for the door. However, the bread at the table distracted Kaden again.

"Are you sure I can't have a piece now?"

Their mother shook her head. "You are quite the nuisance."

"Just like in Tarvin Hall," Kyrin chimed in, giving her brother a wry look, "except the cook there loved to feed him. I think she liked the flattery."

"You can have a piece of mine, Kaden." Meredith came around the table and took his hand.

"You made bread?" he asked in a surprised tone that delighted her.

Meredith nodded. "Look. See?" She pointed out the perfect little golden-brown loaf.

"Meri, I would love to have a piece of your bread." He bent down, whispering by her ear, "My mother won't give me any."

Meredith giggled, and Lydia tried to give him a look of annoyance, but it was lost in a smile.

"Kyrin, can you cut it for me?" Meredith asked.

"Of course."

While Kyrin sliced the loaf, Meredith ran over to get a little plate from the cupboard and put a piece of bread on it for Kaden.

"Mmm," he breathed as he took his first bite. "You know, Meri, I think you're going to have to bake bread for me all the time."

Meredith twisted her hands together, her face aglow with a grin as she watched him eat. Then she remembered, "Oh, I need to take a piece to Warin. Can you help me find him?"

21

Kaden swallowed his last bite. "Sure."

Meredith rushed for another plate, asking Lenae for help with the butter. Kyrin stepped closer to her brother. "I think she has a crush on you."

He smiled, loving every minute of it.

When Meredith had her coat on and had retrieved the bread, which included a slathering of butter sure to make Warin smile, she and Kaden headed out the door with Talas. As it closed on their happy chatter, Kyrin chuckled, and her mother and Lenae joined in. Kyrin cherished these moments. They had gone through so much to get here. The thought of it ending pinched her stomach. She looked at both her mother and Lenae.

"So, now that spring is here, are you going to stay or leave for somewhere safer?"

They processed the question for a moment, and Lenae spoke first.

"I just talked to Jeremy about this. This camp has become home. I don't have any intention of leaving unless I have to."

That gave Kyrin a good measure of comfort, and she turned her gaze to her mother, who smiled.

"Don't worry, dear; we're not going anywhere. We're all in this together."

THE WEATHER COULDN'T have been better for a celebration.
After almost a week of rain, Kyrin and Kaden's eighteenth
birthday had arrived with splendid springtime weather, full of
sunshine and warmth. And for the first time since the sacrifice,
Jace found his spirits lifting. The joy radiating from Kyrin's
smile alone lightened his mood. He liked to see her having a
good time. It was their first outdoor community meal of the
year, and Anne and her parents had come out to celebrate. Cheery
talk and laughter filled the campsite, and Jace quietly enjoyed it
from the background. He would personally wish Kyrin a happy
birthday later when some of the fuss had died down.

He watched her from his seat at one of the tables they had
carried out from the cabins. Her mother had given her a new
dress the color of forget-me-nots. Not only did the short-sleeved
garment complement her slender figure, but it brought out the
color of her eyes like he had never seen. Meredith had also
provided her with a crown woven of snow violets. It made her
look so innocent and almost childlike, but he was keenly aware
that she was a woman, growing in beauty and maturity every
day.

He let out a light sigh and tried to silence the possibilities and
what-ifs that rose up from a longing in his heart—a persistent

longing that both scared and shocked him. Feeling it grow over the last few months showed him just how careful he needed to be, determined to bury them so deep they would never find their way out. After all, she was his closest friend. He didn't know what he would ever do without her and wouldn't jeopardize that. There were too many reasons why he could never let it become anything more than it was now.

After the meal came the gift-giving. Everyone had something for the twins. A smile tugged at Jace's lips as Kyrin accepted each gift with delight. His anticipation grew to give her his own gift. He hoped she would like it. He'd spent the last few weeks working on it. Once most of their friends had come forward, Jace murmured to Rayad, "I'm going to get my gift."

He nodded and smiled as Jace rose and headed off to the supply shack where he had kept it. The laughter and voices lingered behind him, fading to a light hum as he passed the cabins, out of sight of the gathering.

"Where're you sneakin' off to?"

The slurred voice stopped Jace. To his right, behind one of the cabins, Mister Hagen staggered toward him, his hair and clothing disheveled. No doubt he had started out looking presentable, thanks to his dedicated daughter, but just like a child he didn't stay neat for long. Jace wondered if the man had somehow gotten into some liquor, but it was difficult to tell. Either way, it was best to try to ignore him, and Jace continued on his way.

"I'm talk . . . talkin' to you," Hagen's halting voice trailed after him. "You took my wife."

Jace stopped at the door of the supply shack and glanced over his shoulder. The man bumbled along behind him. He frowned, his tone low. "I had nothing to do with your wife."

The man didn't seem to hear him. "You're a . . . murderer."

Jace's eyes slid closed in a grimace. He couldn't refute that.

He breathed out slowly. *Just get the gift and go.* He couldn't let himself stand here and think too long. Guilt was too quick to take hold of him these days, and he didn't want Kyrin to sense him sinking back into a dark mood.

A sound invaded his consciousness; a mere whisper of a sound that sent a prickling sensation down his back—the chilling hiss of metal. He spun around right as Hagen dove at him with a dagger. Jace sidestepped and shoved Hagen away. If not for his swift fighting reflexes, the blade would have plunged right into his chest.

The man stumbled, and then crashed to the ground. He let out a muffled groan.

Jace stood, clenching his fists as warmth stirred his blood. He willed it away. The man wasn't in his right mind. He didn't truly know what he was doing. Jace waited for him to rise. He needed to make this man understand that he wasn't an enemy. But Hagen did not get up.

A breath-halting cold gripped Jace, extinguishing all traces of anger. He rushed to Hagen's side and rolled him over. The man gasped, his eyes rounded and uncomprehending. Slowly, his gaze slid down to the dagger hilt protruding from between his ribs. Glaring red seeped through the fabric of his shirt.

Jace's heart stopped. No! "*Help.*" His plea came only as a whisper, but he forced his voice to break free. "Someone help!"

He couldn't tear his gaze from the stain overtaking Hagen's shuddering chest. No, not again. Not more spilled blood.

"Please!" he prayed in desperation.

Wheezing, Hagen reached for the dagger, but Jace held his hand away. The blood would flow more freely if the blade were removed. Footsteps rushed up behind him. He looked up, a horrible ache gripping his stomach as his friends approached. Rising, he backed away from Hagen to let Lenae and the others near him. She knelt down, inspecting the wound, but her grave expression offered Jace no comfort. After all, she wasn't a trained physician. If only Leetra were back from gathering information in Valcré. Perhaps she could have done something.

"What happened?"

Only now did Jace take his gaze from Hagen, meeting Rayad, who stood at his side. "He came at me with the knife. I pushed him and he fell. I didn't mean to. . ." His voice broke off. If only he had just dodged the attack instead of pushing him!

Rayad rested his hand on Jace's shoulder and started to speak, but a cry cut off his words.

"Father!" Hagen's daughter, Alice, broke through the growing crowd. She gasped, her face sickeningly white, and dropped down beside him. "Father!" she cried again, tears choking her voice.

He wheezed out her name, and she took his hand. His eyes locked on her a moment and then slid closed. With a final, shuddering breath, he went still.

"No! Father!" She shook him as everyone backed away to give her a little space. "Please, Father, no!"

Her anguished cries ripped gaping wounds in Jace's heart that immediately filled with guilt. It was one of his nightmares come to life. Real and irreversible. There would be no waking up to find it only a dream.

Sobbing, Alice looked around as if trying to find an answer. Her gaze came to Jace, locking with his, and pain-fueled anger joined the grief in her eyes.

"You!" She stumbled to her feet. "You did this!" She rushed at him, and beat her fists against his chest. "You killed him! He was a harmless old man, but you just killed him. Murderer!"

Jace couldn't move, couldn't find a way to explain that he hadn't meant for this to happen. He hadn't meant to kill him. Her fists were nothing compared to the sting of her accusations. They pounded into his head, and soon he didn't think he could deny them. A man was dead. If he had not been there, it never would have happened. It *was* his fault.

Holden stepped in, prying the young woman away from Jace and holding her back. She struggled against him, still shouting her accusations until she finally dissolved into tears. Lenae came forward to comfort her, and Holden turned to Jace.

Now Jace noticed Rayad, Kyrin, Kaden, and the others gathered around him.

"Jace, are you all right?" Kyrin looked at him, her eyes wide and full of emotion.

He couldn't answer, Alice's agony still digging into him, tearing him up inside.

"It was an accident," Rayad told him.

This finally broke Jace from the paralysis of shock. He backed away from them. They could say what they wanted, tell him it was an accident, but the rising guilt told him otherwise. He could have done something different—*anything* different—and Hagen would still be alive.

"Jace, stop."

Rayad reached out to him, but Jace shook his head and turned away. He headed straight toward the forest, ignoring Rayad's plea to wait. Then came Kyrin's desperate voice.

"Jace, come back."

His steps faltered, but he couldn't bear to face her. Not after what he had just done. She called to him again, and a fierce ache pressed into his heart. Still, he pushed on, not looking back. When he reached the edge of camp, he walked faster and faster until he was almost running. He paid no attention to direction or location; he just went—trying to escape, just like in his dreams. And just like the many nameless faces in his dreams, Alice's voice echoed in his mind, convicting him of all the lives he had taken.

Warm air soaked into Kyrin's damp cheeks as she stepped inside the cabin and dispelled a little of the chill that had overtaken her. She pushed back her hood and untied the strings of her waterlogged cloak. Out of the corner of her eye, she caught the questioning looks her mother and Lenae sent her way. The knot in her stomach bunched more tightly and the moisture in her eyes rose a little farther. Facing them, she shook her head.

"Nothing. We looked everywhere. The stream and everywhere he usually goes, but he wasn't there, and any sign that he was has been washed away by the rain."

She rubbed her sore eyes. She'd hardly slept last night. Jace had been gone for almost twenty-four hours. He had never disappeared for so long before, not while she had known him.

Hanging her cloak by the door, she sank down in a chair at the table where the other women worked on sewing.

Her mother offered her an encouraging look, optimism lighting her eyes. "I'm sure he'll turn up soon and will be just fine."

Kyrin breathed out a deep sigh. Her own optimism had grown rather dim. "Normally, I would believe that, but he went off without any warm clothes, food, or even a weapon. It's cold out there. Too cold to wander around in the rain dressed as he was when he left. I know this sounds crazy, but what if he got lost? It could happen to any of us, especially if he wasn't paying attention to where he was going."

And in his state of mind, she doubted he had. She sighed again, her shoulders sagging under the weight of grim possibilities. If only he had stayed and let her and Rayad help him through this! "I'm sorry. It's just that I keep seeing the look on his face when he left, and I hate to think of him out there alone."

"Don't forget Tyra is with him," Lenae said gently. "Even

if she isn't human, she can provide comfort, warmth, and protection, and guide him back if he is lost."

A small flame of comfort finally grew amidst Kyrin's doubt. Lenae was right. At least Jace's wolf had been able to follow him when none of the rest of them could. This comfort intensified when Lenae added, "And he may not think so, but you know and we know that Elôm, too, is out there with him."

How Kyrin prayed He would keep Jace safe and bring him back. She couldn't bear to lose someone else, especially not Jace. She cared for him too deeply.

After a moment of silence, Kyrin's mother suggested, "Why don't you go work with Timothy? I'm sure it will help you feel much better while you're waiting."

Kyrin considered it. She did have some questions to ask Timothy. With a nod, she stood and went to the door, where she slipped on her coat as she stepped outside. Hurrying through the rain, she reached Trask's cabin and knocked.

"I came to see if Timothy was working," Kyrin said as Trask let her inside. Sure enough, the half-crete sat at the table surrounded by scrolls and parchments. A few candles illuminated his workspace. Such a young man looked a bit out of place in such a scholarly position, yet his love for it shone in his dark eyes.

On the way to the table, Kyrin exchanged a glance with Rayad. He stood near the fire talking to Warin as he warmed up from the search with her and Kaden. He offered a small but reassuring smile. While everyone worried about Jace's wellbeing, it wasn't quite the same as the concern she shared with Rayad.

Timothy gave her a warm smile as well when she took a seat near him. He and his brother, Aaron, had returned a couple of weeks ago from spending the winter with their crete relatives in Dorland. Once they had settled in, Kyrin had begun helping Timothy make copies of the King's Scrolls, something they had discussed late last fall. The process of copying each line of Scripture was long, but worth every moment, especially with Timothy there to explain difficult passages so knowledgeably. He had a real gift for that.

"How are you?" he asked.

Timothy was one of the kindest and most caring individuals Kyrin had ever met. He looked a bit tired this morning, and Kyrin had no doubt he had been up late praying for Jace and his safe return. He always put others before himself that way.

Kyrin breathed out slowly. Just being around Timothy made her aware of her spiritual shortcomings, yet it was a good awareness. One that made her strive to do better. That was another thing Timothy was good at—inspiring the faith of others.

"Honestly, I'm struggling. My mother thought this would be the best use of my time while I'm waiting. She's right, of course. Sitting and worrying won't make Jace show up."

Timothy nodded in understanding. "I'm sure he'll be here before long."

Kyrin wanted with all her heart to believe that. Before she really thought about it, she said, "I'm just afraid he won't come back at all." Deep down, it was her greatest fear.

"He will."

Kyrin lifted her brows at his confidence. After all, he hadn't had time to get to know Jace very well.

With the same confidence, Timothy explained, "You're here. You're too important to him to leave behind."

Kyrin let the words sink in. It warmed her inside to think that she meant so much to Jace. Still, she didn't just want him to come back; she wanted him to live without his pain and fears. It was heartbreaking to see him dragged down by them so often. What kind of life was it to live with such uncertainty? He missed out on so much joy.

"Timothy, have you come across anything in the Scrolls that might help him? Anything about ryriks? If they have souls or . . . if they don't?" Just saying it sent a stabbing pain through her heart. She would never believe that he had no soul.

"No. I've not found anything that distinguishes between the races at all, which only leads me to believe more strongly that ryriks are just the same as all the other races. We all have our good and evil, and we all have souls that need Elôm."

"If only there was a way to convince him of that. I'm afraid he'll go his entire life wondering and fearing. I don't want that for him. Maybe, if you told him what you told me, maybe coming from you it would make a difference."

"I can try, but you're the one he trusts most."

Kyrin nodded. "Will you pray for him? For peace and assurance?"

Another comforting smile reached Timothy's face. "I already am, and I will continue."

Jace didn't realize just how far his escape into the woods had taken him until he started back. He had just walked, on and on, for hours, until he collapsed near a tree, panting. Only then had he noticed that Tyra followed. She had just stared at him with her loyal, trusting eyes, not knowing what pain had driven him out here.

They had spent the night by that tree, all the many regrets of Jace's past flooding up around him. He couldn't stop the way they tormented him, growing his guilt. If only he could escape it.

An early morning storm finally drove him back toward camp. He had managed to stay warm with Tyra during the night, but it was impossible in the downpour. At first, he'd looked for shelter, but the rain soon drenched his clothes, so he trudged through it.

The morning passed before anything looked familiar. By now, his soaked clothing clung to his skin and shivers gripped him. If he didn't get dry and warm soon, he risked getting sick. The way his lungs already felt in the cold, damp air, an illness could quite possibly do him in. It didn't really matter to him except that it would devastate Kyrin. That and he had a promise to keep to her father. He couldn't protect her if he was dead.

At last, the glow of cabin windows beckoned through the mist, and he entered camp. There was little activity in the rain. With his head down, he made his way toward the shelter.

"Jace!"

He stopped, his stomach balling into an aching knot, and looked up. Kyrin rushed toward him from the direction of Trask's cabin. Relief washed over her face, but faded to concern when she reached him. After a quick look at his wet clothing, her gaze rose to his face.

"You must be freezing. Go change and then come to Lenae's cabin. I'll make sure there's coffee and a good fire going."

She turned to carry out her mission without giving him a chance to decline. He watched her go and battled the conflict in his mind. He hadn't been ready to face her just yet—wasn't ready now—but she had left him no choice. With a hard sigh, he moved on.

He paused at the door to the shelter, hesitancy seizing up his muscles. Did he dare hope it would be empty? How could he face any of the others? Little choice he had now that he'd returned to camp. He couldn't stand out here forever with Kyrin waiting for him. Grimacing, he pushed open the door and found Kaden and Trev there with Liam. Kaden said his name in surprise as he walked in.

"You all right?"

Jace glanced at him, but didn't answer. What could he say that they would understand? An awkward silence settled in the small dwelling. He focused on the task at hand, peeling off his wet clothes and changing into a dry pair. He then grabbed an old towel and scrubbed the majority of the moisture out of Tyra's soaked fur. The others were still uncomfortably quiet as he worked. Jace gritted his teeth. It was too reminiscent of his early days in camp when he had been nothing more than an oddity and object of scorn. *It's your fault.* The condemning voice heaped more guilt on his already severely burdened conscience. Always his fault.

The weight of discomfort grew too heavy, and he left the shelter. Tyra followed. Outside, his eyes strayed once more to the trees. He shouldn't have come back. Fighting the urge to be alone, he turned toward Lenae's cabin. He couldn't ignore Kyrin waiting for him. At the door, he hesitated, then knocked. Kyrin was right there to answer it and usher him inside.

"Come, sit by the fire." She gripped his arm lightly and guided him to a chair near the hearth. "I'll get you some coffee."

He sank down with a heavy breath, and Tyra claimed her favorite spot on a rug near his feet, unaware of the tension coiling inside him. If only Kyrin wouldn't treat him so generously, as if he was innocent. He wasn't, and it made him feel that much more despicable, like an impostor. Pretending to be otherwise was too difficult.

Kyrin brought him a mug of coffee and then stood by—watching, waiting. Silence stretched between them. Jace stared down into the mug, unable to look at her. Everything that was so wretched about him would surely be visible to her.

Finally, she asked, "Are you all right?"

Again, he had no answer for that question. Oh, he could tell her he was fine as he always did, but what would that achieve? It would only be a lie, and she would know it.

After another long, painfully silent moment, she left him alone at the fireplace. Still, he watched her from the corner of his eye. Her face was drawn, yet had a determined set to it. At the table, her mother, Lenae, and Meredith conversed quietly, but she did not join them.

Several minutes later, she came to him again with a bowl. "Here's a little soup left from lunch."

He stared at it. Even after twenty-four hours, he had no desire to eat.

"I won't let you stop eating again."

Her quietly firm voice drew his gaze to her face. At the knowing look in her eyes, he gave in and took the bowl. With her looking on, he forced himself to eat. His stomach and fatigued muscles did welcome the warm meal. Once she seemed satisfied that he would keep eating, Kyrin also retrieved a bowl of torn up bread pieces, milk, and some meat for Tyra, who was much more enthusiastic about her food than Jace was. He gave Kyrin an awkward nod of thanks for tending to Tyra as well.

Now that he had eaten and was warm enough that the tremors had ceased, restlessness set in. It was too quiet, just like in the shelter. Life and joy usually filled Lenae's cabin, but the women only spoke in subdued murmurs, as if they were uneasy around him.

Swallowing the tight lump in his throat, he weighed his options. It was either here or the shelter. Nowhere would be empty on a day like today. At last, he pushed to his feet and pulled on his coat. He would rather be in his own place, even if it meant facing Kaden and the others. With them, he wouldn't feel such guilt for not speaking as he did with Kyrin.

"Thanks for the soup," he murmured as he passed the table.

He caught the way Kyrin straightened, her eyes growing a bit wide.

"Where are you going?"

"To the shelter." He avoided her gaze and walked out after Tyra before she could say more.

Pulling his collar closer to his neck, he started across camp. A moment later, the cabin door opened and closed behind him and footsteps hurried to catch up.

"Jace, wait."

He looked over his shoulder and stopped as Kyrin reached his side.

"Come back inside. It's warmer and drier than the shelter. You need to stay warm or you'll get sick."

"The shelter will be fine."

Her gaze darted to the shelter, and then slid back to him. A weak little smile grew on her face. "Maybe, but if you come back to the cabin, you'll be there when my mother's cookies are finished. They're always the best when they're warm and fresh."

She tried so hard to make things seem all right—to make things normal, as if a man hadn't just died because of him. Why did she try so hard?

"You shouldn't be so kind to me," he said, raising his voice just above the patter of rain.

Her smile drooped, and the encouraging light died in her eyes. Weariness overcame her expression and carried to her voice.

"Why not, Jace?" She put her hands out helplessly. "Why would I ever want to be anything but kind?"

He tried to loosen the tightness in his throat. "Because . . . I don't deserve it."

Again, her expression changed, tensing. A spark returned to her eyes, but not one of determination. He'd angered her— angered and wounded. The tightness spread to his chest. She had endured so much with him, exhibiting untold patience, but it seemed he had finally exhausted some of that patience.

35

She shook her head, her voice strained. "I can't believe you're doing this again, after all this time and all we've been through. If you try to push me away again—"

"I'm not." It surely would have been in her best interest but, selfishly, he couldn't make himself do it. She would never stand for it anyway. She was stubborn that way.

His voice rose as frustration gave way. "It's just, you always try to see the best in me, but you have to understand and accept that it isn't there. And if it was, then it's so sullied by blood that it's worthless." He paused, drawing in a sharp breath that ached in his constricted chest. "I'm not the man you want so much to believe I am."

In less than a moment, tears welled up in her eyes, glimmering with pain, and he hated himself even more.

She shook her head, her words choked. "I don't believe that. Whatever you say, I'll never believe it."

He held her watery gaze. "That doesn't change anything."

Now the tears fell. Even with her cheeks already wet with raindrops, he could see each one as they trailed down to her chin. Crushing defeat left an empty look in her eyes that cut right into him. Out of words, she took a wobbly step back, and then turned away, her head bent as she trudged back to the cabin.

His heart beating a heavy, painful rhythm, Jace forced himself in the opposite direction. He'd just crushed the one person who meant everything to him. He was a cruel, heartless monst— He bit down hard, but the word floated tauntingly through his being. How he could ever have allowed himself to wonder about the two of them? How could he have ever hoped that, just maybe, he could be good enough for her? What foolishness. Had he been anyone else, he would have been horrified to know a man like him had any feelings for her. He shouldn't be anywhere near her.

Kyrin swiped her hands across her cheeks as she neared the cabin. At the door, she paused and glanced back at Jace's retreating form, but that just caused more tears to overflow. With a sob catching at the back of her throat, she pushed the door open and stepped inside. Her hands trembled as she returned her coat to the peg. She fought mightily to compose herself, but all her emotions clamored for her to yell, and cry, and let it all out.

"Kyrin?"

She turned slowly to her mother, determined to hold it together, but it all crumbled in the next heartbeat, her tears starting fresh.

"Oh, honey, are you all right?" Her mother rose and stepped away from the table, her arms open invitingly.

Kyrin gave her head a pitiful shake. "For once, I just want him to be happy and believe he's worth something, but he won't. He just keeps going back to the lies no matter how hard I try to stop him." She choked down another sob. "I just wish he'd listen to me."

JACE ROLLED RESTLESSLY on his cot and scrubbed his hands over his face, letting out a deep sigh. The birds had just begun to sing outside. Had he even closed his eyes once all night? Kyrin hadn't left his thoughts since the fight. What a fool he was. Everything he had thought and said still held true for him, but now that he'd had all night to let the emotions settle and think more reasonably, he could have kicked himself for how he had handled it. Why hadn't he kept his mouth shut? Of course such careless and cold words would hurt Kyrin after how much effort she spent trying to help him. That look of defeat just before she had walked away ate at his sanity. He had never hurt her like this before.

Grumbling to himself, he yanked back his covers and got up to get dressed. No rain pelted the shelter, so he only pulled on a warm shirt and his jerkin, leaving his coat hanging on the wall. Kaden rolled over as he passed him, but remained asleep like the others, blissfully unaware of any turmoil like that which darkened Jace's mood.

Outside, he couldn't quite see any sun through the trees yet. The air was cool and still damp, as expected, but fresh and smelling sweetly of spring. A beautiful morning if he could just be rid of the personal cloud hanging over him. His gaze

39

automatically sought Lenae's cabin. If only Kyrin were standing there like when she used to wait for him to go hunting. She wasn't, of course.

Turning his back on the cabin, he walked slowly through camp with Tyra. Candlelight flickered in some of the windows as the other inhabitants started to stir. A few minutes later, a cabin door opened, and Jace looked up to see Rayad. He hadn't seen him since returning yesterday, though someone must have told him he was back. Rayad spotted him and approached with an encouraging smile. He wore no look of disapproval or lecture—though Jace deserved it this morning—only concern.

"Jace." He spoke his name as if glad to see with his own eyes he was back. "How are you?"

Jace blew out a long breath and shook his head. "I feel like a fool."

Rayad's forehead wrinkled.

"Kyrin and I argued when I got back yesterday." Jace winced. "I said things I meant, but now wish I'd kept to myself. I hurt her, and I hate that I did."

Understanding replaced Rayad's frown. "You know, things like that can almost always be fixed by a simple apology."

"I know." Jace planned to do just that as soon as he had the opportunity. He glanced at Lenae's cabin again, still hoping to see Kyrin there. Jace faced Rayad again, his thoughts turning painfully toward another person he had hurt. "How is Alice?"

Rayad answered slowly, as if trying to spare Jace further guilt. "Well, she's grieving, as any of us would."

Jace hung his head. He was well acquainted with grief, and to cause it for someone else . . .

"You do understand it's not your fault?"

Jace's gaze rose back to Rayad, but he wasn't sure he could accept that. It wouldn't have happened if he hadn't been there.

"Really, it wasn't," Rayad insisted, knowing him too well. "Hagen attacked you, and you defended yourself. Anyone, except maybe Alice, would agree there was nothing you could have done differently."

Yes, there was.

"I didn't have to push him. I could have just dodged the attack and walked away."

"Did you have time to do anything but react?"

The moment replayed in Jace's mind. Though he wasn't ready to let himself off so easily, he could only answer with the truth. "No."

Rayad nodded in affirmation. "You are not to blame in this. Not in the slightest."

Perhaps, but that didn't relieve Jace's conscience and the guilt eating at it. However, he did not try to dissuade Rayad. Arguing had already caused enough damage. He wouldn't be at odds with him too.

Jace waited for Kyrin most of the morning, his gaze constantly going to the cabin, watching for her to come out. It was unusual for her to remain inside on such a lovely day. Kaden said she was busy helping Lenae, but he seemed to know things were off between them. She was probably still angry, and he didn't blame her. He debated going to see her, but what if she turned him away? Or worse, didn't forgive him?

By lunchtime, the truth was obvious—she was avoiding him. With regret and lack of sleep weighing on him, he sank down heavily on a bench outside the shelter. He fixed his gaze on the cabin for a long moment while he scratched Tyra's head. Then he looked down at her. At least she would never understand enough to be angry with him.

Holden walked out of the shelter, and Jace looked up when he offered him a plate of beans and pork.

"Thanks." He stirred the beans, sighing before finally taking a bite.

Holden sat down next to him, but didn't say anything for a long moment.

"She's still inside?"

Jace met his eyes and gave a short nod. If Holden had noticed, then he wasn't just paranoid.

Holden motioned toward the cabin. "You should go talk to her."

Jace heaved another sigh. Of course, in a close community like this, he couldn't hope the rift between him and Kyrin had gone unnoticed. Anyone could have witnessed their argument yesterday.

"I don't think she wants to see me."

Holden shrugged and gave him a pointed look. "Or maybe she's just waiting for you to come."

The look of defeat and hurt that had flashed in Kyrin's eyes returned to Jace and didn't reassure him that she was waiting to see him this morning.

"You know, Jace, when you've been scarred by a past like you and I have, it can shadow things and make it difficult to differentiate between who we are now and who we were in the past. We're not the men we were. You can't let yourself fall into the trap of thinking you are. It'll only ruin you."

Jace stared down at his dish, mulling this over. Out of everyone in camp, Holden would understand his struggle the best. The two of them had the most in common as far as past bloodshed and the regret of it, but the one thing they didn't share was Jace's ryrik blood. None of them would ever know how much it tortured him and held him captive to his fears. He alone carried that burden.

The whooshing sound of dragon wings passed overhead before he had a chance to reply. A moment later, Leetra and her dragon descended through the trees and landed at the edge of camp. She would surely have news. Jace and Holden rose and set their bowls aside to meet her.

"Welcome back," Holden said as they approached.

The crete girl gave a nod, her lavender eyes cool as always, and slid down from the dragon.

"What's the latest from Valcré?" Holden asked.

"A lot that Trask will want to act on." She reached up to unstrap her things from her saddle without giving them any further information.

Jace exchanged a look with Holden. Winter had been quiet, but now that spring had arrived, whatever plans Emperor Daican had for the domination of Ilyon would inevitably resume. There was no sense in hoping he had somehow had a change of heart.

In silence, Leetra gathered up her things and headed straight for Trask's cabin. Jace and Holden followed along. Whatever news she brought would no doubt affect them in some way, despite how Jace hated such disruptions. For once he would just like to find a place to live in peace, but that seemed as unlikely as the emperor suddenly declaring them all friends and fully pardoned.

At the cabin, Leetra knocked, and Trask opened the door to greet them.

"You're early today," he said as she strode inside. Usually she returned from trips to Valcré in the evening, not midday.

"I started out late yesterday," she explained, setting her things down by the door. "I planned to fly through the night, but the rain got heavy and I set down for a while."

"Have you eaten?" Timothy asked.

"Not since yesterday."

He pulled out a chair for her at the end of the table and moved to the fireplace to dish her up a bowl of soup.

Meanwhile, Trask asked, "So, what's the news?"

Leetra gave Timothy a brief thanks for the soup and, after taking a bite, her focus fixed again on Trask. "Sounds like Daican is setting his sights on Samara."

Trask made a face. They had always suspected it would be the first place the emperor would seek to conquer. As far as Jace knew, the country was small and still predominately devoted to Elôm. He couldn't see them standing against a country the size of Arcacia for very long.

The door opened again. He looked over his shoulder as Kaden, Trev, Talas, and the other prominent members of their group walked in. Kyrin entered last. Anything the others said was lost as Jace locked eyes with her. Just as the day before, she looked tired, and her eyes were red from crying. His stomach knotted around the little bit of lunch he'd eaten. He had caused her this pain. She, however, offered a brief, tentative smile as she stepped farther into the cabin and stood near Kaden at the table. Her attention turned to Leetra, and she didn't look at him again, but he watched her for a long moment. Her smile gave him hope that things would be all right between them once they talked it out. He would have right this moment, but Leetra's voice reminded him of the reason they had all gathered here.

". . . been sending correspondences back and forth with Sir Rothas Cantan. Aric thinks they're planning something."

Trask nodded in agreement. "From what I know of Sir Rothas, he's a brilliant strategist. If Daican is planning war on Samara, it would make sense for him to involve Rothas to form an attack strategy. Does Aric have any idea what kind of information they are trading?"

Leetra shook her head. "Daican keeps things pretty secretive these days. As far as Aric can tell, he only involves that vile Sir

Richard. Not even Foss has been able to get a look at any of the letters."

"I sure would like to know what Rothas is helping him plan," Rayad said. "It must be something big if he won't even let his secretary in on it."

"Why don't we intercept one of their messengers and find out?" Holden suggested.

Trask let out a long breath. "I don't think that would be wise. The emperor would know someone close to him has tipped us off. That would only put Aric at greater risk and, if Daican knew we discovered his plans, who's to say he wouldn't just alter them?" He folded his arms, his expression thoughtful. "What we really need is a way to get a look at those correspondences, either at the palace or at Sir Rothas's home, without either of them knowing."

"Perhaps we could sneak someone in," Talas suggested. "Rothas's home can't be as secure as Auréa. If we could get someone inside, we could probably gather all sorts of useful information."

"It would be risky. Just the time needed to go through whatever we might find would make it nearly impossible."

"Not if you sent me in."

All eyes went straight to Kyrin, and Jace felt as though he'd taken a blow to the gut. The danger of such an undertaking was unthinkable, yet her expression was calm and matter-of-fact.

"I would only need a quick look at the letters and could go through it in my mind later. I wouldn't need much time."

"It's good of you to offer, but we can't put you at risk like that," Trask said, shaking his head, and Jace released the breath he was holding. "And anyway, we'd have no way of getting in. If I were not a fugitive, then it would be possible, but Sir Rothas won't invite just anyone into his home."

This seemed to settle the discussion, thankfully. The more conflict and danger Kyrin could avoid, the better.

Jace's attention shifted once more to Leetra when Talas asked, "Any news of Falcor?"

Leetra's eyes glittered coldly, the icy tone of her voice matching. "Aric sees him at the palace now and then. He and his group of traitors are still training the firedrakes and their riders in a camp near Fort Rivor. They'll have an estimated sixty ready for combat within the next couple of weeks."

"Just in time for an attack on Samara," Trask murmured.

"No doubt that's the plan," Rayad said.

Trask looked at Kaden. "Would you get Marcus for me? If war is coming, we need to be prepared so we're there when Samara needs us."

Kaden turned to go, as did Jace and several of the others. Kyrin was just ahead of him, following her brother. They stepped outside, and Jace worked up his courage before calling her name. She stopped to look back at him. He waited until everyone had walked off, and then approached her as she faced him. It was hard to read her guarded expression, but her blue eyes stared up at him, projecting hopefulness. His heart rate picked up, and he licked his lips. Suddenly, everything he wanted to say seemed inadequate. How could a few words fix the pain he had caused? He frowned down at the ground, berating himself, before dragging his gaze back to hers.

"I'm sorry."

Those two little words hardly seemed able to convey his true remorse, but they had the power to erase all sign of hurt from her face, warming her expression.

He swallowed and pushed on. "I shouldn't have said what I did. Your kindness has seen me through some of my worst times, and I wouldn't want to lose it. I know I hurt you. Can you forgive me?"

A tired but ready smile graced her lips. "Always."

Jace let out a deep sigh, and now Kyrin took a turn to speak.

"I just want to help you. I was worried when you were gone."

Jace hung his head. He should have thought about her before he left like that. "I know . . . I'm sorry." He rubbed the back of his neck. "And I'm really sorry I ruined your birthday."

Kyrin shrugged. "There will be others."

And Elôm knew how Jace prayed there would be. He, of all people, understood how fragile life was. It could end in a moment, without warning.

"I'm just glad you're safe . . ." she paused, ". . . and came back."

"I would never leave for good." Jace didn't know where the promise came from, but he meant it. There had been a time when he'd contemplated leaving, but as long as she was here, that wouldn't happen.

Her smile returned, brighter this time, but it faded again into seriousness as she searched his eyes. "Are you all right?"

Jace broke eye contact, his gaze wandering around camp as he contemplated how to answer. After last night, he didn't want her to see the doubt, fear, and turmoil that still boiled up inside him and have it come between them again. Struggling, he let his gaze return to her.

"I don't know," he answered truthfully, and shrugged.

"I understand, but please, try to realize that none of this was your fault." She spoke with gentle earnestness. "Yes, it is tragic. I have all the compassion in the world for Alice because I know what she feels, but it doesn't change the fact that her father tried to kill you. *That* would have been murder." She paused, and Jace caught a glimmer of moisture in her eyes. "Do you know how many times I've imagined coming to find you lying there dying? Maybe it's selfish, but I thank Elôm constantly that you're still here. I know this is hard for you, but we've been through hard times before. I just need you to believe we can get through this one."

Jace stared down at her. Maybe he could get through this and maybe he couldn't, but he nodded. For her sake, he had to try.

SPRING WAS TRASK'S favorite time in Landale. It always brought him back to his childhood when he and his friends had run off to the woods to build their forts and have grand adventures. They had spent all day in the forest, always reluctant to return home in the evening. He'd often wished he could live in one of their forts and never leave. He chuckled, taking in the view of camp from just outside his cabin. Though he couldn't say he liked the circumstances, that wish had come true.

Across camp, his eyes snagged on movement that brought a wide smile to his face. There was one thing that could make a day like this even better, and she was riding in right now on a white mare. He set off to meet Anne, his heart light in spite of the matters weighing on his mind. Her smile further buoyed him up. He had known her since they were toddlers, yet she still captivated him like no other. One of these days, he would make her his wife.

"Two visits in one week. Aren't I lucky?" He took hold of her horse's reins while she dismounted.

Anne gave him her familiar amused smile. "I came to see if Jace was back and how Kyrin is doing."

Trask tipped his head. "Why is it that you never seem to come just to see me?"

"You're the one who cautioned me about being seen too often on the forest road. I have to pick and choose my times."

Trask glanced at the playful curve of her lips, tempting him to kiss them.

"So, what about Jace?"

He raised his eyes back to hers, completely unabashed, noting her arched brow. "He returned two days ago."

"Good," Anne said in genuine concern that convicted Trask to take her questioning more seriously. "How is he?"

Handing her horse to one of the boys he had put in charge of the stable, Trask took Anne's hand, and they walked slowly around camp. He could do this all day.

"About as well as can be expected. There was some strain between him and Kyrin, but they've worked it out. I think it's just going to take time for him to put this behind him."

"It's so unfortunate. He looked so happy at the party."

Trask winced. "I should have done something about Hagen before it came to this."

Anne squeezed his hand. "I don't think there was anything you could have done. You couldn't turn them away. I'm sure Jace doesn't blame you for what happened."

Trask agreed, though he still contemplated possible ways he could have prevented it. Despite how Jace viewed himself, Trask valued him as an important member of his inner circle and didn't want him thinking otherwise.

Putting it aside for now, he said, "Leetra returned yesterday."

"What news did she bring?"

"Not good, I'm afraid." He stopped to face Anne. "Looks like Daican is planning to move against Samara. He's been in contact with Sir Rothas Cantan. The man is a brilliant strategist, and we can only assume that he is helping Daican plan a war."

"But you don't know specifics?"

"No. Daican is taking all precautions and only sharing with Richard."

"There's no way to find out what they're up to?"

"The only thing any of us have come up with so far is getting someone into Sir Rothas's home to gather information. Kyrin offered, since all she would have to do is get a look at things, but not only is it dangerous, we have no way to get anyone inside. If I still had my position, it would be easy to manufacture a reason to visit him, but he's not going to take in just anyone."

"What about me?" Anne's question blasted right through Trask's thoughts. "As the daughter of a fellow knight, he'd be obliged to offer me hospitality if I were, say, passing through the area to visit a friend."

"No." He wouldn't even consider it. "It's too risky."

Anne frowned. "Is that based on the chances of success or just that you love me?"

"It's dangerous. If you were to be discovered, you'd be arrested and executed."

Anne's brows rose. "How is that different from my situation now?"

"It *is* different," Trask insisted. "It isn't lying low; it's putting yourself in danger."

"But what if it's Samara's only chance for survival?"

Trask hesitated. He didn't have a good argument for that beyond what he had said already. Before he could try again, she pressed on, her voice softening to an almost pleading tone.

"All of you risk your lives in trying to protect people from the emperor. Well, I want to do my part. I fully understand the risk involved, but if this could aid the people of Samara, then how could we just let the opportunity pass because of the danger? If Kyrin is still willing to take the risk, then so am I. Think about it. This is far bigger than you and me."

Trask grimaced. Why hadn't he kept his mouth shut? The last thing he wanted was to admit that she was right. He blew out a heavy sigh.

"You need to talk to your father. Without his permission, we're not doing anything."

A smile grew on Anne's lips and determination lit in her eyes. Trask's last hope was that Sir John would never agree to this, but, since Anne had already persuaded him to consider it, he had little hope that she wouldn't persuade her father as well.

A prickle of unease crawled along Jace's skin as he followed Warin and the others to Trask's cabin for another meeting. It wasn't like Trask to gather them just before supper. Jace knew he had ridden to Marlton with Anne earlier in the afternoon, and it upset his empty stomach to consider what news he brought back.

As they gathered inside the cabin, Jace sensed the tension in the air. Whatever this was about, it had Trask on edge as well. Once everyone from their group was present, Trask faced them, his usual good humor buried tonight.

"I'm sorry to interrupt you so close to suppertime, but I'll make this brief." His eyes sought one particular member of the group. "Kyrin, are you still willing to gather information from Sir Rothas?"

Jace's heart thumped, and "no" almost left his lips, but he couldn't speak for her. He watched her expression lift in surprise, silently pleading with her not to say yes.

"I'm willing."

Jace let his shoulders slump. He had been so relieved when they'd decided against this course of action. Why had Trask changed his mind?

"I spoke with Anne on the matter today, and she has offered to use her status to get an invitation into Rothas's home."

So that was reason for Trask's sullen mood—he didn't want Anne in such danger any more than Jace did Kyrin. No doubt he had tried to talk her out of it, but, knowing Anne, she had likely insisted.

"I've spoken with Sir John and we're both in agreement that we should make every effort to gain this information for Samara's sake, though neither of us are particularly comfortable with the risk." Trask paused as if rethinking the entire thing before pressing on. "The best way to combat this is to make sure Anne and Kyrin have a strong security force. That's where the rest of you come in. Unfortunately, Sir Rothas and I have met, so I am unable to join you, but I trust that you will take care of them." He turned. "Rayad, unless you have any objections, I'm placing you as head of security."

Rayad nodded in acceptance.

Trask scanned the others present—Jace, Kaden, Trev, Mick, and Holden. "Do any of you have objections about going?"

Jace shook his head, as did the others. He would follow Kyrin anywhere to make sure she was safe.

"Good, that makes five, plus Rayad. I'd like to add one more man. It will look more professional that way. I'm open to suggestions."

"I'll go." Aaron's voice came from the back of the cabin where he stood listening in with Timothy.

Trask looked at him, appearing pleased by the offer. After all, Timothy's brother was resourceful in tricky situations and a master with a bow. His skills as a half crete had already come in handy before. "All right."

"When will we be leaving?" Rayad asked.

"You'll have tomorrow to prepare. Sir John will gather Marlton security uniforms for you. You'll need to travel by horseback."

His gaze shifted once again to Kyrin. "You'll go under the guise of Anne's maid. She will provide you with the necessary clothing."

Jace worked the hard-bristled brush over Niton's warm black coat, loosing the mud and thick winter hair. The stallion stood, one back leg propped restfully, enjoying the attention. The two of them hadn't been on any sort of mission together since the dragons had become part of camp. Jace had grown very fond of his dragon, Gem, but he was eager to use the horses this time. Though he had become accustomed to flying, he still had no love of heights.

Glancing over the horse's back, his gaze caught on Kyrin as she left Trask's cabin, from working with Timothy, no doubt. They spent a lot of time together . . . His brows pulled together. Not that it should bother him. There was no better man in all of camp than Timothy. Kyrin would do well to take interest in him. Still, that didn't stop the discomforting twinge in Jace's chest.

When she turned in his direction, toward the stable, he fixed his gaze back on Niton. She would read more in his expression than he wanted her to know. He focused on his brush and a stubborn patch of mud. A couple of minutes later, Kyrin appeared again, leading her dappled buckskin, Maera, out of the paddock to tie at the rail near Jace. She smiled brightly as she caught his eyes.

Why did his heart have to do that flip, making his breath hitch in his lungs? It happened too often lately. He cleared his throat to settle it and managed to smile back normally, or so he hoped. She turned to brush her horse, and he let his breath seep out without a sound. What a ridiculous fool he was being.

They were both silent for several minutes, but Jace's thoughts continued to revolve around Kyrin as they had been almost nonstop since the meeting with Trask last night. If only they had never found out about Daican's correspondences with Sir Rothas. He tried to bite his tongue, but the words tumbled out anyway. "Are you sure you want to do this?"

Kyrin straightened and met his eyes. She looked so calm in spite of the impending danger. For once, he couldn't help but wish she wasn't so brave.

"I want to help Samara. I don't think we have much of a choice."

"You don't have to do it." He should be thinking of the greater good like everyone else, but the last time an Altair had attempted a dangerous mission, he had been caught and executed. Jace couldn't abide the thought of losing Kyrin the same way. Yet, as much as he wanted to stop her, he couldn't. She would have to decide for herself.

"I know," she responded quietly.

And he knew her mind was made up. He couldn't combat her courage and compassion. All he could do was go along to protect her or die trying. Resigning himself, he bent to finish grooming Niton.

An hour later, neither one of them had said much. Kyrin certainly knew of his feelings about the mission. Finished with the horses and full of dust and horsehair, they returned the animals to their paddocks and walked back to the cabins.

"I better get cleaned up and start packing." Kyrin's voice was light, as if she were trying to dispel the heavy mood and cheer him up.

Jace only nodded and they parted ways, but then he stopped. If she wasn't going to change her mind, then he had something to do before they left in the morning. "Kyrin, before you go in, I want to show you something."

She turned to him curiously, and he glanced down at his dirtied hands, his tongue suddenly becoming clumsy. "I never had the chance to give you your birthday present."

Her face lit up, and he led her toward the supply shed.

"I was going to get it when . . ." Jace cleared his throat. "I met Hagen."

At the shed, he told her to wait outside and stepped in to retrieve a long, burlap-wrapped item from the back corner. His heart beat a little faster as he brought it out to her. Would she like it? It wasn't a typical gift for a girl. Some would probably think it a very odd gift, but Kyrin was different.

Her expression once again lifted in curiosity. She took it from him, glancing once at his face while she untied the twine that secured the cloth. Jace held his breath, his uncertainty rearing up again. Maybe he should have gone to Trask or Lenae for ideas for something else, something more befitting a young woman . . .

The wrapping fell away, and Kyrin's eyes grew huge at the oak staff it revealed—stained and polished, with flowers carved into the top and vines winding down toward the middle.

"Oh, Jace!" She ran her fingers along the intricate carvings.

Jace shifted, unable to shake his awkwardness. "I know it's not like your other gifts, but I hoped you would like it."

"It's beautiful. Where did you get it?"

He cleared his throat. The last thing he wanted was to make this about him. If only he didn't have to answer. "I made it."

Her wondrous eyes rose to his. "You made it? When did you learn how to do that?"

"Aldor taught me." He shrugged. "We used to work on pieces together. It's been a while since I practiced."

She shook her head. "It's incredible."

"You probably can't take it with you," Jace said, shifting the attention away from himself, "but I wanted you to have it before we left." A stirring of satisfaction did settle inside him at the smile that grew on her lips.

"Thank you." She stepped forward to give him a hug.

Jace returned her embrace, and his pulse quickened again. She fit so perfectly and comfortably in his arms . . . as if she were meant to be there. With a jolt of alarm, he reined those thoughts back and pulled away before the embrace could linger too long and cause him to do something altogether crazy . . . like kiss her.

His heartbeat doubled in panic. He needed an escape. "I should go pack." Heaven help him, he hoped his voice wasn't as hoarse as it sounded to him.

Kyrin nodded, a little grin peeking out. "Me too. Thank you so much for this. It's one of my favorite gifts I've ever received."

Jace ducked his head. "I'm glad you like it."

With a glowing smile, she turned away. When she had disappeared, Jace sagged back against the shed, hanging his head. What was he doing? What was happening to him? He wasn't supposed to feel like this. After what had happened with Hagen, he should have pushed these feelings aside for good. Instead, they just kept growing harder to resist. What was he to do with them? He knew *nothing* of such things. All he knew for sure was that, if he wasn't careful, it could ruin everything between him and Kyrin, and he didn't want to risk that any more than he wanted to risk her life.

THE FIRST PALE glow of dawn was just lighting the horizon when Jace followed the others up to Marlton Hall the next morning. Most of the countryside was still asleep, and they hoped to be off before too many people who might report to Captain Goler noticed their departure. Trask dismounted first and knocked on the back door. Sir John answered it, spilling light into the yard, and invited everyone inside. Anne and Lady Catherine greeted them as they entered the candlelit main room.

"I have the uniforms for each of you." Sir John closed the door behind them and gestured to the dining table, where seven bundles of dark fabric lay.

While Anne took Kyrin upstairs to change, the men stepped to the table and donned their uniforms—a deep blue and black tabard with a white dove in the center of the chest. Jace pulled his on over his shirt and buckled on his belt. Looking over the others, he found they made a diverse group but, in matching uniforms, no one would ever guess their true identities or intentions. They were simply a security escort for a noblewoman.

He glanced at Trask and Sir John, who stood watching. They may have agreed to this, but neither one looked comfortable with it. If he thought it would make them feel any better, he would have told them that anyone intending harm to either

Kyrin or Anne would have to kill him first. The same went for every man in the group. Jace tested his sword in its sheath, making sure it didn't stick if he did have to use it. He had just put a razor edge on it and his dagger the night before, though he prayed it would be unnecessary.

A few minutes later, Anne returned with Kyrin, who wore a nondescript gray traveling dress and white cap to hide her still-too-short hair. She looked the part of a servant, although it didn't make her any less attractive. Jace quickly forced this thought away. He would not let his feelings overshadow his reason and common sense as they nearly had yesterday. Especially not when he needed all his wits about him to make sure she stayed safe.

"We're ready," Anne announced. "We'd best get started. I would hate to have this be the one morning Goler decides to visit. That's just the sort of thing he would do whether he realized it or not."

Trask and John picked up her belongings, and they all gathered out by the horses again. Here, Anne said goodbye to her parents before coming to Trask.

His hands on her shoulders, he looked down into her eyes, his tone uncharacteristically somber. "Be careful."

She gave him an understanding smile. "I will."

"If you get any sense at all that Rothas is suspicious, get out. You have to promise me."

"I promise."

Jace could hear Trask's long exhale. It must be killing him to have to remain here. Jace didn't know how he did it. He watched Trask place a soft kiss on Anne's forehead. Anne, in response, rose up on her toes and gave him a quick kiss on the lips instead. Trask's grin finally emerged, and Jace looked down at Niton's reins to resist the tugging urge to glance at Kyrin. Fighting these feelings was going to drive him mad yet. Why couldn't he just feel the same as he had last year when she'd simply been his closest friend? Why the unwelcome complications now?

With their goodbyes said, Trask guided Anne to her horse and helped her mount, while giving a few final instructions. "We decided on Kyrin going by the name Corinne, and Kaden will be Caleb. They're close enough to their real names to be easy and familiar, but won't raise suspicion."

Anne nodded.

The rest of the group mounted, and Trask addressed the men. "Be cautious and keep a low profile. Thanks to Falcor, the emperor knows a great deal about us, but we can only pray Rothas doesn't have the same details. Like I said, if there is any hint that he's on to you, I want you all to leave." His gaze shifted back to Anne. "Don't stay any longer than you must."

"Don't worry. We'll find an excuse to leave." She gave him a playful smile. "Perhaps his food won't agree with me."

Trask's lips lifted in return, but it was short-lived. "Right then, you should go."

Anne took up her reins and, with a final goodbye to him and her parents, she turned her horse to take the lead with Rayad. Kyrin and the rest of the men fell in behind them. When they reached the road, they turned north, and a twinge passed through Jace's stomach. Would the next few days go as smoothly as they hoped?

Around noon, the entire group paused for a rest and lunch after an uneventful morning. So far, they had not passed any other travelers on the road. An hour ago, they had left the forest behind, coming to a landscape of gentle rolling hills, which grew more pronounced the farther they headed north. It appeared to be good farmland, though Jace preferred more trees. There were some pockets of them, but nothing like the seemingly endless wilderness around camp.

Gathering at the side of the road, they each ate from their saddlebags.

"What do you know of this Sir Rothas?" Rayad asked Anne.

Everyone looked at her for her response. Jace wanted to know exactly what sort of man they had to deal with and what Kyrin was walking into. The fact that he was a brilliant strategist was not comforting. What if he saw right through their ruse?

"I've only met him once at a banquet held in Landale. We barely more than greeted one another, but he didn't strike me as a friendly sort." Anne wrinkled her nose. "But I hear he's got quite an eye for the ladies."

The hair along Jace's arms prickled. Not what he wanted to hear. Hopefully Kyrin wouldn't spend much time near him.

"He actually grew up in Tarvin Hall," Anne continued, giving Kyrin and Kaden a look, "and was knighted shortly after his promotion. Daican was apparently quite impressed. I wouldn't be surprised if he's been a driving force behind the emperor's plans all these years."

"Is he married?" Holden asked.

Anne nodded. "His wife is Lady Rachel, the daughter of Henry Ilvaran, Earl of Dunrick."

"I know your mother did, but isn't it rather rare for the daughter of an earl to marry a knight, even a prominent one?"

"Well, I don't know the details, and I've never met her, but rumor has it that Lady Rachel had a child out of wedlock and the marriage was a rushed arrangement. I hear Sir Rothas was the only suitor still interested, though, from what I know of him, I suspect it had more to do with the prestige and wealth it bought him than saving her reputation."

"Poor woman," Kyrin murmured.

"Yes, despite the rumors and circumstances, I do hear she's very kind. In any case, I'm sure it will be an interesting meeting."

Interesting and dangerous. Jace sighed.

With the sun setting behind them, Jace and the others approached Ashwood, Sir Rothas's grand estate. According to Anne, it was part of Lady Rachel's dowry. Acres of soon-to-be tilled farmland spread out around them, dotted with cottages and barns. The center point of it all was the magnificent stone manor house with ivy weaving up the three stories to the roof.

Following the rutted path that branched off the main road, they passed through a low rock wall, the horses' hooves clacking when they hit the stone courtyard. Here, they all reined to a halt. Jace's gaze traveled up the height of the manor house, its many windows blazing in the red-orange sun. In a way, it reminded him of an estate he had belonged to during his childhood. Rothas sounded very similar to one of his old masters. Once again, a chill crawled along his skin, and he shook away the old memories. This mission was unpleasant enough already.

A door closing drew Jace's attention back to the manor's entrance, where a middle-aged man with dark features had just exited and descended the steps to meet them. Dressed in a red security uniform with gold trimming, he carried himself with confidence and authority, no doubt a ranking member of Ashwood's security. His face was strong and serious, and he eyed each of them in turn.

Rayad, as the head of the group and expected to handle Anne's affairs, nudged his horse forward. "Lady Anne, daughter of Sir John Wyland to see Sir Rothas Cantan."

If Jace hadn't known him, he never would have guessed that Rayad had been a simple farmer and horse breeder all his life. But then, he'd always had a commanding air about him when the occasion called for it.

The guard's attention shifted to Anne. Jace glanced at her. She was already playing her part as well, projecting herself as the opulent daughter of a fellow knight. She had said it would make Rothas less likely to suspect her or them of duplicity. Amazing how something as simple as posture could change her entire appearance. Just the way she perched in her saddle, her chin at a slight angle, exuded superiority.

The guard nodded. "Please, come inside, my lady," he invited, his deep voice surprisingly soft-spoken.

As they dismounted, he motioned to two young men, who had come from the stables to tend the horses. He then led them all into the manor house. When they stepped inside, Jace's gaze was drawn to the furnishings, and he compared the manor to Baron Grey's castle in Landale. The castle had been too dark and stifling for him, but Ashwood clearly had a woman's touch. Lady Rachel had filled it with warm, rich colors that made it seem homey and welcoming in spite of its intimidating size.

With the tap of footsteps, a distinguished older gentleman met them in the entrance hall.

"Walton, this is Lady Anne of Marlton. Will you please see that she is comfortable?" the guard requested. "I will inform Sir Rothas and her ladyship of her arrival."

"Of course." The butler focused on Anne. "Right this way, my lady."

Off to the right of the hall, he admitted them into a comfortable parlor that overlooked the courtyard.

"Is there anything I can get you, my lady?" Walton asked.

"I think I'll just sit for now."

"Of course. Make yourself comfortable."

He left them to wait, and Anne took a seat on a nearby sofa, while the others stood off to the side. She arranged and smoothed her skirt before trading a wry look with Kyrin, who didn't quite hide a smile. The act would be amusing if not for the knotting and churning in Jace's gut. Now that they were here, he just wanted to get things over with as soon as possible. He didn't feel as confident as he wanted to about being able to keep Kyrin safe here. In a house this size with all the staff and security, there were too many variables.

"So far so good," Anne whispered.

Only moments later, footsteps echoed in the hall. Jace straightened as the door opened. A lordly man and woman stepped inside, and the security guard entered behind them. Anne rose from her seat as the first man greeted her.

"Lady Anne, welcome to Ashwood."

She nodded to him and his wife. "Sir Rothas, Lady Rachel."

"We were not expecting company." Rothas's voice was smooth as glass and equally cool.

His presence made Jace distinctly uneasy, and he sized the man up. He was tall, fit, and dark. No doubt he could handle himself, being a knight. But that wasn't what disturbed Jace—it was the look in his iron-like eyes. Jace had known men like him before. He had the look of a predator. Jace barely restrained himself from stepping closer to Kyrin.

"I'm on my way to Mareby to visit Lady Hamilton," Anne responded. "My father thought some time away from Landale and all that dreadful talk of rebellion would do me good, but I'm afraid my constitution just isn't built for travel."

Again, she amazed Jace with how well she played her part, even making her voice a bit breathy.

"If you would be so kind as to allow me a day or two to refresh myself before I travel on, I would very much appreciate it."

65

The man could hardly say no to her persuasive tone. "Of course you may stay, for as long as you wish."

Rothas's cool, dark eyes traveled up and down Anne, and Jace gritted his teeth. Trask would be infuriated were he here. Even the security guard gave Sir Rothas an unseen look of disgust.

Working to cool his own emotions, Jace shifted his gaze to Lady Rachel. Though in her mid to late thirties, she had a very youthful beauty—her long hair dark and silky, the perfect complement to a pair of violet blue eyes. Yet, hidden behind them was an underlying hint of sadness. Somehow, Jace just knew she had seen hard times, and his scorn for Sir Rothas grew. How could a man ever have an eye for other women when he already had a lovely wife right at his side? Every sense of decency burned in indignation.

At that moment, Lady Rachel glanced toward their group, and her eyes met Jace's. They held for a second before Jace looked away. His face flushed. He shouldn't have been caught staring. When he glanced up after a moment, she still watched him. Ice traveled down his spine, and this time he dropped his gaze to the floor, holding it there as he fought not to fidget. What if she suspected he was a ryrik? It could jeopardize their entire mission. Had his mere presence just endangered everyone? The possibility made him sick.

After several minutes, in which he heard nothing Anne or Rothas said, he risked another glance at Lady Rachel to gauge her mood. Her attention had returned to Anne, but her expression worried him. Only a hint of her earlier smile remained in place, and she seemed to have paled. What it meant, he couldn't say, but he feared the consequences. If only he could pull Rayad aside and let him know of the possible danger.

At last, Lady Rachel's smile returned full-strength as she spoke with Anne. "I'll show you to a room. Once you're settled in, a servant will show your maid to her room . . ."

"Actually," Anne cut in smoothly, "I'd prefer her to stay in my room should I need her."

Jace let out a quiet sigh. The idea of Kyrin alone, especially in the household of a man like Sir Rothas, had given him a moment of panic. Knowing she was with Anne would ease his nerves.

"Then I will have extra bedding brought in for her." Rachel turned to the security guard near the door. "Elian."

The man stepped forward.

"See that Lady Anne's men are looked after and her belongings are brought inside."

"Yes, my lady." He spoke in a quiet, almost warm tone of respect.

Comparing the two, Jace found him to be the opposite of Sir Rothas. While both were very capable and potentially formidable men, Elian embodied a distinct humility whereas Rothas oozed arrogance and power. Though both shared dark features, it took little more than a glimpse at their eyes to see the difference—Rothas's cool, hard, and predatory while Elian's were a warm, yet perceptive deep brown. The look Elian had given Rothas before suggested he could be an ally . . . if things didn't fall apart on their first night here.

They moved to follow him. Falling to the back of the group, Jace glanced over his shoulder at Kyrin, who gave him a brief smile. It was torture to leave her, but he had to believe she would be safe with Anne. As his gaze swung around to the parlor door, it met again with Lady Rachel. She knew something, and he could only hope she wouldn't share it with her husband.

Outside, Elian instructed servants to bring Anne's bags inside and the stable boys to bed down the horses. Collecting their things, Jace and the others followed him around the manor and through a side door to the downstairs level. The commotion of voices and activity came from down the hall, and Jace got a strong whiff of savory meat roast.

"The servants' hall is straight ahead to the right and the kitchen beyond that," Elian told them. "Supper will be served after Sir Rothas and her ladyship have finished around eight."

Now he guided them down a long hall to the left, pausing to open two doors. "These will be your rooms for your stay. Should you need anything, ask one of the staff or find me at the guard house."

"Thank you," Rayad responded.

Elian gave a short nod and strode away.

Jace glanced into the rooms. They were whitewashed and sparsely furnished with a washstand, wardrobe, and four beds, but they looked clean. Splitting up, Jace, Rayad, Kaden, and Holden took the first room while Aaron, Mick, and Trev occupied the second. Setting his bag down on a bed, Jace turned to Rayad.

"We may have a problem."

Rayad frowned. "What is that?"

"Lady Rachel." Jace grimaced. "She may be suspicious of me and think I'm a ryrik. She noticed something when she looked at me."

Rayad rubbed his beard, thinking. "You're sure?"

Jace nodded.

"Then we'll keep you out of sight. If nothing is said at supper, we'll let Anne know about it and pray it doesn't become an issue before we can leave."

Jace released a heavy sigh. If their mission failed because of him . . . "I'm sorry."

Rayad shook his head. "It's not your fault. I'm sure everything will be fine. Their focus will be on Anne anyway."

"WELL, THIS IS quite spacious," Anne remarked as she and Kyrin took in the sight of the bedroom.

Kyrin gazed at the lovely pale gold walls and dusty pink accents. The large, four-poster bed was dark wood, but had a dreamy, sheer canopy and lush bedspread. "It reminds me of my old room back at Auréa Palace . . . but less dark." And less intimidating.

"I suppose I better change if I'm going to be down in time for supper." Anne rummaged through one of her bags and pulled out a peach-colored satin evening gown. "A bit wrinkled, but it will have to do. Perhaps tomorrow I can have the others pressed."

She reached back to loosen the laces of her dress, and Kyrin stepped up to help. If she was pretending to be Anne's maid, she might as well play the part.

"Thank you," Anne said.

Helping her into her evening gown, Kyrin spoke in a hushed voice. "So, now that we're here, what's our plan?"

"Well, I intend to do a little exploring tomorrow. No doubt Sir Rothas has a private office where he keeps all his letters. Hopefully I'll find it quickly. I don't want to be here any longer than necessary. The man is just as insufferable as I remember. Thank heavens Trask isn't here or we'd have a duel on our hands."

Kyrin had to smile, though it faded in a moment. The way Sir Rothas had looked at Anne sent skitters across her skin. She hesitated and swallowed, a little heat rising to her cheeks. "Are you sure you're safe around him?"

Anne glanced back at her. "Don't worry. Thanks to my mother, I still outrank him and could cause quite a bit of trouble if I had a mind to. He's not going to risk his standing with that sort of scandal. We know he's anything but stupid."

This did ease Kyrin's mind.

Once Anne was dressed, Kyrin helped her tidy her hair and cosmetics. Putting on a rather gaudy pair of gold and peach earrings, Anne frowned at her reflection in the dressing table mirror.

"I do hate these things . . . and the dress."

Kyrin gave her an odd look, and Anne smirked wryly. "Most of what I brought are birthday gifts from suitors trying too hard to impress me."

Kyrin laughed and helped her slip on a pair of heeled shoes that she seemed much more comfortable in than Kyrin would be.

"Will you be all right on your own this evening?"

Kyrin straightened. "I'll be all right." If she could handle Auréa Palace, she could handle this.

A couple of minutes later, a light knock brought them to the door. Anne opened it to a blonde-haired servant girl, who curtsied deeply.

"Excuse me, my lady, I was sent to inform you that supper is near ready."

Anne nodded curtly. "Thank you."

"And I can show your maid down to the servants' hall if you'd like. Supper'll be there later."

Anne glanced back at Kyrin and nodded again. The two of them left the room. Downstairs, Walton met them to show Anne to the dining room, while Kyrin followed the servant girl. Hopefully Jace and the others would be down in the servants' hall as well. She didn't want to have to try to socialize with the other servants without them, especially if anyone had questions about Anne.

"I'm Tina, by the way."

Kyrin looked into the servant girl's striking green eyes and infectious smile. "Corinne."

"Have you always worked for Lady Anne?"

"No, not always." Kyrin paused, and Tina waited for her to elaborate, but she kept silent. The less anyone knew of the situation, the better.

Undeterred, Tina wrinkled her nose. "She's a bit of a prig, ain't she?"

Kyrin barely choked back a giggle. That was so not Anne. Tina must have taken her silence as disapproval.

"I mean no offense."

Kyrin shook her head. "She's actually quite nice when you get to know her."

"Well, in any case, it must be nice to work in a smaller house like Marl—"

Tina's mouth snapped shut as a young man strode around the corner ahead of them. His dark blue eyes landed on her first, but then shifted to Kyrin, locking on her boldly. He was certainly no servant, dressed richly as he was. His gaze did not leave her until they had passed each other. A cold shiver raced down Kyrin's back. He had the same leering look as Sir Rothas. She swallowed, her mouth dry, and looked over at Tina. The girl had her head ducked. When she did look up again, Kyrin read an unsettling discomfort in her eyes, perhaps even fear.

"That's Sir Rothas's son," Tina murmured. "Best stay clear of him."

Nausea bubbled in Kyrin's stomach, and she silently reached out to Elôm for security. It was hard enough to be wary of Rothas without having to worry about the threat of his son too.

Down in the servants' hall, Tina invited Kyrin to sit at one of two long tables. Kyrin did so, rubbing her moist palms across her skirt when Tina joined her. She wasn't good at small talk. Thankfully, Tina was a talkative sort, and Kyrin managed to say just enough to keep her going and avoid any risky topics.

Sometime later, the chattering Tina's attention suddenly shifted. "My, he's a handsome one."

Kyrin looked over her shoulder and breathed a sigh as her friends entered the room. Tina's exuberance was starting to give her a headache. Kyrin looked at her again. It was Kaden the girl had her eyes on.

Her face alight with curiosity, Tina asked in a low whisper, "Is he your brother?"

"Yes, Caleb."

Tina's admiring gaze returned to Kaden. "Goodness, look at those shoulders. Your father must be huge."

Kyrin's throat squeezed, the ache radiating down into her chest. "No, our grandfather," she murmured, but Tina was no longer listening.

Kyrin breathed in hard, shaken by the mention of her father. After all, he had died on a mission not too unlike this one. Coldness crept into her core with a sudden homesickness for camp and safety, and every part of her that didn't want to do this cried for escape. But then someone sat down beside her. She looked over into Jace's eyes. At once, she was comforted and felt safe. He would protect her.

The rest of the evening passed as they congregated in the servants' hall. Someone always had an interest in their presence. Tina didn't leave until one of the older maids showed up and scolded her for neglecting her duties. However, she didn't seem the slightest bit contrite when she sent a wide smile in Kaden's direction on her way out. He was either oblivious or pointedly ignoring the girl's interest. Kyrin wasn't sure which yet.

Suppertime brought the whole staff together, crammed at the tables with their guests. Kyrin was thankful to have Rayad there to handle all the questions.

"So, Marlton," an older man, the gardener, said. "That's right near Landale, isn't it?"

Rayad nodded. He never said anything more than he had to.

"There's quite a rebellion going on there. The baron's son turned traitor, isn't that right?"

"That's what they say," Rayad responded casually.

"Word has it your Lady Anne was sweet on him."

Rayad glanced at him. "It's Lady Anne's safety that is my concern, not her personal life."

The gardener shrugged.

"What do you think of this rebellion?" another man asked. Kyrin didn't care for him. He was a sneaky sort.

Rayad leveled him with a stern gaze. "Like I said, I'm not much concerned with the affairs of Landale. My job is to protect Lady Anne. That keeps me busy enough."

No one mentioned Landale again after this.

When the meal ended and the crowd dissipated, Kyrin rose. If only she could stay with Jace and the others, but it was getting late. Anne would be waiting for her, and she didn't want anyone getting suspicious if she didn't play her part. Aside from Tina, the staff here seemed very attentive to their duties. Jace rose with her, and they met Rayad and Kaden near the door.

"I should be getting up to Anne's room. She may be there already."

Rayad agreed. "It will be interesting for you to find out how supper went."

"Yes, I'll let you know about it tomorrow." She glanced at the table. Tina still lingered there. Kyrin couldn't help giving her brother a wry look. "In case you haven't noticed, Tina has quite an eye for you."

"Oh, I noticed." He released a longsuffering sigh.

Kyrin gave him a half sympathetic, half amused smile. "Well, goodnight then."

Rayad and Kaden both said goodnight, and Kyrin turned to Jace. They hadn't spoken at all since arriving, but the deep shadows in his eyes said he was troubled.

"Be careful," he told her in a solemn voice.

"I will." She gave him a quick smile before leaving the hall.

As she climbed the steps back upstairs, she didn't think much about being alone until the sounds died away behind her. She let the door close and found the main hall dim and quiet. Taking a deep breath, she reined in her imagination. Still, Tina's words when they had passed Sir Rothas's son whispered at the back of her mind. She cast another cautious look around before walking on.

Kyrin forced herself to maintain a moderate pace through the hall and up to the second floor, but her steps did quicken the closer she came to Anne's room. The candlelight peeking under the door was a great relief. After a light knock, she let herself in. Anne sat at the dressing table pulling pins from her hair.

"There you are." She turned to face Kyrin. "How was it?"

Kyrin shrugged. "There were a lot of questions and curiosity about Landale, but we let Rayad do the talking. He did want me to warn you that Lady Rachel may suspect Jace of being a ryrik. Did she mention anything?"

"No."

After making certain to lock the door, Kyrin pulled off her cap and ran her fingers through her hair as she sank into the stuffed chair near the bed. What a long day. "How was your evening?"

"All right," Anne replied. "Lady Rachel is a wonderfully pleasant hostess. She makes up for everything Sir Rothas lacks. I almost feel sorry deceiving her. Their daughter, Elanor, is also very nice. She offered to show me around tomorrow."

Pulling out the last pin and fluffing her hair, Anne made a face in the mirror. "Their son, James, however, clearly takes after his father. He flirted with me all through supper, never mind that I'm five years older than him."

Kyrin drew her brows together, Tina's warning coming back again. She would certainly heed it. "What about the child you mentioned earlier?"

"I don't know. It was only the two of them, and they were clearly Rothas's."

Mulling this over, Kyrin and Anne changed into their nightgowns and finished preparing for bed. Sometime earlier, servants had brought extra bedding to the room. Kyrin picked up a blanket from the pile to construct a bed on the floor, but Anne stopped her.

"Never mind that. This bed could hold three of us."

Kyrin smiled as Anne pulled down the covers, and they both crawled into bed. For a moment, her mind wandered back to Landale. Meredith would be asleep by now. She and Kyrin always shared a bed. Maybe she would sleep with Lenae tonight instead.

"This reminds me of when my cousins used to visit years ago," Anne said as they settled in. "We'd stay up until all hours talking and giggling. Mother even had to come in and shush us a few times."

Kyrin grinned, and Anne continued, "They would tease me just terribly about Trask, or worse, talk about catching his eye themselves."

They shared a laugh now, and Anne propped herself up on her elbow. "What about you? Anyone interested back at camp?"

Kyrin shrugged against her pillow. "Well, Jeremy still likes to hang around as much as he can, but I think he understands that I'm not interested. And now he has Kaden, Marcus, *and* Liam to contend with."

"Poor boy," Anne mused with a laugh. "So that's it? No one else?"

"Not that I'm aware of."

Anne just stared at her for a moment, as if trying to draw something more from her. "Anyone you wish was interested?"

Jace's face jumped immediately to Kyrin's mind and a strange feeling of longing fluttered through her chest. She breathed out slowly, and pushed it away. It was a silly thought. Jace didn't think that way, and she shouldn't either. Finally, she looked at Anne. "No one who ever would be."

"I THINK SHE'S in love with you."

Kaden shot Trev a dark look in answer to his amused tone and grin. Though Jace tried, he couldn't hold back his own amusement, even if it was at Kaden's expense. He was just glad he wasn't the one Tina had set her sights on. He wasn't equipped to handle that awkward situation.

Kaden grumbled under his breath and sat down hard on his bed, where he flopped back against the pillow.

Aaron leaned casually against the doorframe. "She's quite a talker."

Kaden scrubbed his hands over his face and released a low groan. "If I have to hide in this room the whole time we're here, I'll lose my mind."

"Not as fast as you would out there." Aaron gestured over his shoulder, earning a chorus of chuckles.

Grabbing the pillow, Kaden chucked it at him. "A lot of help you are."

As Aaron bent down for it, Rayad returned to the room from meeting with Anne and Kyrin. The mood changed immediately, and Jace straightened. He needed to know about Kyrin. He hadn't slept well last night, not knowing for sure if she was safe. How could he protect her if he couldn't even be on the same floor as her?

"What's the word?" Aaron asked.

"Rothas's daughter, Lady Elanor, has offered to show Anne around. Anne hopes to discover Rothas's office that way. In the meantime, we need to lie low and keep things quiet down here. No drawing unnecessary attention."

"That might be difficult if Kaden has to break a certain servant girl's heart."

Kaden scowled again at Aaron, who tried, unsuccessfully, to hide a smile.

"I'm afraid, Kaden," Rayad said flatly, "you'll just have to put up with it for the time being."

Kaden released another groan.

Footsteps echoed in the hall, and everyone fell silent. A moment later, Elian appeared at their door. He scanned the room, and Jace tensed. It would be entirely too easy to be caught in this dangerous masquerade of theirs.

"Can we help you?" Rayad asked.

Elian glanced at him, but his eyes settled squarely on Jace. "I need him to come with me."

Jace's heart stalled before beating rapidly in his throat.

Silence surrounded them until Rayad spoke up, calm, yet firm. "What for?"

Elian's gaze did not leave Jace. It was as if he were searching for something. Proof, perhaps, of Jace's ryrik lineage? It wouldn't take much for him to find it. Though nothing about the man spoke of ill intent, everything inside Jace shouted to escape the situation.

"Her ladyship wishes to speak with him."

So it was as Jace feared. Why couldn't he have been wrong about Lady Rachel's reaction? Why hadn't he done everything possible to keep a low profile and never given her a chance to notice him? His folly had doomed them all. He could feel it in his gut.

He steadied himself. No. He would do whatever it took to keep Kyrin and the others out of this.

"May I ask why?" Rayad questioned.

Now Elian did look at him. "That's not for me to say. I was only sent to bring him to her." He paused for a moment, and his tone lowered. "But I do know it is important."

He sent another glance at Jace, though whatever thoughts filled his brown eyes were impossible to guess. Something about them almost looked imploring, yet Jace was no great judge of emotions. If only Kyrin were here.

Rayad's voice rose a little in intensity. "You must have some reason you can give us. Why would she need to see one of Lady Anne's guards?"

"She only wishes to ask him a few questions."

"Then I'm going with him," Rayad said decidedly.

Elian shook his head. "She asked to speak with him in private."

Jace sensed the tension rising between them. This was exactly what they needed to avoid. Kyrin's safety depended on it.

Before Rayad could argue further, Jace stepped forward. "I'll go."

If this concerned his ryrik blood, then he would take whatever consequences it brought. He would not let the others get involved and jeopardize the mission. Maybe, once he explained that he was only half ryrik, Lady Rachel would understand and there would be no trouble. Somehow, though, he didn't see it being that simple.

Both Rayad and Elian looked at him. Rayad had an expression of protest on his face, but Jace shook his head and focused determinedly on Elian. "I'll go with you."

The man gave a slow nod. "Thank you."

He gestured to the door. Jace glanced around the room. Not one of his friends looked happy about this, but it had to be this way. Rayad had just said that they needed to keep things quiet.

Elian turned, and Jace followed him out of the room. The guard didn't say a word as they walked down the hall and up the steps. Jace drew a restricted breath, doing what he could to prepare himself. There was no telling what this meeting would lead to. Strange that Lady Rachel would wish to see him in private. Then again, it was probably better than facing Sir Rothas. Lady Rachel might be more understanding of his situation.

At the top of the stairs, Elian opened the door and paused, checking the hall before motioning Jace to follow. Jace frowned when he did it at several other points on their way through the house. Why such secrecy? Needle pricks crept along his arms. Something just wasn't right about this whole thing. If they suspected he was a ryrik, why not just arrest and question him? Elian certainly wasn't treating him as a potential threat.

Jace's heart thudded, heat threading through his arms and warming his hands. There were too many unanswered questions. He wasn't sure whether to be relieved or even more apprehensive when they finally stopped at a door. Elian opened it and motioned him inside.

Jace squeezed his right fist. His instincts rebelled at entering an unknown situation without a weapon, but resisting now was not an option. He stepped cautiously into the small parlor and took it all in with a sweeping look. No immediate threats jumped out at him. Lady Rachel stood near a large window, where sunlight filtered through a set of sheer curtains. Beside her was an older woman—tall, thin, yet regal. A picture of poise and refinement. By the similarities between the two of them, Jace guessed that this other woman was Lady Rachel's mother, adding a new level to the oddity of this meeting. What in Ilyon could they want with him?

The door clicked shut. Jace darted a glance over his shoulder. Elian stood there, blocking the exit, though it may not have been intentional. Jace's attention swung back around to Lady Rachel, who took a step forward. She seemed almost as tentative as he was.

"Jace?"

He drew his brows together. How did she know his name? Of course, one of the servants could have informed her . . . but the way she said it—it was more of a question than merely addressing him.

"Yes?"

She drew in her breath and put her hand to her mouth as she looked at the other woman. Then Jace caught a whisper from her lips, something so slight, only he could possibly have heard it.

"*Oh, Elôm.*"

Jace's heart skipped a beat. What was going on? His thoughts a jumble, he spoke the first thing that came to mind. "How do you know my name?"

Lady Rachel faced him again, her hand dropping to her chest. Tears pooled in her deep blue eyes, and her voice trembled. "I know because . . . I named you."

Everything stilled. There were no thoughts, no sounds, nothing. Just those words, hanging in Jace's consciousness with all their many implications. *I named you.*

His breath rushed out and a swell of emotions flooded in. A million different thoughts crashed into his mind, but one rose to the top, throbbing through his entire body with the intensity of what it meant. He drew a halting breath, his throat threatening to close up. Something akin to both terror and a deep hopeful longing took hold of him. He opened his mouth and fought to make his tongue work. All the while, she watched him, tears glittering on the very edges of her lashes.

"You're . . ." The one word barely made it past his lips. He couldn't seem to form the rest.

"Yes," Rachel whispered, but it didn't fully sink in until she said, "I'm your mother."

Jace took a shallow breath as he watched her tears finally spill over, sliding down her face one after the other. His own eyes burned, and he had to blink to keep her in focus. Could it be true? Did he dare believe it? How could it be? Then it hit him, the realization slamming into his chest like a hammer blow. *He* was the child Anne had mentioned on the road.

Weakness gripped his legs, and questions assaulted his mind, all clamoring for answers at once. He could only stand there, barely breathing, not knowing what to say or if he could even speak at all. How did he process it, coming face to face with the mother he had no memories, no knowledge of? Could he trust her?

Tears still falling heavily, she approached him, one slow step at a time, until she stood looking up into his eyes. Her tears and the emotions . . . they were real. He couldn't deny that. With a trembling hand, she reached up and laid it softly against his cheek. He flinched inside, but the warmth of her touch kept him from pulling away. Her other hand covered her mouth again as a weak sob broke free. Then she put her arms around him, drawing him into her embrace. Almost numb, Jace held her lightly as she cried against his shoulder.

He stood at a loss for a moment until something inside him—something that had lain dormant in his heart for all these years—awakened. He had a mother. He wasn't just some outcast orphan, a nobody with no name or ties to anyone. He was a son. His embrace tightened, and he closed his eyes against the pressure building in them.

"I thought you were dead," his mother's voice choked out, barely audible.

Dead. A fear Jace hadn't even fully realized yet eased. If she had thought he was dead, then she couldn't have simply abandoned him.

After a long moment, she finally pulled away, her eyes red and cheeks wet. Jace stared down at her and struggled to contain the most intense emotions he had experienced in a long time.

"How?" he asked, his voice raw. It was all he could manage, but it encompassed so much. How could he have grown up as a slave without even the slightest scrap of information about his own mother, especially when she had such standing?

Rachel breathed out a heavy breath, her shoulders drooping as if the weight of that question were almost too much for her. She wiped her cheeks and shook her head. "Oh, Jace, there is so much to tell you, and so much I must know myself."

A gnawing desire took hold of Jace to hear every bit of it, but one concern rose above it.

"My friends." His voice still came out hoarse. "They need to know . . . they need to know I'm all right."

Rayad was probably pacing their room right now, and if Kyrin found out what had happened, she would be worried sick. Despite the overwhelming need for answers, he could not let them suffer such a wait, for it would surely take hours.

Rachel nodded and swallowed hard as if still trying not to burst into tears again. "Of course." Her gaze shifted. "Elian, please show him back downstairs." When her gaze returned to Jace, her eyes held an earnest plea. "Then would you consider returning to talk?"

Jace didn't hesitate. "Yes." He needed answers as much, if not more, than she did.

A teary smile flashed across her face, and she touched his cheek once again before pulling back. Finding it difficult to tear his eyes away from her, Jace turned slowly. When he faced Elian, he witnessed clear emotion in the other man's expression. Even his eyes appeared unusually moist. He cleared his throat and turned to open the door.

As before, Elian led the way cautiously, though Jace hardly noticed, still reeling. It was like a dream, but he knew enough about dreams to know this was very real. Walking in a daze, he slowed to a stop when they neared the bedroom downstairs. He glanced at Elian, and the man gave him an affirming nod, seeming to understand how overwhelmed he was.

Jace moved on, his friends' voices drawing him to their room. Kyrin was there now, questioning them about him.

"Jace!" she exclaimed when he stepped in.

Her face wasn't the only one that lifted in relief. They all looked as though they had been debating whether or not to come after him.

"Well?" Rayad asked.

Jace quietly closed the door and leaned back against it. Where did he even begin? Silence reigned, and everyone's expressions grew more and more serious with every second he didn't speak. Finally, Kyrin stepped forward. Her eyes searched his with a look of deep concern.

"Jace, what is it?"

Breathing out slowly, he spoke the words he never once imagined uttering. "She's my mother."

They all gaped at him in bewildered silence.

Kyrin shook her head, frowning as if she had not heard him right. "What?"

"Lady Rachel is my mother." Each slowly spoken word tasted foreign to Jace. He could hardly wrap his mind around it himself.

"How?"

"I . . . don't know. We didn't get to speak much yet, but she recognized me last night."

Her face still slack, Kyrin sank down on the edge of the bed. Jace understood how she felt. It was a lot to take in.

Rayad spoke now, his voice cautious. "Are you sure about this?"

Of course, Rachel could be anyone. Jace had hardly spent five minutes with her, but he felt surprisingly confident of his answer.

"Yes."

Whether it was an innate sense or simply the emotion she had displayed, he just knew. She had touched something in his heart the moment she'd hugged him.

With this declaration of surety, questions started to pour from everyone. He had little information to give beyond what his mother had already told him. That would have to wait until after they spoke again. Anxious for these answers, he soon excused himself. Elian was waiting for him at the end of the hall, and led him back upstairs.

Jace's heartbeat kicked up on the way to the parlor. Now that it was sinking in, his nerves took over. He had lived with questions about where he'd come from all his life. Now, in one unexpected turn of events, he was about to gain the answers. Part of him feared them. What if knowing was even more painful than not? However, floating at the back of his mind like a warm security blanket were the whispered words only he had heard his mother speak. She had called out to Elôm—not Aertus or Vilai—Elôm, the true God.

When they reached the parlor, Elian let him go in alone this time. He scanned the room, finding only Rachel. The older woman had gone.

"She thought it would be good for us to speak alone for now," Rachel said, guessing his thoughts. She gestured to a chair. He sat on the edge of it and rested his hands on his knees. His mother sat across from him. "She's my mother, Evelyn . . . your grandmother."

Shock hit Jace again. This should have been obvious, but it had not yet occurred to him that his mother wouldn't be the only family he had gained from this reunion.

Already pressure built at the back of his throat. He cleared it and stared at his mother. Neither of them seemed sure where to begin, but Jace had something he needed to know before things went any further. It was a risk, but necessary.

"I heard you speak the name of Elôm."

Rachel's eyes grew wide, fear flitting through them, and that was enough for Jace.

"It's all right," he assured her, and paused for only a moment. "I believe in Him too."

Rachel gasped, the fear melting into tearful joy. "Truly?"

Jace hesitated, but nodded. He couldn't tell her what he believed about his soul. Right now, just the fact that he believed was enough.

Tears dripped down her cheeks, and she dabbed her eyes with a handkerchief. "I have no words to express the joy that brings me, especially with how things are around us." She took a deep breath to compose herself. "I want very much to know how you came to believe, but I realize you must have the most questions. Please, ask me anything."

With this invitation, a multitude of questions poured into Jace's mind, but one above all had always plagued him.

"How did I get here?" He paused, reluctant. He could think of only one explanation for his next question, and it already made him sick. "I know I'm half ryrik. How did that happen?"

Rachel's gaze flickered away from him, but then she looked him in the eyes, her voice quiet and solemn. "I was attacked."

Jace's stomach lurched. It was just as he had expected, but having it confirmed was even more painful than he'd imagined. He breathed hard, a fire kindling inside him at the atrocity.

Fighting to come to terms with the violent way he had come into this world, he once again noticed his mother's youthful beauty. She must have been young when it happened.

"How old were you?"

"Sixteen."

Jace clenched his fists. She'd barely been more than a girl. Younger than Kyrin.

"It was a result of significant foolishness on my part," Rachel admitted, surprising him. "I was upset with my father and rode off alone. The only reason I survived was because my brother and Elian rode out looking for me."

This explained, in part, Elian's emotional reaction to the reunion between Jace and his mother. He had been there at the beginning.

Jace shuddered at what it must have been like to find her. If it had been Kyrin . . .

He cleared his throat again, but his voice was still rough with the rage of emotions he tried to suppress. "The man who attacked you . . . is he dead?"

Rachel looked down again, wincing. "Yes, he was killed."

Jace clenched his jaw and nodded. He couldn't summon any sympathy for the man who was technically his father. Not after what he had done. Only hatred burned inside him—hatred for the man's actions and for the accursed blood he had passed on to Jace. It took all of his strength to let the anger cool, but even that struggle pointed straight to his father. All he wanted was to force thoughts of the man far away.

"Then what happened?"

His mother slowly let out her breath. "Then I tried to deal with it. I've been through some hard times, but that will always be one of the darkest. I could barely eat, or talk to anyone for weeks. I couldn't sleep without having nightmares."

Jace's heart squeezed with compassion at the shared affliction.

"Just when I was beginning to cope again, that's when I realized . . . I was pregnant." She shook her head, and Jace couldn't even imagine the horror she had experienced. "I was terrified. I hid it for days, but I only made myself sick until I finally broke down and told my mother. My father immediately sent for the physician, who gave me a drug to end the pregnancy."

She paused, and Jace just stared at her, one thought drumming in his mind—how was he even here? Was it his ryrik blood? Had it kept him alive, just like all the other times he had wished to die, but hadn't?

She continued slowly, "That vial sat on my dresser for days. I would sit and stare at it for hours. Finally, one day, I dumped it out the window."

"Why?" The question broke from Jace. Right or wrong, the fact that she hadn't taken it, knowing what he was, shocked him. He was a monster, at least according to society. How could she have made that decision?

A faint smile grew on Rachel's face. "I wondered that myself at first. I wondered how I could ever go through with it; but you see, after the initial fear, I began to see things differently. I knew you were part of the man who'd attacked me, but you were also part of me. You were *my* child. And you were just a helpless, innocent baby growing inside me. You hadn't done anything to deserve to die just because I was afraid."

Jace stared at his mother, as if seeing her again for the first time. It took his breath away. She had *chosen* to keep him. Despite his race and the circumstances, she had chosen to go through with it.

She looked at him, moisture pooling in her eyes. Her voice wobbled as she said through a full smile, "Oh, Jace, you were such a beautiful baby with your black hair and the most beautiful blue eyes I've ever seen. That's how I recognized you. The moment I saw your eyes, I knew." She shook her head, her lips trembling. "And you were such a good baby, always so happy. How I loved you. From the first moment I held you in my arms, I knew you'd have my heart forever."

Overcome, Jace bowed his head and pressed his fingers against his eyelids. His breath hitched as he drew it in. His mother loved him. What a profound, unimaginable thing.

At last he looked up again, blinking her into focus. What had gone so wrong? After all she had told him, he should have grown up here with her—nurtured, loved. But that was not his past. The only memories he carried of his childhood and young adult years were those of slave yards, grueling days, cruel masters, and the never-ending hatred he'd endured for his mixed blood.

His voice cracked with the pain of those times. "What happened?"

Her expression changed with this question. She had spoken of the past with a surprising amount of peace, despite its darkness, but the peace disappeared. Her lips pinched, and now her eyes revealed a deep hurt and anger. She looked away, smoothing her hands against her skirt as if trying to gain better control over her emotions. When she spoke, her tone was low and taut.

"I had you for three months . . . three wonderful months." She took a deep breath. "My father still tried to get me to give you up, but I refused. Then, one day . . . I woke up and you were gone."

An invisible hand clamped around Jace's throat, digging in and cutting off his air. He had been taken from her?

"I don't know where my father had you taken; I only know he did." A choked sob slipped out, and she couldn't hold back any longer. Drooping forward, she put her face in her hands and cried.

Propelled by his growing love for her, Jace stood, drawing her up with him, and held her tightly. But he shook inside with his raging feelings. That familiar hot burn of anger battled to take hold. How could his own grandfather have separated mother and son so cruelly, dooming both of them to such pain? It willed him to lash out in some way, but the quieter, yet persistent voice of reason reminded him it was not the way. It took several minutes, but he finally tamped down the anger enough to think calmly again. By this time, his mother had worked her tears under control.

She looked up at him. "The last time we were together I could hold you, and now you're holding me."

She wiped her eyes, and they returned to their seats.

"I tried to find you," Rachel said, her voice now tired. "My brother, Charles, he looked, but my father hid you too well. At the time, my father was trying to get me to marry Rothas. I was so desperate to find you that I agreed to the wedding if he brought you back. That's when they told me you had died of fever."

Bitterness crept into her tone, but, like Jace, she looked to be trying hard to fight it. "I grieved over you for so long. By that time, I was too worn out to resist my father's plans and married Rothas. The rest of the story is right here in this house. Until I saw you last night, I truly believed you were dead."

Sagging against the back of his chair, Jace let the whole thing process. It was almost too much to take in at one time, and it mentally exhausted him. After a few moments, he noticed how intently Rachel watched him and met her gaze.

"I can tell you this, Jace," she said. "Now that I've found you, I'm not going to lose you again."

ONCE JACE HAD shared the details of his life, he wasn't sure his mother had any tears left to shed. It was significantly painful for both of them—for him to tell it and her to hear it. Yet some things he couldn't share. He had left vague his recent history and the events that had brought him to Landale. He hadn't even told her about Kyrin—something he deeply wanted—but he first must discuss the wisdom of it with the others. So much danger and risk surrounded them already.

Wiping her face with her already-soaked handkerchief, Rachel said, "I must meet Rayad, properly, so I can thank him for what he's done."

Jace nodded, eager for them to meet. "If he had not found me, I wouldn't be alive right now." He paused and drew a long breath. He had never told anyone this before, not even Rayad. "Right before he showed up and paid for my freedom, I had decided to lose my next fight. I didn't intend to ever walk out of the arena again. Even after he freed me, I snuck away that night while he was asleep and almost ended it. I just didn't want to face the world anymore."

"Oh, Jace." Rachel touched her chest as if her heart were in great pain. "Thank Elôm for leading him there when He did and for stopping you."

Jace didn't respond. He still struggled, wondering if Elôm had truly led Rayad there for him, but he couldn't tell his mother this. It would only hurt her more.

"You know, Jace," she said gently, "if I could go back and change everything, I would do it in a heartbeat to prevent the things that you have endured, but I find comfort in the way Elôm has clearly worked in this. I could never choose for it to be this way, but it is what He used to guide me to Him. After I lost you and made it through the wedding, we moved here and I was so lonely and broken, struggling with learning to be a wife and still desperately missing you. My maid—dear girl—saw how I was suffering, and found the courage to tell me about Elôm. I was so desperate for hope that I devoured everything she told me. It's the only thing that has kept me going all these years."

She gave a weary smile. "In turn, I've shared with my mother, Charles, and Elian. I tried to raise James to believe, but he follows too closely after his father. Elanor, however, does believe."

"James?"

"Oh, I'm sorry. James and Elanor are my children . . . your half brother and sister."

Of course, Jace knew this, yet it was hard to believe he had siblings now. He had always wondered, watching Kyrin interact with her brothers, what that would be like.

"So does Rothas know you believe?"

"He did. He was furious when he found that I was teaching James, and promptly went to work reversing it. Now he thinks I let the whole thing go a long time ago, and I work to keep it that way, especially now. He has no idea about Elanor, thank Elôm."

A light knock at the door interrupted them. Jace tensed as it opened, but relaxed when Elian let Rachel's mother inside. She smiled at them, carrying a tray.

"I had tea brought up. I thought you could use it." She set the tray on a small table near them. Her gaze fell on Jace and lingered as if soaking in the sight of him as she backed away.

"Mother, please stay," Rachel invited.

The older woman's eyes lit up and she smiled as she joined them. Again, she just looked at Jace before shaking her head apologetically. "I am sorry. It is still hard to believe what my eyes are seeing."

Under most circumstances, Jace would have felt uncomfortable, but this was far from a normal situation. "It's all right."

"I still remember you as the little baby you were before." Though refined and rich in dignity and poise befitting a noblewoman, her voice trembled and her eyes glimmered, the rims red from tears she must have shed in private. "I'm sure Rachel has told you what happened, but I do hope you know that I had no part in the plan to get rid of you."

"Oh, none at all," Rachel quickly added. "She was one of the only ones who supported me. She, Charles, and Elian."

At least his mother hadn't been completely alone at such a hard time.

"Speaking of Charles, will you send for him?" Rachel's mother asked.

Rachel's eyes sparkled joyfully. "Yes. He will be so surprised." Her gaze then shifted to Jace, the sparkle dimming to a question. "That is, if you would like to meet him."

Jace's stomach flipped over at the thought. He had never been good with new people, yet he had a growing desire to know his family.

"I would, yes."

Rachel smiled. "Good." She looked back to her mother. "I'll tell Elanor as well. She would want to know. But Father and Rothas must not find out. I can't trust what they will do after they took Jace from me once. Unfortunately, we can't trust James either. He's too close to his father, and I don't think he would respond well."

"It's quite magnificent." Anne truly admired the loveliness of Ashwood as she walked side by side with seventeen-year-old Elanor through the second floor. Her uncle, the Earl of Belford, had a large estate as well, but Anne found Ashwood more to her liking.

Elanor nodded. "Yes, though I must confess, having lived here all my life, I take it shamefully for granted most of the time."

Anne gave her a smile. She quite liked the girl. Taking after her mother in both appearance and manner, she was mature for her age and well-spoken. Anne particularly liked her kind and bubbly personality. Had they lived closer together and had the opportunity to visit, she could see the two of them becoming good friends. It was difficult to keep up an act with her, and Anne often found herself slipping into enjoying the moment.

As they passed by a closed door with particularly impressive moldings, Anne asked, "What is this room?"

"Oh, that's Father's private office."

Anne's heart gave a thump, and at once her mind focused on the mission.

"Best not to disturb it," Elanor warned. "He's very particular about that. Not even Mother goes inside."

Careful to maintain her act, Anne chuckled. "Men and their offices."

Elanor just smiled, and they continued their tour. Anne, however, gave the door one final glance, making mental notes on its location to give to Kyrin later.

Come lunchtime, Anne followed Elanor into the dining room where the rest of the family gathered. She pointedly ignored the flirtatious smile James sent her way, and focused on Elanor, who introduced her grandmother, the Countess of Dunrick.

As they took seats at the table, Anne noticed that Rachel didn't look well. Her eyes were noticeably red-rimmed. Even Lady Dunrick appeared pale. Elanor noticed too. Anne caught the concerned glances the girl sent her mother's way, but Rachel answered with a reassuring smile.

Rothas, however, did not seem to notice at all, and if he did, he wasn't the least bit concerned. How many other times had Rachel come to the table with signs of tears? Anne's stomach burned with indignation and stole her appetite. The man was a louse and entirely unashamed of it. Lady Rachel deserved better. Thank Elôm that Anne's father did not intend to arrange her marriage, though she was well past the age that most girls married. She would rather die than be married to a man like Rothas.

Having Lady Dunrick at the table was a breath of fresh air. Sir Rothas was a dominant conversationalist, and Anne had grown quite weary of him. However, the countess had preeminence, and kept Rothas's contributions to a minimum. Anne couldn't help but feel a great deal of satisfaction at seeing the man put in his place. If only Lady Rachel had her mother around all the time to keep the loathsome man in line.

Once the meal concluded, Anne excused herself under the pretense of wanting to rest for a bit. The sooner she made plans with Kyrin about getting into the office, the sooner their mission would be complete and this charade could end. She hurried upstairs. When she entered the bedroom, she found Kyrin waiting.

"Good, you're here. I . . ." She stopped. Tear smudges glinted on Kyrin's cheeks. A gnawing ache mangled Anne's stomach. "What happened?"

A smile blossomed on Kyrin's face, sending a wash of surprised relief through her. Surely she wouldn't smile over anything terrible.

"You'll never believe what Jace discovered this morning."

Anne waited. She couldn't even begin to guess. For all she'd known, the men had just been sitting around waiting for this to be over.

Kyrin stepped closer, her voice low and breathless. "Lady Rachel is his mother."

Anne's mouth fell open. "What?" She sank down in a nearby chair, her head spinning. "She is?"

Kyrin nodded. "She recognized him when she saw him last night, and then she asked to speak with him this morning. They talked for hours."

Anne breathed out a long breath. It would take some time for this to sink in. "How is he taking it?"

"He's still in shock, as you can imagine, but . . . I think he's very happy. I've never seen him quite like this." Kyrin shook her head. "When Rayad questioned him about her truly being his mother, he was very sure. That's unusual for Jace."

Anne sat, her mouth still open for a moment. "Out of all the people in Ilyon, *Lady Rachel* is his mother?"

Kyrin gave a small laugh. "I know, it's incredible. Oh, if you could have seen his face. He's struggled so much with his identity. How I pray this will help him. And not only is she his mother, but he also found out she's a believer in Elôm. Lady Elanor too."

"Well, that's the one part in all this that doesn't surprise me. She has to be getting her strength from somewhere to endure a husband like Rothas."

"Jace would like to talk to us about what he can tell her. Rayad thought we could meet outside."

Anne nodded. "That's a good idea. We need to discuss things anyway. I found the office."

"I trust her. She won't give us away." Jace had never trusted people easily, but he'd experienced enough cruelty to spot true goodness when it was there, and his mother had it in abundance. Even after just a couple of hours, he trusted her with their secrets.

Rayad nodded. "I'm willing to trust her too, but we'll see what Anne and Kyrin have to say first."

Jace agreed. He wouldn't proceed to share more information without their consent. Safety had to be the priority.

Reclining on one of the beds, Holden gave Jace a thoughtful look. "You do realize now that you're of noble blood? You outrank all of us here, except Anne."

Jace hadn't considered this. All his life, the focus had been on his ryrik blood. It was strange to think the other half was that of nobility. Even so, his illegitimate birth would have annulled any privileges and status that would have afforded him.

"It doesn't matter." He could never see himself above the others, and didn't want them to either. "I'm just the same as I always was."

To be treated any differently would be uncomfortable.

A moment later, Aaron stepped into the room. "Kyrin and Anne are waiting outside."

Rayad thanked him, and he, Jace, and Kaden left the servants' quarters and walked outside. Across the courtyard, near Sir Rothas's grand stable, the women waited. When they reached them, Anne gave Jace a wide smile.

"I want to say how happy I am for you."

"Thank you," Jace replied. "I'm still trying to take it all in."

"Kyrin said you wished to talk."

He nodded. "I want to know how much I can tell my mother about us. She doesn't know yet that I have anything to do with the resistance in Landale. I can keep most of it to myself, but I would at least like to tell her about Kyrin." He paused and cleared his throat. Was that making his hidden feelings too clear?

Glancing at Kyrin, he found a sweet smile on her face. He continued, "I trust her. She won't tell Rothas."

Anne considered a moment. "If she knows the truth about you and Kyrin, she may suspect our motives for being here."

"If it's too great a risk, I'll just leave it at what I've already told her." It was a disappointment, but somehow he would have to find another way to tell her about Kyrin. After all, Kyrin had done as much for him as Rayad had. He might not have lived without her either.

"I don't want you to have to keep things from her," Anne said, surprising him. "If you're sure about her, and everyone is in agreement, then you can tell her what you wish . . . at least about Kyrin."

Jace looked at Kyrin and her brother, and then at Rayad. None of them spoke against it.

"Now, that brings me to the reason I wanted to speak with you." Anne turned to Rayad. "I found Rothas's private office, which means we can proceed. We just have to determine when to act."

"What about tonight while everyone is asleep?" Rayad suggested.

"That was my thought, but Kyrin pointed out how suspicious it would be if she were caught wandering around so late. Much more so than earlier in the evening. There's no telling what habits the staff have at night."

Rayad's brow furrowed. "True, but to try earlier would run the risk of Rothas showing up while Kyrin is in there."

Jace's stomach twisted into a knot. If it were up to him, Kyrin wouldn't go at all. However, her face was calm and resolute. If she was afraid, she didn't show it. *Please, Elôm, protect her.*

His gaze shifted to Kaden. He didn't look particularly at ease with this either, but he hadn't spoken against it. Jace didn't doubt that Kaden's concern was any less strong than his own, but, like the rest of the group, Kaden was thinking of Samara and the importance of the information Kyrin could gather. Jace could only think of Kyrin. She was what mattered most to him.

"That is why we're thinking late evening around suppertime," Anne drew Jace's attention again. "Then Rothas will be occupied."

"Sounds like a plan," Rayad replied.

Anne turned to Kyrin. "What do you think? Are you up to it this evening?"

Kyrin pulled in a slow, deep breath, and now Jace did catch the briefest flicker of nerves in her eyes. Even so, she spoke steadily. "Yes, I'll do it. I'd like to get it over with."

"All right, then." Anne looked at Rayad again. "Perhaps you can come up to my room shortly after supper has begun so you can be there when Kyrin heads out and returns."

"I want to be there too," Kaden said.

Jace had had to bite his tongue not to say it first. "So do I."

Rayad was a little hesitant, but he gave a nod. "We can't have everyone heading upstairs, but I think we could manage you two without undue suspicion."

"Good, we're all set then. I'd better head back inside before someone wonders." Anne turned and walked back toward the front of the manor house.

Jace, Rayad, Kyrin, and Kaden followed several paces behind. Halfway across the courtyard, a young man strode in their direction. His gaze swept Anne as he drew near, much the same way Rothas's had when they'd arrived. Heat crept through Jace's muscles. The young man gave Anne a bold grin. "My lady."

Tilting her chin, Anne didn't check her stride.

Unaffected by her rebuff, the young man's smile lingered as they passed each other. Then his gaze fell on the group behind her. His dark blue eyes—a cross between Rachel's indigo and violet and Sir Rothas's hard ice blue—locked on Kyrin. Every muscle in Jace's body went taut when the man didn't look away.

Instead, he perused her in a way that was by no means honorable. The more he looked, the hotter Jace's blood flowed, working its way through his arms, right down to his fingers, which curled into fists.

Finally, they passed by, and Jace was hard-pressed not to grab the young man by the collar and warn him never to set eyes on Kyrin again. Jace glanced down at her, where she walked between him and Kaden. She had her head ducked to avoid eye contact and looked up again once the man was past them.

"That's James," she murmured.

This hadn't occurred to Jace in the heat of the moment. He twisted around for another look at his half-brother. James was looking over his shoulder as well, his predatory gaze still fixed on Kyrin. But then it caught on Jace. They stared at each other, and Jace sent him a glare that left no uncertainty as to the threat behind it. In spite of this, an infuriating little smirk grew on James's face.

JACE JOINED HIS mother in the parlor again that afternoon. Lady Dunrick had gone back to Brandell, her nearby home estate, and would return later with Charles. As they settled in, Jace said to his mother, "There are things I didn't tell you earlier, and some things I still can't share, but I want to tell you as much as I can. You'll understand the complications when I do."

Rachel nodded slowly to this, her expression open. "Go on."

"You know the so-called rebellion in Landale? Well, I'm part of it."

His mother's eyes flickered with surprise, but she didn't react openly. "I see."

"The reason I want you to know this is because I want to tell you about another of my friends. Like Rayad, without her . . . I'm not sure I'd still be here."

He had her full interest now. Having received both Kyrin and Kaden's go ahead, Jace went forward with the truth. "Lady Anne's maid—we call her Corinne—is really Kyrin Altair."

Her eyes widened now. "Oh?"

For the briefest moment, Jace's stomach clenched with the awful feeling that he had just put Kyrin in grave danger, but he mentally reinforced his trust in his mother and nodded. "I went through a dark time after Kalli and Aldor died. Kyrin is the one who helped me through it." Her face filled his mind along with the memories of that time. "I'm not sure what I'd do without her."

A soft smile touched Rachel's face, and Jace told her about the previous summer, when both he and Kyrin had come to Landale. Certain parts were difficult. He couldn't quite bring himself to tell her everything he had thought then—everything he still believed now. Perhaps he was afraid of disappointing her. He had already confessed to the number of people he'd killed. He hated to add any more stains to his image.

They talked for a long time about Kyrin and Landale. His mother was curious, but never pushed for more information than Jace was willing to give.

A couple of hours later, Elian stepped into the room. "Lady Dunrick and Lord Ilvaran have arrived, my lady."

Rachel rose, and Jace with her.

"Wait here," she told him. "I'll go find Elanor and bring them in."

Jace nodded and watched his mother leave. Once he was alone, he blew out a long breath. This was it. What would they think of him? His mother said they would love to meet him, but what if she was wrong? After all, they didn't know his story. Would that change their opinion of him?

He tugged at his jerkin and smoothed the front, but then winced. After lunch, he had changed into the best clothes he had with him. It felt only right to try to make a good impression when his mother introduced him to more of the family. Still, his clothes were suited for a more rugged life at camp, not for social gatherings in a house like this. Even Elian was dressed more appropriately. Jace had asked Kyrin what she thought. Her response was a smiled declaration that he looked quite handsome. Another surge of warmth built in him as it had then. He would take her word for it.

Setting his mind on the matter at hand, he rubbed his palms against his pants and moved about the room to try to loosen the tension. After several long minutes, he picked up the sound of faint footsteps. He returned to his place near the chairs and exhaled slowly, his heart rate defying him again. What would the new faces that came through the door be like?

The footsteps neared and the door opened. His mother stepped in first, along with Lady Dunrick. Right in after them came a young woman and a man around Rachel's age. He resembled her closely, but his hair was a shade lighter, and his eyes deep green like Lady Dunrick's. A couple days' worth of stubble shadowed his chin, and though his clothing was clearly of fine quality, it was much simpler than Jace would have expected for a nobleman. This helped put him more at ease, but what further aided this was the man's kind face. The slight crinkles at the corners of his eyes and around his mouth suggested that he liked to smile and laugh—an encouraging sign.

The two newcomers regarded Jace curiously as they waited for Rachel to make introductions. She stepped between them, appearing just as nervous as Jace. She took a breath.

"Elanor, Charles . . . I want you to meet Jace . . . my son."

Their eyes rounded, their expressions going slack. Charles's mouth opened as if he wanted to speak, but nothing came until his gaze shifted back to Rachel.

"I thought . . ."

She shook her head. "Father and Rothas lied."

"Merciful heavens," Charles breathed.

He approached, and Jace had to fight the ingrained instinct to maintain more distance. Charles offered his hand, and Jace clasped his forearm. Gripping him with both hands, his uncle looked him over, his eyes still wide.

"Forgive me," he said finally. "It seems words have failed me, but it's as if you've returned from the dead."

"I understand." At last Jace's hesitation subsided.

"And you can speaking freely," Rachel stepped in to tell her brother. "He is a believer too."

Delight lit Charles's expression. "Then praise the King for not only bringing you back to us, but guiding you to His truth."

Jace couldn't help but smile even when he had his doubts. The pure joy his uncle drew from this meeting gave him an indescribable feeling of peace and belonging he rarely knew. When had anyone ever accepted him so readily?

Elanor stepped forward, her smile genuine and eager. She took his hand, squeezing it gently. "Jace, I am so very pleased to meet you."

Jace was just as pleased to meet her, his *sister*. He could sense the same kindness in her that he did in their mother and uncle.

With the initial greetings past, they took seats—Jace and his mother on the sofa, while the others sat in the chairs facing them.

"How did you find him?" Charles asked, his voice still echoing disbelief.

"I didn't," Rachel replied. "He arrived last night with Lady Anne from Marlton. Elôm's work, clearly. I recognized him right away, but then had to wonder if the very thought was foolish. That's why I sent for Mother this morning. I needed her advice. But as soon as I spoke with Jace, I had no doubt."

Charles shook his head. Jace could just imagine what a shock it was on the other side of this as well. His uncle's gaze turned to him.

"Incredible. So, where have you been these last . . ." he glanced at Rachel, "twenty-one years?"

Jace couldn't suppress a wince and the desire to avoid that question. It wasn't that he wished to hide the answer, but the shame of the things he had done in his past weighed heavily. As of now, his image was unmarred for his uncle and sister.

"I apologize," Charles said. "That was insensitive of me. I should have realized you may not wish to share."

"No, it isn't that so much . . ." Jace hesitated. He did want to share—they were family, after all—but would their view of him change? Would their acceptance disappear?

"He was a slave," his mother supplied quietly. She laid a gentle hand on his arm as if she knew of the uncertainty gnawing at him. "Father must have given him away to a slave trader."

Charles and Elanor looked at her aghast. The muscles in Charles's jaw tightened, particularly when Rachel added in an even quieter and more regretful tone, "He was then forced to be a gladiator."

Jace dropped his gaze to his hands, unable to stop the way his mind tried to scare him into believing they would think the worst of him. After all, didn't he think it himself? To see it in their faces would break him.

Elanor let out a little gasp. "That's horrible."

Jace forced himself to look up. The repulsion on their faces was clear and terrifying, yet it was not for him. It was for the evil he had endured. The compassion and sympathy growing in their expressions proved that.

"It's barbaric," Charles ground out, his eyes hard until they fell back on Jace and softened. "I am so sorry it happened to you."

Jace swallowed hard through his thickened throat. "Thank you."

"How did you escape it?" Elanor's eyes were large and riveted on him.

Once again, Jace condensed a retelling of how he had met Rayad and their life at the farm. In those moments that his sister and uncle focused on him so intently, he marveled over the rarity of meeting a group of people where not one of them looked at him as something strange and different. They each knew of his ryrik blood, but it was as if it didn't even exist.

Sitting in this room with these four people, for the first time in his life, he was normal.

He was family.

Anne pinned up a final curl and smoothed the bodice of her evening gown, this one a spring green brocade, and turned to Kyrin. They were both more than a little on edge this evening.

"I'd better go down. Will you be all right?" They all risked a lot by being here, but none quite so much as Kyrin.

However, she nodded with a look of intense determination. Anne could only imagine what sort of thoughts she might have lurking underneath, especially after what had happened to her father in Valcré. Still, she was willing to go through with it. The Altairs were certainly a brave family.

"You are confident you can find the office?" Anne had been very specific about its location, but Kyrin had seen little of the manor house. Rothas's office was clear in the opposite wing of the place. The more time she spent wandering around looking for it, the greater the chance of being caught and having to try to talk her way out of it.

"I'll find it," Kyrin said with enough confidence to reassure Anne. "It's not like I can forget your directions."

They both broke into smiles, relieving some of the tension.

"I'm sure Rayad will be along shortly. Remain here a bit just to be sure supper has begun."

Kyrin nodded again, and Anne turned to go but looked back. "I'll be praying for you."

"Thanks."

Anne stepped out of the bedroom and walked down the hall. After a plea to Elôm for Kyrin's safety and the success of their mission, she set her thoughts on enduring yet another meal at Sir Rothas's table. Tonight she didn't dread it as much as she might have. She had a keen interest in meeting Jace's uncle, the popular Viscount Ilvaran. She had not seen him before, but many in her parents' circles spoke of him with high regard.

When she entered the dining room, she spotted him easily. He was a handsome man with a genuine smile—quite the opposite of Sir Rothas. The viscount followed his sister around the table for introductions.

"Pleased to meet you, Lord Ilvaran," Anne greeted him.

"And you as well, my lady," Charles responded kindly.

If only his brother-in-law could learn from his manners.

Just as the night before with the countess present, Sir Rothas was forced to behave himself, and even James ceased with his incessant flirting. The one time he did attempt to charm Anne, Charles sent him a disapproving frown. She found it quite refreshing, if not a bit amusing. How nice to know the family had one man of honor.

She quickly corrected herself. They had two. Jace was a part of the family as well.

As pleasant as it was in Charles's company, Anne didn't have much of an appetite tonight. Though she was careful to keep up appearances and remain outwardly attentive to the conversation, her mind always centered on Kyrin. If only she could know when she made it to the office and was safely back in their room. It was hard to stomach anything, what with the churning dread of what would happen if any of them were caught.

Not too long into the meal, the butler approached Rothas.

"Excuse me, sir, this just arrived for you."

He handed him a sealed letter. Anne caught only a brief glance, but her pulse spiked at the gold seal that could only belong to Emperor Daican. Rothas tore it open and scanned the contents in intent silence. After a moment, he snorted in apparent disgust.

"Word from the emperor?" Charles asked casually.

Though Anne avoided looking too curious, she listened closely.

Rothas only murmured confirmation as he perused the rest of the letter. Finally, he looked up. "News from Samara, specifically. Apparently, there is a man masquerading as some sort of miracle-worker. The unenlightened Elôm worshippers in the area are claiming he's some sort of savior."

He sent his wife a condescending glance. Though Rachel's face remained poised, Anne caught a glint of curiosity that grew inside her as well. Timothy's words concerning a Savior at the sacrifice she and her parents had attended came back to her. Surely this couldn't be what he spoke of, could it?

Rothas gave another rather undignified snort and rose abruptly.

"If you will excuse me, I have some business to attend to. I'll be in my office."

Anne's heart slammed her ribs. *Kyrin!* She gripped her chair with her free hand, resisting the urge to jump up.

Rothas's gaze fell on Charles and his mother. "My lord, Lady Dunrick, I will be late so allow me to bid you good evening."

They each nodded, and Rothas strode from the room.

Working hard to suppress a rising flood of panic, Anne folded her napkin and laid it on the table, using that time to banish the fear from her voice.

"Actually," she said, praying to sound normal, "I'm afraid I am suffering from a bit of a headache and can't find my appetite. Would it be very rude if I excused myself as well, just to rest for a bit?"

"No, not at all." Rachel smiled, but a curious look in her eyes suggested that she might know something was up.

"Perhaps you will feel up to joining us in the drawing room later?" Charles said graciously.

Anne forced a smile despite her urge to run upstairs and find Kyrin. "I hope so."

Leaving her chair, Anne walked from the room in as poised a manner as she could manage. Only after she was out of sight and earshot did her steps hasten. *Please, Lord, let her still be in our room!*

Jace fought to keep still. He wanted to get up and pace— no, he wanted to be the one to go instead of Kyrin—but he stayed in his seat as Kyrin and Rayad discussed what to look for in the office. He didn't wish to make her any more nervous by his own fidgeting. His thoughts were so focused on what she was about to do that he almost didn't hear her speaking to him.

"What was it like, meeting your uncle and sister?"

His gaze jumped to her, taking in her calming smile as he gathered his thoughts. "I'm not sure how to describe it . . . I've never truly belonged like that."

Her smile widened. "I hope I can meet them all one day."

"So do I." More than she probably even realized.

She studied him for a long moment, and his heart skipped strangely. Just because of concern, surely.

"I can see your mother in you," she said finally.

"Really?" All he and others ever saw was the dominance of his ryrik blood.

Kyrin nodded. "Yes, you have her smile . . . and her eyes. Well, not the color, but there's something of her in them."

Jace let this sink in, and found it a comforting thing. It was something to hold on to whenever he thought of his birth father and the undesirable traits he had inherited from him.

A few moments later, Rayad spoke up. "I think we've waited long enough."

Kyrin pushed up from her chair and took a deep breath. Jace rose too. He would never be able to sit still while she was gone.

"Just find what you can, but don't linger," Rayad instructed her. "And remember, make sure to leave everything as it was."

"I will."

Rayad walked her to the door. As she stepped out, Jace said, "Be careful."

It was not what he wanted to say. He wanted to beg her to stay and pull her back into the safety of the room. Somehow he stopped himself, though everything about it felt wrong.

She looked back and gave him a quick smile and a nod. Rayad closed the door behind her. The room grew quiet. Jace ran his hand through his hair and looked over at Kaden. Unspoken concern passed between them. They would both lose their minds before she returned.

Rayad returned to his chair and rested his head in his hands, praying. Jace wanted to pray too, but the only words that formed were, *Please, Elôm, protect her.* Over and over, he spoke them in his mind. This would be one of the longest evenings of his life.

Not three minutes later, the door opened and he jerked around. In walked both Anne and Kyrin.

Rayad frowned at them. "What happened?"

"Thank Elôm that I met Kyrin in the hall," Anne said breathlessly. "Rothas just went to his office."

A sick feeling tangled Jace's stomach. Kyrin had almost been caught! She would have walked right in on him.

KYRIN LOOKED OUT the window, but even the abundant morning sunshine couldn't shake the coldness that crept in whenever she thought about last night. She hadn't slept well, and every dark hour she had lain awake she couldn't stop herself from imagining Rothas catching her. They would try it again tonight. Her scalp and arms prickled, and she shivered. If she wasn't careful, she would talk herself out of this.

She turned resolutely. Anne had just left for breakfast, so Kyrin went about tidying their room. Staying active would help her ignore the increasing nerves, at least until she went downstairs to join the others. She wanted to make sure all the members of the Cantan family were occupied with breakfast before she left the room. The last thing she wanted was to cross paths with James again. The looks he gave her scared her as much as Rothas did.

Praying quietly to herself, she arranged Anne's dresses and gathered up the ones she needed to have washed. A light knock came at the door. Kyrin froze and stared at the knob. Her heart throbbed in her throat. What if it was James? Her gaze darted around for a place to hide, but then came Rachel's voice. Kyrin sagged, a bit faint, and pressed her hand to her chest. She needed to not let her panic take hold so easily.

Kyrin quickly crossed the room to let Jace's mother inside.

"My lady." Her voice was still breathless from the fright.

Rachel smiled kindly, helping to calm her. "I was hoping you were still up here. I would love to talk for a bit."

"Of course." Kyrin couldn't turn down what might be her only chance to speak with Jace's mother. He had told them all about her, but Kyrin wanted to get to know the woman for herself.

Rachel stepped inside and closed the door. When they had taken seats, she said, "It's good to meet you more formally. Jace has spoken of you so fondly."

Kyrin smiled, warmth spreading up through her chest. "He means a great deal to me too. I am overjoyed that he has found you and has family now." In her mind, she relived the moment shortly after they had met when she had asked him if he knew if he had any family and his pained answer that he didn't.

"From what I hear, you and Rayad have been his family for the last couple of years. I can't tell you how grateful I am for what you've done for him."

Kyrin shook her head. "I haven't really done anything, just striven to be his friend."

"But that's just what he needed—someone to accept him and help him find his place."

"I am more than happy when I can help him." Kyrin thought back over their friendship so far. Her influence over Jace was only one side of it. "I think he underestimates what a source of strength he has been for me. He too has seen me through some hard times."

Her words caught a little at the back of her throat as the emotions kicked in.

Rachel's eyes filled with compassion. "News from Valcré always travels fast. I'm sorry for what you've lost."

Before she could even hope to stop them, tears rushed to Kyrin's eyes, and she took a quick, hard breath as an unexpected sob rose out of her heart. The lady's tender words, coupled with the strain she was under, broke the wall enclosing her pain, and though she tried to force them back, two tears spilled over. Almost six months had passed since her father's death, but the pain still came in waves that were unbearable at times. Wiping her cheeks, she murmured, "I'm sorry."

"Oh, no, dear, don't be." Rachel reached out to rub her shoulder. "I understand the pain of loss."

Pressing the heels of her hands against her eyes to stop the flow, Kyrin breathed deeply and cleared her throat before looking at Rachel again. "Jace was there for me, and for my brother, the whole time."

"He's a good man."

Kyrin sniffed and gave her a wobbly smile of whole-hearted agreement.

"But he doesn't see it, does he?" Rachel's voice took on a sad tone.

Kyrin sighed. It was always what pained her most about Jace. "No, he doesn't."

"Because of his past and his ryrik blood?"

"Yes. He can't seem to let go of the lies he's heard all his life. Rayad and I try so hard to help him, but . . ." Kyrin shook her head, thinking back to the fight in Landale. "It's never enough. It just won't leave him. He needs proof and assurance that we just can't give him." She shrugged, helpless. "Maybe you can try."

Rachel reached out to squeeze her hand now. "I certainly will."

Jace little more than picked at his breakfast. His insides had been in a tumult ever since last night. This was such a bad idea. Kyrin shouldn't have to risk herself like this. In fact, he had spent most of the night tossing about in bed, trying to find any way he could to get her out of it. He should have put up more of a protest back at camp . . . not that it would have changed anything.

A welcome distraction came in the form of Elian walking into the servants' hall. At this point, only Jace and the others from Landale were present. Elian approached the table and told Jace quietly, "Your mother can see you now."

Jace rose to follow him. Talking to his mother wouldn't erase his fear for Kyrin, but at least he wouldn't have to sit around all day, powerless and fretting about what he couldn't change.

Elian looked back at him as they turned in the opposite direction of the stairs. "She thought it would be nice to talk in the garden."

Jace liked the sound of this. Fresh air and open space would be much more soothing than sitting indoors. Maybe it would even ease the tension and worry over Kyrin's second attempt at the office tonight.

As yesterday, Elian was careful about their path and who saw them along the way. Jace sighed. If only there was no need for secrecy. The sneaking around didn't help his nerves.

Behind the manor house, they reached a sprawling garden. Various shrubs, rose bushes, and hedges lined the gravel walkways, highlighted by the bright green of immature leaves. A few early blooming flowers added splashes of white and yellow, but the real beauty wouldn't show itself for another month or so.

Following the winding path, they came to a secluded area behind a grouping of tall shrubs. A stone bench sat under a decorative arbor, where Rachel waited. Her smile blossomed with the love of a mother for her child. It gave him a moment of peace, despite the circumstances.

"Good morning," she said.

He echoed her, and then she glanced at Elian, who said, "I'll keep watch and alert you of anyone nearby."

"Thank you," Rachel told him.

Elian nodded, his gaze lingering before he turned to go. Jace watched him until he took up his guard position several yards away. There was something in the way he looked at Jace's mother. Not inappropriate, but something sad, wistful. He gave Jace similar looks. Jace frowned a little as he and his mother took seats on the bench. What story did those looks hold?

Rachel drew a deep breath, and Jace looked over at her. She appeared to gather her thoughts, and then shifted so she could sit facing him.

"I think you should know that Elian and I have a long history." She must have seen the curiosity and questions in his expression. She winced as if unburying painful memories. "My father hired him when I was fifteen. Obviously, as the daughter of an earl, I shouldn't have taken any interest in him, but he was so kind, friendly, charming, and yet always honorable. He was also good friends with Charles. We hardly spoke beyond simple greetings and occasional small talk, yet somehow we grew to love each other."

A smile flashed briefly across her lips, but faded. "Then, after the attack and my decision to keep you, Elian came to me—it was probably one of the first times we truly talked alone—and he asked me to marry him. He wasn't a noble, but he promised to do whatever it took to take care of me, and that he would raise you as his own."

A hollow ache rose up inside Jace's chest as he absorbed this information, and his gaze shifted to Elian. The man could have been his father. *Wanted* to be his father. How much different would life have been to be raised and loved by a man of honor and integrity? Pain pierced his heart to contemplate what could have been and the horrors he could have avoided.

"Of course, my father wouldn't allow it," his mother continued sadly. "He almost fired Elian, but I convinced him to let him stay."

Jace returned his gaze to her, his eyes burning. "How do you do it? How do you endure so much from Rothas when . . ." He didn't know what to say. In his heart, he knew it would be wrong for his mother to leave her husband to be with Elian, or even entertain such thoughts. Yet, he couldn't imagine the deep heartache she must experience to know the man who truly loved and respected her was the not the man she had married.

And Elian. No wonder he had been so disgusted by Rothas's perusal of Anne. Jace clenched his fists, heat coursing down his arms with the intense desire to somehow make things right.

Rachel sighed at his question, many long years of weariness and struggle behind it. "Because Elian and I both know what is and what can never be. We've had to be on constant guard over our hearts. It hasn't been easy, but I know Elôm's desire for me is to respect, remain faithful, and even love Rothas. There are many times I feel I'll surely fail, but those are the days I must trust Elôm to carry me."

Jace rested his elbows on his knees and put his head in his hands for a long moment, fighting bitterness, despair, and one choking question—why? Why had both he and his mother had to suffer so? Had she married Elian, everything would have been different. She would have a husband who loved her, and he would have a father, and they would be a family right now. *Elôm, what purpose could this serve?*

"Jace."

At his mother's gentle voice, he straightened and let out a long breath, but the question still burned into him.

"It's all right," she told him, her voice earnest. "It may not appear to be, but Elôm has a way of working things out."

Jace had no reply. If only he could see evidence of that, but all he had ever witnessed was how cruelty was always winning over those too weak to fight it—how cruel men always got what they wanted, leaving those beneath them to suffer.

His mother drew his attention again, certainly having guessed his thoughts. "I realize after everything I've told you, you must hate your grandfather very much and think him very hard and cruel."

Jace ground his teeth together. That was just what he thought. The man had ruined both of their lives.

"I'm sorry," Rachel murmured. "That was never my intention. He isn't that way, he's just . . . he's very set in his ways. He loves me and Charles very much, and in all that he did, he truly believes he has acted in my best interest. And while I don't condone his actions for a moment, I have, in time, forgiven him. I hope you can too."

Jace bowed his head. Such a difficult thing to ask of him. Sensing his mother's gaze, he finally choked out, "I'll try." But it wouldn't happen overnight.

Hope took hold in her eyes, and her face lit up in a smile. "I spoke with Kyrin this morning."

Jace's heavy emotions lifted some, eagerness to know what his mother thought taking hold. Kyrin was one of the most important people in his life. If his mother didn't think as highly of her as he did, it would probably crush him.

Rachel's smile brightened as if she knew this. "She's a lovely young woman."

Jace didn't realize he'd held his breath until he let it out in relief. "She is."

"And quite remarkable, especially for someone so young."

"She's been through a lot, and has dealt with it far better than I could have." As strong as Jace was physically, it was Kyrin's strength of character and faith that he most admired and envied.

His mother's expression softened. "You love her, don't you?"

Jace blinked. He hadn't even been so direct with himself yet. Of course he loved her—she was his best friend. He was closer to her than anyone, but he knew that wasn't the love his mother meant. Did he even know what that sort of love was? How could he love her if he didn't know? Yet, even if it was love, it could never work.

He cleared his throat, avoiding the question. "There are better men for her than me."

His mother drew her brows together. "I don't believe that."

Jace sighed. His mother didn't truly know him. How could she after less than two days? He cared more deeply for Kyrin than he ever had for anyone, but he could never be the sort of man she deserved. She was too special. She needed someone exceptional. Not someone who constantly struggled the way he did.

He tried to shrug off the sting of those facts. "Besides, there's someone back at camp she spends a lot of time with. He's very strong in his faith. He's a good man." *Everything I'm not.* Still, it was surprisingly difficult to talk of Kyrin and Timothy together.

"Jace, you're a good man."

He looked at her, unable to hide his doubt.

"Why don't you believe that?"

He swallowed hard, trying to loosen the stranglehold around his throat that made his voice crack. "Good men aren't guilty of murder."

"Those sins are in the past." Rachel reached out and laid her hand on his arm. "Elôm doesn't want nor expect you to still carry them now." She stared for a long moment into his eyes. "You do have a soul, Jace."

The words plunged into his heart and then rippled through him. He hadn't intended for her to know about this fear.

"Yes, I know how you struggle," she said quietly. "I can see it every time we speak of Elôm. It's as if you are trying to hide yourself from Him, believing you're too broken and lost for Him to love. Oh, Jace, that just isn't true. He *does* love you."

Jace ground his teeth together. Why was it so hard to believe that? Perhaps because so many people believed the opposite. How did he know for sure what was true?

"Jace, look at me." He did, and she raised her hand to his cheek. "Always remember this: Yes, you are part ryrik, but you are also part of me. You are my son, *my* flesh and blood. How could Elôm love you any less than I do? I know I did not give birth to a soulless monster."

Jace's breath trembled past his lips, the words soaking into his mind.

His mother's eyes grew teary. "And just look at how Elôm brought us together. It wasn't by chance. How could it be? He cares about us; about me, and about you."

Deep inside his heart, a small fissure opened up in the thick walls he always tried to use as protection, and a little light streamed into the darkness. Maybe she was right. If he couldn't trust his own mother, who could he trust?

"My lady!"

Elian's sharp warning jerked their attention to the sound of approaching footsteps. Striding straight toward them was Rothas, his eyes dark with rage.

JACE HAD JUST enough time to reach his feet before Rothas's fist latched onto his jerkin and slammed him back against the arbor. The impact forced the air from his lungs, but his ryrik blood kicked in, flushing through his body in preparation for a fight. A sharp blade flashed in front of his face and hovered dangerously close to his throat. He balled his fists, drawing on every ounce of willpower to keep from taking swift and decisive action. He would have liked nothing more than to do the man serious bodily harm. However, he knew the trouble it would bring.

"You dare touch my wife!" Rothas snarled.

The temperature of Jace's blood rose another few degrees at such an accusation coming from an unfaithful boor like Rothas. Elôm help him, he wanted so badly to plant his fist in the man's face.

"Rothas!"

But the man was too intent on Jace to notice his wife. His dagger pricked Jace's throat, and Jace was one second from acting in defense when Elian reached them. He grabbed Rothas's wrist, prying the dagger a few inches from Jace's neck.

"Rothas!" Rachel tried again, more forcefully. Again, she went unheeded.

Rothas's burning glare fixed on Elian. "Unless you want to find yourself mucking out horse stalls for the rest of your life, you'll stand aside."

Elian did not budge, his expression just as set and fierce as Rothas's.

"No, Rothas, listen to me," Rachel pleaded.

Yet Rothas snarled in Elian's face, "Stand aside!"

Jace's stomach twisted. This was going to end in bloodshed—either his own or Elian's. He could see it in Rothas's violent eyes. But then his mother spoke again.

"He's my son!"

Rothas's head whipped around, and he fixed his flashing gaze on her now. She stood, unflinching, her voice dropping back to a normal volume, but low with seriousness.

"He's Jace. Let him go."

No one moved for a long moment. Rothas continued to stare wide-eyed at Rachel, who held his piercing look without wavering. At last, the man's hold loosened, and Jace pulled away while he had the chance. Elian too stepped back, standing near Jace, ready to step in and shield him should Rothas advance again. Jace rested his still curled fingers where his sword should have been. It had been hard to leave it sitting in his room, and this was why. One way or another, trouble always seemed to find him.

Rothas shot Jace a cold look. Jace could almost see the gears of the man's cunning mind turning as he returned his attention to Rachel.

"That's impossible."

Rachel shook her head. "No."

"The boy died of fever," Rothas insisted, but even to Jace it was clear he spoke what he knew to be a lie.

A cool light kindled in Rachel's eyes now. "So you and my father both told me."

Rothas stepped closer to his wife, his voice a low hiss. "He could be anyone."

Jace bristled at the man's threatening stance, but his mother drew herself up.

"I know my own son."

"This is ridiculous." Rothas spun on his heel, giving Jace a scorching look before striding away.

"Where are you going?" Rachel called after him.

"To send for your father," he threw over his shoulder.

"So you two can conspire to get rid of him again?"

Rothas didn't respond this time. Rachel stood rigidly until he was gone. The shudder of every hard breath she took filled the following silence. Jace sensed the internal battle she fought, especially in light of all she had just said about her faithfulness to Rothas. When she finally turned to him, her eyes displayed it plainly. Guilt struck him for being the source of the conflict.

He hung his head. "I'm sorry. I—"

"No, Jace. You're not to blame." She drew a slow breath, her anger dissipating in a moment as concern overwhelmed her expression. "Are you all right?"

"I'm fine," Jace assured her.

Her gaze dropped to his neck, just to be certain. She then turned to Elian. "Will you stay with him? Who knows who else Rothas will tell about this. I don't want any of his men making trouble. I must try to reason with him before my father gets here."

Elian nodded firmly.

To Jace, she said, "Don't worry. I'll get this sorted out . . . somehow."

Jace said nothing as she turned to leave. The cold suspicion inside him warned that she wouldn't succeed. Things like this just didn't work out in his favor.

Rachel tried everything in her power to get Rothas to soften on the issue; however, he all but refused to speak with her. Forced to give up and wait to try again when her father arrived, she passed on lunch and secluded herself alone in a back parlor to pray. She begged Elôm for His hand in this, to soften the hearts of both Rothas and her father toward Jace, and for them to see how desperately she loved and wanted him in her life. She also prayed for a good deal of patience and restraint. It was too easy to be angry and bitter. Without Elôm's strength, she was likely to say something she would later regret.

She was still deep in her prayers when someone tapped on the door. She rose from her knees and opened it to a servant girl in the hall.

"Lord Dunrick has arrived, my lady."

"Thank you." Rachel offered a quick smile and drew a calming breath. Time to head off to do battle once again for her son. She strode down the hall, whispering last-minute prayers along the way. Memories of the morning she had woken up to find Jace gone relived themselves. Her heart ached as much as it did then to think of losing him again. But he wasn't an infant. They couldn't just secret him away from her. She wouldn't let them.

Her father's voice echoed loud and clear when she neared the drawing room. He had a habit of speaking louder than necessary on most occasions, but especially when he was agitated. Most people considered him a rather blustery man if they weren't well-acquainted enough to see his gentler side. Rachel had hoped for that gentle side today. No doubt Rothas was at work, riling him up. Her father openly admitted that he and Rothas didn't see eye to eye on most things. Unfortunately, this was the one thing they had and would work together on. *Oh, Lord, I need Your intervention and strength.*

Pulling her shoulders back and shoring up her resolve, Rachel stepped into the drawing room. She spotted her mother first. The older woman offered her a sympathetic, yet encouraging look. Charles wasn't present, and Rachel's heart sank. He must have been away when Rothas's messenger arrived at Brandell, or surely he would have come. Rachel had counted on his support, but at least her mother was here. It would be up to the two of them to defend Jace's place in this family.

Finally, her gaze settled on her father's daunting figure. He wasn't tall exactly—a sliver under six foot—but he was burly. Though he had become a bit rounded in the middle over the years, it wasn't quite so noticeable in comparison to his broad shoulders and chest.

The moment he spotted her, he stepped forward, a storm brewing in his indigo eyes. "What's this I hear about a strange man claiming to be your son?"

Rachel cast a sharp glance at Rothas. Of course, he wouldn't wait for her to discuss the matter.

"He isn't *claiming* anything." Rachel met her father's eyes. "He *is* my son."

"Nonsense. The child is dead," he blustered as if, after all these years, he had convinced himself it was true. "The man is an impostor. He probably heard you lost a child and is here to gain whatever he can from you."

Rachel drew in her breath and let it out slowly to make sure she was calm before speaking. "He is not just any man. His name is Jace. Furthermore, he never approached me with any of this. I recognized him when he arrived in Lady Anne's security detail. *I* approached him. He had no idea who I was."

"You don't know that," Rothas cut in. "You could be playing right into his plans."

Rachel narrowed her eyes. "You weren't there. You didn't see his face when I revealed who I was. Not everyone is manipulative and conniving."

His face darkened at her accusation, and Rachel felt her conscience pricked. *I'm sorry, Lord.* She bit her tongue, reminding herself to guard her words.

She faced her father again. "He's clearly half ryrik. There's no question of that. How many half-ryriks do you think there are? I doubt most women are as fortunate to be rescued as I was."

Her father grimaced at the memories, but said, "That doesn't make him yours."

Rachel put her hands out. "And you think all half-ryriks have the name Jace?"

Her father bumbled for a response, but had none. Finally, he huffed. "Even if it is true—and I'm not saying it is—he's the unfortunate consequence of a despicable act. A painful reminder."

Rachel shook her head. "The act was despicable, yes, but Jace is the blessing in it, not the consequence."

Her father waved his hand, addressing her in the same tone he had used when she was a child. "You're being ridiculous. You should have ended things when I first told you to and then you wouldn't have had the opportunity to become attached. You should let this go and forget about him."

Ire rose inside Rachel again, and she worked very hard to control it, though her voice trembled in the process. "I am a grown woman and old enough to decide how I feel about my own child."

Her frustration grew further when Rothas interjected his unwelcome opinion again.

"Whoever he is, let's not forget he is half *ryrik*, as you say. He's dangerous and should be sent away at once if not imprisoned."

"No!" Rachel gasped, her voice a tad desperate. She quickly controlled it. "He is not dangerous." She glared at her husband. "Why are you so against him? He's no threat to you. Is it because he's outside your control?"

Rothas glowered at her, and his jaw twitched. Of course, she was right. Her husband was a man of power. He desired to control everything—her, their children, their household. He had proved it in his accusations and threats against Jace in the garden. Though he held himself to no standard, taking advantage of any willing woman who came his way, woe to his wife if she dared to even look at another man.

Her voice low and even, she said, "Jace is my son. I carried him and gave birth to him, and I love him. I will *not* let either of you take him from me this time."

Her gaze remained fixed with her husband's, driving home her point. She would not back down in this. Once she was satisfied, she turned back to her father, now needing to rest her case with him.

"There is no deception here. Jace truly is my son, and you would see that if you would only take the time to know him. You never did. Not from the day he was born. You may not wish to acknowledge it, but he was your first grandchild. He's no different from James or Elanor, and no less worthy of your love."

"Henry, she is right," her mother joined in now, speaking with soft persuasion. "I sat with him, talked with him. He's a wonderful young man."

Her father peered between the two of them, his face sour at being ganged up on.

"Fine," he muttered. "Bring him in here and I shall form my own opinions."

Rachel's heart tripped, not sure whether to rejoice or cringe. She wanted him to meet Jace, of course, but her father could be very abrasive. It had been her hope to present Jace to him when he was in a much kinder mood. Poor Jace.

She glanced at her mother, who gave a nod of assurance.

"Well?" her father snapped impatiently.

Taking a deep breath and sending out a desperate prayer, Rachel turned for the door.

Somehow, the news of Jace's identity had already traveled throughout the house. At lunch, every set of eyes in the servants' hall was on him, along with a steady stream of murmurs and whispers. Many were only exclamations of surprise and curiosity, but others weren't so innocent. He caught snatches of suspicion about his mixed blood and intentions. It quickly became clear which members of the staff were more loyal to Rothas than to his mother. Most were sure Rothas would have him thrown out at the earliest opportunity.

The others did their best to encourage him. Kaden looked ready to get into it with some of the men, but Rayad gave him a cautioning look. Despite their support, Jace soon couldn't take the unease anymore and left the table. He needed sunlight and the freeing touch of fresh air. Just outside, he found a bench and sank down. Elian remained close, as Rachel had asked, though they spoke little. Jace wasn't in the mood to talk.

A short time later, a lavish carriage pulled into the estate. Jace's stomach turned over. A sense of doom seemed to follow as the carriage rolled out of sight. Now his fate would be decided. How could his mother convince both Rothas and her father to accept him? She had already tried once in the past. They all knew how that turned out.

Jace bent forward with a sigh and rubbed his forehead. He didn't often get headaches the way Kyrin did, but he could feel one building now. Just imagining what might be taking place inside sent tension through his shoulder, up his neck, and into his skull. If only he could know what was happening.

"Jace."

He jerked his head up. His mother stood near the door, her expression hopeful, yet strained. How could she be out here so soon? This didn't bode well.

"My father wishes to meet you."

Jace lifted his brows. "He does?"

"Yes," his mother winced slightly, "but I don't think he's convinced of your identity, and is suspicious of your motives. I wish I could present you under better circumstances, but if I put it off now, he may decide not to see you at all. However, I don't want to force you to see him."

Jace hesitated. He had no desire to meet the man responsible for his life of slavery. Just the thought of facing him set fire to his blood. Yet, if there was a chance at resolving things, he had to take it. Considering his mother's desire for him to have forgiveness for his grandfather, he forced a nod.

"Good." She looked at Elian, who stepped closer. "Your presence would only agitate Father, but I would appreciate it if you would be nearby. I don't think my father has ulterior motives or some sort of plan with Rothas, but I might need you if they do."

Elian nodded. "Of course."

Rachel then motioned to Jace. "Come with me."

Together, they walked inside. Along the way, she said, "I just want to warn you that my father can be loud and gruff when he's upset. I don't know what he intends to say or ask you, but just be honest and yourself."

Jace absorbed her words and tried to prepare himself. In his life, he had faced men from one end of the spectrum to the other—both kind and cruel, though mostly cruel. Such experience should have helped in this situation, but his nerves still kicked in. After all, this meeting could decide the future he had with his family—or whether or not there would be a future.

At the door to the drawing room, Jace's heart rate spiked, and he froze. What if this was a bad idea? What if, as his mother feared, there was some plan in place to get rid of him again? Could she stop them? Could he? What would that do to their mission here?

His mother rested her hand on his arm, and he looked down into her earnest eyes.

"Whatever happens, I want you to remember that it doesn't change who you are to me."

With this assurance, she opened the door and stepped in. Jace still hesitated. It was as if he were entering an arena again. The emotions were eerily similar. Fighting to banish them, he steeled himself and followed, immediately taking in the surroundings. There, in the center of the room, stood a man with a hard, ill-tempered look. A knot tightened Jace's stomach as his mother drew him closer.

"Father, I want you to meet your grandson, Jace."

In silence, the two of them stared at each other. For all his life, Jace had assumed his physical attributes had come predominantly from his ryrik blood, but that was not quite true. His grandfather was a strong-bodied man with a stern jaw set, just like Jace, and though their heights differed and Jace was leaner, their builds were similar. The biggest shock was to realize he had his grandfather's straight nose. Despite the obvious differences, they looked very much alike.

It took Jace a long moment to process this. His grandfather's granite expression lifted just a little as he too made the same shocking discoveries. If he'd still had doubts about Jace's lineage, he couldn't dispute them now. It was too obvious. Jace was family.

Lord Dunrick cleared his throat. Jace caught a glimpse of a brief breakthrough in his hard exterior, but he had it back in place in an instant.

"What is it you want from us?" His deep voice was edged in a growl, but it seemed forced.

"Father," Rachel scolded.

The man's gaze never wavered from Jace.

"Nothing." Jace pulled his shoulders back. "Only to know my family."

Lord Dunrick's eyes narrowed, unconvinced. "No money?"

"No," Jace answered.

"Not a position among the nobles?"

"No."

"Revenge?"

Jace sucked in his breath at the blunt question. Had he learned about his mother a few years ago, before meeting Rayad, then yes, he would have wanted revenge. However, he knew now that it would only hurt him and his mother.

Despite the internal tugging to seek retribution, he answered quietly, "No."

"Father, you heard him," Rachel stepped in. "He just wants to get to know us—his family."

Lord Dunrick frowned at her, but then his face portrayed a subtle hint of softening. Just maybe he was beginning to believe it. Jace wasn't so foolish as to hope the man may eventually feel sorry for what he had done, but as long as they were on civil terms, he could live with that.

Rothas stepped forward. Jace had almost forgotten he was here, and he braced himself. The man had been too quiet during the exchange between Jace and his grandfather.

"Well then, it appears we were wrong in our suspicions."

Jace eyed his too-wide, almost smug smile.

"It is only fitting that we make amends," Rothas continued. "We'll have a room prepared immediately and get you out of the servants' quarters. And tonight, at supper, we shall celebrate your return to the family."

The way he said *family* dripped of sarcasm. The man was up to something. After all, his cunning and plotting had brought Jace and the others here in the first place. He had a motive hidden behind his apparent change of heart. Jace glanced at his mother. She shared his look of suspicion.

Hoping to avoid the brewing trouble, Jace said, "That won't be necessary."

A ruthless light glinted in Rothas's eyes. "You decline our desire to right the wrongs that have been done?"

Cold slithered along Jace's skin. He could hardly resist now without it appearing to be out of spite. Rothas had maneuvered him exactly where he wanted him, and they both knew it. The question now was the man's end game. What devious plan did he have in mind for Jace?

Rothas's gaze turned to his wife, a smarmy smile pasted on his face. "We should tell James and Elanor. I'm sure they will be delighted."

Rachel glanced away and murmured, "Elanor knows."

"Does she?" Ice laced Rothas's smooth tone. "We'd best not leave James out any longer then."

With a sigh, Rachel walked to the door and instructed Elian to send for James and Elanor. As she turned back into the room, Rothas addressed Lord and Lady Dunrick.

"You must stay for supper. Then, if Charles can make it, the whole family can be together."

Jace ground his teeth together. He really hated the way the man spoke about family. There was no love in it. He glanced at his grandfather. Even the earl seemed wary of Rothas. If only his grandfather were on his side and an ally in this.

A few uncomfortable minutes passed before the door opened. Elanor stepped in first. She gave Jace a quick smile, but must have sensed the tension in the room.

Then came James. Jace traded a cool look with him. James's entire being radiated an infuriating air of superiority. All Jace could think of for a moment was how this half-brother of his had leered at Kyrin the day before. It still heated his blood.

Rachel stepped forward, her mouth open to speak, but Rothas swiftly cut in.

"James, it seems you are the only one who was left out of your mother's news."

James frowned. "What news?"

Rachel again tried to speak, but Rothas spoke over her. "About your brother, Jace, the half-blood child she had before she married me."

Jace clenched his fists. How tempted he was to use one on Rothas, not only for his rude, bullying behavior toward his mother, but for the way he spoke, as if she were somehow to blame for Jace's birth.

James's eyes grew round before his brows scrunched low. "What?" He looked Jace up and down. "*This* is my half-brother?"

Jace's ire shifted to his brother now, just as tempted to use a fist on him.

"James," their mother said soothingly, "yes, he is your brother."

"What does he want?" James looked on Jace with both suspicion and loathing.

"We're his family. He just wants to be part of it."

"He's the issue of some ryrik."

"James," Rachel said more sternly. "Do you forget that I am his mother?"

James just glowered at Jace, and instead of trying to calm things, Rothas stood in silence, clearly pleased with his handiwork.

"WILL YOU BE all right with this?"

Jace looked over at Kyrin, who stood in the doorway as he packed up his things. "I have no choice. If I refuse, Rothas will use it against me. I don't know if Lord Dunrick will ever accept me as his grandson, but if I'm not careful, I'll destroy any credibility I do have with him."

Kyrin sighed and bit her bottom lip. "Just beware of Rothas. Men like him are dangerous. You have no idea they're manipulating you until it's too late."

And didn't Jace know it.

"I will." He hoped he sounded more confident than he felt. She had enough to think about without worrying over him on top of it.

"At least Anne will be there tonight."

He wasn't sure if Kyrin said this for his benefit or her own. Either way, he would be glad to have someone from their group present. He needed all the allies he could get to face Rothas again.

Gathering up his pack and sword, he stepped to the door and looked down at Kyrin. Even more troubling to him than his issues with Rothas was the grave danger she would face come suppertime.

"We may not get to talk again before tonight. Please, be careful." His throat ached with the plea. "Don't take chances."

If only he could stay with her! Instead, he would be stuck sharing a meal with some family members who wished he didn't even exist.

"I won't," Kyrin murmured.

She stared up at him, and he stared back. It was the first time all day that his mother's question came back to him. This crazy mix of fear, confusion, and admiration that squeezed and throbbed in his heart, robbing him of a decent breath . . . could it be love?

But now was neither the time nor the place to hash that out.

"Just . . . don't get caught," he said finally.

She gave a flicker of a smile. "I won't."

She stepped back, allowing him to pass through the door.

In the hall, Rayad met them. His eyes expressed sympathy, and he put his hand on Jace's shoulder.

"I know this is difficult for you, but I want you to keep in mind that Elôm works in even the most difficult situations. We've all seen that. He has some plan in this that goes far above Rothas's. And, Jace, He wants the best for you. You can be assured of that."

Jace glanced down at the floor, but nodded. He would try to believe it.

Looking Rayad in the eyes again, he said, "Take care of Kyrin."

"I will."

Jace forced himself to move, and strode down the hall. As he climbed the stairs, hesitancy took hold of him. Though they were all in the same house, it was almost as if he were leaving his friends behind. If he gained acceptance from his family, was this how it would always be? Would he have to choose one or the other? This new prospect deeply disturbed him.

Upstairs in the hall, his mother met him with a gentle smile. Such a kind woman shouldn't have to live such a hard life. If only Jace could find some sort of understanding in all this. What could Elôm be doing?

His mother motioned to him, and he followed her down the hall.

"I'll show you to your room. I was going to prepare one near the rest of ours, but I didn't think Rothas would appreciate that . . . or James."

Jace agreed. It probably wasn't a good idea for him and James to be in close proximity. Like his father, James had a way of pushing Jace dangerously close to rash action.

"But I don't want you to feel that you're only a guest." His mother looked at him, her expression earnest, as they climbed the stairs to the second floor. "You're not."

Jace held back a sigh. He felt even lower than a guest. More like an intruder, but he kept this to himself. He wouldn't destroy her effort to make him feel welcome.

In the upstairs hall, Rachel opened a door a couple of rooms down from Anne's. At least he would be nearer to Kyrin. This gave him some comfort.

He followed his mother into the room and looked around. It was more masculine than the other rooms he had seen. A wide bed with a navy blue canopy sat perpendicular to him. The other furnishings included a large wardrobe matching the bed's dark wood frame. Straight across the room, heavy drapes were thrown back to let sunlight through a pair of wide windows. He'd never stayed in such a large, rich space before. To come from slave yards to this was staggering.

"I hope you'll be comfortable."

Jace snapped out of his thoughts to face his mother. She looked hesitant.

"I'm sorry you were forced into this. I know it must make you uncomfortable."

"I'll manage." Jace tried to smile for her and looked about the room again. "It'll just take some getting used to."

He set his pack in a chair and propped his sword against it. If Kyrin was successful tonight, he might not even be here long enough to get used to it. A sudden ache throbbed inside him at the thought of leaving his mother. What if he only had one more day with her? If so, why did it have to be marred by tonight's supper and whatever ill plans Rothas had for him?

Behind him, his mother said, "I don't know what you want to do this afternoon, but Charles arrived while you were downstairs. He wants to see you, and I know it may not be pleasant, but I think the more my father gets to know you, the more he'll open up."

Jace drew in a breath, forcing aside the longing to sit and visit privately with his mother as he had the last two days. He wanted to see Charles, but it came at a heavy price if it meant facing his grandfather and Rothas again. Yet, if that was what his mother wanted, he would do it. "I'll come down."

The proud look she offered buoyed him up.

Back down in the drawing room, the family was still gathered, this time including Charles and Anne. She gave him an encouraging smile. She might not be able to help him much, but there was some comfort in the fact that she knew more about this lifestyle than he did.

Charles offered a friendly greeting as Jace took a seat in the chair his mother indicated. He made a quick sweep of the room. His grandparents sat together on the loveseat across from him while Elanor and Anne occupied another. Rothas and James each had a chair at the far end. Jace could only see his brother's profile, but the young man seemed intent on brooding. Rothas, however, watched him, and Jace once again got that sense of a predator from him.

The conversation was slow and awkward at first, but gained momentum. Charles, being the gentleman he was, attempted to keep things light and cheery. Between him and the four women, they had the other men well outnumbered, which helped. Lord Dunrick didn't have much to say, but Jace strove to leave him with something of a good impression. Rothas was surprisingly silent as well, and Jace worked hard to ignore his constant scrutiny.

He didn't have to work at it long. After less than an hour, Rothas stood. He offered no excuses, but motioned to James, who followed him out. Though everyone pretended not to notice, Jace stared at the door they had exited. Unease crept through his stomach. While the oppressive mood had followed them out, the saying held true about keeping your enemies close. Who knew what schemes the two of them might be hatching off in private? They would surely get rid of him if they could, and the hair rose along his arms.

Still, with the two most hostile forces now gone, things livened up. Since the majority of them knew Jace's background already, they focused more on their own lives. Jace enjoyed learning more about each of them, particularly Elanor. He discovered they shared a common love for horses and riding. She made him promise to take her out to see Niton and his tricks when they had the chance. He also found she liked to hunt, thanks to their uncle. She and Kyrin would get along well given the chance.

The afternoon passed by much more quickly than Jace had anticipated. He had overcome one hurdle, but an even greater was fast approaching. A formal dinner was not something he had any experience dealing with.

When Elanor and Anne excused themselves to prepare for dinner, Jace took the opportunity to go to his room for a short time of solitude. Though the afternoon had not been overly taxing, he was still drained. The amount of energy it took to sit in the same room with the man responsible for his past and not hate him for it was exhausting. If only his grandfather would display even the smallest hint of remorse, or at least goodwill toward him.

Once behind his closed door, he sagged back and rubbed his eyes as he released a sigh. He just wasn't made for this. Letting his arms fall to his sides, he stared down at his clothing. While the women would show up to dinner in their evening gowns and the men would be dressed in their lordly attire, he would arrive in rough linen and scuffed leather. He would be as a peasant showing up at the table of nobility. It had never mattered before, and he didn't like that it did now.

A knock sounded behind him. He turned and pulled the door open to let his mother enter. In one hand, she held a white shirt and had other black articles of clothing draped over her arm.

"Rothas sent me with these for you."

Jace eyed the outfit and raised a brow. Rothas had sent clothes for him?

Rachel shook her head, her expression tired. "I don't know, Jace. I don't know what he's doing."

Jace had his suspicions. Maybe, by offering the clothes, Rothas wanted him to feel indebted, and therefore gain some measure of control over him. Either that or he just knew how uncomfortable Jace would be wearing them. A cruel way to make the evening even more unpleasant.

He peered at the clothing in disgust. Should he take them and follow right along with Rothas's game? Either choice had its drawbacks. At last, he took them from his mother. If Rothas thought this would gain him any power, he was mistaken.

His mother gave him a weary smile. "You did well this afternoon. I think my father just might be thawing."

Jace struggled with unwillingness to believe that, but she didn't appear to have said it just for his benefit.

"I'll see you downstairs." She turned and left him alone again.

Jace closed the door and laid the clothing on his bed. He scowled as he started changing. With any luck, the clothing wouldn't even fit him. He murmured a prayer that it would be so; however, the shirt was only a little snug across the shoulders. Not quite enough to prevent him from wearing it. He grumbled under his breath.

As he fastened the ornate silver buckles of the well-tailored suede jerkin, he stepped in front of the mirror to inspect himself. The black pants and jerkin contrasted sharply with the pristine cotton shirt. He tugged the jerkin down, smoothing any wrinkles. The way it was constructed, fitted at the waist and tapered to a point, emphasized his muscular chest and shoulders. He shrugged his shoulders. The rich material didn't feel right. He glanced down at the toes of his boots. The worn leather stood out against the dark pants, but he could do nothing about that.

Fighting not to sink into too dark a mood, he walked over to the windows to get a good view of the shadowed twilight. The gardens lay below. Had he just talked with his mother out there this morning? How did things change so quickly in the space of a day? It was enough to destroy anyone's delusions of control over their lives.

Jace remained at the window as the darkness grew, until it was time to go down. He turned for his door and paused to brace himself, but could not shed the growing doom that settled around him. Rothas and James had had all afternoon to scheme. Would they pounce on him during dinner, or would they let him sweat for a while? He loathed the waiting. He'd rather just face them now, head-on. But this was no physical battle he could fight. These mind games were a form of battle he had no skill in.

Resignation hardened inside him, and he stepped into the hall. Just down from him, Anne's door opened. She walked out, and Kyrin stood in the doorway. When they noticed him, Kyrin appeared to do a double take, her gaze making a quick sweep of his outfit. What was that reaction? Could it be . . . appreciation? He chided himself. Things were complicated enough already.

"Good," Anne said, gaining both their attention, "we can go down together." She turned to Kyrin, who stole another quick glance at Jace. "Are you all set?"

She nodded and drew a breath. Her gaze once again slid to Jace, and he marveled over how brave she was, taking on this mission. He wanted to say something before he had to go, but what had he not said already?

In a low, quiet voice, he told her, "I'm praying for you."

Her eyes glowed with the comfort of those words. "I'm praying for you too."

Trading brief smiles, they parted. Dinner was waiting, and it would do Jace no good to arrive late. However, halfway down the hall, he glanced back. Kyrin still stood in the doorway, and he experienced a sudden attack of powerlessness to protect her. His heartbeat grew shallow and faint. *Elôm, please protect her tonight.* Whatever she found in that office, he just wanted her safe. That was all that mattered.

The heaviness of concern pressed on him all the way downstairs. As they neared the dining room, Anne whispered, "Is there anything you want to ask before we go in?"

Jace had never attended a formal dinner in his life. Kyrin had given him some information on what to expect, but he had difficulty remembering it now.

"No." Nothing Anne could tell him in these last few moments would make much difference in the end. As long as

Kyrin was safe at the end of the night, he didn't even care what sort of impression he made at dinner.

His mother stood at the door waiting for him when they entered the dining room. With a smile, she looked him over. "Whatever the circumstances, you look very handsome tonight."

"Thanks," he murmured. He thought of Kyrin. Had she thought so too?

His mother led him around the table, indicating a chair to her right. In another minute, the rest of the family appeared, and everyone took their seats. At least Rothas and James had places at the far end of the table. It might be overly tempting to stab each other with their dinner knives if they were seated together.

The servants circled the table to serve the first course of the meal, and Charles talked casually about Brandell and local news. He even managed to get his father talking after a few attempts. Soon it was almost as if Jace were not present, which suited him just fine. He would have preferred it to stay that way, but surely Rothas wouldn't let an opportunity ripe with the chance to humiliate him pass by. He could almost sense the man biding his time, working up to his moment.

Then came a lull in the conversation. The man's icy eyes pinned on him, and Jace went rigid. Here it was.

"So, tell us, Jace, what have you been doing these past years?"

A coldblooded smirk crept across his face. Jace just sat for a moment. Since the man had likely been involved in stealing him away from his mother, he no doubt knew the answer already. In fact, the only one who probably didn't know he had been a slave was James, and Jace had no desire to enlighten him.

Careful to keep his voice even, yet cool, he met Rothas's piercing gaze. "I think you know what I was doing."

Rothas didn't back down. "Well, you're clearly no slave now. How did you get free?" His eyes glinted dangerously, as if he had just discovered a weakness in Jace. "Are you a runaway?"

Don't you wish? "No." Had he been, Rothas could have had him arrested and shipped back to his master, solving all his supposed problems.

The man appeared only marginally disappointed. "How then?"

Jace continued to hold his gaze, determined to prove he wasn't intimidated. "A friend bought my freedom."

Rothas barely nodded and finally took a bite of his food, certainly plotting his next course of action. Turned out he had James to do some of the work for him.

"How much did he pay?"

Jace's attention switched to his half-brother. The worm was just begging for a beating. "Everything he had."

James imitated his father's loathsome smirk. "He must have been awfully poor."

Elanor gave their brother a scolding look. "James, don't be so horrid."

But James just smiled insolently. Jace glared long and hard at him. Little did his brother know that, had Jace fought the way his master wanted, he would have been worth a fortune. He didn't lift his intense gaze until James grew visibly uncomfortable and looked away. Now Jace allowed the smallest hint of a smirk.

Rothas, however, was not about to let him gain any ground, though this time his words weren't aimed directly at Jace.

"Lady Anne, were you aware you had a half-ryrik in your security detail?"

Of course, it was only a matter of time before he attacked Jace's bloodline. Jace looked over at Anne, sorry to see her dragged into this. Yet, Anne wasn't a woman to be pitied or trifled with. She sat very straight, her eyes sparking.

"I was," she responded primly, "but I don't judge a man based on his blood. I judge him on his character and actions, whether or not he is honorable. Men of that quality seem to be increasingly rare these days."

They traded a cool look at the implication of her words. Glancing around the table, Jace caught the not-quite hidden smile on Charles's face and the look of admiration he sent Anne. Thanks to Jace's family and Anne, the evening didn't seem to be going quite the way Rothas planned it.

PANIC COURSED THROUGH Kyrin's body, growing stronger with every solid thud of her heart. She had only come down to the servants' quarters to get something for the headache tightening at the base of her neck. After all, it would be hard enough to sift through Rothas's office without having to focus through the pain. What she hadn't planned on was meeting Tina. The girl was determined to talk to her about Kaden, which led to an array of other things. No matter how often or how strongly Kyrin hinted at needing to go, it seemed to fly right over her head. Now it was getting late. If Tina didn't run out of words soon, Kyrin might just shake her.

Her heart drummed even harder, and she wasn't even in the office yet. How many chances would she get at this? They couldn't remain at Ashwood much longer without Rothas suspecting something. He was already in a foul mood since discovering Jace. *Elôm, please, help.*

In that moment, Rayad appeared, and Kyrin only just held in a sigh. His face was grim, reinforcing her own desperation to get to the office and get this done. When he reached the two of them, Tina finally fell silent.

"Corrine," his voice was deceptively stern, "I need to speak with you about some things Lady Anne has brought to my attention."

This was exactly what they needed to end Tina's chatter. She gave Kyrin a sympathetic look and murmured, "Excuse me," before scuttling off.

Now Kyrin did blow out a sigh. "Thank you." The girl was incessant.

Rayad only nodded as he ushered her toward the stairs.

"Do you think there's still time?" Kyrin whispered.

Rayad glanced at her, his serious expression twisting her stomach. "I hope so. The meal hasn't ended yet. You just have to work quickly."

They met Kaden at the stairs.

Kyrin gave him an exaggerated look of pity. "Just so you know, I'm much more sympathetic to your situation with Tina now."

He huffed and rolled his eyes as they followed Rayad cautiously upstairs. When they reached the second floor, they stopped at the top of the staircase. Here, Rayad faced Kyrin and handed her a candle.

"Kaden and I will be waiting in your room."

Kyrin glanced down the dim hall that would lead to the office. This was the moment. Her skin tingled.

"Are you all right?"

Kyrin looked at Rayad again, giving him a quick nod. She caught eyes with Kaden, noting his worry-knit brow, before forcing herself to move. She had to do this, and she had to do it now.

With light footsteps, she hurried across the manor house to the opposite end—the family's wing. Her hands quivered almost as much as the small flame of the candle she tried to shield along the way. To calm herself, she whispered some of the words she had recently read in the King's Scrolls.

*"For I have heard the slander of many, Terror is on every side;
While they took counsel together against me, They schemed to take
away my life. But as for me, I trust in You, O Lord. I say, 'You are
my God.' My times are in Your hand; Deliver me from the hand of
my enemies and from those who persecute me. Make Your face
shine upon Your servant; Save me in Your lovingkindness."*

In just a couple minutes, she arrived at the door Anne had
described. She drew a shaky breath and put her hand to the
knob, praying. If it was locked, their mission was as good as
over. Carefully, as if the slightest sound would bring Rothas
down on her, she turned the knob. It turned easily, and the
door pushed open a crack. Kyrin's heart thudded.

Casting a nervous glance over her shoulder, she slipped
inside and closed the door silently behind her. The room was
dark. Her candle only cast a small circle of light, leaving the edges
of the room cloaked in wavering shadows. Cold wafted across
her skin from the open window across from her, the thin drapes
billowing like specters. She closed her eyes for a moment and
gathered her courage. Her imagination would not get the best
of her.

When she opened them again, she focused on the large
desk and crossed the room. Candles, books, and parchments
dotted the surface, but everything was very neat. Rothas was a
man who liked things just so. Kyrin would have to be
meticulous about leaving things just as she found them.

After fixing a clear mental picture of the desk in her
mind, she set the candle down and went to work. She flipped
through the parchments, looking for Daican's seal before
scanning the contents. From what she could tell, they were all
local correspondences.

"Kyrin?"

Her heart jumped into her throat, and she choked on a gasp
as she spun around, nearly knocking over the candle. There, just

stepping over the window frame, was Aaron. Kyrin put her hand over her drumming heart and gripped the desk, a little faint. She couldn't get her voice to work.

"Sorry," he said as she stood and gaped at him. "I didn't mean to scare you."

"How . . ." she managed at last, though the words were breathless. "How did you get up here?"

"I climbed."

He climbed? Up the side of the manor? She had to remind herself that he was half crete and this wasn't the first time she had seen him climb a building.

"I thought you could use some help," Aaron said, snapping her from shock.

Truthfully, she would be very relieved not to be alone here. "Thanks."

She turned to the desk again, willing her hands to stop shaking.

Aaron came to her side. "Find anything?"

"No, but he probably wouldn't leave important information lying out, even if it is his private office."

Arranging the stack of parchments just as she had found them, Kyrin pulled open one of the desk drawers. Again, she took a good look before touching anything. "He's very organized, so we have to be careful to leave things exactly as they were."

Aaron nodded and let her do the searching.

Praying to get this over with quickly, Kyrin fingered through the contents of the drawer.

Jace took a sip of his wine, the tart liquid sliding over his tongue. He wrinkled his nose. He'd never had a fondness for the taste of alcohol. But this minor discomfort was nothing compared to the tension straining his insides. His gaze drifted again to the drawing room door. It took every effort to resist the powerful urge to leave. Was Kyrin back safely from the office yet? It was difficult to concentrate on anything without knowing for sure.

A small sigh crept past his lips as he dragged his eyes back to the others. He didn't want to cause any suspicions with his distraction. Unwittingly, his gaze met with Rothas. The man was a master at the death glare. Its burn reached all the way across the room, carrying with it a dark promise of retribution. Jace held it for a moment. He refused to be cowed. Whatever the man had planned for his next assault, Jace wouldn't take it lying down. However, after Rothas's failure to destroy him at the table, his coming attack was sure to be doubly vicious.

With the continued black looks and the rest of the family working hard to keep things civil, tension thickened the atmosphere. They had only finished the meal just over half an hour ago, but Lord Dunrick apparently grew tired of the oppressive mood. He rose abruptly from the sofa.

"It's getting late. It's time we returned to Brandell."

Lady Dunrick quietly followed along as he bid everyone goodnight. His gaze lingered a moment on Jace. It wasn't a kindly look, but neither was it hostile. The acknowledgement encouraged Jace. After all, the earl could have simply ignored his existence.

Charles chose to leave with them. When he came to Jace, he gripped his arm and smiled warmly. "We'll win my father over yet. You just watch and see."

Jace had to smile at this. If his grandfather was willing to forget the past, then he would do his best to forget it as well.

Now that the guests had gone, Jace resumed his seat, half-listening to the remaining women talk amongst themselves. With each minute, it grew ever harder to sit still. Every instinct inside him screamed to check on Kyrin.

These feelings doubled when Rothas stood. He paused near James and whispered something. If only Jace were a bit closer and could hear it. The man then walked out without a word. James did not move at first, absently swirling the leftover wine in his glass. Finally, he downed it in a gulp and followed his father. On the way out, he gave Jace a smoldering, squinty-eyed glance. Though he walked steadily enough, he seemed to have had a bit too much to drink. Jace narrowed his own eyes in disgust, but his nerves tingled in warning. Twice now, Rothas and James had slunk off in private.

Now that they had gone, Jace didn't think he could stay still much longer. Who knew where Rothas was headed? Kyrin had better be out of that office. If he didn't find out soon, the unknown would kill him. Moisture welled around his neck and soaked into his collar, which seemed to tighten around his throat. He had to work hard not to appear too relieved when Anne gave her excuses to retire for the evening. They all rose.

"I think I'll head up too," Jace said.

Rachel smiled at him and nodded. He turned to go, but she touched his arm.

"For what it's worth, it was good to have you at the table tonight. You handled it very well."

"Thank you." Jace would have liked to linger and speak with her and Elanor more, but his thoughts and concern for Kyrin overwhelmed the desire. "I'll see you in the morning."

"Good night," his mother's soft words trailed after him as he left the room.

Hurrying, Jace caught up to Anne at the staircase. They said nothing, but shared apprehension passed between them. Jace wouldn't relax until he set eyes on Kyrin's face. *Please, let her be there.* Anything could have happened in the time he sat dining with his family.

Jace's heart was thrashing by the time they reached the room. Anne pushed open the door, and they both walked in. Rayad and Kaden's anxious expressions sent Jace's stomach to his feet.

"Kyrin's not here yet?" Anne asked.

Rayad shook his head. "No."

Jace's mind went into a spin, but he forced himself to focus … to breathe.

"How long has she been gone?" Anne questioned.

"About an hour. She was detained by that young maid, Tina, and got a late start," Rayad answered. "Where's Rothas?"

Anne shook her head. "Lord and Lady Dunrick left about fifteen minutes ago, and Rothas disappeared shortly after that."

"Did he mention going to his office?"

"He didn't say."

Jace had heard enough. Visions of Kyrin being hurt or even killed by the monstrous man swarmed his mind. He turned for the door. "I'm going to get her."

"Jace, stop."

He spun around, his entire body rigid. Rayad had a hand to Kaden's shoulder, apparently restraining him from following after Jace. He looked at both of them.

"If either of you get caught near that office, with or without Kyrin, it will be just as dangerous and disastrous as Kyrin getting caught herself."

"We can't just sit here and wait to see if she comes back all right," Kaden said, voicing Jace's thoughts exactly.

"I don't think we have much choice," Rayad replied. "By going after her, we could place her in even greater danger than she is in already. If Rothas doesn't go to the office, and we don't know that he will, then the best thing is to let Kyrin sneak out as planned without raising any suspicion. Now, if something does happen, you both know we will do whatever we must to protect her. That's why we're here, but right now, we have to trust Elôm to take care of her."

Sweat rolled down near Kyrin's eye. She brushed it away and breathed out hard. Frustration and panic threatened to make her careless. She shook her head, fighting them back.

"There's nothing here. Nothing about Samara." In every document she skimmed, she hadn't found the country named once.

She pushed the last drawer of one of the cabinets closed and rose from her knees to face Aaron. He looked around the room. Though he appeared much calmer than she was, his eyes gave away a little of his own frustration. They were risking everything for this. How could she return to the others empty-handed?

Kyrin put her hands out helplessly. "What if Rothas isn't helping Daican plan a war?"

After all, she had come across several missives from the emperor, but none of any real importance that she could tell from a quick scan of the contents. But then why had Rothas left the table last night if the message hadn't been urgent?

Aaron shook his head. "I have a hard time believing that if he's such a brilliant strategist."

Kyrin agreed, but what could they do? She had searched everywhere. She cast her gaze about the office. Had she missed something obvious? *If this is Your will, Lord, guide us.*

Neither of them said anything for a long minute.

"We should go," Kyrin murmured at last. She hadn't kept track of the time, but she had a sickening feeling in her stomach that they had tarried too long.

She turned to retrieve the candle, and her gaze snagged on

the bookshelf along the wall. A dark leather spine stuck out a little farther than the rest. An inexplicable sense drew her to it. With the candle in one hand, she walked closer and pulled the book out. When it came free, she found it was not a book at all, but a thick leather satchel. Her heart fluttered. She carried it to the desk, unbound the tie, and flipped it open to reveal a collection of parchments. Daican's royal seal jumped out at her. She traded a glance with Aaron as she lifted the parchment to skim it, immediately picking out the name Samara.

"This is it!" *Elôm, thank You!*

She took a more careful look at the top letter to commit it to memory before laying it aside to scan the next one. Systematically, she worked through each one, picking up bits and pieces without taking time to read the whole thing. Then she came to one with phrases and details that sent a prickling cold along her skin.

"Here, read this." She handed it to Aaron. "It looks like a lot of information we want to know."

As he read, Kyrin worked through the remaining documents.

Near the end, Aaron gave a low whistle. "Oh, he's definitely planning—"

His head jerked around to the door, and Kyrin froze, her breath caught in her lungs. Then his wide eyes darted to her. "Someone's coming!"

Kyrin's heart sped back into motion—a wild, crashing beat. She grabbed the letter from Aaron, tucking it into place. She scrambled to arrange the letters the way she had found them, but her fingers trembled so much they kept slipping. Slapping the leather cover shut, she fumbled with the tie. *Please, Lord, help!*

Aaron took over in an instant, tying the knot and putting it into her hands. His calm, decisive expression helped her think clearly. She rushed to the shelf and shoved the satchel into its place, forcing herself to make sure everything was perfect. By this time, faint but steady footsteps echoed in her ears.

The room went dark. Kyrin turned as Aaron stepped out the window. Her blood flushed cold. Where would she go? She would never get out unseen. Her eyes searched the darkness for a place to hide.

"Come on."

Aaron's whisper brought her darting gaze back to the window. He motioned to her. Her heart tripped. He wanted her to go out there? But she couldn't climb! She was not crete or even half-crete.

The footsteps neared, threatening to stall her heart again. There was no time. She dashed to the window and peered out. Just below, a narrow ledge ran under the window leading off in both directions around the manor. A knot formed in her throat. The ledge was barely more than two handbreadths. Her feet fused to the floor.

"It's all right," Aaron's voice was calm despite the situation.

She looked into his reassuring eyes. He offered his hand. The footsteps reached the door.

Kyrin grabbed Aaron's hand and stepped over the sill. He drew her toward him. Gasping in a breath, she pressed herself against the rough stone beside the window. Aaron put his arm around her, holding her securely back against the manor. She squeezed her eyes shut, terrified to look down. For a fraction of a second, she realized this must be the same terror Jace experienced when it came to heights.

The door opened, and heavy footsteps entered the room. Kyrin hardly dared to breathe. *Please, Elôm*, the words repeated as a desperate cry in her heart.

Rothas's desk chair scraped the floor and creaked as it took the man's weight. What if he was there for hours? Kyrin gulped. She would fall before being able to wait him out!

The door opened again and a second pair of footsteps crossed the room.

"Are you prepared?" Rothas's low, menacing voice came from right inside.

After a brief pause came James's response. "I'll go find her when things get quiet."

"You're sure she will do as she's told?"

"Oh, she knows better than to defy me."

A chill tingled Kyrin's skin that had nothing to do with the night air.

Rothas's chair creaked again. Kyrin could just imagine his ruthless expression.

"Good."

The chair scraped back. Papers shuffled. "I'm going to bed. I trust you will have things under control."

James released a short, cruel chuckle, and they both walked out. The door closed and the room grew dark again.

Kyrin didn't move—not a muscle—as she listened to the deafening drum of her heart. A minute or two passed. Then, Aaron shifted.

"I think we can go in."

Kyrin's eyelids wouldn't budge at first, but she pried them open, careful not to look down. Aaron gripped her hand again like a lifeline, and she reached for the windowsill with her other. Holding to it with a death grip, she shuffled along the edge. When she stepped into the security of the office, her legs nearly buckled. She braced herself against the desk as Aaron came in after her.

"Are you all right?"

Kyrin only nodded, her voice trapped in her throat. She never wanted to do this again.

"Is there anything else you need to see here?"

Kyrin shook her head, forcing a winded, "No." All she wanted was to get out.

"All right; I'd better head back the way I came. Will you be all right?"

Kyrin drew a deep breath into her depleted lungs. "Yes." She turned to the door, her legs still wobbly, but glanced back. "Aaron . . . thanks."

He nodded, giving her a comforting half-smile before leaving her on her own once more.

KYRIN SLIPPED OUT into the darkened hall, pulling the door silently closed behind her. Far down the hall, a candle flickered in its wall sconce. No one was in sight, yet goose bumps rippled up her arms. Rothas and James had been here only moments ago and could still be close by. What if a door opened and one of them stepped out? She had no excuses for being in this wing of the house. Was this the way a rabbit felt venturing out at night?

She reined in these thoughts and set off down the hall with swift, yet careful, steps. Her thudding heart urged her to move faster. She took deep breaths to slow it down. Still, it would be a while before it settled completely. Certainly not until she reached her room.

Halfway there, she rounded the corner and collided with a hard male chest. She gasped and looked up. Her heart jumped back into the same place in her throat it had occupied in the office.

James peered down at her, an unnerving little half-smile raising his lips—the very opposite of the one Aaron had just given her. Kyrin tried to swallow her heart back into place, but it stuck, sucking the moisture from her mouth. James eyed her, and she took a step back. A tremor passed through her at the spark of satisfaction kindling in his eyes.

"Where are you off to in such a hurry?"

Kyrin swallowed again and wrinkled her nose at the sour sting of alcohol coming off his breath. She worked hard to disguise the fear in her voice. Cowering would surely encourage him.

"Lady Anne is waiting for me."

Her only relief was that she was far enough from the office now that he probably wouldn't suspect that's where she'd come from. He clearly wasn't thinking along those lines anyway.

She set off to walk past him, but he slid sideways to block her path. So much for trying to slow her heart rate. It spiked again. She looked up at him. That sickening smile had widened.

"Surely she can wait a bit longer."

Kyrin stood rigidly and scrambled for an escape. If only Kaden or Jace were here with her. But she was alone, and only too aware of it. She didn't even have a weapon to defend herself. Still, she somehow managed boldness.

"Please, excuse me; Lady Anne cannot wait."

She made another attempt to bypass him, but this time he caught her by the arm, stopping her in an iron grip.

"I didn't say you could go yet."

Breathing hard, Kyrin spoke through clenched teeth. "With respect, sir, I am not one of your servants."

"But you're in my house," he responded, his tone low and entirely too much in control.

A thread of terror shivered through Kyrin. She strained against his grasp, but he drew her closer.

"Let go of me, now." Kyrin hated the way her voice quivered at the end.

James gave a low chuckle of sinister amusement, just like in the office. Reality crashed in on Kyrin. No plea would be effective with him. He was a man used to getting exactly what he wanted and wouldn't take no for an answer. The urge to scream rose up in her throat, but would anyone who cared even hear it?

Eyeing her lips, James leaned toward her. She jerked against his hold and turned away, but with contemptuous ease, he grabbed her other arm and yanked her around to face him again. She tried to knee him, but it grazed off his thigh.

His lips curled in frustration. "You won't get away from me."

Tears bit at Kyrin's eyes and helplessness washed over her like ice water, but she would not give in. Not without a fight. Drawing back her foot, she aimed hard at his shin this time. He grunted and spat out a curse as he hopped back on one foot. Kyrin ripped out of his grasp to run, but his right hand caught her sleeve, tearing it away from her shoulder. It slowed her down just enough for him to grab her around the waist.

She sucked in a breath and screamed as loud as she could. "Jace!"

James's hand clamped over her mouth, smashing her lips against her teeth. His fingers dug painfully into her cheeks.

"Shut up!" he hissed in her ear.

She clawed at his hand, struggling with all her might.

"If you don't cooperate, I'll see things go very badly for you."

James turned, dragging her down the hall. She fought to resist, but her efforts grew weaker as a nauseating horror enveloped her. Tears trickled out. *Elôm, please!* She could hardly breathe with James's hand covering her mouth and the growing terror of what was going to happen.

A whimpered cry clawed its way out. In the next instant, something ripped James away from her. Kyrin tumbled to the floor. She looked up just in time to see Jace's fist land a solid blow to James's jaw. James staggered and would have landed flat on his back, but Jace grabbed him and slammed him up against the wall, pinning his forearm against James's throat. James choked in an attempt to breathe.

Kyrin just stared at them, her entire body shaking until someone took her by the arm. She flinched and looked up into

Kaden's eyes. The last time she had seen them so dark and intense had been when she'd stood on the execution platform. Snapping from the paralysis that had taken hold, she looked past him. Anne and Rayad had just shown up. It only took one look for them to know just what had happened. Carefully, Kaden helped her to her feet.

Her gaze jumped back to Jace, who spat in his brother's face, "Give me one good reason I shouldn't break every bone in your body."

Kyrin had never heard such a dangerous edge to his voice before. Fear pierced her heart again. If Jace had a mind to, which he certainly did, he could beat James to within an inch of his life. And if Kaden were to join in, well, there would be nothing left. Rothas would kill them both.

"Jace," she tried, her voice wobbly, but another voice broke in.

"What is going on?"

Rachel stood in the hall now, her eyes rounded. She looked from Jace and James to the others, her gaze resting on Kyrin, specifically her torn sleeve, and understanding dawned. She paled.

"Jace, let him go," Rayad murmured.

But Jace would not move, and James struggled to breathe.

"Jace, please," Kyrin said softly.

Her voice seemed to get through to him. Breathing heavily, he jerked himself away from his brother and turned, locking eyes with Kyrin. She sucked in her breath at their fierce glow. She'd only seen it once before when they had faced a group of ryriks, but that had been a fighting will to survive. This time it was hatred. Hatred for his brother and what he had done; all mixed with the outrage and concern he must feel for her. Never had she seen him so angry.

He stood between her and James, ready to leap in should his brother even look at her. James pushed away from the wall, dabbing at the blood that oozed from his lip, and glowered at him, but it was Rachel who moved in.

"How dare you do this? How *dare* you? Have I not done everything in my power to raise you better?"

"She's just a servant girl."

"Don't you *ever* use that sorry excuse with me. She's a defenseless young woman, just like the others." Her voice wavered. "Just like I was."

James scowled. "I'm not some ryrik animal." He cast a loathsome glance at Jace.

Kyrin sensed Jace tense and reached for his arm, hoping to keep him from doing something he would later regret and get himself in trouble. She could only imagine how furiously Rothas would respond to find that Jace had beaten his son to a pulp . . . or worse. Tremors passed through Jace's taut muscles.

"Oh, so that makes it all right then? Do you think it makes a bit of difference to any of these girls?" Rachel shook her head, her eyes filled with a deep heartache. "No, James. Ryrik, human, it makes absolutely no difference at all. The act is just as unspeakable."

James scoffed. "I'm done with this." He pushed past his mother and skulked down the hall.

With pain etched all over her face, Rachel turned to the others. She focused on Kyrin. "Are you all right?"

All eyes turned to Kyrin now. She took in each probing look, and reached for her torn sleeve to cover her shoulder. Suddenly she felt exposed, vulnerable. She forced a nod, working to set her mind on the positive.

"He didn't really hurt me," she murmured, though her cheeks and lips throbbed.

"I am so sorry." Tears ran down Rachel's face.

"It's not your fault," Kyrin replied, her own eyes stinging.

"But he's my son," she cried. "I tried so hard . . ." She hung her head.

"We know," Kyrin whispered.

Rachel wiped her cheeks and drew a breath to calm herself. She stepped closer to Kyrin with an understanding, motherly look. "If there is anything I can do, tell me."

Kyrin nodded. "Thank you. I think I'll be all right." However, her words sounded hollow. Could one be all right after such an encounter? It would take a long time for the horror and paranoia to diminish, just like after the ryrik attack. The sinister and terrifying feelings now associated with the memories would never truly fade.

Rachel gave her a long look. If anyone understood, she did. She then looked at Jace. His eyes still flickered torturously. They parted then, Rachel walking off with her head bowed and her shoulders drooping.

Everyone else turned. Kaden put his arm protectively around Kyrin's shoulders as they walked back to the room. She was safe now, yet James's menacing presence seemed to lurk in every shadow. By the time they walked in, her knees wobbled. She sank down in a chair, hugging her arms around herself, and shivered. Now she felt cold. Anne draped a blanket around her shoulders and knelt in front of her.

"Are you sure you're not hurt?"

Kyrin nodded, though her breath still caught at how close she came to that not being so. "He only grabbed me and covered my mouth to stop me from screaming." She rubbed the sore spots on her cheeks.

Jace forced out a hard breath. She glanced up at him. He clenched his fists so tight that his fingers turned white aside from the red scuffs on the knuckles of his right hand. The fire still lit his eyes, but it had an even rawer, pained look to it now. This would torture him for days.

Kyrin cleared her swollen throat. For his sake, they needed to stop talking about it. If not, he might still go after James. "I got the information."

Her quiet words brought a startled look to their faces, as if they had forgotten all about the mission.

"It doesn't look good for Samara. Rothas is definitely helping Daican plan an attack. I don't know the details yet, but you can ask Aaron. He read more than I did."

"Aaron?" Rayad asked, voicing the confusion displayed in their expressions. "How in Ilyon did he get into the office with you?"

"He climbed in through the window."

Rayad's brows shot up.

"Thank Elôm he did or Rothas would have caught me. Both he and James came in as I was finishing, but Aaron helped me out onto the ledge outside the window." Her mind went back to that moment, and the brief conversation between Rothas and his son. "The two of them spoke while they were in there. Rothas asked James if he was prepared, and James said he would go find someone after it was quiet. They were talking about a woman, because Rothas asked if James was sure *she* would do as she was told."

Kyrin paused, and a deep chill shuddered through her body. Could they have been talking about her? Had James been intending to come after her? She shivered again, but halted her runaway thoughts. It couldn't be her. James's words pointed to someone he knew personally.

"I don't know what it was all about, but we have to be careful."

Rayad exhaled slowly, trading a look with Jace and Kaden, and nodded. "At least now we can get you and Anne out of this place. The sooner the better."

Anne agreed. "We'll discuss it and make plans in the morning."

165

Rayad turned to Kaden. "We'd better get back downstairs."

Kaden stared at Kyrin, his face set and his stance immovable.

"I'll be all right now," she assured him. "You can go."

It still took him a moment to move. Rayad stepped out into the hall, and Kaden followed. Jace, however, remained. Kyrin met his eyes, trying to convince him he could go too. Finally, he walked out after the other men, and the door closed.

Kyrin hung her head. She didn't want Jace to see her cry and fuel his anger, but moisture welled in her eyes now that he was gone.

Once Anne had locked the door, she returned to Kyrin and gently rubbed her shoulder. "It's all right. You're safe now. We won't let anything else happen."

Kyrin looked up, blinking her friend's face into focus. Her mind was too quick to replay the scene and what could have happened had they not shown up. "Did you hear me scream?"

Anne shook her head. "No. None of us did except for Jace."

"I won't just leave them here alone." Kaden's voice hissed sharply in the hall.

Neither would Jace. He didn't want to let Kyrin out of his sight until they left Ashwood. "Don't worry. I'll keep watch from my room."

"I'll stay with you," Kaden replied.

Rayad shook his head. "No. We need to keep things quiet and not draw any more attention, especially tonight when we don't know what is going on with Rothas and James."

Kaden's jaw hardened, an argument brewing in his eyes, but he refrained. Jace met his fierce gaze and sent a clear message of his own. No one would pass through the women's door and live to tell about it.

Sighing hard, Kaden nodded.

"Go on," Rayad told him. "I'll be there in a minute."

Trading one more look with Jace, Kaden trudged down the hall.

When he disappeared around the corner, Rayad turned to Jace and looked him directly in the eyes. "I need you to promise me something."

Jace narrowed his eyes. He knew already what was coming and didn't like it.

"Promise me you won't leave your room unless someone is breaking down this door. Not for any other reason, do you understand? Promise me that."

It was clear why Rayad would request such a promise. Probably the same reason he wanted Kaden downstairs where he could keep an eye on him. Simmering right under the surface was Jace's belief that James deserved far more than one punch to the face for what he had done tonight.

"Jace, retaliation won't solve anything and won't erase what has already been done. You have to promise me that you will stay in your room."

Jace shifted his jaw. A man shouldn't be able to attack a woman and just walk away. But Rayad continued to stare hard at him.

"I promise," he ground out, but it took much effort.

"Thank you." Rayad sighed and squeezed his shoulder before turning away.

Jace watched him walk down the hall and then went to his own room, leaving the door open a few inches.

Here, everything he had been fighting to control let loose. His breaths came hard and fast, shuddering in his lungs as he relived the moment he had come upon that vile worm of a brother dragging Kyrin away. His fists clenched again. If James had truly harmed her . . . To think of Kyrin scarred for life in such a way and what could have resulted . . . she could have ended up just like his mother.

Jace nearly lost his supper. Thoughts and impulses he hadn't felt in years took hold. His blood boiled in his veins. He hadn't felt it this hot, this driving since . . . the day he had killed Dane. His heart raced. He was losing control.

No, a very faint voice whispered inside him. *Don't*. He pressed his palms against his burning eyes. *Don't*, the whisper came again. For several minutes he stood as stone, afraid that if he moved at all, he would grab up his sword and go after James.

After a long, agonizing struggle, his heart stopped pounding so hard. His breaths came more evenly, and his mind cleared, no longer driven by thoughts to avenge Kyrin. The blood in his limbs cooled, leaving them leaden and aching. He hung his head, his shoulders sagging. He had almost done it. Almost given in. Guilt riddled his heart, but not nearly so much as if he had acted. Ashamedly, he still wished harm on his half-brother, but to exact revenge would only cause more harm, especially for Kyrin.

A light knock tapped his door and he straightened, spinning around to pull it open. Kyrin stood just on the other side. Even in the dimness of his room, her eyes glinted with a watery sheen.

She cleared her throat. "I wanted to make sure you were all right . . . that you wouldn't do anything."

She stared earnestly at him, no doubt reading every thought leaking through his expression. She knew him too well.

"I wanted to, but I won't." He'd given Rayad his word, and now he gave it to her.

She attempted a small smile, but it wobbled almost immediately, breaking down as more moisture filled her eyes. Jace's blood grew hot again, but he fought to keep it in check. Still, to see her so traumatized and be powerless to do a thing about it was worse than torture.

Before he could say a word, she stepped closer and her arms slipped around him as if still seeking protection. Jace embraced her tightly, his heart thudding with a vengeance. If he could, he'd keep her right here with him until they left this place. He glanced out into the hall. Anne was watching from their door, and Jace would make certain Kyrin didn't leave the sight of someone within their group for however long they remained here.

A moment later, Kyrin pulled away. Her cheeks were damp, but she managed to offer him a more stable smile. He tried, but couldn't quite return it. The emotions were still too raw.

"Goodnight," she whispered.

Jace murmured in reply, and she turned. He watched until she was once more with Anne. The hall grew dark as their door closed, and Jace listened for the click of the lock. He then turned and grabbed a chair from near his bed and set it at the door where he could watch the hall.

Glancing down, he realized he still wore Rothas's clothes and scowled. He yanked the buckles loose on the jerkin and changed back into his own outfit, tossing Rothas's into a heap on the floor. Once he sat down, he fixed his gaze on the door to Kyrin and Anne's room.

RAINDROPS TICKED AGAINST the window. Jace listened to the hypnotic sound and let his mind wander aimlessly. It must have started around one or two in the morning, but it was after dawn now. He shifted in his chair, wincing at the soreness in his body, and rubbed his gritty eyes. The fire of the night before had died to a cold and weary emptiness inside him.

He sat a bit longer and then pushed to his feet, stretching to work the stiffness out of his limbs. Over at the dresser, he poured a basin of water to wash his face. No doubt the family would expect him at the table for breakfast, though to be in the same room as James and not want to strangle him would take every ounce of willpower. The cad deserved nothing less.

Jace sighed. Today would also decide when they would leave. Like Rayad, he wanted to get Kyrin and Anne out as soon as possible, but the thought of leaving also left his heart heavy. He didn't want to leave his family—not those he cared about— and he'd never imagined feeling so torn over it. It wasn't as if he could stay. Rothas would never stand for that, but he desired deeply to have his mother, his sister, his uncle, and his grand- mother in his life, the way Kyrin had her family. Yet what hope was there of that?

Footsteps echoed loud and heavy in the hall. Jace stiffened, darting a glance at his sword as the hair along his arms rose. Fighting away paranoia, he left it where it lay and walked to the door. He pulled it open just as two household guards showed up on the other side. Before a full thought could form, they grabbed his arms and dragged him from the room.

His instinct to fight kicked in, and he jerked against them. "What are you doing?"

"You're under arrest," one of the guards announced gruffly, tightening his hold.

"For what?"

The guards would not answer. He wrenched his arms back, but what good would a struggle do? Fighting them would only land him in worse trouble than he apparently was in already. First, he had to find out what was going on. Then he could fight.

Anne's door opened as they hauled him past, and she looked out. "Jace?"

He struggled to look back. Kyrin stood there now, her eyes huge.

"What happened?" Anne asked.

Jace shook his head. "I don't know."

And he didn't. He had honored his promise and hadn't set foot outside his room all night.

As they dragged him downstairs, Jace fought to keep a cool head. Rothas was behind this, but if he let himself think on it too deeply, his anger would kindle. With a forceful shove from the guards, Jace half stumbled into the drawing room. Straightening, he came to face Rothas. Just to his right stood James. A bruise darkened the younger man's jaw, working up toward his cheekbone. Perhaps that was what this was about. Well, Jace had a thing or two to say about last night.

"What is this?" he ground out.

Rothas's lips upturned in a vicious smirk. Before he could

answer, a group of people rushed in—Anne, Rachel, and Elian. Kyrin had probably gone for Rayad.

Rachel stepped toward her husband. "What are you doing?"

Now Jace might finally find out himself.

"Your son has taken our generous hospitality and welcome and thrown it back in our faces by committing a deplorable crime under my roof."

His gaze remained locked with Jace, enjoying every moment of it. Jace glared back at him.

"What crime?" Rachel demanded.

Rothas only broke eye contact when he turned to the other door and opened it. At his bidding, Tina stepped meekly into the room. The breath died in Jace's lungs. Tina's eyes and cheeks were red and puffy as if she had been up all night crying. Her sunny, albeit overly friendly, disposition was gone. But the most disturbing of all was the ugly purple bruise under one eye.

Rothas drew her farther into the room. She kept her head down, but cast a quick glance at James, who gave her a cold, narrow-eyed glare.

"All right, Tina, tell them what you told me." Rothas's deceptively soothing voice sickened Jace. "Tell them what this man did."

Tina peeked up at Jace, but instantly dropped her pained eyes. "He . . ." Her voice wobbled. She bit her lip, and two tears dripped down her cheeks. "He . . . attacked me."

Jace went cold. He stared at her standing there, trembling, broken, violated. The smoldering embers inside him burst into flames. His gaze rose once more to Rothas. So this was his scheme.

His voice vibrating in intensity and restraint, Jace ground out, "I did no such thing."

"Are you calling this poor girl a liar?" Rothas asked in mock outrage.

Jace longed to hit him. He shook his head. "I'm saying you are a cruel, black-hearted man and you've forced her into this to get at me."

"How dare you accuse me in my own home," Rothas snarled, but his eyes betrayed his pleasure. This was all a game to him. A cruel, vicious game—one he was far too good at. "I see only one suitable response to this outrage. Hanging."

"Rothas!" Rachel gasped the same moment Jace's heart nearly failed. "You can't hang him."

"I didn't ask for your permission." Rothas literally brushed her aside to address the guards. "Take him out and lock him up."

The guards grabbed Jace's arms again, but he refused to move. He and Rothas traded searing looks. If Jace could just get his hands on him . . .

They yanked Jace back, forcing him toward the door. He resisted a moment longer, this time catching James's eyes. His brother did not attempt to conceal his triumph. It was probably a good thing the guards restrained Jace, because his every muscle tensed to lunge at the younger man and do him serious harm.

At last, Jace gave in and turned with the guards. His eyes locked on Kyrin's fearful face. Both she and Rayad were present, though when they had arrived he couldn't say. He wanted to reassure her, but had no words to do so. He would have to leave that to Rayad, who had his hand on her shoulder.

Jace now looked into his mentor's grim expression. Rayad would believe he hadn't left his room last night, wouldn't he? That there was no possible way he could ever do what Rothas accused him of? Of course he would. He knew both what Jace was and wasn't capable of doing.

"Jace, we'll take care of this," Anne murmured to him as they passed her.

He nodded, but what could they possibly do or say to change Rothas's mind? Nothing. Not with a man like that. No, they would have to find another way. Either that or he would shortly face a noose. He swallowed involuntarily. He would rather die at the end of a sword.

As the guards guided him down the hall, Anne's voice filtered after them, but the words were lost as the distance increased. They led him outside, where the rain still fell steadily. Jace ducked his head and hunched his shoulders, but moisture quickly soaked into his shirt. They marched across the courtyard, not slowing until they reached the back of the guardhouse. Built up against it was a small, but sturdy structure. It had only one window in the door that was barred.

Pulling open the door, they shoved Jace into the dark, musty interior. The door slammed, and the lock bolted. Jace stood in the center of the cramped space and looked around. Old straw, reeking of mold and mildew, covered the dirt floor, and a steady drip came from at least three places in the roof. Memories floated in, sending a shiver down his back. It was just like the confinement cell his master had thrown him into right after they had beaten him for killing Dane.

He breathed out a heavy sigh and used his foot to brush away some of the straw to find a dry place to sit. Sinking down, he rested his head back and rubbed his face. It was all up to his mother and friends now—what fate he would face when he left this prison.

Kyrin tried to rub the knots out of her stomach and blink away the prickling in her eyes. Rayad had assured her that they would find a way to save Jace, and she trusted him and Elôm. Even so, it hurt to think of Jace locked up and how bent Rothas was on eliminating him. His threat to hang Jace echoed in her mind all the while Rayad explained things to the other men down in the servants' hall. She couldn't help thinking of her father. They hadn't been able to do anything to save him. What if the same held true now? She shivered hard. She couldn't lose Jace too.

Kaden put his arm around her shoulders, and she gave him a weak smile. Everything about his expression said they would figure this out.

"What are we going to do?" Holden asked.

They all focused on Rayad.

"The best thing we can do for now is let Anne and Lady Rachel work on Rothas. And, of course, pray."

"Not to be the pessimist," Aaron said, "but chances seem pretty slim that Rothas will budge on this. Do we have a plan if he doesn't?"

Each man had a light in his eyes, proving they were willing to fight for Jace if it came down to it.

"Not yet," Rayad murmured. "First let's see how things play out."

He was right, of course. Any action by them now would only make things worse. Still, impatience pricked at Kyrin. Anything could happen. Lives could be lost in a heartbeat. What if they waited too long to stop this? *Elôm, help me, but most of all, help Jace. Protect him and rescue him, please.*

She couldn't let these thoughts overcome her. She had to stand firmly in her trust in Elôm. Searching for a distraction, she said, "Rothas has been planning this since yesterday, probably from the moment he discovered Jace's identity. Last night, that's what he and James discussed in the office. They had to be talking about Tina."

"So James is clearly in on this," Aaron replied.

Kyrin nodded. His smug look in the drawing room was proof enough. She shivered again just thinking of it.

Holden scowled. "I'd like to sit that boy down for a long talk."

"Or more," Kaden grumbled.

He and the rest of the men had hovered around Kyrin like her own personal army since she had come down. While she certainly felt safe, her concern for Jace outweighed it.

"Tina is obviously lying," Holden said. "Maybe, if she would tell us the truth, Rothas would have to let Jace go."

Kyrin shook her head. "She would never go against Rothas and James."

"But does she realize her words could get a man killed?"

As if summoned, Tina stepped into the room. She took one look at them and spun away.

Kaden rose from his chair. "I'll talk to her."

Kyrin hurried after him. He wouldn't be cruel, but she didn't think he realized how intimidating he could be. He might scare the poor girl to death, and she had clearly been through enough already.

"Tina, can we talk?" Kaden asked.

Under normal circumstances, the girl would have been positively giddy to have him initiate conversation, but she refused to face him. Kaden and Kyrin trailed her out of the servants' hall.

"Tina, wait."

Kaden reached out to stop her, but she jerked away as if burnt.

"Don't touch me!"

Her wide, red eyes locked on them, so full of torment and pain, Kyrin couldn't breathe for a moment. Kaden took a step back and raised his hands non-threateningly. Tina's eyes darted between him and Kyrin. She trembled like a small, wounded animal seeking an escape.

Kyrin touched Kaden's arm, her voice low and firm. "Go back to the hall."

He hesitated, but did as she asked. Once they were alone, Kyrin approached Tina, who appeared torn between staying and fleeing now that she had the chance.

Kyrin spoke gently. "Tina, I know Jace didn't hurt you. Can you please tell me what happened?"

The girl stared at the floor, tears rolling down her cheeks, and she shook her head.

"Please. Jace will be wrongfully hanged if you don't."

Tina raised her chin slowly, her terrified eyes meeting Kyrin's. "I'm sorry, but it's not Jace I'm worried about."

Kyrin swallowed hard. "Is it James?"

Tina cringed, a shudder shaking her shoulders. Kyrin's stomach turned inside out. With the mood James had been in when he had left her last night, she didn't want to imagine how he had taken it out on Tina. That bruise on her face hadn't just appeared there. What a horrible, vile man.

Neither of them said a word, but they shared understanding. Then Tina's gaze dropped a little. She must have noticed the bruises that had shown up on Kyrin's jaw and cheeks. Her eyes flitted back up.

"He came after you too, didn't he?"

Kyrin rubbed her arms as a chill raced across them at the memories of last night. Memories that would always be as vivid and clear as if she were living it. Now she shuddered. She nodded slowly. "But Jace stopped him."

"You're lucky. You've got people watching out for you." Tina's voice quivered. "I don't."

RACHEL FLUNG HER cloak over her shoulders and knotted the ties as she strode toward the door. Halfway there, Rothas stepped into the hall.

"Where are you going?" His voice bit through the quiet.

She paused as he walked up to her. "I'm going out for a while."

He narrowed his eyes. "It's raining."

Rachel just stared back at him. She didn't care if it was pouring.

The suspicion grew in Rothas's eyes. Rachel drew herself up. She had nothing to lose by trying once more, though she and Anne had already exhausted their efforts.

"Please, Rothas, let Jace go. We both know he's innocent."

His jaw set stubbornly. "No."

Rachel breathed hard. "So that's it then; you're determined to falsely accuse and hang him, *my son*, for a crime you and James commit on a regular basis?"

Rothas took a sudden step closer, his eyes flashing. Rachel just managed to keep from flinching. If her husband hadn't feared her father, she had no doubt he would have struck her. She was betting on that fear to save Jace.

She stared up into her husband's fiery expression for a moment, and then walked on with hardened determination. A shiver passed down her spine. Would he forcibly keep her here? She held her breath, but his footsteps didn't follow. Once outside, she released a heavy sigh. She had never so openly defied him before, but Jace was her son and she would protect him this time.

Rachel pulled up her hood against the unrelenting rain and hurried to the stable, undeterred. One of the stable hands met her.

"Saddle my horse for me," she instructed. "And I want a regular saddle, not a sidesaddle. I'll be back in a couple minutes."

"Yes, my lady."

Rachel turned out into the rain once more, this time heading for the guardhouse. Elian must have seen her coming and stepped out to meet her. She looked up at him from under her hood.

"I'm riding to Brandell. If anyone can stop Rothas, it's my father."

"I'll go with you."

He turned for the guardhouse, probably to grab his own cloak, but Rachel caught his arm to stop him. She quickly let go. It would be far too easy to let her emotions get the better of her in her anger with Rothas and concern over Jace. She must take care.

"I need you here to watch over Jace. I don't trust Rothas while I'm gone."

Elian frowned. They both knew what had happened the last time she had ridden off on her own. His gaze flickered to the house before falling on her again.

"Then let me send Gabe with you."

Their newest guardsman was young and sweet, and not yet corrupted by Rothas and turned into one of his spies. Elian must trust him enough to guard her. She nodded her acceptance.

"I'll send him to the stable," he said.

Rachel turned, but paused when Elian continued.

"Don't worry. Nothing will happen to Jace while you're gone."

She looked back to give him a tense smile. How did a woman keep her heart from loving a man whose every action spoke of how much he cared for her? *Elôm, give me strength.* "Thank you."

She rushed back to the stable, setting her mind firmly on Jace. As long as her son was safe, she could be content with the rest of her life, painful as it might be.

The stable hand had her surefooted gelding saddled and waiting for her. She instructed the man to saddle a horse for Gabe, and then stood stroking her own horse's neck while she waited. Letting out a deep breath, she closed her eyes. *Please, Elôm, let my father want to help Jace. And if not, please provide another way to save him.* She bit her lip. *I can't bear to lose him again.*

Gabe jogged in a moment later. Water dripped from the young man's shaggy blond hair, but his bright-eyed expression was eager to please. How she hoped Elian could keep him from being corrupted by Rothas's influence.

"Thank you for accompanying me in this weather, Gabe," Rachel said.

He grinned. "Not a problem, my lady."

His horse arrived shortly, and they both mounted. Rachel tied her cloak a little tighter, and then nudged her horse's sides with her heels. Once out of the courtyard, she urged him on as fast as the rain and mud-slicked road would safely allow.

Jace wrapped his arms around his chest, but to no avail as the chill air sank deeper into his body. Tremors raced up and down his limbs. The rain continued to drum against the roof, no longer a soothing sound, but one that beat his spirits even lower.

He let his head hang, hopeless thoughts of the gallows lurking in his mind.

He chided himself. If it were Kyrin or Rayad in this situation, they would turn their despair into prayers. Why was that so hard for him? Why was it so hard to believe his own mother when she told him Elôm loved him? He groaned. Why couldn't he feel Elôm? Why instead did he feel so alone, so helpless? The only logical answer pointed to his soul, or lack thereof. He propped his elbows on his knees to rest his head in his hands. He was so weary of this despair. How many times had he fought to escape it, only to find it still had a hold of him?

He breathed a hard breath that dragged against his throat. The deep, desperate ache inside him grew in intensity until it forced equally desperate words to his lips.

"Elôm . . . show me. Show me the truth."

Pressure built behind his eyes in the deafening silence.

"Jace."

He snapped his head up, his gaze lifting to the dark silhouette in the barred window, and pushed to his feet. Now that he could see better, he recognized Elian.

"Here." The man stuffed a bundle through the bars.

Jace took it in his hands and shook it out to find a heavy woolen cloak. He put it around his shoulders, and warmth built underneath.

Next through the bars came another linen-wrapped bundle and a canteen. Jace didn't have to open the bundle to smell the food. His stomach gurgled. He hadn't had anything to eat since supper last night.

"Thanks," he told Elian, truly grateful. A thought struck him. Had this been Elôm's answer? How could he know?

"How are you doing?" Elian asked.

Jace shrugged. He had faced worse conditions and predicaments, but it didn't diminish the heaviness of the situation. Even if Rothas didn't kill him, this forever erased any hope he had for a close relationship with his family.

"Your mother rode to Brandell a bit ago to try to get Lord Dunrick's help in releasing you."

Jace fought the immediate hopelessness as he considered this. Perhaps his grandfather would help, but had he made enough of an impression in one evening to secure sympathy from the man?

Not likely.

Elian must have read the doubt in his eyes. "Don't worry. If he doesn't, your mother will find a way, and she won't be without help."

Jace stared at the man who could have been his father, recollecting the way he had stood up to Rothas in the garden and risked demotion or worse to protect him. How had people like him, Kyrin, and Rayad come to care so much? Jace thanked him again, his voice coming in a rough murmur.

Elian nodded. "I'll be around again in a while if you need anything more."

Jace returned to his spot. At least it was still dry. He set the canteen of coffee to the side and opened the bundle of sliced bread, cheese, and cold sausage. It looked far more appetizing than any of the fancy fare he had consumed during supper. His stomach growled again. He reached for one of the sausages, but his hand stalled. If this had been Elôm's answer, how could he not express gratitude?

Guilt rose up inside him. He cleared his throat and closed his eyes, but struggled for words. If only he didn't feel like he was only talking to himself.

"Thank You," he forced out. It was all he could say, but he hoped his sincerity was enough if Elôm did hear him.

Rachel stormed into Brandell, her wet, mud-spattered skirt tugging against her legs. She swiped back the bedraggled strands of hair that fell in her eyes. Halfway here, she had ceased trying to keep her hood up. This was not the day for maintaining her image as a lady. But she must have looked like quite a sight when she went marching into the drawing room where her family was gathered. Both her mother and Charles lifted their brows at her, but Rachel fixed her gaze on her father, who had a stack of letters in his hands and peered at her over his spectacles.

"Were you aware of Rothas's scheme against Jace?" She had realized on the way that her father could very well have played a part in it, though she tried not to sound too accusing. She did need his help, after all.

His forehead wrinkled deeply. "What scheme?" He seemed genuinely surprised.

"Rothas has falsely accused Jace of attacking one of the servant girls and now wants to hang him."

Her mother gasped, and Charles exclaimed, "What?"

"I've tried talking to Rothas," Rachel went on, still focused on her father, "and so has Lady Anne, but he will not listen. I need you to change his mind."

Silence hung deafeningly. Her father didn't move, and Rachel stared hard at him. Now was his chance to make up for what he had done in the past. He could save Jace this time, instead of taking him from her.

Finally, he asked, "Why?"

Rachel's mouth dropped open. "Because he'll hang Jace if you don't!"

"If he attacked the girl, then I'm sorry to say that he's getting what he deserves."

Rachel balled her fists. How could her father be this way? "But he *didn't* attack her. Rothas made it up."

Her father pulled off his spectacles, giving her an impatient look. "Can he prove that he didn't? Was anyone with him last night?"

The blood heated in Rachel's face, and she had to remind herself to hold her temper. Going off on him in desperation wouldn't solve anything. "Jace wouldn't do that."

"You've known him for how long? Two days?"

"Father, please, I am begging you for help to save my son. You took him from me once; please don't allow him to be taken from me again."

He scowled and broke eye contact. "This is an Ashwood matter. I will not get into it."

Rachel drew a breath, unsure of what words might come out next, but her mother spoke first.

"Henry, I love you, but right now I think you're wrong and being impossibly cruel."

"What?" he growled. "There is nothing that proves to me that he didn't attack the girl."

"Of course he didn't. We both know this is Rothas's doing to get rid of him. Don't sit there and pretend you didn't see it written all over his face last night."

Rachel's father stared stubbornly at his letters, apparently trying to ignore both of them.

Her mother's eyes narrowed. "I hope you know that I love Jace as my grandson, and if you allow Rothas to go through with this, it will be very hard for me to accept." Her voice dropped a bit lower. "I don't want to go back to the days after you took him away the first time."

Rachel remembered those days. Her parents had barely spoken. It was only her mother's eventual conversion to faith in Elôm that had repaired the marriage. She wanted to slap Rothas for possibly turning them against each other again.

Her father stiffened, but he was an incredibly stubborn man. "This is not my problem." He shoved his spectacles farther up his nose and set a stern frown on his letters.

Rachel just stood for a long moment, her entire core shaking. She had really thought she could convince him to help. All the hurts she had experienced in losing Jace the first time flooded back.

"Fine," she ground out, "but don't think I won't do whatever it takes to save him. Then we'll see if it becomes your problem." Whatever she did, Rothas would be furious, and her father may just have to step in to protect her from his wrath.

She spun around and strode out. Her time here was wasted. Now she needed to get back to Jace and form some sort of plan. She would die before she let her husband kill her son.

"Rachel."

She halted and looked back as Charles caught up to her.

"Let me gather a few things and I'll go with you. He can't hang Jace if I object."

A wobbly smile broke out on her face, and she squeezed his arm. She wouldn't have to face Rothas alone. "Thank you."

The next time Jace heard his name, his heart jumped, for it was the soft lilt of Kyrin's voice. He scrambled to his feet, meeting her at the door. Rayad stood with her. Wrapping his fingers around the bars, he peered down into her eyes that were almost the same color as the misty sky. They lacked their usual cheery light.

She searched his face. "How are you?"

"I'm fine." He ducked his head sheepishly. He had to stop doing that to her. "It's not too bad. Elian brought me a cloak and some food."

"Good," Kyrin breathed out, looking much relieved. She licked her lips and glanced down at the puddle just outside the door. "Your mother returned."

Jace's heart pounded hard again. "Was Lord Dunrick with her?"

Her face cast down, she shook her head.

Jace exhaled. He hadn't gotten his hopes up, but the disappointment still stung. His grandfather didn't want to save him.

"But your uncle came," Kyrin hastened to tell him.

As future Earl of Dunrick, Charles had nearly as much power as his father. Even so, Jace had gone through many scenarios in his mind, yet hadn't come up with one that had a perfect ending.

Kyrin reached up and put her hand around his. The feel of her soft fingers, warm despite the murky weather, sent a pleasant tingling all the way up his arm. It would probably be in his best interest to pull away, but he couldn't manage it.

"We'll get you out of this, Jace." She gazed up at him, a promise in her eyes.

"I know you will," he murmured. He looked at her hand again, wishing it could stay there always.

Then she pulled it away, ducking her head as if embarrassed. As the warmth she left behind slowly faded, Jace looked at her solemnly.

"Earlier, I wish I could have assured you that I am innocent of Rothas's charges." He searched her eyes for any sign of doubt, finding none, and then glanced at Rayad. "I never left my room last night."

At Rayad's nod, Jace returned his focus to Kyrin. "I would *never* do anything like that."

He didn't know why he had such a passionate desire for her to believe him.

"Of course not," she replied. "I know that. I didn't think for a moment it was true."

Jace slowly let out his breath as a weight he didn't even know he was carrying lifted.

Rayad stepped closer. "We'd better go. I don't know what Rothas would think of us coming out here to see you."

Jace nodded, and they both left him. He remained standing at the door for a moment, and even though the drizzle still fell, things didn't feel quite so bleak with Kyrin's face in his mind and the memory of her hand on his.

ROTHAS STORMED FROM the drawing room, the door slamming in his wake. Charles shook his head. And he used to think his father was the most stubborn man he knew. Though he had used every bit of his persuasion and diplomacy skills to reason with his brother-in-law, Rothas wouldn't budge. Charles could use his superior position to his advantage, but that would only anger Rothas further. No, he would save that for if the man actually made a move to hang Jace. Then he would use every avenue of power at his disposal. It wasn't like him to pull rank, but he would for Jace, and Rothas wouldn't risk ruin. Still, he had a little time to try to resolve this in a more peaceable manner.

Moments after Rothas's heavy footsteps died away, the door opened again. Rachel and Lady Anne peeked in with anxious expressions. They entered slowly, as if Rothas's very presence still lingered in the room.

"Well?" his sister questioned, her eyes hopeful.

Charles shook his head. "He's determined to go through with it."

Rachel's face fell, and she sat down on the couch with a heavy sigh. Charles drew his brows together, visions of her despair after Jace had disappeared the first time revisiting his mind. He wouldn't let her lose him again.

"I won't let him hang Jace."

Their eyes met, and she nodded slowly, but didn't appear heartened. So many terrible things had happened to her. He couldn't blame her for fearing the worst in this situation. Still, he meant it as a promise. One way or another, he would stop this from happening. He even had a plan forming.

He looked over at their guest. "Lady Anne, you believe he's innocent, don't you?"

"Of course. I've known Jace for a while. He would never purposely harm an innocent person, especially not a woman."

Charles nodded and posed another important question. "How far would you be willing to go to ensure his safety?"

"As far as it takes."

He smiled at the surety of her answer. This was a woman of spirit and strength. "Good. What about your men?"

"They will do whatever necessary to protect Jace. They are all very close."

That would certainly help for Charles's plan. "Who is in charge?"

"Rayad. He's like a father to Jace."

"Do you mind if I speak with him?"

"Not at all."

"What are you going to do?" Rachel asked.

Charles looked down at her, considering. "I think I'll keep that to myself for now. That way Rothas has no one to blame but me." Not that he wouldn't place blame on anyone else involved, but at least Charles would be the mastermind. Elôm willing, he could stop Rothas from going on the warpath after this.

He left the women in the drawing room and headed downstairs, praying silently. This seemed to be the best course of action, though, if Elôm had other plans, he prayed He would make them clear. The situation was dangerous enough already.

At the bottom of the stairs, he met Walton. The butler's eyes rounded at the sight of him in the servants' quarters. He bumbled, flustered over such a thing. Poor man. The butler back in Brandell had grown used to Charles among the servants, making sure all was well.

"Can I help you, my lord?"

Charles smiled kindly. "Yes, if you would send for Elian, I'd appreciate it."

"Right away, my lord. Shall I send him to the drawing room?"

"No, I'll speak with him here."

Walton hesitated. "Very well, my lord." He moved off with a confused look.

Charles just smiled and made his way down to the servants' hall. When he stepped into the room, he paused at the door to look around. A diverse and unfamiliar group sat around the far end of a table. Their tense faces left little doubt that they were the ones Charles sought. He approached them and addressed the oldest man of the group.

"Rayad?"

"Yes?"

They all watched Charles, no doubt trying to determine whether he was friend or foe.

"I am Charles Ilvaran. I wondered if I might speak to you in private." He glanced over his shoulder. The group was alone in the Hall, but he lowered his voice. "It's about Jace."

"Of course, my lord."

Rayad stepped away from the table and followed him. Elian met them on the way to the men's quarters where they could talk in secret.

"I just finished speaking with Rothas," Charles told them. "He has every intention of hanging Jace as soon as possible." He had gone so far as to mention the next morning. No doubt he wanted to minimize the time in which they could put together a rescue plan.

Neither Rayad nor Elian responded, but their eyes said it all. They would never allow it.

"There's no reasoning with him, so that leaves it to us to take action," Charles continued. "I believe the best thing we can do is simply remove Jace from the situation."

"What do you have in mind?" Rayad asked.

"I will remain here tonight, and once everyone is asleep, you two can help me get him out. We'll prepare his horse and supplies, and Elian, you can make sure there are no patrols at the main gate tonight."

Elian nodded. "I can do that."

Rayad too gave a nod of agreement. "Sounds good to me, but I would like someone to go with him. I'd go myself, but I can't leave Lady Anne. It won't be easy for Jace to leave like this."

Charles understood. He hated to see Jace go this way. He would never be able to return with Rothas around. But right now, saving Jace's life was the most important. "Would one of your men go with him?"

"Yes, I'll talk to them."

"Good. Have Jace's things ready, and I'll meet you at the stable tonight when everything's quiet."

Jace paced the cell, his boots squishing in the mud. Though the rain had finally ceased, he had lost any dry ground to sit on. Not that he could have sat still for long anyway with his pent-up nerves. He glanced out the window. The sky was black, and it was at least midnight by his reckoning. When Elian had brought him supper earlier, he had filled him in on the escape plan. Surely, they would come for him any time now . . . if Rothas hadn't stopped them.

He should be glad of the opportunity to escape, but the moment Elian had given him the news, a heavy weight settled inside him. This would make him a fugitive to his family, and fugitives did not come for visits. He didn't know how he had expected it to end, but not with such painful finality.

Soggy footsteps approached outside a moment before Charles whispered his name. They had made it. The bolt on the door slid free and the door swung open. Jace stepped out. His uncle, his mother, Elian, and Rayad gathered around him. Holden stood behind them, holding Niton and his own horse, both saddled and ready.

"Elian has stationed the guards so that there will be none on the main gate," Charles said, keeping his voice low. "You shouldn't have any trouble slipping out undetected."

Jace hesitated. He might get away safely, but that left the others in a dangerous position. "What about Rothas? He'll know I didn't get out on my own."

"He will have to contend with me," Charles answered. "I won't make it any secret that it was my doing."

But what if he couldn't stop Rothas from taking his wrath out on someone else? Someone like Jace's mother or his friends who would still be here? Maybe he shouldn't go.

Rayad stepped forward with instructions for him. Even if he protested, they would never let him stay.

"We don't know if Rothas will send men after you, so you need to keep riding until you reach the forest. You'll have plenty of cover there. Holden is going with you. The rest of us will meet you there. I talked to Anne, and she plans to leave in the morning."

This eased Jace's mind a small fraction. At least they wouldn't be around Rothas for much longer.

Silence settled. The nature of this escape plan pressed for haste, but Jace couldn't bring himself to face goodbye. This was where it would all end, but he had only just begun to get to know his family.

Finally, Charles offered his hand, and Jace gripped his arm.

"It has been good to get to know you, Jace, even if the time was brief. Whatever happens from here, you will always be part of this family."

Jace fought the swelling emotion that tightened his chest. "I wish we could have had more time. Thank you for doing this for me."

"I'd do it again and more." Charles smiled, and then hauled Jace in for a hug.

Jace embraced his uncle and blinked hard. Charles did the same as they parted.

"It is my hope and prayer that we'll meet again," he said.

"And mine." Jace cleared his throat and shifted his gaze to Elian. He would never forget the moment the man had come for him and this all started, nor the way he'd sought to defend him from Rothas. The ache of knowing they could have been father and son would never heal completely.

"Thank you, for everything." Jace didn't know what more to say. The situation was just another cruel twist of the life he had struggled with for so long.

Elian merely nodded, and they grasped each other's arms. Unspoken understanding passed between them.

In a quiet voice, Elian said, "Take care of yourself."

Now the final, most painful farewell loomed. Jace turned to his mother. Moisture pooled in her eyes, glittering in the sliver of moonlight that peeked through the clouds. The stinging pressure in his eyes took hold in his throat. He wasn't ready for this. Three days—to know his mother for only three days—it wasn't nearly enough time. He swallowed once, and then again, to work his throat loose. He had never experienced such emotions before, this longing for his family.

His voice was deep and low, but carried the cry of the child inside him, once thought orphaned and unloved. "I don't want to go."

A quivering smile touched his mother's lips. "I know. And I desperately wish you could stay." She dabbed her eyes. "But I'm thankful we had the time we did. I can rejoice now to know you are alive and I've been able to see you."

Jace struggled to breathe. His voice came out hoarse. "It just doesn't seem fair." But then, how much of his life had ever been fair?

"No," his mother replied sadly, "it doesn't. Many things don't, but remember, we can't see the whole picture."

Jace released a hard sigh. If only he could believe this would all lead to something good.

His mother stepped closer. "Jace, I know this is difficult for you, especially after the life you've lived. It breaks my heart. I just want you to have peace, and it is my belief that only Elôm can give you that. Please, do this one thing for me. Please don't try to hide from Him anymore. Bring Him everything—everything that has and does hurt you. Let Him take it all. He is more than willing."

Jace hung his head. Such a heavy burden that request was. To do so would mean opening the doors on the deep down vaults where he tried to hide all the dark memories, guilt, regrets, and shame that continually leaked out. Things of which his mother didn't truly know the extent.

"Jace."

He grimaced as he raised his eyes back to her, but told her with all the strength he could manage, "I'll try."

She breathed out slowly. "And I will pray for you."

She opened her arms, and Jace stepped into them, soaking in her embrace. If this were the last, it would never be enough—never soothe the ache of being deprived of such love for so long.

"Every day, I will pray to Elôm that I will see you again, but if I don't, know that I love you so much. I always have, and I always will."

Jace's voice choked past his swollen throat. "I love you too." It was the first time in all his life he had spoken those words.

Reluctantly they pulled apart, and his mother's cheeks glistened.

She gave him a teary smile. "I'm so blessed to have you as my son."

Jace dropped his gaze again. She surely deserved better.

"Truly," she stressed. "You don't realize your worth; not just to me, but to all those around you, and most importantly to Elôm. Somehow, someday, you'll see."

Jace would have to take her at her word.

She drew another shaky breath. "Goodbye, my son."

Already the dagger of separation tore through his heart, almost robbing his voice, reducing it to a hoarse whisper.

"Goodbye, Mother."

It was too painful to linger any longer. Willing his body to respond, he moved toward the horses, pausing when he came to Rayad. The man gave him a look of deep sympathy. Jace cleared his throat, though his voice still came out rough.

"Keep watch over Kyrin. Make sure she's never alone."

Rayad nodded firmly. "We'll keep her safe."

His heart heavy and sluggish, Jace reached Niton and pulled himself up into the saddle. Holden mounted beside him.

Looking down on the small gathering, he said to his mother, "Say goodbye to Elanor for me."

"I will. She will be very sad that you have gone. She grew quite fond of you."

Jace pictured her face and how she had defended him at supper. How he wished he could have gotten to know his sister better and show her Niton.

Controlling the sorrow as best he could, Jace took up the reins and looked off toward the wall. Freedom didn't draw him quite the same as it had in the past. The pull to remain was almost as strong.

"Jace."

He looked once more to his mother.

She stepped closer. "Ilvaran. That was my maiden name, your name. Jace Ilvaran."

Jace couldn't take a full breath for a moment. For twenty-one years, he had lived without a family name. No more.

"Thank you," he murmured, and forced himself to prompt Niton forward.

He told himself not to look back once he passed them, but after a few yards he did. The same sort of grief he had experienced at Kalli and Aldor's deaths coiled around his chest, constricting the air from his lungs. This wasn't death, but it still hurt unbearably. When he looked ahead again, it took a few moments before his eyes cleared enough to see, and each breath he drew was small and halting.

The hundred yards to the gate stretched on, each one tearing at his heart. Pain fought to consume him, but he tamped it down with all the strength he could manage. The only way he would get through this was to block his family and what he left behind from his mind and focus on the objective—safely escaping Ashwood.

He and Holden drew near the five-foot-high surrounding wall. Once through, they could pick up the pace and leave the estate behind. Just before they reached it, a solid shape formed from the shadows on the other side and blocked their exit. The horses stopped, and Niton snorted, tossing his head at the sudden movement. Jace squeezed the reins and narrowed his eyes.

"Slinking off into the night just as I suspected."

James's hateful voice stoked a fire that burned away the sorrow for a moment. Jace struggled to contain it. He scanned the wall, expecting Rothas and his men to make an appearance, but it was only James.

"Step aside," Jace ground out. His uncle and the others had risked a lot to help him escape. He would not let James make it all for naught.

The younger man shook his head, his fists on his hips. "We have unfinished business."

So this was personal. No wonder he hadn't brought his father out with him.

James took a step forward, slowly withdrawing the sword at his side.

Jace scowled. "You don't want to do this."

"You think I'm afraid of you?"

"I think you should be."

James snorted and tipped his chin up. "I am the son of a knight. I've been trained since I was a child. I'm not afraid of a slave."

Jace glared fire at him. His *brother* had never had to fight day after day for his life. Stiffly, he dismounted, his blood warming in anticipation.

"Jace," Holden said in a low warning. "The sound of swords will bring every guard on the estate down on us."

Jace kept his gaze locked on James. He stepped toward his brother, leaving his sword where it hung on Niton's saddle, and only stopped when James's sword hovered a mere inch from his chest.

"Last chance. Step aside."

James shook his head. "No. We're going to have this out right here." His sword point pricked into Jace's skin. "Now take up your sword."

The familiar flow of raw energy surged from Jace's blood into his nerves and muscles. His brother had made the wrong choice. Using his forearm against the flat of the blade, Jace batted James's sword away and threw a right-hand punch before his brother could react. James staggered. Jace reached for his wrist, ripping the sword away, and tossed it into the bushes beside the wall. This left him open for a brief moment. His brother's fist smashed into his ribs, driving the air from his lungs, but it only fueled the fire. He backhanded James hard across the chin.

Stumbling away, James's hand dropped to the dagger on his belt. Jace reacted in a moment and kicked his legs out from under him. James landed in a gasping heap just outside the wall. He scrambled to his hands and knees, but Jace kicked one of his hands, sending him back down. He pressed a knee down on his brother's back and neck to pin him in the mud. James fought to wiggle free.

"You are going to pay for—"

Jace grabbed his wrist and wrenched his arm up behind his back. James groaned through his teeth, powerless. Here, Jace could have left him in a state he would never forget, exacting full revenge. He had wanted nothing more the night that his brother had tried to attack Kyrin. The fury of it still stirred within him, but as vile as James was, the fact remained that he was Jace's brother. As much as he wished it didn't matter, it did. Even after all he had done, Jace suddenly found it impossible to do him serious harm.

Breathing loud and hard through his nose, James waited for Jace to act, a defiant scowl on his face. Jace looked down on him, a despicable, pathetic individual, but family nonetheless.

His anger changed from loathing to disappointment and frustration.

Jace pushed to his feet and hauled his little brother up with him. Dragging him along, he shoved him none too gently up against the wall. James struggled against him, but Jace grabbed the dagger still on his belt. James stilled when it flashed in front of his face. At last, fear lurked in the younger man's otherwise petulant expression. Jace leaned close, looking him straight in the eyes. The fear grew at what James must have seen in his.

"I know you despise the fact that we're brothers. Well, so do I. You think I'm nothing because I'm half ryrik, but I would far rather be who I am than a vile man like you who preys on helpless girls. You think I'm an animal, but which of us is behaving just like the man who attacked our mother? I would *never* harm a woman like that, but you do it on a whim."

Jace breathed heavily after this impassioned speech, waiting for James to respond, but his brother just stared blankly. Prompted by a strong desire to make his brother understand, he acted on impulse. Before James could even flinch, Jace sliced the dagger across James's cheek. Though not deep, it would surely leave a noticeable scar. James gasped out a cry, grabbing at his face as blood trickled from the wound.

"What did you do!"

"I'm making sure my point is well understood." Jace brandished the dagger in his face again, gaining his full, wide-eyed attention. "Every time you take advantage of a woman, you scar her for life. Maybe you'll remember that now every time you look in the mirror."

Satisfied at last, Jace released his hold on James and turned away. He took only a couple of steps before he spun back and said icily, "And if you dare lay so much as a finger on Lady Anne's maid again, I will come back and finish this."

James seemed to wilt against the wall, any trace of arrogance evaporated. He didn't respond, but Jace took his silence and cowering as submission.

Tossing the dagger off with the sword, Jace mounted Niton again. As he and Holden rode out, James stayed backed up against the wall, his hand to his face as blood dripped onto his shirt. For that brief moment before they left him behind, Jace felt sorry for him.

KYRIN STUFFED THE last of her maid's dresses back into her pack and then rubbed her sore eyes. She wasn't sure she had closed them at all last night with Jace on her mind. Had he made it out safely? They hadn't received confirmation from Rayad yet, and she would remain on edge until she knew for certain. Anything could have happened between when Rayad had escorted her to her room for the night and now preparing to leave this morning. Surely they would have heard if something went wrong.

She sighed and prayed once again for Jace's safety. But he wasn't the only one who drifted into her mind as she spoke to Elôm. During the night hours when she wasn't praying for Jace, she had worked on mentally reading all the letters she had seen in the office. Things did not look good for Samara. Thank Elôm that they were returning to camp today. Trask needed to hear what she knew so they could warn Samara's king of the danger. The fate of an entire country rested on the information she had locked away in her brain. The sooner she could share the burden, the better. She also had much to consider and discuss with the others about certain rumors coming out of Samara. The very thought of it filled her with questions as well as excitement over the possibilities.

A knock tapped the door—Rayad's knock. Kyrin's heart stuttered a little as Anne let him in, and she immediately searched his face for news about Jace.

"How did it go?" Anne asked.

"Good." Rayad lowered his voice. "As far as I know, Jace and Holden rode out just fine."

Kyrin let out a deep breath. *Thank You, Elôm.* Had she slept last night, she was sure she would have had nightmares of Rothas hanging Jace. Even now, the thought sent a chill down her arms.

Anne closed the door to make sure no one would overhear them. "Does Rothas know yet?"

"I'm not sure, but if he doesn't, he will shortly."

"Well, Kyrin and I are all packed. You can let the others know to be ready. As soon as breakfast is finished, we're leaving."

Rayad nodded and picked up two of Anne's larger bags. Kyrin took the smaller one containing her things, and they followed Anne out of the room. Downstairs, Rothas's upraised voice boomed from the drawing room.

"This was Elian's doing, wasn't it?"

"No." Charles's voice was quieter, but firm. "It was mine."

"But he helped, didn't he?" Rothas snapped.

Anne glanced at Rayad and Kyrin and tipped her head. Setting the bags down, they trailed her into the drawing room.

Charles stood in the center of the room, facing down his brother-in-law. "He couldn't exactly refuse my request for his help."

Rothas glared at him, his eyes like an enraged bull. "Oh, but I'm sure he was more than willing." His gaze jumped to Rachel, who stood at her brother's side. "And you were there too, weren't you?"

Rachel stood rigid and would not answer.

Disgusted, Rothas went back to railing at Charles. "This is my estate. What happens here is my business, not yours."

"Yes," Charles acknowledged, "but Jace is my nephew, and there's no way I was about to let you hang him."

Rothas's face turned a few shades darker. He reminded Kyrin of Daican when he had gone off on Prince Daniel in the palace library. She stayed close to Rayad in case the man lashed out in his anger.

Suddenly, amidst the tension, Anne cleared her throat. Everyone turned to her, but her attention was on Rothas.

"I've been informed that Jace is gone and another of my men with him."

"Have you?" Rothas replied in a condescending voice. "Or perhaps you were there too."

Anne straightened her spine. "Excuse me?" Her voice was razor sharp, and Kyrin almost smiled at the flicker of uncertainty in Rothas's eyes. "Are you accusing me of some sort of conspiracy? Because I don't think my father would be pleased by that, nor Lord Dunrick, should I take it up with him."

Rothas almost shook, his voice tight with suppressed fury. "Of course not. Forgive me."

Anne tipped her chin up, not allowing him off that easily. "It seems that's all you've done since my arrival—accuse my staff, and now accuse me. If you want to know if I believe Jace is guilty, then I certainly do not. I do know your son made highly inappropriate advances toward my maid. If you *truly* wish to find the guilty party, Sir Rothas, then I suggest starting with him."

Rothas opened his mouth to speak, but Anne wasn't yet finished.

"Now, I shall leave immediately after breakfast. Since you've driven away two of my security force, I don't see that I have any other choice but to postpone my trip to Mareby and return home. Clearly, you care very little for the wellbeing of servants, neither your guests' nor your own. If I can't be assured of my people's safety, then there's no point in staying. And don't think I won't let my father know exactly what went on here, as well as my other acquaintances."

The room rang with silence. Kyrin could have applauded Anne for putting him down so soundly. Rayad's wry expression agreed, and Charles looked to be fighting mightily to hold back a smile as he stared at the floor.

When Rothas couldn't come up with any response besides glowering at her, Anne turned to Rayad. "Go and prepare the men to leave."

Rayad nodded, and Kyrin caught the subtle hint of amusement in his voice. "Yes, my lady."

An hour after the incident in the drawing room, Kyrin followed the men outside to the courtyard, where their horses were prepared. Several minutes later, Anne joined them. Kyrin breathed a little easier now. There was no telling what Rothas could have done when she and Rayad had left Anne in the drawing room.

"How was breakfast?" Rayad asked as they gathered around her.

"Tense. But the curious thing was James. He came in sulking, and it looked like someone beat him up pretty good. He has a nasty cut on his face."

Kyrin sent a suspicious look toward Kaden. He, however, appeared just as surprised as the others, if not more than a little pleased over the news.

"Lady Rachel questioned him about it, but he wouldn't say what happened. Even Rothas seemed surprised. All I know is that James was awfully moody and didn't look at me once. He barely touched his food either." Anne paused, glancing toward the road.

"Are you sure nothing happened when Jace and Holden left last night?"

Rayad shrugged. "Not that I'm aware of." But his eyes narrowed in thought.

Kyrin turned her gaze to the road as well. Had Jace and James gotten into a fight last night? Had Jace been hurt? What if James had prevented Jace from escaping? A knot twisted in her stomach. Surely Rothas wouldn't have been so angry this morning if they had Jace hidden away somewhere. Everything Kyrin saw led her to believe that his rage was genuine. If only they didn't have so far to go to find out.

A few minutes later, Rachel, Elanor, and Charles came out to say their goodbyes, followed shortly by Elian. As relieved as Kyrin would be to leave, it was sad to bid them all farewell. She would have liked to get to know them better. After all, they were Jace's family, and that was important to her.

While the others shared their parting words, Rachel approached her with a smile.

"I'm glad we had a chance to talk the other morning, however briefly."

Kyrin smiled in return. "So am I." Rachel was so kind and wonderful to talk with. Now she knew exactly where Jace got it from. If only he realized what a good man he was.

"Jace has a very special place for you in his heart."

A happy warmth filled Kyrin's chest, and her smile widened. "He has one in mine too."

"I'm glad. It was very difficult for him to leave. He's going to need you."

Kyrin nodded, promising, "I'll be there for him."

Her eyes misting, Rachel hugged her, and Kyrin returned the embrace readily. Her own eyes grew watery. Jace needed this love from his mother. It seemed so cruel for him to lose it so soon.

Please, Elôm, let it work out someday. Please don't let him lose it forever.

They parted, and Kyrin asked, "Is there anything that can be done about Tina?"

She couldn't get the girl's broken look out of her mind.

Rachel nodded, deep regret in her eyes. "I'm sending her to Brandell. Charles will make sure she is well treated there."

"Good," Kyrin murmured. At least now she would have someone to look out for her, even if the damage had already been done.

They then traded sad goodbyes, and Kyrin drew a deep breath to loosen up her chest. Blinking several times, she focused on Anne and Charles. The viscount gave Anne a wide smile.

"I'm quite impressed with how you've handled your time with my brother-in-law. If I were a bit younger, I would seriously consider going to your father for permission to court you."

Anne arched her brow in amusement. "I'm afraid you would have some very serious competition to contend with first."

Charles chuckled. "Well, whoever he is, I hope he knows the treasure he is pursuing."

"Oh, I think he does."

Everyone concluded their goodbyes, and Kyrin turned to Maera. She froze when she caught sight of James watching her from several yards away. A chill crept over her skin, but it lessened with curiosity. Now she could see for herself the new bruises on his face and the cut along his left cheekbone. The inflamed edges were clean and straight, obviously the result of a blade.

James's gaze flitted past her, and his jaw went taut. He looked at her once more and turned away. She looked over her shoulder to find Kaden's menacing glare trained on the other man until he disappeared.

Leaving thoughts of him behind, she mounted up and followed the others away from the manor house. Once beyond the wall, Kyrin glanced back, again with mixed feelings. Ashwood could have been Jace's home . . . but then she would never have known him and that was a painful thought.

Jace downed his fourth cup of coffee and contemplated another. Though he had taken Holden's suggestion to rest shortly after reaching the cover of the forest and setting up a temporary camp, he had only slept for an hour, maybe two. Not nearly enough to make up for three sleepless nights.

Needing to move around, he rose and rubbed a tender spot on his ribs.

"You all right?"

Jace glanced down at Holden. "It's nothing."

The dull soreness didn't come close to the pain he had experienced with broken ribs last winter. And it was his own fault for under-estimating his brother.

He gritted his teeth and bit back a sigh. All day he had tried not to think of his family and the pain of leaving, but how did one do that? It was as if he had left behind a part of himself he could never go back for, leaving a horrible wound inside him. One he wasn't sure would ever heal.

"The others should be here any time now."

Jace's attention snapped back to Holden, and then he looked down the road. Midday had come and gone, adding to his nerves. What if Rothas had flown into a rage after his disappearance and imprisoned everyone? If they didn't show up soon, he would be sorely tempted to ride back and find them.

The road blurred, and he rubbed his eyes.

"You really should sleep while you can," Holden said.

Now Jace's sigh did escape. "I can't."

After those first couple of hours, sleep had eluded him. It had given him a taste, a brief escape, but no more.

"It's not easy leaving family."

Jace clenched his fists. Holden wanted to help, but Jace didn't think he could. Despite his clear lack of desire to talk, Holden pressed on.

"When I left the emperor's service, I knew I would be severed from my family, likely for good. Now they probably believe I'm dead, and what's more, most of them probably don't care." He shrugged, as if he had long since accepted it, and looked up at Jace. "But you've got family that loves you whatever the circumstances, and while that does make it harder to leave, their love is still with you, and you know they're pulling for you, praying for you. And when this all comes to an end, you'll be together and won't have to be separated again."

Jace imagined his family together for eternity, but a black cloud of doubt shadowed the blissful scene. Would he be part of it, or would he be the only one missing from that picture?

Stop it. Hadn't he promised his mother he would try to leave all these fears to Elôm? But, right now, the very thought of lifting those dark fears out of his heart was exhausting. He just didn't have the will.

Overwhelmed and frustrated with his own weakness, a welcome distraction came in the sound of approaching horses. Holden pushed to his feet, and they both peered down the road. Jace gripped the hilt of his sword, just in case.

In a few moments, the riders appeared, and Jace recognized Rayad's horse as well as Anne's white horse in the lead. The tension inside him relaxed. When the riders reached them, they all appeared relieved and dismounted.

Kyrin was the first to reach Jace, her expression serious and searching. "Are you all right?"

"Yes." But she looked at him so earnestly, he asked, "Why?"

"James looked like he got into quite a scuffle. We were worried something happened when you left last night."

Jace's mind turned back to the confrontation. Kyrin must have picked up the subtle change in his expression.

"Did something happen?"

Slowly, Jace nodded. "I don't know how he knew I was leaving, but he was waiting at the gate. It was just him, and he wanted the two of us to have it out." Kyrin's brows lifted, and he continued, "We had a . . . brief discussion, and then Holden and I left."

"So you're not hurt at all?"

Jace shook his head, drawing a sigh of relief from her.

JACE NEVER SLEPT in. It just wasn't in his nature, but lying on his own cot the next morning, he had little ambition to rise. They had reached camp late last night. As soon as he had finished unsaddling Niton, he'd gone straight to the shelter and fallen into bed. At least he had slept well, but lingering fatigue weighed down his limbs. The heaviest of all, however, was his heart. His mother was his last thought before falling asleep and his first thought upon waking. A yearning ache stabbed his chest. He would probably never see her again.

Jace rubbed the stinging from his eyes and glanced around the shelter. Kaden and the others had left several minutes ago. Only Tyra remained. Other than the wolf, he was alone with his thoughts. Not the best position to be in—not in this state. But he was tired. Too tired to summon the energy and force himself to face the day.

Don't do this, a tiny fighting spark urged. If he didn't take charge now, he would only sink deeper, something he knew well. Besides, Kyrin was going to meet with Trask and the others this morning to share her findings concerning Samara. No doubt these findings would shape any future plans for the group, including him. Things could just never seem to stay peaceful for long.

With a sigh that turned into a soft groan, he pushed himself out of bed and grabbed his clothes. Tyra jumped to her feet, eager to follow him out.

"Sorry," he murmured at making her wait.

Outside, they stepped into the bright morning sun and headed toward the central fire pit, where many of the men congregated for breakfast. This would be the norm now, what with the weather improving. Jace grabbed a bowl and served himself from the pot of porridge. When he looked up, he caught some of the men watching him before averting their eyes. A sharp cramp pinched his stomach.

They were the newer men in camp—those who had arrived last fall and in the recent days. He read the questions in their eyes, their suspicions. After all, Hagen's death was little more than a week old. Jace may have been gone for a while, but the incident was still fresh in the minds at camp. And maybe he wasn't responsible, but he couldn't erase his connection to it. Not everyone had accepted him as fully as the others had. The Korvic brothers, who had beaten him up last summer, kept their distance, especially since Holden was on his side now, but it didn't completely stop their threatening looks. They had probably done some whispering while he was away.

Jace moved away from the fire and drew closer to his sheltermates and friends. At least he didn't have to worry about accusing looks from them, but even here, he didn't feel entirely comfortable. They would all tell him that was ridiculous and that he was one of them, but . . .

He shook his head. More thoughts he shouldn't be having.

He stared down at his bowl and whispered a short prayer of thanks, admitting how weak it was. Those looks had stolen his appetite, and he tasted little as he battled his destructive thoughts. His old enemy despair jabbed and pried at every weakness he had. He recalled his mother's encouragement and the peace she wanted for him, but that did little more than increase the ache in his heart. Either way, he couldn't win.

"Jace."

His attention jerked to the men, to Marcus in particular. If they had said anything before that, it hadn't registered.

"Thank you for saving Kyrin," Marcus told him. "If you hadn't heard her scream . . ." He shook his head, his face solemn.

Thoughts of Kyrin and the encounter with James pushed everything else to the back of his mind for the moment. He nodded slowly. Contemplating what could have happened only darkened his mood.

"I'm still glad you had a few more words with James before you left," Kaden said.

Jace glanced at him. Only Holden knew the details of their "discussion," and the man gave him an amused look. Jace wondered briefly if he had gone too far, but if what Anne and Kyrin had told him of James's behavior in the morning was any indicator, perhaps he would think twice before taking advantage of another woman. If so, then Jace really couldn't regret his actions.

The focus of the group shifted when Rayad joined them. Behind him, Trask and Warin strode across camp to the meeting hall, rolled-up maps and parchments under their arms. Kyrin's talcrin friend Sam and his nephew Tane followed.

"As soon as Kyrin is ready, we'll all meet inside," Rayad informed the group.

They finished their last bites of breakfast and then followed him to the nearly completed meeting hall. A long table was set up in the back, and the men gathered around it. Captain Darq and his lieutenant, Glynn, spoke in the corner. The two cretes must have arrived from Dorland while they were in Ashwood. Once Aaron and Timothy joined them, they only awaited Kyrin.

Jace noticed her arrival only moments later. She carried her own stack of parchments, which she laid on the table near Trask. Her face was quite serious, but also tired, especially her eyes. Had she slept much last night?

"These are the copies I made of the letters from Daican to Rothas. I have a few more to do, but these contain the most pertinent information." Kyrin slid a map over to refer to, and everyone else gathered in close to see as she went on. "From what I can tell from the letters, Daican intends to attack the fortress of Stonehelm, here, on Samara's southern border."

"I thought that fortress was nearly impenetrable," Holden said. "Didn't the giants build it for them?"

Sam nodded. "Yes. There's a wall running from the mountains down to the marshlands. Between that and the river, an army would have a hard time reaching Samara. They'd lose a lot of men."

"Unfortunately, that isn't Daican's only plan." All eyes turned back to Kyrin. "Rothas has something else in mind. The attack against Stonehelm is basically a diversion. Daican intends to send half of his force by ship to Amberin, Samara's capital. With Samara's resources gathered at Stonehelm, they could take the city with minimal force and then march on the fortress to attack it from both fronts. They wouldn't even have to fight. They could merely starve Samara's army out, since no supplies could be brought in."

A silence settled, heavy with impending doom. Jace admitted with some shame that he hadn't thought much about Samara's plight—he'd been too focused on other things—but it was real now, and it didn't just affect the people of Samara. If the emperor succeeded in his invasion, he would control more than half the continent. Who could stop him then?

In a low voice, Trask asked, "Does Daican say when he's going to enact this plan?"

"He doesn't say specifically, but the last letters sound pretty set, so I don't see why he wouldn't act immediately."

"We have to warn Samara," Sam said. "If they can split their forces between Stonehelm and Amberin, then just maybe they can hold Daican off."

Trask agreed. He looked about to say something, but Kyrin spoke first.

"There is a reason he has chosen to attack now."

They focused on her once more. Jace found her expression odd, almost hesitant or questioning.

"The emperor has been hearing rumors from Samara. Anne told me that Rothas mentioned it at supper one night, and I have found several mentions of it in Daican's letters. There is a man in Samara named Elon. Apparently, he has been teaching and miraculously healing people."

"Miraculous healings?" Trask said. His voice held a tone of doubt.

Jace looked between the two of them, discomfort stirring inside of him. Such things belonged in stories told around campfires at night. Not in real life.

Kyrin nodded. "The letters don't contain much detail beyond that, but . . ."

Jace found himself holding his breath as she paused.

"There is talk among the people of Samara that he could be their Savior."

Complete silence overtook the room, and Jace resisted the urge to fidget. Talk like this was unsettling. There was too much unknown in it.

Timothy spoke up for the first time, his eyes alight. "You mean *the* Savior? The One sent to redeem us?"

Kyrin lifted her shoulders in a shrug. "That's what it sounds like they're saying. Of course, Daican doesn't believe it, but I think he wants to destroy the rumors before they embolden

Samara, which is why he'll probably move against them as soon as possible."

Trask nodded, and looked at Jace and the others who had gone to Ashwood. "Leetra went to spy out Fort Rivor. She should be back in a day or two. Once we know what's going on there, we'll bring all this information to the king." His gaze then fell on Marcus. "When Daican does attack, they will need all the help they can get."

Marcus stood up taller and nodded. "We may not have a large force, but the men are ready. I'll see that they are prepared to march as soon as you give the order."

So this was it, then; they were going to war. Jace glanced down at Kyrin, who watched her brother with a mix of admiration and concern.

"Good," Trask said, now turning to Captain Darq. "Daican's men may not be able to easily breach Stonehelm's walls, but it is imperative we take into consideration the firedrakes. Samara will have no way to defend herself against them."

Darq didn't even pause to consider. "I will return to Dorland immediately and gather as many riders as are willing to join me. We'll meet your men in Samara."

"Thank you. Last we heard, Daican has about sixty firedrakes ready for combat. We will need as many dragons as we can get to face them."

Jace slid the whetstone down the edge of his sword blade over and over again, lost in the motion of it. The sword didn't really need sharpening, but it was something to do with his hands while his mind argued with itself. He should focus on Samara and the days ahead, but his heart was still stuck back in Ashwood and dwelling on the situation here in camp. He had seen Alice when he'd left the meeting hall earlier. She still blamed him. It was clear in her eyes, driving deeper his growing unease. And, more and more, he kept catching the same types of glances from the other men that he had received at breakfast.

With a scowl, he admonished himself for going down this road again, sinking into the lonely pit of despair he had been in when he'd first come to camp. But this back and forth between his emotions, this constant battle, was wearing on him. He didn't want to be this way. He wanted more for his life, wanted to *be* more, but he didn't know if he was strong enough to attain it. Every attempt on his part in the past had met with failure, no matter how hard he fought for it. He breathed harder. Why did peace elude him so?

And then there were these rumors from Samara. He gritted his teeth at the uncertainty that swelled up inside him. He didn't know enough from the Scrolls to understand much of what Kyrin and Timothy had said, but they both seemed very excited about it. They had talked for a long time after the meeting. What would such a thing mean for all of them? For him? It left a tight knot in his gut.

A voice broke his concentration. His hand slipped and the heel of his palm just below his thumb slid across the freshly sharpened blade. He hissed at the fiery sting of sliced flesh and dropped the whetstone. Blood rolled along his skin.

"Jace!" Kyrin knelt at his side and grasped his hand. "I'm so sorry. I didn't mean to startle you."

At her regretful tone, Jace shook his head. "It's not your fault."

"Come on. We'll get it cleaned up and bandaged."

But Jace pulled his hand away. The awareness of her touch only complicated his already muddy thoughts.

"There's no need." He pressed his other thumb to the cut to stop the bleeding.

In the heavy silence, it occurred to him how insensitive and short he'd been. Guilt took hold. Here he was, taking his frustration out on her and possibly hurting her again. Meeting her questioning expression with his own apologetic one, his voice gentled. "Really, it will be fine. It's just a shallow cut. Nothing serious. I'll clean it later."

Her face cleared of confusion, but concern remained.

Jace cleared his throat. "Did you need something?"

Kyrin sat back, watching him. "I just wanted to see how you were doing."

Jace sighed and stared at the small pool of blood in his hand. Surely, he didn't have to say anything for her to know the answer. It must be written plainly across his face.

"It's hard," he admitted, though to do so was difficult. He looked at her again, into her eyes, and the unceasing compassion she had for him.

"It is," she murmured. "When I left Kaden in Valcré, not knowing if I'd ever see him again, it was one of the hardest things I've had to do."

Jace winced and looked away. She had handled separation so much better than he was. Outwardly he might appear so strong, but inwardly he was a weakling in the things that really mattered. He rubbed his forehead with the back of his hand. He was used to keeping things locked up inside, but was just worn out enough to let his thoughts slip out.

"I just wish I could be with them." He shook his head. "When I was, my ryrik blood meant nothing. It didn't matter."

Kyrin leaned closer to see his face. "It doesn't matter here either."

Jace released a hard breath. "But it does. It always does. Was it not a factor you considered when you chose to go hunting with me?"

Her gaze wavered, but she answered in a low voice, "Yes."

"And Rayad had to consider it when he chose to help me, and Kalli and Aldor when they opened their home to me. They would have been foolish not to. But my family . . . for the first time in my life, my ryrik blood was not a factor. I was part of them. I belonged with them."

"You belong here too."

She said it so earnestly, and maybe it was true for her, but he didn't feel it. He never had.

He shook his head, his chest tightening and growing warm. "No, it's not the same. I—" He stopped and squeezed his eyes closed. This discussion was heading down the same path as the one they'd had after Hagen's death. He couldn't take another argument coming between them right now. Breathing steadily, he tried to speak more calmly. "I just . . . I need time."

The sad look in her eyes pierced his heart, but at least she wasn't angry. She nodded in acceptance and swallowed before speaking in a soft voice.

"I wish with all my heart you didn't have to be separated from them. I hate that you've lost and endured so much. If I could somehow change things for you, I would."

He stared at her, caught up in the way moisture gathered in her beautiful, smoky blue eyes—those eyes that displayed her inner beauty and everything about her that he loved more than life itself. His voice, along with his breath, stuck in his throat for a moment. When it released, he murmured, "I know you would."

She breathed out slowly and looked away as she wiped the corners of her eyes. Pushing to her feet, she looked down at him. "Just remember . . . if you need help you have people here too."

She turned to go. Immediately, an intense ache throbbed in Jace's heart. He called her name. When she faced him again, he struggled for what to say, afraid of what might come out. Just why *had* he stopped her?

Thankfully, he remembered something he wanted to talk to her about. He cleared his throat. "Do you have a minute?"

She nodded, and he rose, setting his sword aside. Inside the shelter, he rinsed his bloodied hands in a bucket of water and retrieved the object he had gotten from Trask earlier. Back out where she stood waiting, he handed her the object—a dark leather sheath and dagger. She pulled the double-edged blade free. The knife was small enough to fit comfortably in her hand, while still large enough to be deadly. She looked up with questioning eyes.

"As soon as there's time, I want to teach you how to use it to defend yourself so you'll be prepared if you ever encounter someone like James again." The possibility made him ill. *Please, Elôm, don't let that happen.*

Kyrin looked back down at the dagger, nodding as she slid it into the sheath. "Thank you. I appreciate that very much. I don't want to be defenseless again."

She gave him a quick smile. Not very wide, but thankful.

When she walked on, Jace's heart constricted again, and he rubbed his chest. After so many years, he should be used to pain, but this was different, forcing him to face facts.

He loved her.

He took a deep breath and sank back down next to his sword. Just as clearly as he knew he could never have her, he also knew he loved her.

OUTBURSTS OF LAUGHTER and good-natured insults drew Kyrin to the shelter belonging to her oldest and youngest brothers. The door stood open, so she peeked inside. In the middle of the dirt floor, Kaden wrestled both their little brothers at the same time. Michael had a half-hearted chokehold around Kaden's neck, while Ronny attempted to squirm out of his big brother's one-armed grasp. There was no telling how it started, but Kyrin watched and grinned. They were obviously having a marvelous time, and she wanted to commit the moment to memory. She loved to see Kaden interact with the boys. His own childhood had been cut so short. This carefree moment might be one of the last they enjoyed in a long time with war looming.

With a shout of triumph, Ronny broke free and jumped on Kaden's back to help Michael try to pin him down. Kaden straightened on his knees and reached back for them. That was when he noticed her in the doorway.

"Kyrin," he gasped, winded.

She put her hands on her hips and gave them her best mock-scolding look. "I thought you three were supposed to be gathering your laundry."

"We are." Kaden nodded to two heaps of clothing near one of the cots—one belonging to Michael and Ronny, and the other to Kaden, who must have gathered his from the other shelter.

"Is that all of it?"

The three nodded.

Breaking into a smile, Kyrin stepped inside and gathered the clothes into her arms. "Carry on."

She caught their delighted faces as she ducked out of the shelter. The tussle continued, and she headed across camp to where the women were washing. Along the way, her brothers' clothing started to slip and she had to readjust her hold. Halfway there, someone came up behind her. She looked over her shoulder. Jace was bending to pick up a shirt she had dropped and already had another in his hand.

"Oops. I didn't realize I was losing some."

Jace eyed the load. "Need help?"

"Thanks," she said as he took half. "Kaden and the boys were supposed to bring it, but somehow it turned into a two-against-one wrestling match, and I hated to interrupt them."

A flicker of a smile crossed Jace's lips. At least another night's sleep seemed to have helped him. It was so hard to see him the way he was during their conversation yesterday afternoon. It had weighed on her all day. If only she could change things for him.

Keeping these thoughts hidden, she led the way to the group of women around the washtubs.

Kyrin's mother looked up from her wash water as they joined her and frowned lightly. "Where are the boys?"

Kyrin dropped her bundle next to the washtub. "Wrestling."

Her mother shook her head with a mild look of exasperation.

Jace stepped up next to Kyrin and set down the rest of the load. She gave him a sweet smile. "Thank you."

He nodded and went on his way. Kyrin stared after him, thinking, wishing . . .

Her mind snapped back to her work. She turned to the wash-tub and found her mother watching her keenly. Kyrin pretended not to notice and grabbed up one of Michael's shirts, dunking it into the water and scrubbing it against the washboard. Though she still sensed her mother's lingering gaze, it wasn't a discussion she wanted to get into. It would be pointless, especially in light of the more sobering things they had to deal with.

After a while, the probing silence ended, and they talked companionably as they tackled the mound of laundry. An hour later, Kyrin turned to hang up a shirt to dry when she spied Marcus.

"Trask has called another meeting to discuss plans for Samara." He gestured over his shoulder to the meeting hall.

Kyrin glanced at her mother and brushed her damp hands on her already water-spattered skirt as she followed him to where the camp leaders waited. Once their core group was present, Trask addressed them.

"I wanted to let you all know that, once Leetra returns and we find out what is going on at Fort Rivor, I plan to deliver our information to King Balen personally. Warin and Sam have agreed to remain here to oversee the refugees and begin preparations for the new camps."

He paused. "This is not like our other missions. I am not asking any of you to join me. That is entirely your choice, as it will be for everyone in camp. I intend to remain in Samara to see this through. Before any of you make your decisions, I want to make sure you have fully considered what we will face there. We might not all make it back, if any of us."

A heavy silence surrounded them. Kyrin glanced around at everyone, and didn't find a single person who appeared daunted by the prospect of such a bleak future. Win or lose, they were prepared to fight. Starting with Holden, each of the men voiced their desire to join Trask, until only Kyrin and Jace were left undecided. Out of the corner of her eye, she saw him watching her. His decision would most certainly rest upon hers. He would go where she went. In that way, she controlled his future as much as she controlled her own. Whatever she decided could potentially lead to his death. Ice built in the pit of her stomach, but she forced it away. Jace's life was not in her hands. It was in Elôm's.

Kyrin gave it a final moment of consideration. She couldn't fight, but she could assist in other ways. As appealing as it seemed to remain in the safety of camp, her closest friends and brothers would be in the fight. After all they had faced, to stay behind now just wouldn't sit right. Besides, the torturous waiting to see if any of them would return made her queasy.

"I will go with you. I'm not sure how I can help, but I'll do whatever I can."

"I'll go too," Jace spoke up right after her.

Kyrin tried to ignore the knot it brought to her stomach, and prayed that Elôm would protect him and the other men. This was not the first time they had faced such grim circumstances together.

Trask nodded to each of them. "I can't say I won't be happy to have the group together in this. I'll spread the invitation around camp. Everyone else who wishes to join us can travel with Marcus and the militia, though I will want some men to remain here to look after things." His gaze shifted to Talas. "Same with the riders. I'll want some here with Warin. The emperor's focus is on Samara, but that doesn't mean he couldn't send a few firedrakes to find us. I don't want camp left defenseless from the air."

Talas agreed.

Turning his attention to Kaden now, Trask asked, "Are the riders ready for combat in Samara?"

Kaden's brows lifted as he glanced at Talas. No doubt he had expected Trask to direct this sort of question to the crete as well. But he nodded firmly and spoke with confidence.

"Yes. A few could use a little more flight experience, but I believe they're ready and willing to fight."

"Good," Trask said, "which brings up the subject of leadership. They will need to be captained."

Everyone looked over at Talas. He was the obvious choice.

"Kaden, if you accept it, I'm commissioning you as Captain of the Landale riders."

Kaden's gaze snapped back to Trask. "Me?"

Kyrin stared at them, matching her twin's wide-eyed expression. She certainly hadn't seen this coming.

Trask gave a nod and a hint of a smile.

"But what about Talas?" Kaden asked. "He has the most knowledge and experience."

Talas smiled at him. "I appreciate your vote of confidence, but I think the men would prefer one of their own to lead them."

"Talas is the one who came to me with the recommendation," Trask told Kaden, "and we all agree that you're the most suitable for the job. You have a rare natural talent for flying that we believe will serve you well in leading the men."

Kaden just stared, his mouth hanging partly open, speechless.

"Do you accept the position?"

Kaden took a breath, exhaling slowly before he nodded. "I accept."

A full smile came to Trask's face. "Then congratulations on becoming our second Captain Altair."

Amidst grins and kind words, the men all congratulated Kaden on his new position. Kyrin's heart swelled in her chest as she watched them. She never would have foreseen this for her twin but, oh, was she proud of him. When he glanced her way, she gave him a wide grin, her eyes smarting. She blinked hard and compared their years in Tarvin Hall to this moment. They both seemed to have grown up so quickly—they'd had to—but, in reality, they were still so young. Yet, here her brother had just received the command over a group of dragon riders heading to war. It was a lot to wrap her mind around. What would their mother think?

"Talas will be your lieutenant for the time being," Trask continued once the congratulating ceased, "unless Captain Darq has other plans for him when we reach Samara. I will address the men when we're finished here, and you can begin to prepare them to leave."

He looked around at the others. "As for the rest of you, we don't know exactly when Leetra will return, but be ready."

Camp buzzed with activity following the meeting as most of the men prepared to journey to Samara. Even the camp refugees were busy getting ready to set off for safer lands to the east, now that much of their fighting force would be absent.

Jace seemed to be the only one without something to do. His weapons were ready, and most of his clothes and belongings were already packed. Besides food for the journey, there wasn't much more to do. So he sat in the sun with Tyra, who had rolled over at his feet for a belly rub. She had been glued to his side since returning from Ashwood, and he hated to leave her again. There was no telling how long he would be away this time, or if he would even return.

Still, leaving camp again might be the best thing right now. It would give him something to focus on, and he needed that. After his conversation with Kyrin and the conclusion he had reached, he'd decided it best to push away all the feelings that hurt so much, including those he had for her. Not that it proved easy. No, nearly impossible was more accurate, but he needed to do it. It was the best he could come up with to cope with the pain and avoid jeopardizing their friendship. He couldn't lose that. It was one of the only things he had left.

Tyra rolled back to her stomach, her ears perked. Jace looked up, and his heart missed a beat. It couldn't be. The turmoil he had been through had to be playing cruel tricks with his mind. He blinked not once but twice before he could truly believe what he saw. Anne had just ridden into camp with Elanor and Elian.

Jace scrambled to his feet. This needed a serious explanation. Elanor gave him a sparkling grin as he drew near, but he was too shocked to smile back.

"What are you doing here?"

Her grin widened. "I am staying at Marlton for the time being."

Jace gaped at her. "Marlton?"

She gave a quick nod, and then dismounted. By this time, many of the others from camp had gathered, all sharing in Jace's surprise.

"They arrived last night, asking to stay," Anne explained.

Jace glanced at her, but fixed a questioning look on his sister.

"You see," she said, as if she hadn't just given him one of the greatest shocks of his life, "I will turn eighteen in just a couple months and, when that happens, Father plans to marry me off to one of his friends. I can't abide the thought of that. Mother and I have prayed diligently for a way out, and I believe this is it."

Jace's mind reeled. Of course, how could he not be delighted at having his sister so close, but what of the danger? If Anne and her parents were ever found out, then Elanor would be caught up in it as well. She could be executed for merely associating with "rebels."

"Are you sure about this?"

"Quite," Elanor answered with a tone of finality. "I'm well aware of the risk. Mother filled me in on your involvement with the resistance. And, frankly, I'd much rather be a part of it than suffering in a forced marriage. Mother agrees."

Jace let out a long breath and looked at Anne again. She must be all right with it if she had brought them here.

"I explained everything that's involved in this decision," she said. "They are fully informed."

Jace gave a slow nod, still considering all the dangerous implications.

"Besides," Elanor jumped in again, "we can't go back now, or at least Elian can't." She winced. "He hasn't said it outright, but Father has threatened his life."

Jace glanced at him. He was very calm about this, but his eyes hinted at sadness. It must have been difficult for him to leave Jace's mother behind.

"How is Rothas going to take this?" Jace wouldn't put it past the man to ride out here to reclaim his daughter and exact his revenge on Elian and anyone else he deemed responsible. "What if he comes for you?"

Elanor shrugged, her voice matter-of-fact. "I'm sure he'll be furious, but Mother and Uncle Charles won't let him come."

Jace rubbed his forehead. "And what about Mother?" He hated the thought of her alone with only Rothas and James. She would have no allies and no one to turn to on hard days.

At this, Elanor's eyes dropped, and she lost a little of her enthusiasm. "She insisted she'll be all right, and Uncle Charles promised to look after her."

Jace shared another look with Elian. Hard as it was, they would both have to trust them. It was clearly what Jace's mother wanted. Finally satisfied, he nodded. As long as he had his sister here, he would try not to worry about the circumstances.

Anne took over then, introducing everyone Elanor and Elian had not met personally. When they came to Kyrin and Kaden, Elanor's eyes widened in surprise.

"You're the Altair twins."

Kyrin smiled. "Yes."

"I'm very pleased to meet you. Father receives a lot of news from Valcré, so I've heard about you. I'd love to talk and hear more."

"I'd like that," Kyrin replied.

It looked like Jace would get his wish after all.

They came last to Trask, who welcomed them kindly. Once greetings concluded, Anne said, "I have a bit of news for you. Goler stopped by yesterday."

Trask's nose wrinkled. "And?"

"He wanted to let me know that he and most of his men are leaving for Fort Rivor. He said it was for training but, considering our information, I'm more willing to believe he's headed to Samara with the rest of the army."

"Probably." Trask quirked a brow. "Maybe he won't come back."

Anne gave him a scolding look until he didn't appear so pleased with the thought.

"All right, maybe I shouldn't be thinking such things. I'm not going to lie, though. It would make things a lot easier around here. At least he wouldn't be showing up in Marlton all the time."

Jace had to agree, especially with Elanor staying there now. Would the captain find it suspicious?

Anne smiled in amusement at Trask and wrapped her hand around his arm. "Don't worry; I can handle it. Now, why don't you show me the meeting hall? Looks like you've made a lot of progress."

As the two of them walked off, the rest of the group exchanged a few kind words with Elanor and Elian before leaving Jace alone with them. He stood for a moment, not quite certain what to say. When had he ever entertained guests?

Before the silence could drag into awkwardness, Elanor noticed Tyra.

"Who is this?" she asked in genuine interest.

Jace reached down to rub the wolf's head. "Tyra."

"Hello, Tyra."

At her name, the wolf wagged her tail and approached. Elanor bent down, rubbing her ears.

"She's beautiful." Obviously, she didn't share most of society's belief that black wolves were evil. She looked up at Jace. "Where did you get her?"

"I found her as a pup. She'd been shot." He stepped closer, ruffling the fur around Tyra's neck. He and his wolf had survived their share of perilous scrapes.

"Poor girl," Elanor murmured. Then she straightened and looked around camp. "So this is your home?"

"I've been here for almost a year now." But even after all those months, 'home' still didn't fit it. "Do you want to look around?"

"We'd love to," Elanor said, and Elian nodded his agreement.

Jace guided them through camp, explaining about the refugees and villagers they had rescued from Goler. Along the way, they met Marcus and Liam. Jace introduced them, and they talked for a bit before moving on.

A short while later they came to the dragons, and Jace introduced Gem. Elanor was especially delighted, never having seen a dragon before. As they admired her, chuckling at her chirps and warbles, Kyrin joined them. She and Elanor soon struck up a conversation and moved off toward the cabins, where Kyrin wanted to introduce her mother, Lenae, and Meredith.

Jace and Elian followed slowly behind.

"Lady Anne told us why you visited Ashwood," Elian said. "I figured Rothas must be planning something with all the letters he received from the emperor. What will you do with the information?"

"Warn the king of Samara," Jace replied. "Trask plans to leave as soon as one of our spies returns, probably in a day or two. We're all going with him, and Marcus will lead the militia there to help fight."

Elian nodded slowly. "If I hadn't promised your mother I'd watch over Elanor, I'd go with you."

Jace could see the desire in his eyes. "It's good you'll be here." He hesitated, pausing to face him. "I'm not sure how many of us will make it back."

Kyrin walked through the lengthening shadows in camp that evening, replaying the day in her mind. She had very much enjoyed her time with Elanor. She was kind, genuine, and lots of fun, not to mention the first young woman Kyrin's age that she felt could be a close friend. Yet, beyond that, she especially enjoyed how Jace was with Elanor and Elian. It brought out his soft, more vulnerable side, and he had smiled more than she'd seen in days.

However, as good as it was to see, it was equally hard to witness his reaction to their leaving for the night. He became a shell again, containing pain and loss and little else.

"Oh, Elôm," she whispered. "Please, guide him through this and give him peace, somehow. He may not know if You are there to help him, but I do."

She sighed. It used to be that she could bring him out of his shell and make him smile, but it didn't seem to work anymore. Instead, he seemed to pull away. Why, when they talked lately, was it as if he would suddenly close himself off to her, as if closing off all feeling? She had worked so hard to get him to

233

open up to her and trust her with whatever deep emotions he experienced. Was she losing that?

She shook her head. Jace would figure this out, and she would always be right there to help. She had to believe things would be all right and not focus on painful possibilities. Instead, she set her mind on her task. Supper was about ready, and she needed to round up her brothers. Their mother wanted them to have a family meal together, since half of them would soon leave. Kyrin didn't want to think of it as one of their last meals. She just wanted to enjoy being together, and that meant not thinking about Jace for now.

Easier said than done.

Out near the edge of camp, Kyrin spotted Kaden. He sat on a large rock, staring into the forest. Kyrin frowned. This wasn't like her brother at all, especially not around suppertime. She changed course, all her concern for Jace momentarily shifting to her twin.

"Kaden?"

When he looked at her, his eyes glinted with excess moisture. He blinked quickly and cleared his throat. "Hey."

Kyrin sat down beside him. "Are you all right?"

Kaden nodded, though his voice was a bit lower than usual. "I'm fine." He stared at his hands. "I was just thinking about Father . . . I wish he were here."

Mention of their father always made it difficult to breathe. Kyrin fought against the tightness that locked around her chest and murmured, "Me too."

A sad little smile came to Kaden's face. "I wonder what he'd think of all this. About me becoming captain of the riders."

"Oh, he'd be very proud," Kyrin said with absolute certainty. She had never known anyone to support them the way he did. To see how far they had all come would have delighted him.

"Probably not what he would have expected. It's not what I expected. I was always the rebellious one." Kaden let out a long sigh, and any hint of a smile faded into seriousness. "Honestly, I don't know if I'm the right one to do this."

Kyrin wasn't surprised he felt this way. She would feel like that too, but she reminded him, "Talas and Trask think you are."

He hung his head. "I've not always done the right thing in tough situations. I've let my temper and emotions get the best of me. Those don't seem like very good qualities for a leader. I'm not coolheaded like Marcus, and this isn't just training exercises. This is war. Men's lives are at stake." He looked at her, his eyes seeking. "You know me better than anyone. What do you think?"

Kyrin considered for a moment, but did not take long to answer. "I think knowing your weaknesses is a good first step in being a leader. You're not perfect, but neither are the rest of us. Talas and Trask wouldn't have chosen you if they didn't see qualities they desired in leading the riders. As for me, I know you can do it. It may take some work, but a willingness to learn is another mark of a good leader."

Kaden gave her a grateful smile, but some of the moisture had returned to his eyes. "That's why I wish Father were here, so he could teach me all that."

Kyrin swallowed hard. "I know . . . but there is still someone who can teach you." She held his gaze. "Marcus would be glad to."

Kaden didn't respond for a long moment. Going to Marcus for help and advice would not be easy for him.

Finally, he cleared his throat and nodded slowly. "Maybe I can talk to him tomorrow."

AT DAWN, CAMP bustled with the activity of a new day of preparation. The men didn't linger over breakfast to chat. There was too much work to be done. Kaden swallowed down his eggs and coffee without much thought, which was unusual, but food wasn't his priority this morning. Today he had to make sure his riders were ready for combat.

His riders.

He shook his head. He wouldn't get used to that any time soon. After all, hadn't he done almost everything possible back in Tarvin Hall to avoid promotion to this sort of position?

Still, he took it seriously—more seriously than he had taken anything else in his life besides looking out for Kyrin. And, all discomfort aside, he was determined to do it right and prove himself worthy of Talas and Trask's confidence, if only to himself.

When Marcus finished his breakfast and walked off with Liam, Kaden gulped down his last swallow of coffee. He followed, but his feet dragged. Why did it have to be so hard to ask his brother for advice? It wasn't that he disliked his brother, but there'd always been friction between them. Marcus always seemed to think he knew best, and most of the time he did. It was aggravating. If Kaden was honest, though, Marcus probably wasn't responsible for most of the friction. Kaden was the argumentative one.

"Marcus."

His older brother turned. "Yes?"

Kaden hesitated. Kyrin was right. Marcus would be happy to answer his questions and help him out, and he wouldn't be smug about it either. He was a better man than that. Though he'd never admit it, Kaden envied him, deep down—envied the calm, level-headed way his brother dealt with any situation thrown at him. He never let his emotions get the best of him, and if he had any of the Veshiron temper, Kaden had yet to see it. He was like their father that way. Maybe that's why this was so hard. Kaden didn't measure up to their father quite the way his brother did.

Trying to shrug off these uncomfortable thoughts, he cleared his throat. "Can we talk a minute?"

Marcus's brows rose just a fraction. "Sure." He looked over at Liam. "Get the men started on drills."

Liam glanced between the two of them, as if debating whether he should stay and act as a buffer, but then walked on to where the militia had gathered. Kaden watched him. On the topic of envy, it would be nice to have his next older brother's good nature right now. He got along well with all five of his siblings.

Kaden shifted his gaze back to Marcus, who waited patiently for him to speak. Though Kaden had three inches on him, his brother's steady confidence could be intimidating.

He breathed out. "Listen, you probably don't have time for this, but . . ." How did he put this without sounding entirely incompetent? "I could use a few tips on being a captain."

Marcus's brows rose higher, but as Kaden expected, there was no smugness or gloating, only genuine eagerness to help. "What do you want to know?"

How about everything? Kaden winced at his total lack of experience. Maybe he should have paid more attention in Tarvin Hall. "Well, I'm used to training them, but I've never really given them orders or had to lead them in any way."

"You've got a good start, especially since you've trained them from the beginning and you all know each other well," Marcus said. "The leading and the orders will probably come more naturally than you think, once you've had a little practice. The key is to lead by example. If they can see by your actions that you're a man worthy of their honor and respect, they'll be willing to follow you anywhere."

Kaden let out a slow breath. It was a tall order. What if he did something stupid in the heat of the moment and got them all killed?

Marcus must have sensed his uncertainty, as hard as he tried to hide it.

"Kaden, I already know you're that man. You just need the opportunity to prove it to them."

Kaden stared at his brother. Such praise meant more than he could say. "Thanks."

Marcus smiled. "Don't worry. You can do it. I saw the way the men responded when Trask gave them the news. They believe in you."

Marcus had worked with enough men over the years that Kaden couldn't doubt his words.

"If you have time," his brother said, "you can stick around for some of the practice drills and get a feel for giving commands. It won't be quite the same as flying, but it might help."

Kaden nodded, finally breaking into a smile himself. "I think I will."

Kyrin rushed outside to the meeting hall. Word of Leetra's return had spread quickly through camp, and she didn't want to miss anything. She met Timothy and Aaron along the way and smiled at them, but turned serious when they joined the gathering inside. Leetra stood in the center of the group, her hands on her hips as she took note of each of them. As soon as the necessary members were present, she shared her news.

"I was able to get close enough on foot to get a good look at Fort Rivor. Daican is definitely gathering his forces. Several companies of men showed up from the south and east while I was watching. I'd say there were almost twice as many men as when I flew over the area last winter. Looks like an invasion army to me."

Trask nodded gravely. "That confirms our information. It's an invasion army." After filling her in on the information they had gained in Ashwood, he asked, "Did it look as though they were preparing to leave?"

"Not immediately, but I can't imagine they'd need more men to invade Samara. There were thousands of them."

"The fact that they're still gathering does work in our favor. It gives us time to reach Samara before they do, and help the king prepare." Trask looked around at the group. "Whatever else you need to finish, do it today. We leave in the morning."

The men nodded, and marched out of the hall with a mission. Kyrin followed more slowly and stopped just outside. She watched her brothers head off in various directions—Marcus and Liam toward the gathering militia, and Kaden with Talas on their way to the dragons. She then looked about camp. Ronny and Meredith played some sort of game nearby. Michael was hurrying after Marcus, always around to watch the men practice.

A sigh seeped past her lips as a sudden wave of heaviness descended. She started when someone touched her shoulder, and looked over to see Rayad.

"Is something troubling you?" he asked, his eyes full of compassion.

"I was just thinking that nothing will be the same after this, will it?" She shook her head. "War can't leave things unchanged."

"No," Rayad murmured, "it can't."

Kyrin breathed hard. For days she had fought to avoid thoughts like this, but she would have to face it eventually. "Whatever happens, I'll probably make it back here, but will my brothers?" Her voice choked up. "Will Jace? Will you?"

Moisture flooded her eyes, building up on the rims, but she somehow kept the tears from falling. She tried to clear her voice. "I don't know if I can take any more loss."

She was afraid . . . no, terrified. That's what it came down to. Her father's death had so utterly crushed her heart that it wasn't even close to fully healing yet. How could it withstand being crushed again?

Rayad put his arm around her shoulders. She gave him a shaky, watery-eyed smile for the gesture of comfort. He was about as close to a father as she had left.

"These are hard and uncertain times we're living in," he said. "You never know what will still be here tomorrow. That's why we must take joy every day in what we do have, so it's something we can carry in our memories when things change."

Kyrin nodded. She knew all about carrying memories.

"I wish I could say everything will be all right," he continued, "but there will be times it won't seem like it. I just know, in the end, it will be. We just have to trust Elôm to get us from here to there."

"And He will," Kyrin said, her confidence returning.

Rayad smiled. "Yes, He will."

That evening, Kyrin and her family gathered at the table for supper, where Marcus led them in prayer. Though still new and growing in his faith, he had slipped into the role as head of the family as easily as his other leadership roles. Kyrin was glad of it. They had all needed that strength in the last months.

Passing around the food, unusual silence settled. Everyone must have had thoughts of the morning's departure, but didn't want to bring it up. Kyrin held onto the things Rayad had told her, but it was hard to keep her emotions from escalating.

Michael finally broke the silence. "I want to go with you."

All eyes turned to him. He looked at each of his older siblings, his face set in determination. When no one responded immediately, he said, "I want to help defend Samara."

"Michael," their mother murmured, "you can't."

Michael's brows scrunched together in stubbornness, reminding Kyrin of both their grandfather and Kaden.

"Why not? I'll be fourteen in a couple of months. Only three years younger than Kyrin and Kaden when they got involved in this. And I'm getting good with a sword. Just ask Marcus." His brown eyes darted to his oldest brother. "Tell her."

Marcus glanced at their mother before focusing on Michael. "I admit you're learning quickly, but . . ."

Anger fueled by hurt deepened Michael's frown. "But what?" His chest rose and fell heavily. "You don't think I'm strong enough?"

"You're not strong enough *yet*," Marcus said. "Trust me, your time will come, but you don't want to rush it."

Michael sat up taller. "But I want to help now. There might not be a Samara by the time you think I'm ready."

Ever calm, Marcus responded, "Remaining here does not mean you can't help. Don't underestimate the importance of this camp. Think of where we'd be without it. Whatever happens in Samara, people will continue to need shelter from the emperor."

He paused. The heaviness Kyrin had experienced all day appeared in his face as well.

"I don't know if we will make it back from Samara. If we don't, Warin will need the young men of this camp, like you, to rise up and help take care of things. You will become a man a lot sooner than you think, and part of that is learning to discern when it's right to follow the things you desire and when it isn't. We all must learn to put the needs of others above our personal wants and desires."

Michael hung his head and stared at his plate, but he didn't argue any further. Kyrin glanced across the table at Kaden. Even he appeared to be taking their brother's wisdom to heart.

Later that night, when only the women occupied the cabin, Kyrin climbed up to the loft with Meredith to get the little girl to bed. She helped her undress and slip into her nightgown before brushing and braiding her hair. When Kyrin pulled back the blankets of their bed, Meredith just stood looking at her, her large eyes watery.

Kyrin frowned lightly. "What's wrong?"

Meredith's lower lip quivered. "I don't want you to leave."

Kyrin let out a long breath, her heart squeezing painfully. She reached for Meredith, and the little girl wrapped her arms around Kyrin's waist. Kyrin held her this way a moment, and then sat down on the edge of the bed, Meredith cuddling in her lap.

"I wish I didn't have to leave you," Kyrin murmured, "but the people of Samara really need our help."

"What if you don't come back?"

"Well, I'm going to do everything I can to come back. And you can pray I'll come back."

Meredith nodded against Kyrin's chest.

"Pray for Kaden and the other men to come back too," Kyrin told her.

"I will." Meredith sniffed.

Kyrin rubbed her arm and then turned, patting the mattress. "Come on, let's try to sleep."

Meredith crawled to her spot, and Kyrin slipped off her boots to lie down beside her, holding her close.

"I want you to be my sister forever," Meredith said.

"Me too."

Kyrin kissed the top of her head and quietly hummed the tune of a lullaby Meredith had taught her that her parents used to sing. Meredith nestled against her, letting out a soft sigh. Kyrin continued to hum until her throat ached too much with emotion. By this time, Meredith's breathing had evened out in sleep. Kyrin lay still in the darkness for another few minutes, and two tears tracked down her face.

Afraid she would lose all composure, Kyrin rolled quietly out of bed, tucking the blankets around Meredith. Wiping her cheeks, she grabbed her boots and left the loft. Her mother and Lenae sat talking at the table.

"She's asleep," Kyrin whispered.

She walked to the door to set her boots down and looked out the window toward the fire pit. A few flames still licked at the logs. Three figures sat around the fire. In the orange glow, she saw Kaden's face and recognized their other two older brothers.

Not yet ready for sleep, Kyrin slipped her boots on and grabbed her coat. She stepped out into the cool night and pulled on her coat. Her brothers' deep voices and chuckles drew her closer. All three looked up when she reached the firelight.

"I hope I'm not interrupting any boy talk."

Marcus shook his head. "We were just remembering some of the things we used to do as kids."

Kyrin claimed a spot next to Kaden. "We sure had some fun."

"Remember the old swamp fort?" her twin asked.

Kyrin smiled fondly. "Oh, yes." Their mother never thought much of them always tromping home muddied and wet, but their father had built them a small fort there anyway, complete with a working drawbridge. Her smile sank into a frown. "Except you three always made me the princess trapped by cave drakes."

Marcus chuckled. "And Kaden was the evil knight standing guard."

"Was not," Kaden protested.

Kyrin lifted her brow wryly. "Actually, you were."

He couldn't argue with her memory so he shrugged. "Well, I had more fun throwing mud at Marcus than pretending to be the hero."

All four of them laughed. Of course, Marcus was always the hero coming to rescue the princess with his trusty companion Liam.

"Those were the days," Kyrin breathed.

Her brothers nodded.

"But I'll never forget that one time we came back plastered in mud and the General had come for a visit." Marcus shook his head. "He was furious."

Kyrin's mind jumped back to that day, but their grandfather's displeasure with them wasn't what stood out to her. It was his heated words with their father. He had tried to get their grandfather to understand that they were just children enjoying their play, but the General wouldn't have any of it. Apparently, he had believed they should act responsibly, even then. That was just before Kyrin and Kaden were taken away to Tarvin Hall.

Kyrin shook off these memories as Kaden murmured, "I wonder if he'll be in Samara."

They all looked at him.

"He'll be there," Marcus said with quiet certainty. "He'll be at the front, leading."

Silence settled as they each came to terms with this. It was the first time Kyrin had considered her brothers facing the General, their grandfather, in battle.

Strong rays of warm morning sunshine filtered through the budding branches into camp. Grabbing the saddle bar, Jace pulled himself up onto Gem's back. As he settled in for the long journey ahead, he looked down at Elanor and Elian. Even now, he wished this was a visit and not a goodbye. Just the other day he had wanted to leave camp, but now he wanted to stay so badly it was painful. If only he could get Kyrin to stay. But she never would, and he couldn't ask that of her. She needed to follow her brothers.

He glanced at her as she gave her mother one more tight hug. Where she went, he would go too. He may not be able to reveal his true feelings for her, but he intended to protect her to his dying breath, even if it meant laying aside his own desires.

When his gaze refocused on her, Elanor gave him an encouraging smile. "We'll be waiting for your return. Remember, you still have to show me Niton's tricks."

This pulled a smile from Jace, though a weak one. Too many uncertainties lay in the future. Trying to share a little of his sister's optimism, he said, "As soon as I get back."

She nodded, and Jace scanned the other mounting riders. Kyrin now sat on Ivoris, just to his right. Her cheeks were damp with tears, and he could understand just how she felt.

On the other side of her, Aaron and Timothy mounted their dragons. Aaron was armed with his bow and a sword while Timothy had a pair of short swords strapped to his back. Apparently, Darq had trained him over the winter in Dorland. Jace had been surprised by Timothy's decision to join them, though not quite so much as Leetra had been. She'd gaped at him for more than a second before recovering her usual stoic expression. It was hard to imagine Timothy as a warrior, but Jace had seen stranger things.

After giving his father, Baron Grey, a hug and Anne a parting kiss, Trask mounted last. From his dragon, he looked at Marcus, who sat on his horse at the head of the militia.

"We'll meet you in Samara," he said, his voice a little husky with emotion. "Make sure to give Ashwood a wide berth. You don't want any of Rothas's men to spot you."

Marcus gave a firm nod.

When Trask's attention returned to those who would remain behind, so did Jace's. They had all gathered in a close group to watch them leave. Most of the women had tears falling. Warin put his hand to Lenae's back as she dabbed her eyes, proud yet fearful to see her son, Jeremy, march off with the militia. So many painful partings, and all potentially separating for the rest of this life.

Jace cleared his throat. He shouldn't think such things. His thoughts were bleak enough already.

Baron Grey stepped forward, addressing the whole group. "We shall pray for all of you. May Elôm bring you back safely and spare Samara."

Trask nodded and, with determined eyes, looked at those willing to follow him into war. "Riders, let's fly."

Amidst final calls of farewell, the dragons took to the air a couple at a time. Jace looked down at Elanor and Elian once more, forcing his voice past his lips. "Goodbye."

"Goodbye, Jace," they replied as they backed away.

Tearing his eyes from them, he murmured, "Gem, *unai*," and soared up through the trees, joining the dragons filling the sky over Landale Forest.

-PART TWO-

ELON

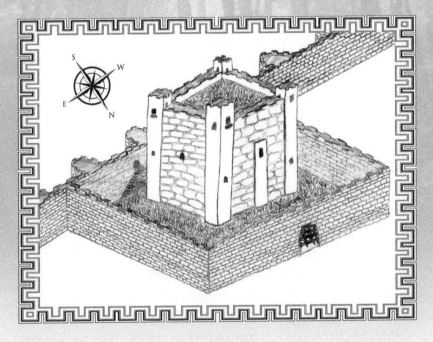

JACE STARED AT the sight before them. Even from more than a mile off, the great fortress of Stonehelm inspired awe. Built of the same type of golden-hued stone as Auréa Palace, it rose high above the horizon, settled on a rise overlooking the northern Arcacian plains. A wide river flowed at the base of the rise, appearing from here as a thin, sparkling, silver ribbon. The giant border wall stretched to the rocky cliffs to the east and then off toward the marshes farther west. It did indeed seem impenetrable, but then, Daican's army didn't need to penetrate it if they could invade by sea.

Grabbing his waterskin, Jace took a long drink as he waited with the others. Trask had taken Rayad, Tane, and Talas on ahead to the fortress to bring their good will. After all, a group of dragon riders could easily be mistaken as a threat, especially considering what they had witnessed just that morning.

His gaze strayed to the burned out homes and buildings smoldering not far from where they rested. An entire village destroyed. Only dragons or firedrakes could leave such destruction, and this wasn't the only devastation they had come upon as they drew near to Samara. It made no sense that the emperor would have Arcacian villages destroyed until Rayad explained that many Samarans had lived peacefully for generations just over the border of their own land, but no more. If the Samarans weren't sure of war before, they would be now.

Capping the waterskin, he hung it back over his saddle and rubbed his eyes. They stung under his eyelids as if they hadn't closed in ages. Five days of travel wore on everyone, but for him it was more. Left entirely to his own thoughts day after day, he had tried to sort through the conflict and confusion in his heart. He wanted to do as his mother asked him, but after the first two days, he just couldn't do it anymore. It left him too disturbed and frustrated.

Maybe that was what had caused the nightmares to start on the second night. So far, he didn't think he had woken anyone but Rayad, thankfully, but the dreams crept in every night. Strangely, they weren't his usual visions of violence and condemning voices. These were vague and dark, and full of despair. In most, he died or was already dead and surrounded by emptiness. It was a deep, black void with nothing or no one but himself and his pain. He would try to run—try to escape, to fight—until he was nearly delirious with desperation. Then he would wake up, gasping and shaking and far more exhausted than when he'd fallen asleep.

He sighed deeply, almost preferring his old nightmares. Maybe because these new ones too closely mirrored his deepest fears. He could not help but dwell on them as they neared Samara to do battle. For any one of them, death could be only a short time away. What then? What would happen to him? Would his soul go to Elôm as he had once believed? Would he simply cease to exist? Or would it be something even worse than that? Would his nightmares become reality? A hard shudder passed through him. Even now, he felt as though he were fighting it, just like in the dreams.

He caught Kyrin watching him, her eyes searching and worried. He cleared his expression, but little good that would do now. She had already seen all. Avoiding her gaze, he turned to Gem and absently worked one of the buckles on her saddle. If Kyrin thought he was busy, maybe she wouldn't try to talk to him. It was just too difficult to explain, and he already knew what she would say anyway.

Neither of them had much time to talk since leaving Landale. They stopped for only short intervals during the day to eat and rest the dragons. At sunset, they set down to camp, ate supper, and turned in shortly after. In that brief time, Jace had begun Kyrin's knife lessons. However, that brought a new challenge he had not anticipated. She learned fast since she never forgot anything, but every time he had to touch her to adjust her stance or to guide her, he struggled against wanting more—wanting to take her hand and not let go, or hold her for more than a brief hug. Even now, he scowled thinking of it. Why must everything in his life be a battle?

At the sound of wings, Jace looked up. Trask and the others had nearly reached the group. Good thing too. Kyrin looked to have been on her way to talk to him. Now all attention focused on the returning riders. They slid down and everyone gathered around Trask.

"Are we welcome?" Holden asked.

Trask nodded. "The captain at the fortress understands that we are allies. He has sent a messenger to Westing Castle just northwest of the fortress to announce our arrival. Apparently, that is where King Balen is staying."

"Not at the capital?"

"Apparently not, but it will be good for us to be able to give him our information right away. He'll be able to put a plan into action immediately. We'll give the rider a chance to get there and then head that direction ourselves."

"How does the fortress look from inside?" Aaron asked.

"Strong. If Daican didn't have other plans, I'd almost believe it could keep him out. They seem to have a large, well-trained garrison there." Trask frowned. "But there were many civilians, most of them wounded in some manner. I didn't ask, but I assume they are from the burned-out villages."

At least some had survived.

For nearly twenty minutes, they waited before climbing atop their dragons once more. In the air, they flew northwest toward the prominently-placed Westing Castle. This gave the riders a good view of Stonehelm from above. The keep was a giant square, with rounded turrets at each of the four corners. A strong curtain wall encompassed it on all sides.

They approached the castle rapidly. Like Stonehelm, it sat upon a hill. A village and many acres of farmland spread out around it like a skirt. Villagers worked busily at tilling the fields and putting in their crops. Jace scanned the land ahead. Aside from the dense forest to their left, there wasn't much for trees— just open plains blanketed in dry, golden grass with the tint of green from new shoots beginning to grow. It had a certain beauty to it, but he much preferred the forest. There was no cover or protection on the plains.

They landed in a vacant, untilled field just outside the village. In only moments, a group of curious onlookers gathered. Leaving Kaden's men to keep an eye on things, the rest of the group followed Trask up the road toward the castle. Though he kept inconspicuously to the center of the group, Jace looked around curiously. He had seen many crowds of people, but this was his first time outside of Arcacia. These people were similar to the villagers of Landale, but more rugged. They looked strong, just like their surroundings, and ready to fight if need be. Even the women were not to be taken lightly.

At the top of the sloping hill, the guards admitted them into the castle courtyard, and Jace looked up at the castle itself. Though it was half Stonehelm's size, it was still very large and impressive. Like the fortress, its design was simple and it appeared that it could withstand a small siege itself.

Before they had crossed half the stone-paved courtyard, a man met their company. He was average height, but strongly built, and had short-cropped black hair. A faint scar cut through his beard on the right side of his chin. He had the appearance and bearing of a military man, dressed in Samara's official burgundy and black.

"Welcome to Westing," he greeted in a deep voice. "I am Mason, commanding general of Samara's military force."

Trask introduced himself, and the two of them shook hands.

"I was with Baron Thomas when he received news of your arrival," Mason said. "He is waiting. I will show you inside."

They followed the general through the heavy oak doors and into the castle. The halls were dim and chilly as Jace expected, but furnished with enough tapestries and other colorful objects to keep it from being too bleak. Still, he would never like castles.

As they neared the deeper interior, the stone walls gave way to wood beams and paneling. Off the main hall, Mason led them into a large meeting room occupied by a long table overhung with three chandeliers in the center.

A man waited there. Like General Mason, his hair and beard were short, but white. He stepped forward to welcome them and introduce himself as the Baron of Westing. Though the lines creasing his weathered face hinted at worry, he had a soft-spoken and calm manner. In ways, he reminded Jace of Baron Grey.

"I've sent for refreshments." The baron gestured to the table. "Please, sit down. I'm sure it's no short trip from Landale, even with dragons."

Trask thanked him, and they all found seats around the table. Jace claimed one next to Kyrin. She offered him a brief smile, but the look in her eyes said she was still thinking about what she must have seen on his face. One of these days, she would start questioning him.

Baron Thomas and General Mason took seats across from Trask, who said, "We heard at the fortress that King Balen is here."

Baron Thomas nodded. "He is in the fields. I sent for him as soon as I received your message. I'm sure he'll be here shortly. No doubt he spotted your arrival. That sort of thing would be hard to miss, especially these days. Everyone is on edge."

"We noticed the burned villages on the way here," Trask said. "I'm terribly sorry."

Thomas sighed heavily, his worry lines deepening. "It is a tragedy. Many lives were lost, and more and more wounded show up every day. We tried to warn people to come back behind our borders, but how could they just leave their homes? I don't blame them for staying." He paused, a look of resignation settling in his expression. "I assume, especially coming with such a large company, that you do not bring good news."

Trask shook his head. "I'm afraid not, but we do hope we can help."

For the next half hour, Trask, the baron, and Mason discussed the developments in Arcacia. The two men took the news with grim acceptance, neither one of them surprised. How could they be, with the steps Daican had already taken to attack them? The villagers in Samara should have heeded the warnings, but hadn't Jace wanted to stay at the farm after Kalli and Aldor died? This was no different.

The hall doors creaked open a short time later, and everyone looked up.

Baron Thomas pushed up from his chair. "My lord."

The others rose as well to get their first look at the king. He was tall and strong, matching Jace closely in height and build, and no more than ten years Jace's senior. His stature befitted a king, but that was as far as his appearance of royalty went. Perspiration dampened his forehead and the strands of shoulder-length, dark blond hair that fell from the rest he had tied back behind his head. At least a couple of days' worth of stubble darkened his jaw, and dirt smudged his skin and sweat-darkened shirt. When Baron Thomas said the king was in the fields, Jace had assumed he meant inspecting them, not working them.

The young king's gaze swept over the group. He could have fooled anyone into thinking he was nothing more than an ordinary farmer or woodsman, but the keen look in his pale blue eyes spoke of something deeper than his simple, rugged appearance.

Baron Thomas stepped forward and promptly introduced Trask. Brushing a rough hand on his dusty pants, Balen offered it to Trask.

"Welcome to Samara," the king greeted, his tone deep and rich, yet not as refined as Baron Thomas's. He took time to look at each of them. "All of you."

257

They nodded, and Trask thanked him.

"Please, forgive my delay," Balen said. "We had but one more row to finish."

Trask shook his head, waving off the apology. "The baron has made us all very comfortable. The hospitality of Westing surpasses that of many in Arcacia."

"Good." Balen's face sobered. "So you bring word of Emperor Daican?"

Trask nodded.

"Is it war?"

"Yes, my lord, unfortunately."

Balen released a slow breath, letting this news settle with the same somber acceptance as the baron and general.

"But we also bring detailed information of the emperor's plans that may help you hold him off," Trask added quickly.

Balen's expression lifted. "I'm anxious to hear it. And now, if you'll excuse me to clean up, I'll be back shortly to discuss it."

"Of course."

As the king left the hall, everyone resumed their seats. No one spoke for a moment or two. Jace still had to get used to the idea of royalty out tilling the fields. To think of the emperor doing such a thing was laughable, but Balen was clearly no ordinary king. Jace looked over at Kyrin, who looked just as surprised. He would have liked to know what she thought of Samara's unique king.

THE KING RETURNED less than twenty minutes later. Though he had changed, his attire was no more regal than before. Just sturdy linen and a simple leather jerkin. Kyrin had met her share of nobles and royalty, but King Balen was nothing like she had expected. He didn't even seem like a king at all, yet his humility was refreshing. If only Emperor Daican had half as much.

When he reached the table, Baron Thomas rose to give him the seat directly across from Trask.

"Thank you," he murmured before his serious gaze focused on Trask. "So what is the emperor's plan concerning Samara?"

Trask laid out all that they knew of Daican's coming invasion, including how they had come by the information and what Leetra had seen of the gathering forces at Fort Rivor. Near the end, he slid a stack of parchments across the table.

"These are the copies Kyrin made of Daican's letters. As far as we know without being able to see the letters Rothas sent in reply, they contain all the details for their attack."

Balen fingered through the letters, scanning the pages before handing them to Mason. He looked at Kyrin.

"Miss Altair, I thank you for the risk you took to secure this information for us. Without it, we would have been ill-prepared for a surprise attack on our capital."

"I hope it is enough to stop Daican from expanding his rule beyond Arcacia." She lowered her voice. "He's done enough harm already."

Balen spoke gently in reply. "I know of your loss, and I am sorry." His ruggedly handsome face displayed deep and genuine remorse.

"Thank you," Kyrin replied, holding her emotions in check. It wouldn't do to get weepy now, especially when an entire country was in peril.

His gaze returned to Trask. "You've all done an admirable thing by coming here when you clearly have enough trouble at home."

"As Kyrin said, we all hope that with Elôm's help we can stop Daican. After all, Elôm has not yet allowed Samara to fall to an enemy force."

At these words, Balen hung his head as if weighed down by a heavy burden. "That is true of more faithful generations, but I fear for this one." He looked up. "It pains me to say the great faith Samara once had is failing. Many have turned to the worship of Aertus and Vilai, or ceased believing altogether. I've done all I can to steer the people back to true faith, but to no avail. I fear what it will take to gain their attention."

Kyrin glanced around at everyone's somber faces. Now was when the people most needed to turn to Elôm. She prayed Elôm would overlook Samara's faithlessness and still give them victory over Daican. To think of Samara falling, after how hard they were trying to save it, left a slight burn of indignation towards those who had abandoned the faith that had kept them safe all these many years.

"I believe the greatest assets we have available to us right now are prayer and preparation," Baron Thomas said.

Balen agreed. "We already have almost half our forces stationed around Amberin. We can send the men from the northern outposts to aid them and ready the fleet." He turned to Mason. "Do you believe we have enough men here to defend Stonehelm?"

Mason gave a firm nod. "It would take more than a half-hearted attempt by the emperor to breach the fortress. If we're not facing the full power of Arcacia, then I believe the garrison we have now will be sufficient."

"Your greatest concern will be firedrakes," Trask said.

Balen turned back to him. "Those are the beasts that destroyed the villages?"

"Yes. Somehow the emperor has discovered how to crossbreed dragons and cave drakes, resulting in these hybrid firedrakes." Trask grimaced. "A group of cretes, about eight of them that we know of for sure, have joined the emperor for reasons unknown to us. They are led by a crete named Falcor Tarn."

Kyrin glanced down at Leetra. The young woman's eyes turned icy at the mention of her former fiancé. None of them had completely gotten over his betrayal and the consequences of it.

"From what we've been able to gather," Trask continued, "Falcor has been training an army of men to ride the firedrakes. We believe he has about sixty of them ready for combat."

"Sixty?" Balen repeated. It was no small number for them to try to defend against, especially when they had never faced such a foe before. "Do they have any weaknesses?"

Trask deferred to Talas, nodding for his input.

Talas leaned forward, resting his elbows on the table. "If you've witnessed them, then you have seen they are nearly twice the size of our dragons and more heavily armored. We faced a small group of them in Valcré last winter. They are fast enough to keep up with our dragons in a straight flight path, but cannot maneuver as quickly. Like any flying creature, their wings are the most vulnerable. Take away their ability to fly, and you take away most of their power."

261

"How do you propose we fight them?" Mason asked.

"Unfortunately, arrows would be nearly useless against them, but we don't intend for you to have to fight them." Talas motioned to Trask, who took over once more.

"We have brought along our dragon riders to help. There are twenty-three of them who have been training to combat the drakes. Kaden," he nodded to him, "is their captain. We are also expecting help from the cretes. Our ally, Captain Verus Darq, left for Dorland several days ago to recruit crete riders willing to come and fight. We hope to have a flying force equal to Daican's."

Balen stared at them in both awe and relief. No doubt he had feared the worst for his country, but they had brought him hope. "Your aid is more than generous."

"Whatever fight involves Daican is our fight too," Trask responded.

Though clearly as thankful as the king to have their aid, General Mason still wore a look of concern. "These firedrakes; what can we do if they decide to attack the villages within our border before we have a large enough force to face them?"

"Well, we would certainly try to stop them, but if Daican wanted to use them to destroy your villages, he would have done it already." Trask rested back in his chair. "Daican is cunning. The destroyed villages were likely a show of strength. I'm sure he wants you to surrender without much of a fight. He wants to rule Samara, not destroy it. It wouldn't benefit him to wreak havoc here unless it was needed to defeat you."

Mason nodded in acceptance of this, and Balen turned to him.

"We must get word to Amberin to the queen."

This was the first Kyrin had heard of any queen, and there was no indication of Balen being married. Now she would have liked to know a bit more about Samara's recent history. She had learned little of the country while at Tarvin Hall, considering its long history of faith in Elôm. Perhaps Rayad or Trask could tell her more later.

"I'll go over these letters," Mason said, "and have someone sent to Amberin to prepare the defense there."

"Yes, good," Balen replied.

Trask leaned forward to gain their attention. "Might I suggest doing this quietly? If we can maintain the element of surprise and keep Daican from realizing that we are aware of his plans, it could work in our favor. He may have spies within your border, so you could use the attacks on the villages as an excuse to fortify without it being known that it's directly to counter the emperor."

Mason agreed. "I'll see to it that only our most trusted captains are aware until the rest of our forces need to know. And the queen, of course. We'll have to take extra precautions to see that she is secure."

Now that their plans were set in motion, Balen stood and addressed them all as a group. "Please, let me show you to rooms where you may rest before supper."

Sliding back their chairs, they all followed him. This was something Kyrin would have expected a servant to do, but Balen showed no aversion to it. Again, it was as if he had no royal standing and was just an ordinary man.

He led them to a long hall on the second floor of the castle, gesturing to the closed doors. "Use as many rooms as you need. There is a sitting room at the end of the hall." He turned to Trask. "Do you want me to send for the rest of your men?"

"Thank you, but we'll be heading down there for our things anyway."

"Do you need help or a wagon?"

Trask smiled. "I think we'll manage. Is it all right for us to leave our dragons outside the village? They'll stay where we command them, but we don't want to cause any discomfort or fear among the villagers, considering the attacks."

"That will be fine. I'll have word spread that they are not a threat, but to give them space. Is there anything else you need? Would you like baths drawn?"

"I think the women might appreciate that." Trask nodded to Kyrin and Leetra. "But the rest of us can make do."

"I'll let the servants know and see that they bring fresh water to each of the rooms. If you need anything else, they'll be around and I'll be with Thomas and General Mason in the meeting hall."

"Thank you again, my lord, for your generous hospitality."

Once Balen had left them, they returned to the dragons to unsaddle them and gather their supplies. Kyrin pulled her unbuckled saddle off Ivy and started arranging her things on it so she could carry it all together. When she reached for one of her larger packs, Jace bent down near her.

"Let me carry it for you."

She looked up with a smile. "Thank you."

He only nodded, avoiding her eyes.

She watched him, even when he turned away. The deep heaviness that had been present for days resurfaced inside her. She still wanted to talk to him about the look she'd seen on his face earlier. What was going on with him? It didn't seem to be anything like she had faced with him before. It was something deeper and darker that she couldn't seem to find a way to fix. Why couldn't he just let these things go and trust her and Rayad for once? Surely his mother had given him encouragement. Had he forgotten it already?

Back at the castle, they divided into their rooms. Kyrin shared one of the smaller ones with Leetra. Setting their things down in the middle of the floor, they inspected the quarters. Warm wood paneled the walls and a large window faced the south. Kyrin walked over to it, leaning on the sill to look out over the surrounding village. Everything seemed so peaceful . . . for now.

Servants arrived shortly with a metal tub. It took many trips to fill it several inches with warm water. Guilt pricked Kyrin about them having to lug so much water upstairs just so she and Leetra could have the luxury of a bath, but they seemed to tend their work happily. Serving such a king as Balen, that didn't surprise her. If Daican had been like him, Kyrin would have loved her job at the palace.

When they finished, the tub half full, Kyrin looked at Leetra. The water wouldn't stay very warm for the second person. But Leetra just waved her toward it.

"You can go first." No great generosity softened her tone, just a simple matter-of-factness that was the norm for her.

Kyrin didn't argue. She was getting used to the cretes' ways by now. Stepping behind the privacy screen where the bath was set, she undressed and slipped into the water. The warmth felt good, and she would appreciate being clean after sleeping on the ground for several nights. She grabbed a bar of soap that was scented lightly with sweet-smelling herbs and scrubbed herself and her hair that was well past her shoulders now. It was still not long enough to be rid of the stigma of shame back in Arcacia, but at least it was easier to hide now.

Kyrin didn't linger in the tub. She wanted to leave some warm water for Leetra. After drying off, she changed into a clean outfit. There hadn't been room for anything fancy, but she put on one of her best embroidered linen shirts and leggings, and a soft suede overdress. Normally, she'd feel out of place among royalty in such garb, but that wouldn't be a factor here. In fact, leather seemed prominent in Samaran fashion, so she would fit right in.

Running her fingers through her wet hair, Kyrin stepped around the screen and stopped. Leetra perched on the footboard of one of the beds and tossed a length of rope over one of the beams in the ceiling. Then she jumped down soundlessly and proceeded to hang up her sleeping hammock. Hands on her hips, she nodded in satisfaction.

Aside from when they traveled and slept on the ground, Kyrin had yet to see Leetra sleep anywhere but her hammock. Even when the dead of winter had forced her inside from her usual spot in the trees, she had hung her hammock in the rafters of Lenae's cabin.

"The bath is all yours," Kyrin said, overlooking the crete's seemingly odd habits. Nothing would surprise her anymore, especially when it came to Leetra.

Leetra grabbed her pack and stepped behind the screen while Kyrin walked around to the other bed. She sat down on the edge and leaned back, sinking into the soft pillows with a sigh. She would be content to stay right here until suppertime.

The sun was close to setting when Kyrin joined the men and followed them down to the dining room that evening. Burgundy cloths draped two long tables that were set with pewter-ware to accommodate all of them. The candles on two grand chandeliers overhanging each table flickered, giving the room a warm glow. Balen and Baron Thomas waited near the door for them, along with a third man about the same age as the baron. Though his hair was mostly white, his eyes were as clear and observant as a man half his age. A kind smile wrinkled his face as they drew near.

Balen met them and motioned to the older man. "I'd like to introduce you to an old friend and counselor of mine, Josef. He's our physician and would-be scholar if he were not so good in medicine."

Josef greeted them all in a warm and friendly way that Kyrin found most endearing. The king's fondness for him was understandable. He had a gentleness about him that would put anyone at ease—a valuable quality to have as a physician.

Spreading out around the tables, they took seats. Silence settled and all attention turned to Balen as he offered a prayer. If only the royalty of Arcacia had such faith! Tears prickled Kyrin's eyes at such a thought. Life would be so different.

When the prayer ended, servants quickly served a mouth-watering meal. They set a large plate before Kyrin that almost overflowed with food. There were butter-glazed potatoes, juicy carrots, a thick slice of fresh bread, and succulent pieces of dark meat smothered in thick gravy. She took a bite. The meat was much like venison, yet more savory and tender.

All around her, the men seemed very appreciative of the fare, especially Kaden. He probably hadn't enjoyed such a meal since dining at Auréa Palace. No one spoke for a good couple of minutes, enjoying it to the fullest. After five days of mostly cold trail food, they must have seemed a bit starved to their hosts.

Finally, Rayad looked up and asked, "What is the meat?"

"Black deer," Balen answered.

"Brought in fresh by the king himself," Thomas added, "right from Feldmor Forest just to the southwest of here."

"It is quite good."

The baron nodded. "It is a staple around these parts, and our cook knows just how to prepare it."

"So Feldmor is good hunting then?" Trask joined in.

"Very," Balen answered enthusiastically. "It may not be as large as the northern forests, but there's plenty of game."

"And he knows it as well as this castle," Thomas said. "He could track a mouse in that forest."

A charming grin rose to Balen's face, his first since their arrival. Kyrin imagined it would be easy to fall quite in love with him were she a Samaran lady.

"Maybe not a mouse, but I am pretty familiar with it. I did spend much of my childhood there."

Though not usually one to jump into a conversation, this piqued Kyrin's curiosity. There was much to learn about this intriguing and unlikely king. "Did you grow up here in Westing?"

"I did. My parents died when I was small, and my aunt and uncle raised me on their farm. That's where I was today, working one of my uncle's fields."

"If I may," Kyrin ventured tentatively, "how did you become king?"

Balen's eyes sparkled in response. "That's a good question. It ties in with Feldmor, actually. I was fifteen and went out to hunt one of the wildcats that come down from the mountains sometimes. It had killed two villagers and quite a few livestock. I have to confess that it was against my uncle's better judgment, but I went out to track it. When I finally caught up, I found it in a tree about to pounce on a group of hunters. I shot it just as it lunged. Only after that did I discover that the man it would have landed on was King Alton. He and his knights had come for a hunting trip."

"He saved the king's life," Thomas said.

"Well, I don't know about that, but he always believed so. In gratitude, he invited me to the palace at Amberin as his personal guest." Balen paused, and his face took on a wistful expression. "After a couple of weeks there, he told me he wanted to adopt me as his son and heir since his wife, Queen Rhosin, was barren. He was so adamant, I couldn't refuse."

He paused for a moment as a sigh slipped out, his voice lowering with true sadness. "Two years ago, he became ill and died, and I was crowned king."

It all made sense now, the king's humble manner. He had grown up as a simple farm boy.

"Personally, I think it was one of the wisest decisions the king ever made," Baron Thomas said after a momentary silence.

"Indeed," Josef agreed.

Though she barely knew him, Kyrin felt inclined to agree as well. She had never known anyone like Balen who held as much power as he did. Of course, Trask and his father were humble and wonderful leaders, but Balen made such an unassuming and unusual king. She had a feeling that if he and Kaden were the same age and had lived in the same area, they would have been marvelous friends growing up.

Balen smiled kindly at Thomas and Josef. "Thank you. I'm not sure where I'd be without your confidence in me."

For a time, they continued to speak of Westing and the surrounding area. Kyrin listened intently, interested to learn as much as she could about the country and its culture. This was the first time she had ever set foot outside of Arcacia. She used to dream of seeing more of Ilyon.

During a lull in the conversation, Timothy's voice came from down the table. Kyrin had sensed his desire to speak, almost since arriving here.

"Daican's letters to Sir Rothas mentioned a man named Elon and rumors about him. Is there any truth to them?"

Josef, who did more listening than talking, turned his gaze to Timothy. "There has been word coming from the mountain villages northeast of here of a man who has been teaching and healing the people. And these aren't traditional healings such as my work, but miraculous healings . . . instant healings of a large variety of ailments, including serious and lifelong afflictions."

"How is that possible?" Trask asked.

"Well, if you've heard the rumors, then you know that many say he was sent by Elôm . . ." Josef paused. "Some even say he's the Savior, Elôm's Son."

Just like when Kyrin had mentioned it in the meeting hall, silence settled around them. A thrilling chill raced along Kyrin's skin. Even if it were not true, the possibility left her breathless and sent her thoughts soaring.

"Do you think . . . could it be?" Timothy asked, as if hardly daring to hope.

Josef's eyes twinkled at his enthusiasm. "I do not know. We've had only secondhand accounts. Not enough to say for certain. We do know that the people hope he will bring an end to Daican's rule and restore peace to Ilyon. That hope alone could lead to misinformation and exaggerated accounts of what's happening. But . . ." the word hung over the table, "we do know Elôm promised a Savior, and if ever we were in need of one, it's now."

DEEP, BLACK DARKNESS *surrounded Jace, so thick it chilled his skin. It consumed him, suffocated him. He struggled to move as heavy weights dragged behind him. Despair saturated the murk, but then a pinprick of light appeared in the distance. It grew to a faint glow, beckoning him, tugging at his spirit. He reached and tried to run toward it, but his feet caught fast in an unseen mire. The light began to fade.* No! *He lunged for it, choking. He couldn't seem to breathe. In spite of his desperate struggle, the light blinked out, engulfing him once more in total darkness. His heart stopped in utter hopelessness. He fell to his knees and gasped for breath, but his throat had closed, leaving him sinking toward death.*

Jace bolted upright. His heart battered his ribs, as if trying to break past prison bars. Dryness scraped his throat. Frantic to break free of the dream's cold grip, he pushed up from the couch and almost fell, his legs entangled in his blanket. He tugged it away and stumbled across the room to the table, where a pitcher sat. Pouring a glass of water, he gulped it down, nearly drowning himself to quench his thirst.

He set the empty glass aside and braced himself against the table. Coldness traveled along his skin, raising goose bumps underneath his dampened shirt. He shivered and spasms darted through his limbs. Now that the adrenaline was wearing off, his legs barely had the strength to support him. He turned and sank back down onto the couch, resting his arms on his knees as he bowed his head. He struggled to breathe evenly, but his heart still pounded and filled the silence with its drumming.

As soon as everyone had fallen asleep in the bedroom he shared with Rayad, Holden, and Trask, he had slipped out to sleep in the sitting room instead. He'd known the dreams would come. He breathed a long, heavy breath, the last of his strength seeping away with it. Would it ever end? His eyes stung, and he rubbed the sensation away with his fingertips, but it only increased at the memories of the dream.

Tonight was the first time a light had appeared. The first time there had been any hope in the consuming darkness. But what good was hope he could not reach? He shook his head. It was only a dream, yet it felt like so much more. Like the manifestation of the struggle raging inside him. A struggle he wasn't sure he could win.

Dawn's light grew around him and illuminated the room. Even then, he just sat and stared. He may be awake now, but the dream's darkness still hung over him. Before long, the door opened and several of the men entered, including Rayad.

"There you are." Rayad's gaze settled on the blanket, and his forehead creased. "Did you sleep here?"

Jace said nothing. He wouldn't discuss it now with everyone gathering. As more of the group joined them, Jace grabbed the blanket and headed alone to the bedroom to change. Just this simple chore seemed to require more energy than he possessed, but what choice did he have except to push on every day for however many were left? A cold sensation seized his gut. Why did he get the ominous feeling it wouldn't be many?

Cleaned up and dressed, but still burdened, he returned to the sitting room. The rest of their company had gathered, except for Talas and Kaden who had chosen to stay with the dragons. Jace caught Kyrin's eyes as he entered, but wouldn't hold them. It was torture to face her these days. He couldn't bear for her to see him like this. He must be such a disappointment to her. She always tried so hard to help him.

When he chanced another glance, sadness weighed down her expression. Pain stabbed his heart. He would do anything for her, yet he was the one who always caused her the most grief. How could he ever claim to love her knowing that?

Kyrin picked at her breakfast, not really tasting any of it. Though she tried to be attentive to the conversation at the table, her thoughts and gaze kept straying to Jace. He hardly ate anything either. Something had happened when they'd left Landale. He was struggling before that, but now he seemed to be on a downward spiral. His life seemed to be falling apart right in front of her. Had he just completely forgotten anything that she, Rayad, or his mother had ever told him? Sometimes she just wanted to grab him and force him to understand. She bit back a sigh.

When the others had finished their breakfast, the entire group left the dining room and trooped outside. King Balen and General Mason were eager to show them around Stonehelm and begin war preparations. Under normal circumstances, Kyrin would have enjoyed a chance to explore the magnificent fortress, but she had no interest for it today. Her thoughts and heart were too heavy.

On the edge of the dragon field, Kyrin slipped over next to Rayad. "Can we talk?"

He stopped, and they let the others pass by them. When everyone else was busy saddling their dragons, she turned to face him.

"Jace is having nightmares again, isn't he?"

Rayad nodded, his face grim. "Yes, since the second night of our journey. Maybe even before that, I'm not sure."

Kyrin bit her lip. How could anyone cope with having their sleep disrupted so terribly every night? No wonder he looked more exhausted each day. "Why now? What caused it?"

"After what happened in Ashwood with his family, I think he is in a very confused and fragile state. The enemy is taking advantage of it and attacking him with everything he's got."

"Is there any way we can help him? I mean, I've tried, but he just won't respond."

"We can fight for him in prayer, but only Elôm can help him truly conquer this."

Kyrin looked over at Jace. He moved and went through the motions as if he were not truly there. Rayad was right. A battle raged over Jace. It was suddenly so clear to her that she almost cried. The enemy fought to destroy him, to tear away his faith and hold him captive until he gave up entirely. Blinking back the burn of tears, Kyrin drew a deep breath. She would pray harder—much harder—and fight for Jace even if he was too weak to do it himself.

"It's not like last time, is it?" She looked up at Rayad again. "Last time he was just giving up under his grief and depression. This time, he's afraid. I see it when he doesn't realize I'm watching. He looks so scared sometimes."

Rayad sighed. "Yes, that is the problem. He is running scared, trying to escape what he can't and too afraid to seek the only One who can allay his fears. Too afraid to seek help and be rejected. I believe that is at the root of it all. He's not yet willing to take that chance."

Kyrin bowed her head, a huge weight pressing down on her heart. "He's too young to suffer so much. He can't go on like this. I'm afraid . . ." She hesitated to speak the words aloud. "I'm afraid if something doesn't change, he won't survive it."

With the admission of this horrible fear, a couple of tears rolled down her cheeks. She brushed them away, but the fear remained.

"I know," Rayad murmured, his voice weary with the burden of the same fear. He reached out and hugged her gently. "But don't forget that Jace has a powerful force on his side. You and I aren't the only ones who see his struggle, and Elôm isn't deaf to all the prayers we offer on his behalf. The battle may be long and painful, but I believe in victory if we don't give up. Jace isn't as alone in this as he thinks."

Never had Jace seen such an imposing structure up close. Stonehelm had looked impressive enough from the air, but from the ground it was even grander. Leaving the dragons outside the wall, they followed Balen and his general to the towering gate. The archway loomed a good twenty-five feet above them. Jace gazed upward as they passed under the points of the raised portcullis. The reinforced iron and wood gates stood open, but could close as a second layer of protection in the event of a siege.

Voices drew his attention to the path ahead as they entered the inner courtyard. He expected to see soldiers, but groups of weary-eyed villagers, many with bandages and soot-smeared clothing, outnumbered the armed men. Their bleak faces appeared hopeless until they spotted their king. As he approached, their expressions lifted, and they bowed their heads in respectful greeting.

One of the first they met was an ancient old woman, who sat on an overturned basket. Balen stopped and took the hand that wasn't heavily bandaged.

"How are you today, Marta?" he asked gently.

Did he know all their names? Jace couldn't imagine it. He couldn't even remember the names of every person in camp.

The woman's wrinkled face lifted to Balen, creasing even more in a smile so bright and cheerful it seemed entirely out of place amid the obvious suffering. "Still alive, by Elôm's grace. That is more than I can say for many."

Balen smiled in return. "Indeed."

Josef came to the old woman's side and rested his hand on her shoulder. "Let's take a look at your arm this morning and see how it's healing."

While the physician tended her, Balen led the group on toward the entrance of the keep.

Trask gestured to the people. "Are they all refugees from the Arcacian villages?"

Balen nodded. "Yes, those fortunate to have made it. This is the best shelter we have for them right now."

They entered the cool, dim interior of the keep and found even more people, many laid out on stretchers. The scent of blood and strong medicinal herbs hung heavy in the air. Jace's stomach churned.

"The seriously wounded are tended here. Severe burn wounds, mostly." Balen shook his head. "We've never seen anything like it."

"It shouldn't be this way," Talas replied, his voice hard and lacking any of his usual humor. "We use our dragons in combat when we must, but never on the innocent. Daican has done a great evil by breeding his firedrakes and using them for such destruction. I'm ashamed that some of my people are involved."

Balen offered him a look of understanding. "It is also your people who can help us defeat them. We are incredibly grateful for that."

They continued through the fortress as Balen explained how they had a fully stocked storeroom, armory, and infirmary, and two inside wells with fresh water. Jace only half listened to the details. The keep was solid stone with almost no windows; good for defense, but such a closed space suffocated him. The dark halls brought back snatches of his dreams, and his heart rate rose. After a while, beads of sweat trickled down his back despite the cool air. The urge to escape clawed deeper and deeper into his chest. But what would he say to the others if he had to leave? How could he explain his fear?

At last Balen opened a door, and they stepped out into the courtyard once more. Jace released a heavy breath, his tense muscles easing. Somehow he had to get a grip on this, and quickly. He couldn't avoid the fortress with war coming.

Across the courtyard, they reached a set of stairs at the border wall. The others immediately followed Balen as he climbed them, but Jace paused to peer up at the towering structure. This gave him no more comfort than the fortress, but at least he wasn't closed in. Keeping as close to the wall as he could, Jace took each of the steps without letting himself look towards the increasing drop into the courtyard just to his right. Fifty feet up, they reached the top of the wall, which spanned an impressive twenty-feet wide. Plenty of room for defenders. The parapet rose to about chest height and, at one-hundred-fifty-foot intervals, rounded bastions jutted out, each equipped with a trebuchet. Daican's army would be hard-pressed to scale these defenses. How long must it have taken to build such a giant structure?

Cautiously, Jace stepped to the parapet with the others to take in the vast view of the Arcacian plains. No army could come upon the fortress by surprise. The wall itself may have risen only fifty feet, but the land sloped away to the river another twenty feet below, preventing any siege engines or towers from getting too close. In fact, to even attempt to storm Stonehelm would be a disaster.

"It's incredible," Trask said for all of them.

General Mason smiled. "When the giants build something, they build it strong. This wall has long discouraged any invaders. If only we had one along our sea border."

"My lord! General!" A soldier rushed to them from one of the bastions several yards away. "Another group approaches the wall." He pointed south.

Looking over the parapet again, they spotted a group of people trudging up the slope to the wall. They moved slowly, and many appeared to carry stretchers.

"More refugees." Balen turned grimly to the soldier. "Get word to Josef. He's in the keep with the wounded. Let him know there are more and make room."

The soldier nodded and hurried off. With Balen in the lead, they descended the stairs again and arrived at one of the only gates that led out of Samara.

"Open the gate," Balen instructed the four guardsmen there. "More refugees have come."

They slid the heavy iron barriers away, pulled open the gates, and raised the portcullis. By this time, the refugees waited just outside. They shuffled in, looking half-dead, their haunted eyes glazed over with fatigue. Not one appeared to have escaped injury.

"Come inside," Balen directed them. "This way."

He took the arm of an elderly man to help him forward. Not far behind him, an older woman stumbled, but Trask quickly stepped in to support her. With his lead, the others offered their help. Jace froze, left standing alone. His first instinct was to shy away from strangers. What could he even do for them? If they noticed he was part ryrik, would they even want him near? But then Holden drew his attention and motioned for him to help carry a stretcher. Jace stepped forward hesitantly and gripped the back of the stretcher. As they lifted it together, Jace glanced down at the man it carried. Though a blanket covered most of his body, deep red burns and a bloody gash along his forehead contrasted against his pale face. His eyes were closed, and Jace might have feared him dead already if not for his shallow, wheezing breaths.

Balen led everyone inside the keep, where they met Josef. The physician looked at everyone, weariness flashing across his expression. He already had so many in his care.

Trask stepped to his side. "What can we do to help? Leetra has been trained in medicine, and the rest of us are willing to do whatever we can."

Josef offered him a grateful look. "Leetra can help me and the rest of you can see to the less seriously injured. Clean their wounds and keep them covered. I'll be around with a salve and bandages. They also need water and food."

With these instructions, everyone spread out to do their part. Everyone except Jace. He shifted, discomfort prickling under his skin. Even Kyrin seemed to know what to do, but this was not a situation he had any experience or confidence in. His only desire was to disappear, but what would they think of him then?

Again Holden came to his rescue, a basin of water and cloths in hand. "Over here."

Jace's neck and face burned with his own incompetency as he followed Holden to a man and his little girl. Ragged bandages wound around the man's hands, and the wide-eyed little girl held her arm close to her stomach.

"Hello," Holden said gently. "Are you burned?"

The father nodded. "My hands and her arm."

Holden smiled at the little girl. "What's your name?"

"Anya," she murmured.

"Anya, my friend Jace is going to clean your arm while I take care of your father, all right?"

He handed Jace a wet cloth. Jace squeezed it in his fist and swallowed before looking down at the little girl. She peered up at him with huge eyes, but he was probably even more nervous than she was. He had never tended injuries other than his own, and certainly never on a child. Trying to think of her as Meredith, he knelt down and reached for her arm. She shrank away, as did he. He wasn't made for this, but he couldn't walk away now. He tried again, and this time she let him take her arm in a gentle grasp. She whimpered when he touched the cloth to the long burn near her wrist, but quieted after a moment. He worked carefully to clean the dust and dirt from the raw skin. His heart raced. What if he hurt her or caused more damage? Glancing up at the girl, he found more curiosity than pain on her smudged face.

When he looked up a second time, she told him, "Your eyes are pretty."

Jace paused. His eyes were always what gave him away. He cast a glance at her father. The man peered at him, but without suspicion.

Jace focused back on the little girl and murmured, "Thanks."

IT TOOK MOST of the day to care for the newly-arrived refugees and those already present at Stonehelm. Kyrin put the skills she had learned from Lenae to use wherever she could. So many people needed attention. Just thinking of what Josef did every day exhausted her. It was a good thing she and the others had shown up when they did. Samara needed far more than just military aid.

When she wasn't focused on one of the refugees, Kyrin's thoughts went to Jace. She had seen his face at first—his uncertainty with the situation. He was completely out of his element, and she felt awful for him, but thankfully Holden was at his side. She was used to dropping everything to help him in hard situations; however, in this instance, she couldn't ignore the inner prompting that the refugees needed her more than Jace did.

By the time they finished, everyone was ready for rest and food. Kyrin wasn't sure what time it was, but she did know the sun had set. Upon Balen's orders she and the others were shown to the mess hall, where food awaited them. It wasn't as extravagant as their supper the night before at the castle, but Kyrin's stomach still growled with anticipation. Sitting at one of the long tables, they ate hungrily.

A few minutes later, Josef joined them, sinking down in an empty place near the head of their table.

"I want to thank you all for your help today. I am the only fully-trained physician in the area, and am spread quite thin with all these new arrivals."

"Anything we can do to help while we're here," Trask replied.

"I appreciate it, and so does the king."

"Is he going to take his meal here?" Rayad asked.

Balen had worked just as hard, if not harder than them, in tending the refugees. Kyrin had seen him still working in the main hall of the keep when they had all left for supper, and he hadn't appeared to have had any intention of quitting.

"Eventually," Josef answered. "He wanted to be sure there was adequate room and cots for everyone."

"He is a remarkable king," Rayad said.

Josef nodded, his weathered face softening in fondness and pride. "Yes, he is. And he could be far greater if he could just make full use of his power and influence over the people."

"What stops him?"

"Queen Rhosin."

Rayad exchanged a look with Trask, and Kyrin listened closely. She had sensed some sort of underlying tension whenever anyone mentioned the queen.

"She never approved of King Alton's decision to make Balen his heir. She saw it as an affront to her inability to bear him a son. Of course, he never meant it as such, but what else could he do? However, many years of disappointment and heartache have made Queen Rhosin a bitter woman. She couldn't prevent Balen from being crowned, but she hasn't made it easy for him."

"That's why he's here in Westing and not Amberin," Rayad guessed.

"Partly. For all intents and purposes, the queen is ruler of this country. The people would choose to follow Balen—he is, after all, one of them—but he has not yet had reason to challenge her authority and take his proper place. He has chosen to avoid conflict for as long as he can." Josef sighed. "But I do wish he could rise up as the king he was meant to be. Samara needs it, especially now. Like Arcacia, the rule of Samara has been in decline. King Alton was a gentle and goodhearted man, but he lacked the strength and conviction to lead us. I believe Balen could change things, given the chance."

Later that evening, the group returned to the castle for the night. Kyrin trudged up the stairs to their sleeping quarters, her legs heavy and aching. The moment they had left the castle this morning seemed liked a distant memory. Her conversation with Rayad, however, settled clearly in her fatigued mind. She set her gaze on Jace, who walked just ahead of her. She wouldn't sleep well without a chance to say a few words to him. However, before she could catch up, he went straight to his room without speaking to anyone. Kyrin slowed and hung her head. Would he just keep shutting her out like this?

Her heart even heavier than her legs, she followed Leetra to their room. Just before they reached the door, Holden called her name. She turned as he approached.

"I was just talking to Timothy and Aaron," he said quietly. "We are going to pray for Jace. I knew you would want to join us."

Kyrin nodded earnestly, buoyed. It was just as Rayad had said—they weren't the only two who'd noticed Jace's suffering and struggle. She followed Holden. To her great surprise, so did Leetra. The crete rarely seemed to give much heed to their group's internal struggles, but maybe she was more aware than she let on. They joined Timothy and Aaron and walked into the room where Trev and Mick waited. The seven of them gathered in the center of the room. Bowing their heads, Timothy led them in prayer.

"King Elôm, we come to You on behalf of Jace and the struggle that surrounds him. We know You are stronger than the lies and doubts that attack him, and only You can bring him victory. Give him peace, and guide him through this. Let him find You in it. We know You hold his life and his soul. Show him the truth, and give him the strength to keep fighting and seek You. Reveal Yourself to him, Lord. He needs You . . ."

Holden grabbed the pillow and a blanket from his bed and walked down the hall toward the sitting room. Jace wasn't going to like this. Holden could already hear his argument. He could be very stubborn in these situations, but Holden had enough stubbornness of his own. Though he wouldn't typically insist, this time he deemed it necessary.

With a quick prayer, Holden stepped into the room. Jace was just settling in on the couch. He looked up, his brow creasing as Holden approached the second couch and unfolded his blanket.

"What are you doing?"

His tone already revealed stubbornness.

Holden glanced at him. "Keeping you company."

Jace's frown deepened, and his voice lowered. "I don't need company."

Holden said nothing. He wasn't here to argue, but he wouldn't be easily turned away either.

Jace breathed a little harder. "You can't stay."

"Why not?"

Jace's expression tensed. "I'm having nightmares again."

"I know." Holden had heard Jace during the nights on their journey.

"I'll just wake you up."

Holden shrugged. "It doesn't bother me." He set his blanket down and faced Jace fully. "You may think so, but you don't have to fight all these battles by yourself. Not when you have all of us around."

Jace stared at him a moment, and then looked away, his jaw clenching. Holden sighed. If only Jace didn't struggle so much with that concept. So many were for him, but he couldn't seem to see it or count himself worthy of it.

Holden opened his eyes and blinked his surroundings into focus. Deep shadows filled the room, but a pale glow at the window hinted of morning. He lay still and heard it again—the sound that had awakened him. A soft groan came from the other couch, and he propped himself up on his elbow. Jace's dark form moved fitfully in his sleep.

"Jace."

But only Jace's hard, erratic breathing and another deep groan answered him.

Holden tried again with no response. Pushing up from the couch, he lit a candle, but even the light didn't wake Jace from the dream. If anything, it only agitated him more. He tossed and turned, his face held taut with a grimace and shiny with sweat.

Holden approached him. Waking a man in such a state could prove dangerous, but he wouldn't let Jace keep suffering under the dream's influence. That was why he was here, after all. He reached out and grasped Jace's shoulder. Jace flinched.

"Jace, wake up." He gave him a little shake.

Jace's eyes snapped open, startlingly blue and lit with a fire that had once terrified Holden. But instead of moving to attack, Jace sat upright and jerked away from him. Disoriented, he bore the look of someone tortured and cornered. Holden grimaced and said his name once more to draw him out of the dream's hold. Awareness slowly settled in Jace's expression. He sank back against the couch, his chest heaving, but that tortured look remained.

Holden brought him a glass of water. Jace's hand trembled so badly he almost spilled some of it, and he drank it down in a couple of gulps. Holden took a seat across from him again and waited for him to speak, but he just sat there, his eyes still flashing in torment and fear. It was hard to see a man with Jace's strength and capabilities brought so low. Holden knew a thing or two about fear. Just a year ago, fear had led him to see Jace as a monster. That's what unchecked fear did: made monsters where there were none. If only Jace could understand that. Closing his eyes, Holden said a silent prayer over his friend.

For several minutes, they sat in silence. Jace's breathing eventually calmed, but Holden watched the extreme exhaustion set in. Jace just sat and stared with a lost, haunted look—the look of someone carrying a burden far too heavy for them to bear. *You don't have to bear it,* Holden wanted to tell him, but they would only be wasted words right now. Somehow, Jace had to learn that for himself.

At last, Holden said, "It's nearly dawn. Why don't we get a little more rest while we can?"

Jace gave him a heavy-lidded glance.

Blowing out the candle, Holden settled down on the couch, but Jace did not move. Holden let out a low sigh and stared at the ceiling. Sleep wouldn't return for him either.

Jace pulled on his clothes and winced at the ache in his sleep-deprived muscles. He had experienced such exhaustion before, just last summer; yet this went even deeper, echoing the days when Jasper had first trained him as a gladiator. Endless days, blurred by pain and hopelessness. He sagged with a sigh and fought to shove those images back into the past. The memories of early this morning took their place. In one way, he was grateful to Holden for waking him from the long and drawn out dream, but he'd been so weak and vulnerable. His skin prickled with the discomfort of having Holden see him that way.

He didn't want to face anyone now, but he had to join the others when they went down for breakfast. If only they were back at camp so he could be alone. This place offered no real opportunity for solitude.

Holden gave him a reassuring nod along the way, but Jace couldn't maintain eye contact.

At the table, conversation drifted from one topic to another, but Jace had no ambition to follow along. He picked at his food, eating small bites here and there, but it took effort. His body begged to lie down, but what relief would he find in sleep? He had no escape.

The door to the dining room swung open, startling him back to attention. An attendant hurried to the table and bowed hastily before King Balen.

"My lord, I've just received word that the one they call Elon is at Stonehelm."

Everyone stared at him.

"At Stonehelm? Now?"

The attendant nodded. "Yes, my lord. Word is already spreading through the village. Many are going to see him."

All around the table Jace's companions rose, their breakfast forgotten. Jace's heart thumped as he pushed slowly to his feet, the last to rise.

"Send for my horse and the baron's," Balen instructed the attendant, "and one for Josef."

With another quick nod, the attendant rushed out, and everyone followed Balen away from the table.

"We'll wait for you at the dragons," Trask told the king.

Outside the castle, villagers scurried about and talked excitedly as many headed toward Stonehelm. Jace remained behind the others as they wove through the crowd. A churning took hold of his stomach as all his uncertainties about the man in the rumors descended.

They saddled the dragons in a rush and waited for King Balen. Looking ahead to Stonehelm, Jace watched a steady line of people stream eagerly toward the fortress. Even around him, he sensed the excitement amongst the others. The ever calm and patient Timothy looked ready to jump on his dragon and leave this very second. He traded a grin with Kyrin, and Jace turned away. Why did such hesitancy grip him, while his friends were so eager? Would there ever come a day he wasn't such an outcast, even among friends?

When Balen arrived with Baron Thomas, Josef, and General Mason, the group mounted their dragons and took to the air. They arrived at the fortress well ahead of the horsemen, but waited outside the walls for the king to arrive. Together, they joined the flow of people into the courtyard.

The large area around the keep was already filling with many people gathered from the village. They had to move slowly at first, but the villagers parted to let their king pass. Jace followed close behind Rayad. Such a crowd put him on edge. Their attention was elsewhere, but he couldn't shake the urge to avoid their gaze.

Near the keep, the crowd thinned to make way for Balen. Jace looked ahead and caught sight of a dark-haired man standing with the old woman the king had greeted the day before. The man smiled down at her, his hand rested on her shoulder, and said something. Her wrinkled face glowed with a smile of her own.

Jace shifted his attention to two other men who stood nearby. Next to the gathering of villagers, they were quite impressive—tall and stoic with dark hair and watchful blue eyes. Their appearance was very similar, twins almost, yet not. There was something foreign about them, perhaps even other-worldly, though Jace couldn't say what. He had never seen anyone like them before.

His gaze drew back to the other man. He took notice of their approach and straightened to face them. Though he was about Balen's age, he was not nearly as tall. A smile remained on his lips as they neared. Jace couldn't see anything that explained the fascination with him, but then the man's warm brown eyes met his.

Jace froze, paralyzed. The courtyard and those in it disappeared. Everything vanished except for the man who seemed to see right into the very deepest, darkest depths of his heart. Instant trembling gripped Jace and images from his past poured into his mind—all the men he had killed and injured, all the terrible things he had seen and done. Just like during the sacrifice, he could almost feel the shed blood dripping from his hands. Looking into this man's eyes, all of it seemed laid bare before him. Every misdeed and sin. Yet no condemnation entered the man's eyes, only compassion. A compassion Jace could not understand as his own guilty conscience convicted him.

Overcome with shame, Jace tore his eyes away, his empty lungs gasping. He shook so violently, his legs almost gave out beneath him. He turned. He needed to hide himself—hide his guilt and unworthiness from the man's sight. Pushing through the people, he fled. He thought he heard Rayad call to him, but he did not look back.

On the other side of the gate he stumbled to the dragons, where he fell to his knees beside Gem, panting. Even here, the man's face stuck in his mind. A numbing mix of awe and fear gripped him. It was undeniably clear. He had just come face to face with Elon, the very Son of Elôm.

THE DARKNESS ROLLED *in, unrelenting, oppressive, choking Jace. But then the light appeared, distant and faint. He stepped toward it, but chains and heavy burdens dragged him to his knees. Gasping, he clawed at the restraints around his wrists. He needed to reach the light. He must escape.*

"Jace."

The voice came from the light, beckoning him. In new desperation, he fought to remove the crushing weight that held him down.

"Jace."

He struggled to release the burden but, somehow, it was inside him. It filled his body like lead and dragged him deeper down into the darkness. The light and the voice grew fainter. He screamed and tried to push to his feet, but was too weak.

"Jace."

He jerked up, away from the hand on his shoulder, his limbs still weighted. His heart thrashed with the panic to escape. He couldn't let the darkness take him! Slowly, the familiar sight of the sitting room sank in. Holden's face hovered in front of him. He choked out one breath and then another. His throat was raw and tight. Had he screamed in his sleep?

Holden handed him a glass of water, though Jace could only manage to drink half of it. His heart crashed painfully against his ribs. It was as if he could still feel himself sinking and fighting.

"Jace, I really think you should talk about this." Holden stared at him, his face grim.

But at the thought of recounting even just part of his dreams, Jace trembled uncontrollably. He squeezed his fists until his nails dug into the skin of his palms and willed the spasms to subside. What was wrong with him? Never had he experienced such terror.

With a heavy sigh, Holden sat down in a chair next to him. "You should talk to Elon."

Jace tensed. When the others had returned from Stonehelm the previous evening, they had come with words of wonder and excitement. He, however, could not speak of his encounter with Elon, of the shame he felt so strongly, even now.

"I saw the people healed," Holden went on. "The refugees, even those we weren't sure would survive." He paused and drew a deep breath as if pondering his own words. "I believe He can heal you too, of whatever troubles you."

Jace shook his head, and his eyes burned. He could not face Elon again. Not in this state. Yet, it sent such pain to his heart that he couldn't breathe for a long moment. Deep down, he longed for that healing more than anything. It just seemed so far out of his reach, like the light in his dreams.

For the next hour until dawn, they both sat in silence. Holden remained in his chair, his eyes closed, but the way his lips sometimes moved told Jace that he prayed, not rested. Jace needed rest—his entire body ached for it—but if he closed his eyes, he would just get sucked into another nightmare.

When everyone gathered in the dining room for breakfast, Jace's attention drifted in and out of the conversations. Talk centered around Elon, of course. They made allusions to His identity, some a little more sure than others. No one seemed sure whether they should say it outright or remain more cautious.

But Jace knew.

From the moment he had locked eyes with the man, he'd known exactly who he faced. The knowledge and memories of it would never leave him, and they burned his insides with a fire both amazing and frightening. Yet the shame of that moment rested most heavily within him. He had never seen his unworthiness as clearly as he had then—how utterly wretched he was. An unrelenting pressure squeezed his throat.

Seeking a distraction, Jace focused on the discussion that had turned to the two men with Elon yesterday.

"Aelos and Riyel, who do you think they are?" Kyrin asked.

"I heard they came with Elon," Aaron answered.

"They certainly didn't seem to be Samarans," Josef said.

Though they discussed the mystery surrounding the two men for another brief moment, conversation quickly returned to Elon.

"I can't wait to go back," Kyrin said, and Timothy eagerly echoed these sentiments. "When Elon was speaking, didn't you just feel like you could sit and listen forever?"

Jace watched their eyes alight with wonder and radiant smiles, and he suddenly felt more alone than he had in a long time. It cut deep into his heart, splaying it open with intense pain. Instead of approaching in awe, he had fled. Instead of eagerly seeking, he had hidden. His stomach convulsed, destroying his appetite, and he left his food untouched.

The moment they finished breakfast, everyone hurried to the dragons, eager to return to Stonehelm. Jace followed, but dread settled on him. Could he do this again?

When they arrived outside the fortress, a crowd of people had already gathered inside. Perhaps they had never left. Jace's heart pounded like a sledgehammer as he slid slowly down from Gem.

Memories of yesterday attacked his mind, and all the deep and torturous emotions reemerged. He stood stiffly beside his dragon as the group started for the gate. After going a couple of yards, Rayad and Holden must have realized he wasn't with them and turned back.

"Are you coming?" Rayad asked.

Jace looked from them to the gate and back, his tongue sticking to the roof of his mouth. He shook his head and managed a hoarse, "No."

Rayad traded a look with Holden and said, "I really think it would do you good."

Jace swallowed hard. "The crowd . . . I can't." He hung his head in shame, the real reason locked away inside him. "Just go."

Rayad and Holden stood for a long moment, but Jace did not look up until their footsteps moved on. Watching them and the others enter the fortress without him was like a knife in the chest. He struggled to breathe, but could not bring himself to follow. His eyes blurred with moisture, and he blinked hard; ashamed of his fear, ashamed of his failure, ashamed of his life.

Breathing out a sigh that turned to a groan, he sank to the ground and leaned against Gem, her warm scales soothing the sore muscles in his back. He rested his head in his hands, too exhausted to make sense of anything or fight the fear that slowly consumed him.

"Jace."

He jerked awake with a gasp, sunlight almost blinding him. Squinting, he looked around and found Gem staring intensely at him, much like Tyra did when he dreamed. He breathed out heavily. Somehow, he had fallen asleep. He glanced at the sun. It was a little past noon. He pushed to his feet and stretched his muscles, heavy with the remembrance of his dream. Though not as vivid as the one earlier, remnants of it clung to him and that voice still echoed in his head, though too faint to recognize. No matter how hard he fought to reach it, he always failed. A shiver raced down his spine. He seemed to spend more and more time in that consuming darkness these days.

Running his hand through his sweat-dampened hair, he turned, his gaze landing on the fortress. His pulse picked up. He thought of Kyrin, Rayad, Holden, and the others inside. Yearning rose up within him, but he grimaced. How could he join them after yesterday? Maybe in the crowd he could stay hidden and at least be near them. Wouldn't that be better than sitting here?

He drew in a hard breath and moved his feet forward before he could talk himself out of it. Though he fought to maintain his courage, his pace slowed when he reached the gate. He peered in hesitantly, but could see nothing past the gathered villagers. However, the hum of a voice reached him and tugged at his heart, drawing him into the courtyard.

Jace inched closer, and the voice grew clearer. Finally, through the people, he spotted Elon sitting in the midst of them. Jace's heart beat faster, and it was as if two opposing forces pulled at him—one to flee and the other to draw nearer. He took another step forward and then another.

In the crowd, he caught sight of Kyrin and Timothy sitting close and listening with rapt attention to everything Elon said. The longing to join them took his breath away, forcing a hard lump to his throat. He swallowed it down. Movement on the other side of Elon drew his attention. The little girl, Anya, approached Elon timidly. The moment He noticed her, He extended His hand, and she came to Him, her face beaming. Smiling down at her, He touched her cheek gently, and Jace's heart nearly failed in yearning for such tender love. Why couldn't he be like that little girl, or Kyrin, or Timothy?

Then Elon looked up and found him in the crowd. Jace stilled, only able to comprehend Elon's presence. For a brief moment, he saw all the love he longed for right in front of him as if Elon were stretching out His hand to Jace. But the darkness of his past was there in a moment to remind him that he wasn't anything like the innocent little girl who had approached. He was stained by blood he never should have shed and filled with a blood he could not control. An animal to most, and unworthy of love.

Jace turned his face away, the shame crushing him. Once again, he fled. If only he could hide himself from all those around him. What if they too could see what he was? Yet every step away ripped his heart to shreds. Back outside the wall, he choked on tears that filled his eyes, but didn't fall. Trying to catch his breath, he sank to the ground in agony.

The following day, Jace refused to return to Stonehelm. He didn't have the strength to bear the pain of it. He had barely slept during the night, but now even his waking hours were almost as torturous as his dreams. He grew increasingly desperate for relief, but could not find it anywhere. The others begged him to come with them, but even Kyrin couldn't change his mind.

He passed the day sitting alone with Gem. She would watch him and make mournful noises when he didn't respond. He wanted to, but the turmoil inside left him powerless to do much of anything. Off and on he would sleep, only because his body shut down, but every moment of it was torment.

That night was the same, and Holden had to wake him multiple times. By morning, he wasn't sure how much more he could take. His hands shaking with weakness, he could barely dress himself. Food would help, but his stomach was so knotted he didn't think he could hold anything down.

Oblivious to anything but the consuming struggle, he followed the quiet group to breakfast, but someone took his arm to hold him back. He looked down into Kyrin's wide, blue eyes. Her jaw and lips were tight, and her skin pale. She waited until the room emptied before speaking in a trembling voice.

"Jace, I'm scared." He didn't understand at first, but she continued, "For you. I've never seen you like this." She stared up at him, searching his eyes and seeing everything he couldn't hide. "What's wrong?"

Emotion rushed into his throat, squeezing off his voice. He opened his mouth, but had no words for her. No words to describe or explain the pain inside. None of them could understand. Overwhelmed, he only shook his head. He closed his eyes, unsteady.

"Sit down." Kyrin guided him to a chair.

He sank into it, and Kyrin stood before him.

"Please, come with us today," she begged. "Listen to Elon. Talk to Him."

Jace hung his head, unable to answer her plea.

"Don't you see?" she urged. "This is what I've been praying for. He can help you, Jace . . . He can answer the questions you have."

Jace's eyes snapped to hers, his heart seizing. That was the very core of the struggle. For the first time in his life, he could finally know. Did he have a soul? Yet, now that he had the chance to find out, it terrified him like nothing he had ever faced before. What if he found out he didn't? How could he live the rest of his life with such knowledge? It was better not to know for sure.

Kyrin knelt down in front of him, taking his hands in hers. "I know you're afraid, but please, you have to do this."

He shook his head, his breath shallow. He wanted to be strong for her, but he was weak. Weaker than he had ever imagined.

She squeezed his hands, her eyes pleading. "Then let me. I'll talk to Him for you."

"No." The word broke out raw and desperate. "Please, don't." He couldn't abide the thought of her discovering he had no soul and how she would look at him then.

"Jace . . ."

"Please," he gasped. "Don't."

Tears gathered in Kyrin's eyes and dripped down her cheeks. "I want to help you."

The anguish in her voice was almost too much to bear.

"I know, but . . ." He swallowed hard. "I don't think you can."

Her eyes slid closed, the tears streaming. After a moment, she composed herself and looked at him again. "I can't force you to, but I am *begging* you to consider going to Elon. Please. You can't go on like this and . . . I don't want to lose you." She drove the plea in with a look of intense desperation.

How could he deny her when he loved her so much? For her, he would consider it, but could not promise. "I'll think about it," he whispered.

Kyrin nodded and wiped her cheeks as she rose. "Come on. I know it's hard, but you must eat. You need the strength." She held out her hand.

Jace gazed at it a moment and then took it, the warmth and connection like a lifeline to his battered heart. She helped him up and did not let go for a long moment before turning and leading the way downstairs.

The sun arched over the sky as Jace wrestled inside himself—yearning against fear, hope against doubt. He was caught in the midst of a battle he had no control over and no strength to fight. Kyrin's words repeated in his head as he paced near Gem. At one point, he nearly got on her back to fly to Stonehelm, but fear crippled him.

Late in the afternoon, he could stand it no longer. He needed relief or he would go mad. He needed comfort. Something familiar. He set his gaze on the distant trees. It had been days since he had been in the forest. He set out toward it as if it somehow held an answer. Gem chirped uncertainly behind him, but he commanded her to stay.

Focusing on the trees, he attempted to leave the struggle behind him, if only for a brief respite. The dark green foliage drew closer with every desperate step, and, after a mile and a half, the shade of the trees engulfed him. Here he paused to catch his breath from the walk, but then pushed on, into the forest.

The sunshine filtering through the canopy gave him the first breath of peace he had felt in over a week. He breathed it in deeply, willing it not to abandon him again. As he went deeper, the forest reminded him of life back at the farm. It had been a while since he had thought about it. Back when life was hard at times, but not a constant struggle. Oh, to be back there. His eyes grew wet, and he rubbed them.

From the farm, his thoughts turned to his mother. He longed for her embrace, but she seemed so terribly far away. Why had their lives taken such painful turns? Why couldn't they have just turned out all right?

Jace wandered on through the forest until the sun grew dim. By this time, his legs burned with exertion, so he sat down at the base of a tree to rest and gazed around the shadows. He was more comfortable in the forest—protected . . . hidden.

And very alone.

He suddenly ached for Tyra. She was always such a faithful companion.

Sighing, Jace rested his head back and closed his eyes. He should get back to the castle. The others would worry if they returned and found him missing. He had quite a ways to go and would have to hurry, but the weariness settling in his limbs was too great to fight.

The courtyard had gone dim and quiet. Most of the villagers had returned home or entered the keep for supper. Trask and the other men had gone to find Balen, but Kyrin remained to watch Elon interact with the remaining people. All day she and Timothy had sat and listened to him speak of Elôm and His will, but she had yet to speak with Elon herself. Her heart desired to have even just a moment alone with Him, but she hung back in reverence. Were her questions worth asking? It wasn't as if they were profound or important to anyone but her personally.

A moment later, He turned and caught sight of her. His ready smile immediately made her feel foolish for thinking her thoughts wouldn't be important to Him. Before she could move, He crossed the courtyard toward her.

"Kyrin," He said in a gentle voice of comfortable familiarity.

The very fact that He knew her name without her telling Him warmed her heart. It struck her how tired He looked. Speaking and teaching all day would tire anyone, but she had never expected Him to be so human, and it drew her even more to Him.

"You have much on your mind," He said.

Kyrin nodded. "My father . . ." She hesitated. What was it that she even wanted to ask? She just missed her father so. Any knowledge of him now would soothe the ache.

Elon put a gentle hand on her shoulder, understanding in His eyes. "I know how you miss him, but your father served Elôm well and is now experiencing a life like nothing you can imagine. Both he and your grandfather."

Kyrin gasped, her heart leaping. "My grandfather, Jonavan . . . he did believe?"

At Elon's nod of confirmation, Kyrin let out a shaky breath. Ever since hearing the story from Rayad, she had hoped her grandfather had turned to Elôm before he was executed. To know was more wonderful than she'd imagined, and she couldn't wait to tell her brothers.

"One day," Elon told her, "you and your family will join them."

Kyrin covered her mouth as tears dribbled down her cheeks. Such a thought left her nearly bursting with joy. One day her family would be complete and never have to endure the ache of separation again.

"Thank You," she managed in a whisper, but her thoughts immediately turned to Jace. He was as much a part of her family as her parents and brothers.

"You think of Jace."

Kyrin lifted her eyes to Elon, holding His gaze as her heart pounded. She thought of Jace's fear that morning. She ached to console him, to discover the truth that could free him from his fears, but he had begged her not to. How could she go against him?

An even worse thought struck fear into her. For the first time, she wondered, what if he didn't have a soul? What if everyone was right about ryriks? How could she bear to know that? It would tear her heart apart. Yet, the mystery of it and watching him suffer so deeply already accomplished that.

Trembling, her mouth went dry and her voice scratched past her throat before she was sure she was ready for the answer. "Does he have a soul?"

"Jace."

He opened his eyes to the shadowy dimness of night. For just a moment, he thought he was back at camp, by the stream, but remembrance flooded in. He was many miles from Landale. He looked around to get his bearings in the strange forest. He'd never meant to fall asleep, especially for so long. Pushing to his feet, he looked up at the sky. Moonlight flickered in the branches. It was late. Kyrin would be worried sick.

Jace turned in the direction of Westing Castle and froze. A cold, slithering sensation prickled along his spine and arms. His senses focused in an instant, his gaze sweeping the trees. Something watched him from nearby, but who could say what? The region was a mystery to him. Balen's story of the wildcat rushed to the front of his mind, and he reached for his sword, only to find air. He grimaced. He'd left it in his room. His hunting knife too, and he called himself every kind of fool.

Taking stock of his surroundings for anything to use to his advantage, he moved slowly in the direction from which he had come. Perhaps whatever it was would let him go without ever showing itself.

Leaves rustled, but there was no breeze. He halted. The heat of his blood rose as adrenaline worked through his body. His gaze darted to the darkest shadows, searching. He breathed slowly and listened for the slightest sounds, but his drumming heart made it difficult.

With a soft thud, something dropped to the ground behind him. He spun around, expecting a stealthy wildcat, but he found himself looking down into a stern face with large, iron-blue eyes. His breath left him. He took a halting step backward, but a blade pressed into his back between his shoulder blades. He glanced over his shoulder to see a second crete, but he focused on the familiar one before him.

"Not a smart move to wander about alone and unarmed." Falcor's piercing eyes glittered threateningly in the moonlight.

A SHARP KICK to the back of the knee sent Jace to the ground. He bit back a groan, breathing hard through his teeth.

"Better," Falcor said, now able to look down on him instead.

Jace glared up at the crete. Right about now he wished for a wildcat instead. He would have stood a better chance of survival.

"Are we going to kill him?" the other crete asked in such a cold, pitiless tone that it sent ice through Jace.

His chest heaved as he fought the way his blood surged and willed him to fight. Had they been human, he would have taken his chances, but he had seen Talas sparring before. Cretes were far too quick to take by surprise. Falcor would have his blade through Jace's heart before he even gained his feet.

The crete's sword caught the moonlight as he placed it at Jace's throat and tipped his chin up. The sharp point pricked Jace's neck. He held Falcor's gaze, finding no mercy. The man had once killed one of his own. Why would he spare Jace's life? Falcor's face hardened even more, as if thinking the same thing. Jace held his breath and waited for him to slice his throat.

However, Falcor pulled his blade away and looked at the second crete. "We'll take him to camp."

In silence, the other crete grabbed Jace's wrist, swiftly tying a rope around it and wrenching his other arm back to secure them tightly. He cut off the excess rope and tossed the extra length to Falcor, who tied a loop in one end. He fitted it over Jace's head and tugged it snuggly against his throat. Jace clenched his teeth. So they were going to treat him like a stray dog?

"Get up."

Defiance took hold, and Jace did not move immediately, but Falcor's warning glare prompted him into motion. He stumbled to his feet, his knees a bit wobbly. Jerking the rope, Falcor plunged deeper into the forest, the other crete trailing behind them.

They moved almost silently through the trees. Under normal circumstances, Jace could navigate a forest with ease, but even after sleep his weariness weighed on his feet. Whenever he slowed or stumbled, Falcor gave the rope a hard jerk, nearly pulling him off balance. The rough cord burned against his neck and made it difficult to breathe.

They marched on for about a mile before Jace caught sight of a fire flickering ahead. Had he kept on earlier, he may have stumbled upon it himself. Not that the outcome would have been any more pleasant. When they drew near, he counted two more figures around the fire—one a crete and the other a man. But a few larger shapes at the perimeter of the small camp grabbed his full attention—three dragons and a massive black firedrake.

As they entered the clearing and neared the fire, the burly man gave him a hostile look. "Who's that?"

Falcor stopped and yanked on the rope. Jace stumbled forward and fell to his knees, coughing. He longed to reach up and loosen the choking pressure. He should have been prepared.

"This is one of the Landale group. The half-ryrik." Falcor's tone oozed disgust.

"What're you gonna do with him?" the man questioned, eyeing Jace as his fingers closed around the large dagger at his side.

"I haven't decided yet." Falcor stepped around in front of Jace and tightened his grip on the rope until Jace looked up at him. "How much do you know of the king's plans?"

Jace glanced past Falcor to the others, just now considering what they were doing in Samara. It made sense that they were here to spy and gather information. He returned his gaze to Falcor and clamped his mouth shut. The crete snorted. Barely giving Jace the time to rise, he strode across camp, dragging Jace with him, and tied the rope securely to the trunk of the nearest tree.

Here, Jace sank down as Falcor joined his companions at the fire to pour himself a cup of coffee. Jace glared at each of them, but a low, rumbling growl drew his attention to the firedrake. He had only seen them airborne before now. The hideous creature bared its teeth at one of the nearby dragons, who hissed back.

At the fire, the man snapped a harsh command. The ill-tempered firedrake released a final growl and backed off, its black eyes reflecting orange in the firelight. Jace shivered. Normally, he had a soft spot for all animals, but firedrakes were an exception.

He shifted his gaze to his captors again, and found Falcor staring at him. He stared back, his muscles tensing. The two of them had been on bad terms from the start, and this traitorous crete was the one responsible for the death of Kyrin's father. Jace's blood heated again, and he strained against his bonds, but knot-tying was an art-form to the cretes. He would never work them loose.

"We'll take him to Valcré."

Everyone looked to Falcor at this sudden announcement.

"Why not just kill him and save the trouble?" the man asked.

"The emperor may have questions for him, and he's been waiting to get his hands on someone from Landale. Would you like to tell him why we didn't bring him in?"

The man didn't respond.

"You two," Falcor looked at the two other cretes, "keep an eye on things here, but find a new campsite. Someone's bound to come looking for him."

They nodded, and Falcor turned to the man. "Hyde, you'll come with me. We leave at dawn."

He probably wanted to have the big man along to help guard and restrain Jace.

With these plans settled, the group gathered closer to the fire. Jace swallowed hard against the rope around his neck. He couldn't decide what was worse—the thought of immediate execution or facing the emperor. Either way, he was a dead man. He considered how far Valcré was. How far away from everyone he cared about. The pressure in his throat doubled. They would never know what happened to him. And Kyrin would be in the midst of war, and he couldn't make sure she stayed safe. He had already failed the very reason he had come here in the first place.

Jace bowed his head. Why had he wandered into this forest? Why hadn't he just stayed at the castle? A desperate, soundless sob burst in his chest. Why hadn't he gone to Stonehelm with Kyrin, as she had begged him to? He blinked the burning from his eyes, but the pain in his heart intensified. He would never see her again. He had watched her fly off with the others, not knowing it would be the last time he ever saw her face. Invisible daggers pierced his chest. In desperation, he twisted his wrists against the rope. Hopeless as it may be, he had to try.

The first chirp of morning birds sent despair deep into Jace's gut. The only thing he had accomplished through the night was to rub skin away from his wrists. If anything, the rope only felt tighter, and his arms burned from the strain.

Falcor stood at the fire, never once sleeping. The other two cretes had for a couple of hours, and Hyde still snored in his bedroll. With his perpetual scowl, Falcor walked over to the man and nudged him with his foot.

"Get up. It's time to go."

Hyde jerked and grumbled before pushing himself up with a gaping yawn. Falcor returned to the fire, where he dished a bowl from a pot of porridge. Striding toward Jace, he set the bowl down and bent to look Jace straight on. He planted his hand firmly on the hilt of his dagger.

"You make one move to escape, and I will kill you."

Jace just stared at him. Part of him wanted to try just to spite him, but wisdom won out. Falcor moved around behind him, tugging at the rope around his wrists until the knots came free. Jace pulled his hands around in front of him and flexed his tingling fingers. He winced when the chilly air stung his wrists.

At the sight of the raw and oozing skin, Falcor snorted in derision. He then gestured to the bowl. "Eat."

With this curt command he walked away, but was ever watchful.

Moving cautiously, Jace worked a little more slack into the loop around his neck and reached for the bowl. Just looking at the sticky substance knotted his stomach, but he wouldn't have enough strength to face the day, let alone the whole journey to Valcré, if he didn't eat something. He took a bite, forcing himself to swallow. The action pained his bruised throat.

Falcor and Hyde ate quickly and were soon saddling up. Jace recognized Falcor's dragon and the scars in its wing, from where Leetra's dragon had ripped it. His gaze shifted to Hyde, who saddled the firedrake. The creature balked at first, but Hyde gave it a stinging rap on the shoulder with a small club, and it submitted with a grumble in its throat. Unfortunate that the beast didn't just snap the man up and then turn on the others. It would create the perfect distraction.

Once their supplies were packed, Falcor approached Jace again with rope in hand. He tied Jace's wrists in front of him this time, heedless of the wounded flesh. Jace ground his teeth. Loosing the other rope from the tree, he pulled Jace up and led him straight to the firedrake.

"Climb on."

Jace's heart surged into his throat. He had only ever flown with Gem. He trusted her, but being in the air on this beast brought his fear of heights rushing to the forefront. It locked up his joints, freezing him in place.

Hyde struck him with the same club he had used on the firedrake, and sharp pain pulsed through Jace's shoulder.

"Get up there!"

Jace sucked in his breath through his teeth. He had no choice unless he wanted them to kill him now. Spasms trembled up his arms and through the rest of his body as he reached for the saddle. His limbs protested every move. Once astride the giant beast, he gripped the saddle, each breath shallow. His tongue was like dry wood in his mouth. It was like the first time he had flown all over again, but he had no friends around to offer encouragement or allow him time to gather his courage. He fought to hide his fear, but must have done a poor job of it. Hyde chuckled cruelly as he climbed up and tied Jace's bound hands to the saddle itself. Jace's heart missed a beat. Actually being attached to the beast was even worse.

Falcor took off first. The lumbering firedrake spread its wide wings and flapped hard three times before gaining any air. It didn't soar gracefully into the sky like a dragon. Each jerking lunge upward sucked Jace's stomach toward his feet. He shut his eyes tightly and struggled not to be sick.

Once above the trees, he finally opened them. The glow of sunlight tinged the eastern horizon. He looked over his shoulder to the north and, in the distance, just made out the dark smudge of Westing Castle. Pain and longing gripped him, but in moments the sight disappeared. After only a short time, they left Samara behind them.

A stomach-churning unease woke Kyrin. She sat up abruptly and looked around. She was in bed, but still fully clothed. Her heart pounded heavily, and her thoughts jumped straight to Jace. They had looked everywhere for him when they'd returned. It wasn't unlike him to disappear in times of distress, but she needed to speak to him as soon as possible. She had been prepared to wait up for him. Rayad was supposed to come for her the moment he returned.

She looked over at Leetra, who stood near the window as early morning sunlight lit up the sky. Even her normally stoic expression held a hint of sympathy and concern. Kyrin slid out of bed and rushed straight to the sitting room. Both Rayad and Holden were there, neither one appearing as though they had slept.

"He isn't here?"

Rayad shook his head.

A cold numbness flushed through Kyrin's body. She took a breath. This wasn't out of the ordinary. Jace did this. He would soon show up. Even so, an uncontrollable panic gnawed at her. She had to find him. She had to tell him.

Rayad and Holden rose.

"We'll go look for him," Rayad said. "Right away."

Kyrin breathed out, glad they would not wait. It couldn't wait. Not for anything.

They joined the others in the hall and went downstairs.

"Has your friend returned?" Balen asked in genuine concern when they met him in the dining room.

"No," Rayad said.

"We could ask around the village. Someone has surely seen him."

"He wouldn't be in the village," Kyrin replied. He would get as far away from other people as he could. "For solitude, he would have gone to the forest."

Rayad nodded. "She's right."

"Let's go then," Holden said.

Kaden and Talas volunteered to join them while the others remained behind in case he showed up. Just as they were about to leave, the door opened, and a guard brought Elon, Aelos, and Riyel inside. Everyone turned to them, and Elon stepped forward.

"I'm here about Jace," He said. "He was captured by enemy spies and is being taken to Valcré by dragon."

These words slammed into Kyrin's heart, stalling it. For a moment, all she could see was the emperor's cruel face, the execution platform, a screaming mob . . .

A tingling sensation she hadn't experienced in a long time worked up through her fingers, and her vision grew shadowed. Kaden grabbed her arm, and she shut her eyes and drew in deep breaths to clear her head. The faintness passed, but the pain in her heart did not. To think of Jace in enemy hands was more than she could bear. Losing him would devastate her. *Please, Elôm, no.*

"Are you all right?"

Kyrin opened her eyes and looked up at her brother. She gave a brief nod, but her body still felt cold and a little numb.

"Are they already gone?" Rayad asked Elon. His voice held the measure of his own concern for Jace.

Elon nodded.

"We have to go after him," Kyrin gasped. Her words barely made it through her throat. If only they had searched for him last night. She had never imagined something so terrible when they hadn't found him after returning from Stonehelm.

Rayad turned to look at everyone. "We can't all go and leave Samara defenseless if Daican sends firedrakes before we return."

"I'll go with you," Elon said, surprising them. "We won't need a large force to rescue him."

Holden stepped up to join Rayad, and they both looked at Kyrin.

"I'm going too." She couldn't stand the thought of waiting here. She had already lost someone dear to her to the emperor. To think of it happening to Jace and not doing all she could to stop it would kill her.

Kaden still held her arm, and she looked up at him again. A battle raged in his expression that she understood immediately. This was his first difficult decision as a captain. He would want to join them, especially since she was going, but he had his men to think about.

She put her hand on his arm. "It's all right. Stay with your men."

The struggle remained in his eyes. He had never willingly let her face danger without him.

"Aaron and I will go," Timothy spoke up. He faced Kaden. "Don't worry. We'll protect her with our lives. You know we will."

Kaden blew out a long breath, finally nodding. "All right."

Now that it was settled, they rushed to gather their supplies and provisions. Trask, Mick, and Tane offered their dragons to Elon, Aelos, and Riyel. Outside, they loaded the supplies and gathered for a rushed goodbye. Standing near Ivoris, Kyrin faced Kaden.

"This doesn't feel right," he said, "staying here."

"I know, but your men might need you."

Kaden grimaced. "Just be careful, all right?"

Kyrin looked into his troubled eyes. It wasn't hard to guess that they were both thinking of their father. Little good had ever come out of their experiences in Valcré, and this was too much like the morning they had watched their father ride away. "I will."

They hugged tightly for a long moment.

"I'll be praying hard for you and Jace," Kaden said just before they parted.

"Thank you."

She managed to give him a quick smile, and then mounted Ivy. Looking over at the others, her gaze fell on Gem. The poor dragon looked lost and confused without Jace. Kyrin's heart squeezed.

"Gem."

The dragon's head perked up, her bright eyes locking on Kyrin.

"*Réma,*" she commanded.

Gem turned, ready to follow. Kyrin let out a long breath and fought back the constant sting of tears. Would they catch up to Jace's captors, or would they bring him all the way to Valcré? How would they ever save him once he was in Daican's clutches? Poor Jace would have no idea they had even tried.

"We will rescue him."

Kyrin jerked around to face Elon and His solemn, but compassionate gaze. Slowly, she nodded and tried to banish her fears and doubts. After all, if she couldn't trust Him face to face, how weak must her faith be?

-Part Three-

Valcré

JACE HUNG HIS head and let his sore shoulders droop. The ache of holding his muscles so tense burned through his arms. Weariness had never weighed so heavily on him, but he didn't dare close his eyes. Not while in the air. He swallowed to relieve his parched throat, and winced at the pain of severe bruising around his neck. The last time he had faced such prolonged ill-treatment was as Jasper's slave. Five days of only Falcor and Hyde for company left him drowning in despair. He had lost hope of ever seeing another friendly face.

Releasing a heavy breath, he glanced at the sun sinking in the west. This glimpse of the surrounding terrain sparked his memory. He looked ahead, past Hyde's broad shoulder, and spied Valcré in the distance. His stomach sank the full three-hundred feet below them, but resignation settled in its place.

Fast approaching the city, Jace scraped together any little strength and resolve he could muster, and struggled to shake off the debilitating heaviness of sleep deprivation. Within minutes, the buildings of Valcré passed beneath them, and the two flying beasts set down in the courtyard of Auréa Palace. Jace's breath caught as he looked up at the splendorous sight, but the chill that raced down his spine stole away any sense of awe.

Hyde turned to release Jace's bonds from the saddle. Moving gingerly, Jace dismounted and sucked in his breath as pain lanced through his chest and abdomen. He had collected a large assortment of aches and bruises, courtesy of Hyde and his rude awakenings when Jace dreamed every night.

Falcor walked up to him and grabbed the rope that had become a permanent fixture around his throat. The crete never grew tired of dragging him around like a dog. No doubt he would miss it now that he was handing Jace over to Daican. It fed his egotistical crete pride and superiority.

Jace followed, his heart pumping hard as they walked to the palace entrance and up the marble stairs. Dread dragged at his feet, but the constant threat of the rope around his neck prevented him from slowing. When the guards admitted them, Jace's eyes grew wide at the sight before him—rich splendor unlike anything he had witnessed before—but he had no chance to stand and gawk at it.

The magnificence of the palace swiftly lost its grandeur, and every step twisted new knots in Jace's stomach. Daican was here, somewhere close by, and Jace would soon face him. He had thought he was ready, but uncertainty flooded in like cold river water. Would he be as brave as Kyrin in facing their greatest enemy?

Down a long hall, they passed through a set of wide double doors into the throne room. Jace gazed across the expansive tile floor to the empty gold thrones, and then up to the towering arched ceiling. The room was empty and silent, save for the three of them and their echoing footsteps. Falcor paused and turned to Hyde.

"Find the emperor and let him know we have a prisoner from Landale."

The man nodded, and left as Falcor led Jace down the center of the room, stopping near the raised dais at the end. Silence fell so fully that Falcor could probably hear Jace's heart knocking. Jace took in the details of the emperor's ornate throne, and then looked just beyond it. Kyrin had stood there once—walked the halls, lived in this very palace. He could almost imagine her standing there. Imagine the despair in her expression. His chest constricted. She must be devastated right now, and it was his fault for leaving.

A side door opened, drawing his attention from these thoughts, and his eyes met a pair the color of fresh honey. Their warmth prompted the smallest spark of desperate hope inside Jace, but it died immediately, snuffed out by the cold glint of satisfaction that appeared as the emperor approached. Jace ground his teeth. How could he be such a fool as to, even momentarily, be taken in by the man's deceptive appearance? He glanced past him, tensing at the sight of Sir Richard. Jace would never forget what the man had done and threatened to do to Kyrin and Kaden.

"What do you have here for me?" Emperor Daican asked in a smooth, rich voice. He stopped before Jace, sizing him up.

"Kneel," Falcor commanded.

Jace refused. His strength might be failing, but so help him, he would not willingly kneel before this man. He braced himself. A moment later, Falcor yanked the rope. The pain brought tears to Jace's eyes, and he was on his knees before he knew it, choking for breath.

"This is the half-ryrik from the Landale group," Falcor said. "Jace."

"Ah." The emperor began circling him, repeating his name.

Fighting past the pain that throbbed mercilessly in his throat, he looked up. Another person had entered the room behind Sir Richard—a young woman about Kyrin's age. Her striking emerald eyes put the image of a snake in his mind—cunning, cruel, and twisted. She appeared to enjoy this immensely. No wonder Kyrin always spoke of her with such dread.

Daican stopped in front of Jace, blocking his view of the princess Davira. Jace's gaze climbed to the emperor's.

"Falcor tells me you and the Altair girl are close. How close? Friends?" Daican's voice lowered suggestively. "Lovers?"

Jace scowled, his skin prickling as heat rose up his neck. The emperor could say whatever he wanted about him, but to suggest such a thing about Kyrin urged Jace to choke him.

Daican smirked at his reaction. "Friends, then, I take it." He started circling again like a bird of prey. "How is she? Concerned about you, I would imagine."

Jace worked to moderate his breathing, but each breath came hard. He hated himself for what Kyrin must be going through. He had promised he would never leave for good. This hadn't been his choice, but would she ever know that? Or would she live the rest of her life believing he had broken that promise?

Daican's voice remained smooth and conversational, masking his ill will. "Tell me, how did Miss Altair react to her father's death?"

Jace's whole body went taut, and he nearly shook in an effort to contain the fire that flared inside him.

"It destroyed her, didn't it?"

Jace glared at him. He had never seen Kyrin so broken as in the days that followed her father's execution. The memories from their time on the mountain just north of here were still hard to bear.

Daican's lips curled in a malicious grin. "You certainly are part ryrik. It's plain in your eyes. So much anger, so much hatred . . . but maybe something more? Something like . . . love?"

Jace's glare slipped before he could stop it. The last thing he wanted was to supply the emperor with more fuel, but it was too late.

Daican released a low chuckle. "Oh, I'm right, aren't I? You do love her." He laughed again, glancing at his daughter, whose grin was even more unnerving. "That is interesting. And how is that working out?"

Jace swallowed, his throat burning.

"I imagine an animal like you doesn't have much of a chance at that sort of life."

Jace ground his teeth together. He shouldn't listen, but trapped here in this chamber with these men stripped his ability to fight.

"That is what you are," Daican pressed on. "An animal. Maybe your friends have said otherwise, but they are only a few. The whole world knows what you are."

Jace hung his head and closed his eyes tightly. The words were so similar to those that had been pounded into him growing up. He struggled to shut them out, but they attacked relentlessly.

"You don't belong with them. Do you really think they'll miss you when you're gone?"

Jace let out a shuddering breath. He knew the answer—he *did*—but the doubts were so heavy.

Daican's voice changed now, subtly, but carried commanding force. "Why don't you tell me what your group is planning in Samara and how to find your camp, and I will let you die a quick and painless death."

A quick death in exchange for the lives of the only people who had cared for him, given him hope, made life worth living. Weak as he was, he would still endure endless torture for them, for Kyrin. Sitting back on his heels, he looked up at the emperor and set his face in defiance. He wouldn't say a word to this man.

The emperor's expression hardened as well. "Your choice."

He motioned to Richard, who stepped forward and grabbed the rope. Jace pushed to his feet as fast as he was able to prevent the man from strangling him. Leaving little slack, Richard strode out of the throne room with Jace and a couple guards in tow.

At the far end of the palace, they opened a heavy door that led down a deep staircase to the dungeon.

The drop in temperature and the dampness sent a chill skittering along Jace's skin. The scent of blood and decay permeated the air, choking him, and his stomach recoiled. Down a long, dark corridor, they arrived at a line of cells. No fellow prisoners occupied them, but perhaps they were elsewhere in this horrible place, or kept at one of the prison camps they had heard rumors of back at camp.

Richard opened one of the barred doors and jerked Jace forward. He stumbled into the cell, and the door slammed shut behind him. Turning to his captors, Jace watched them walk away, carrying the only torch. The light faded and finally disappeared with their distant footsteps.

Jace looked around the cell. It was empty save for a tattered, rat-chewed blanket near the back. He shuddered. Though not completely dark, the thick and heavy air reminded him eerily of the dreams that wouldn't leave him.

He shook his head as if it could rid him of such thoughts and sank down at the back of the cell in exhaustion. His heavy breaths echoed around him. No other sounds of life reached his ears. His stomach pinched. Falcor had fed him just enough to keep him going, but never enough to satisfy his hunger.

Reaching up with his still-bound hands, Jace took hold of the rope around his neck and carefully worked it loose. He lifted it over his head and cast it away as if it were a venomous snake. The raw skin around his throat burned. With a long breath, he leaned back, too spent to try to free his hands. It wouldn't matter anyway.

For several minutes, he just sat and listened to his heartbeat, but then his thoughts roamed to the future. Torture and execution were certain. Pain he did not fear, but death . . .

His heart missed a beat. Once he had not feared it, but with such uncertainty and the plague of his nightmares, it now left him cold and desperate. But what hope did he have? His friends and any rescue were hundreds of miles away. He may have an ally or two in this palace, but what could they do for him?

No. Rescue wasn't coming for him. Best accept that now.

THE MINUTES STRETCHED out long and lonely in the dungeon. Occasionally, Jace caught the pattering and scratching of rats, but otherwise all was still. The unnatural quiet ate at his mind, but it couldn't have been more than an hour before footsteps and light reappeared.

The torches drew near, and Jace tensed in recognition of Richard. No doubt the pain would soon begin. He gathered his will to endure it.

Two of the three guards opened the cell and strode in. Grabbing Jace by the arms, they dragged him to the center of the cell, where they left him on his knees as Richard stepped inside. Jace looked up at him and maintained a stony expression. They wouldn't get anything from him.

A long silence drew out between them before Richard's cold voice filled the stillness. "You were part of the Altair twins' escape in Landale."

Jace just stared at him, but Richard went on.

"Then you can tell me who this arrow belongs to."

The man revealed a dark shafted arrow with blue fletching. Jace's heart gave a thump of recognition. It was one of his.

Richard watched him closely. "You know who it belongs to, don't you?"

Jace swallowed, but kept his mouth shut.

"This arrow has caused me considerable . . . discomfort." Richard flexed the fingers of his right hand, and then bent down, looking Jace in the eyes. "Whose is it?"

Jace held his cold gaze, never wavering. Richard rose with a snort and rolled the arrow between his fingers.

"Well, I may just exact my revenge on Miss Altair when she's caught. It may not be her arrow, but she is the reason I was there."

Mention of Kyrin and vengeance by this horrible man stalled Jace's heart. "It's mine." He had never wanted to speak, but he couldn't remain silent if it meant danger for Kyrin. Besides, what did it matter? He would be tortured regardless.

Richard snorted. "You would say that to protect her."

Jace shook his head. "The arrow is mine. I shot you from your horse in your right shoulder as you tried to charge one of our men."

The skepticism in Richard's expression faded, his jaw hardening. "So it *was* you."

Stewing over this information, Richard walked slowly around him. Jace breathed hard in anticipation of the revenge that would surely come. One tense moment passed, then two.

Searing pain almost forced Jace face first to the cell floor. He couldn't restrain a cry as Richard drove the arrow deep into his shoulder, sending burning waves across his back and down his arm.

"How does it feel?" the man growled near his ear.

He twisted the shaft and dug the arrowhead deeper into Jace's shoulder. Jace choked on the pain and groaned through his teeth, his eyes flooding with tears. He curled over, his face almost to his knees, but couldn't escape the agony ripping through him. Richard viciously wrenched the arrow before jerking it out again. It tore another cry and Jace's breath from his throat.

Jace gasped and tried to straighten, but the pulsating pain left him dizzy. Richard bent in front of him again, and held the arrow before his face. The arrowhead glistened red, and drops rolled down the shaft.

"A fitting trophy, is it not? I'll display it in my office." Richard turned for the door, but paused. "I nearly forgot. Something to make your stay in Auréa more *comfortable*."

Jace slowly raised his head. One of the guards placed a shallow metal basin in the hall across from his cell. Using the torch, he lit the contents, and white smoke curled up around the basin. Jace's already pounding heart kicked up another notch.

"Being you're half ryrik, this should be very interesting."

Richard slammed the door shut. As they marched away, Jace stared at the smoke growing like a phantom outside his cell. Already the acrid scent of incense tickled this throat. Gathering his strength, he gritted his teeth and moved farther back in the cell. He let his breath out in a hiss. His arm was leaden and his fingers numb, but pain jolted through his shoulder at the slightest movement. Blood warmed his back.

The first of the smoke cloud rolled through the bars of the cell. Jace lifted his shirt up to cover his nose and mouth, fighting the pain it caused. But how long could he really protect his lungs once the incense saturated the air?

The burning in Jace's throat and the heaviness of his lungs told him his attempt to filter clean air was failing. Smoke filled the corridor, searing his eyes. Hazy, suffocating darkness hung around him, becoming ever more like his dreams. He shook his head and squeezed his eyes closed, trying to shut it all out. Time passed unmarked by all but the steady rhythm of his heart. The dry irritation in his throat increased until he couldn't hold back a cough. A groan cut it short as pain ripped through his back, leaving him breathless.

Somewhere in the midst of the struggle, footsteps came again. Torchlight wavered in the haze. Richard returned, but this time Daican had joined him. They stopped at the door and peered in as if he were a caged wild animal they were experimenting on.

"So, it does affect you," Daican said. "Perhaps you've reconsidered your unwillingness to supply me with useful information."

Jace just glared at him.

The emperor stepped closer to the door, his eyes narrowed cruelly. "How long do you think it will take before you're suffocating in your own blood?"

Jace swallowed hard and dropped his gaze to the floor. He couldn't let the man get to him.

"Is this how you want to go?" Daican persisted. "To stay down here and slowly suffocate? Because it means nothing to me. What do I need with another public execution of a ryrik?" The emperor gripped the bars of the cell. "We can end this here and now if you cooperate *or* . . . you can drag this out slowly and painfully for however many hours you think you have left."

A tremor passed through Jace. It wouldn't be many hours before he could no longer breathe, but he would not give in. He lowered his shirt from his face for just a moment.

"I won't tell you anything."

Daican's jaw ground tight, but he still spoke in a controlled tone. "Perhaps not about your camp, but tell me of this Elon."

Jace locked eyes with him.

"Yes, I've heard the rumors and claims. Rumors that He is the Son of Elôm and is coming to destroy me."

With a sudden upwelling of conviction he didn't know he had, Jace said, "He is who they say, and if He does mean to destroy you, you can't stop Him."

Daican looked at him, as if contemplating whether or not he was insane. He then laughed a harsh, yet not altogether convincing laugh.

"Falcor tells me He's just a man with a few showy tricks. You only prove that a doomed people will believe anything."

Jace stared at him, measuring his words. If he weren't mistaken, he would say that underneath all his arrogance, the emperor was rattled by the news of Elon. Rattled and threatened.

A dark look overcame Daican's expression. "Well, you will die here by the incense of Aertus, and we'll see how powerful your so-called Savior is."

Aric strode down the hall toward the emperor's office and spotted Falcor ahead of him. It wasn't unusual to see the crete these days, but he tensed. He had just come from supper with a group of captains to learn of Falcor's arrival from Samara with a prisoner. Aric's stomach turned. The last time something like this happened, he had lost one of his closest friends.

Aric passed Falcor, trading a cool look. He had never pretended to like the crete. It was because of this traitor that William was dead. He forced away this thought and the deep pang in his chest when he arrived at the office. After knocking, he entered to find the emperor alone at his desk.

"I hear Falcor brought a prisoner." He was careful to control his voice, though his heart pounded. Who would it be this time?

Daican nodded, but he seemed unusually distracted. "Yes, one of the Landale group."

Odd that he wouldn't be more pleased.

Speaking with concealed dread, Aric asked, "Who?"

"The half-ryrik they call Jace."

His stomach sinking, Aric projected a look of satisfaction. "One of the inner circle then. That's good."

"It would be better if he provided any useful information." Daican forced out an irritable sigh, uncharacteristically bothered. He sat up straighter and focused fully on Aric. "But he is close to the Altair girl. Loves her, even. If she feels half the same, she'll be devastated by his capture."

Aric fought back a grimace. He had heard enough about Kyrin's friendship with Jace to know that it would kill her. "What do you plan to do with him?"

"Richard put incense down near his cell to see if he would react the same as a full-blood ryrik, and it appears he does."

"So you intend to let him suffocate?"

"Why not? It's slower than execution, and there's no advantage to killing him publicly. He won't break under torture."

"What about using him as leverage?" It didn't matter who the emperor had; Aric couldn't see anyone from Landale giving up anything that would endanger the camp, but at least it would buy Jace more time. Perhaps even enough to form a rescue plan.

Daican merely shook his head. "They won't let the Altair girl give herself up, and aside from her and a couple of others, no one cares enough about him to give me anything worthwhile. Unfortunately, he's the least useful of the group. The only thing he's good for at this point is what his death will do to the Altair girl. And if she suffers, her family will suffer with her. Besides, he deserves what he's getting."

Aric didn't believe the majority of the group had such a low opinion of Jace, but he kept this to himself. Any argument might lead to suspicion. The emperor seemed overly paranoid lately.

"Of course, Your Majesty. Is there anything you need?"

"How was the meeting?"

Aric shrugged. "Nothing of any great interest."

Daican nodded, and Aric took his leave. He didn't need to

know anything more about the emperor's plans for Jace. Moving with deliberate casualness that had become the norm for him, he left the office and made his way across the palace. He checked to make sure no one else was around and let himself down into the dungeon, grabbing a small torch on the way. Only a few feet down the hall, the overpowering stench of incense assaulted him. Even he could hardly breathe in it.

The cells appeared in the thick haze, and he arrived at the only one holding a prisoner. Jace huddled at the back, but his eyes locked on Aric, fierce in their defiance, yet watery and blood-shot from the smoke. He probably expected more questioning.

"Jace, I'm Aric."

The defiance melted to reveal a bone-deep weariness. Moving as one four times his age, Jace rose to his feet with a gasp and barely suppressed a groan. With shaky steps, he approached the door and grasped at the bars with one bound hand to steady himself. Aric's stomach twisted at his sorry condition—the blood staining his sleeve and the side of his shirt, the ugly bruises and raw flesh around his throat and wrists, but most of all, the hollow look in his eyes. Aric had seen much cruelty in his years at Auréa Palace, but he had never witnessed such a crushed spirit.

Aric swallowed hard and said the only thing he could think of. "Is there anything I can do for you?"

His eyes glinting with pain, Jace's voice came in a hoarse whisper. "Water, please."

He curled over and coughed, a soft cry of pain escaping with it. His balance wavered, and Aric reached in to help steady him. When Jace straightened, blood stained his lips. Aric's chest squeezed. Bringing water would be risky, but how could he deny such a desperate request?

"I'll get you water," he said.

He turned away from the cell, fighting the emotions that churned inside him. Thank Elôm he met no guards along the way and was able to return to Jace with a waterskin. The young man sat near the door when he reached him. Aric knelt down and helped him bring the waterskin to his lips. He drank eagerly, but choked and coughed after every few sips. By the time he'd downed most of it, he looked spent.

Aric released a heavy sigh and bent his head. "If there was time, I'd try to get you out of here." Even if he had a way now, Jace hardly looked fit for escape. "I'm sorry."

Slowly, Jace shook his head. Total acceptance settled in his eyes. No sign of hope. If only Aric could do more. His gaze fell on the tight ropes around Jace's wrists, but even something as simple as freeing them was impossible. It would only alert the emperor that someone with rebel sympathies still inhabited the palace.

Aric glanced up the hall. He could not linger. No doubt Richard would soon come to check Jace.

"I must go." But he loathed the thought of walking away and leaving him to die alone.

Jace nodded weakly.

Aric rose and looked down at him. "You have my prayers, Jace." Prayers for peace, comfort, and less pain as he neared the end.

Jace's eyes locked with his. "Thank you," he whispered.

Taking a deep breath, Aric left the cell, but a heavy weight rested on him. He couldn't stop this any more than he could stop William's execution, and just like that time, it would haunt him.

The water Aric had brought was now a distant memory. Jace's throat felt as though he had swallowed broken glass. He tried with all his might to fight it, but he had to cough. The pain of his shoulder and lungs consumed him. Blood filled his mouth, trickling past his lips. He spit out the rest and struggled to draw a breath, but his lungs only filled to half their capacity. He swayed, his head buzzing.

It was just as Richard intended. He would either suffocate or die of blood loss. Whatever hadn't been lost from his shoulder was filling up his lungs. His heart punched his ribs as a wave of panic took hold, but he had no way to fight this.

He blinked hard. Was his vision growing dim or was the incense only thickening? He gave up trying to block it with his shirt. It only prolonged the inevitable. His breaths grew shallower. Numbness crept in, almost welcoming as it threaded through his limbs, erasing the pain. He let his head droop and his eyes slide closed.

His whole body gave a violent jerk of panic, agony tearing through him, but fear gripped him even stronger. He was dying. The truth of it crushed down with terrifying force. He had minutes—an hour, at most. He was going to die.

Tremors passed through him until he shook uncontrollably. He gasped for breath, desperate for the air to keep him alive, but he wrenched over, coughing again. Blood spilled from his mouth, creating a pool at his knees. He couldn't breathe.

"No!" the hoarse cry broke out. He wanted to live. For the first time in his life, he was desperate to hold on to life.

Darkness swirled around him. He tried to rise and escape it, but was held down. The dreams had become real. He cried out again. The darkness pulled him down, and he had no strength to stop it. He was helpless. He had nothing left. Death wanted him, and he couldn't fight it. Tears filled his eyes, and he barely had enough breath to force whispered words past his lips.

"Elôm, help me."

The wavering darkness grew deeper, but then a faint light appeared. Jace focused on it, though it wavered in his vision. Was his mind playing one last cruel trick on him before the end came? Would the light taunt him and then disappear, just like in his nightmares, and leave him to slip into death with despair?

JACE SQUINTED AND blinked hard. Surely the light would leave him. It always did.

However, it grew, drawing nearer to his cell. The echo of footsteps accompanied it, and dark shapes appeared in the murk.

The first person visible was Richard. Jace's weak heart sank to the floor, any tiny spark of hope crushed. He tried to find the strength to hide his weakness, but he had none left. Whatever the man planned for him now, he didn't think he could endure it. For the first time since he was a child, he cowered.

As Richard unlocked the door, Jace's gaze drifted to a second man. His heart stilled. Time ceased. He didn't think he could believe what he saw, on the edge of death, yet the eyes that bored into his were like a fire, burning, yet soothing to his heart. Elon had come for him.

Guards took Jace by the arms and pulled him up. He choked in agony and stumbled out of the cell where they left him standing before Elon. Again, their eyes locked, and the familiar and crushing unworthiness consumed the awe from moments ago.

"Lord," he gasped. He tried to lower himself to his knees, but they buckled and he fell hard, his head bowed.

Richard stepped to his side with a growl. "Get up."

He drew his foot back. Jace tensed.

"No." The authority in Elon's voice was like a physical force, driving Richard and his guards back a step. "You've harmed him enough."

Jace's heart beat sluggishly in the following moment of silence. Why would Elon come here for him? He was nothing—worse than nothing. A murderer. A sinner.

"Jace."

He took a trembling breath. That voice—tender, loving—it was the voice from his dreams. Elon's voice. He recognized it now, but he couldn't raise his head; he was too ashamed.

Elon knelt in front of him. Jace still didn't lift his eyes.

"Why do you try to hide from Me?"

The question cut deeply into his heart, and tears clogged his throat, filling his eyes. "I've done so much. Failed . . . so many times." He couldn't breathe, the pain was so great.

"I've been calling you. Calling you away from the hold of your past."

"I tried to reach You."

"Jace." Elon said his name with such care that he finally looked up. "You didn't have to reach Me. I was always there. You only had to answer Me."

Jace trembled as these words sank deep into his heart.

"You are loved, Jace."

With this declaration, something changed inside him. His heart broke with how long and desperately he had yearned for such knowledge, but at the same time, it was healed. And in that moment, the tears he had held inside for so many years let loose, flowing warmly down his cheeks, and he cried—cried as all the pain in his heart slowly drained away.

Elon reached for his hands, untying the rope, but it was more than his hands that He freed.

"You have always been loved, by both Me and My Father. From the moment you believed, your soul was safe. You don't have to carry the fears and shame inside you anymore, and you don't have to try to carry them to Me. Just let them go, and I'll take them for you. You were never meant to carry the weight yourself or do this on your own. You don't have to fight alone. Do you understand?"

His tears still falling, Jace nodded. At last, he did.

Elon rose to His feet again and extended His hand. Jace looked at it with the realization that it had always been there for him through all the pain and darkness of the last couple of years. He had only failed to take it, but no more. He grasped it, and Elon drew him to his feet, holding him steady.

"You never have to doubt again."

Elon placed His hand on Jace's chest, and all the pain, including the numbness in his hand, vanished. Jace gasped in a great breath as his lungs freed, and he could breathe easily again. Strength surged into his body.

Richard's voice cut in, reminding Jace it wasn't only him and Elon.

"He's released. Now it's time for You to hold up Your end of the bargain."

Jace glanced back at Richard, his heart giving an uneven beat, and then focused again on Elon.

"What bargain?"

Elon did not answer, but turned and motioned. Only now did Jace notice Aelos and Riyel waiting behind Him.

"Go with them," Elon said. "They will take you safely out of the city."

A fresh wave of cold dread built inside Jace. "What about You?"

Elon faced him again, but a little of the light in His eyes was gone. Something accepting and troubling had replaced it, and Jace's stomach twisted.

He put His hand on Jace's shoulder and urged, "Go on."

Jace hesitated, but walked with the two strong, stoic men down the hall. After a few yards, he looked back. Richard was locking a pair of shackles around Elon's wrists, and Elon did not resist him. Jace halted. Surely, Elon had not given Himself up so that Jace could go free, had He?

"No." Jace turned to go back. This wasn't right. He wasn't worth this, but Aelos held his arm.

"Come," he said, and though it wasn't forceful Jace did not feel he could resist.

At the far end of the dungeon, a group of guards let them into a small room with one chair and a table. Candles glowed, lighting up a pitcher and a large plate of food. The door closed, and Aelos and Riyel stood on either side of it. Jace turned to them.

"What is Elon planning to do?"

Surely, He had a plan. He had just healed Jace with a simple touch. Richard and Daican could never hold Him against His will.

"What He must," Aelos answered, his voice low and deep. He had the same troubling look in his eyes, though his expression barely changed. It did not comfort Jace, or lend much certainty to his previous thoughts.

Before Jace could question any further, Riyel spoke.

"You should eat." He gestured to the table. "You need strength for the rest of the day."

With such unease cramping his stomach, Jace didn't know if he could eat, but one look at the food—a hearty slab of meat, thick slice of bread, and large wedge of cheese—sent hunger pangs to his stomach. He took a seat at the table, but then just sat there for a long moment as it all sank in. Minutes ago, he had wavered on the very edge of death. Now he sat healed, with enough food before him to satisfy his hunger and, by all accounts, appeared to be rescued. Tears welled once again, and he bowed his head, closing his eyes.

"Thank You," he whispered. It hardly seemed enough, but he had no other words to describe the gratitude overflowing his heart. He shook his head. *I'm sorry I failed for so long to understand, and for losing my way when all I should have done was follow Your guidance. I'm sorry for letting fear control me.* He let out a long breath as Rayad, Kyrin, and Timothy's faces reached into his thoughts. They had tried so hard to help him see. If only he had truly let himself hear them. *Thank You for giving me a second chance to live the way You want me to. I will try my hardest not to waste whatever days You give me.*

Raising his head, Jace wiped the dampness from his face and cleared his throat. Never had he been so certain that his prayers were heard. And, despite the unease of the situation, the peace that slowly filled him surpassed any he had experienced before.

Jace reached for a fork and ate hungrily, the first time in over a week he had filled his stomach. However, his mind remained caught up in Elon and what he had seen while leaving the cells. There must be a plan in place. Elon was far too important, too needed, to give Himself up for Jace. It made no sense. He was deity—the Son of Elôm—and Jace had lived a life to this point brimming with failures. He deserved to reap the consequences of it, and now that he had Elon's assurance, he was willing and unafraid. Now he could face death without dread.

When his plate was empty, Jace sat and waited. How long would he be here, and what was going on outside this room? Would Elon come to get him? He glanced at Aelos and Riyel, but they stood as statues planted on either side of the door. Aelos's vague answer to his question earlier didn't give him hope that he could get any definitive information from them.

Settling back in his chair, Jace silently talked to Elôm. It felt awkward at first, but he kept on, praying longer and deeper than he ever had before. And the more he prayed, the more his heart seemed to open, letting in light and cleaning out dark corners where he had buried his fears and torments for so long. This time, instead of trying to deal with them himself he just let them go and left them in Elôm's hands, as his mother had wanted him to. How he ached to let her know that, finally, he understood.

Footsteps echoed in the corridor outside, and Jace jerked his head up. The door opened a moment later, and a guard stepped in.

"Come," he commanded.

The disquiet inside Jace returned. As much as he wanted to know what was going on, uncertainty settled in full force. He stood and joined Aelos and Riyel. They walked on either side of him as they followed the guard up the stairs that opened to the palace courtyard. Jace squinted in the mid-morning sun. Then his gaze locked on a waiting group of guards, and his heart thudded. He remembered Kyrin's description of her escort to the execution platform by just such a group.

"Do not fear," Aelos said. "King Elôm holds your life secure."

Jace let out a slow breath, willing his pulse to regulate as the guards surrounded them. They marched forward, out of the courtyard. Jace trusted Elôm, but he did wonder what lay at the end of this. Was it simply an escort out of the city? It seemed like a lot for one man, and where was Elon? He scanned the streets and the buildings overlooking them. Kyrin and her father came to mind again. Both had walked this path, and one had died. Their bravery awed him. How desperately he wanted to see Kyrin's face again.

The rustle and murmur of people reached Jace's ears even before the crowded square came into view. He sucked in his breath. Kyrin had described such a scene, but it was even more disturbing than anything his imagination could conjure. How could so many thousands of people be so eager to see death and pain or whatever else the emperor had planned? Even the largest crowds he had seen as a gladiator didn't compare to this.

The crowd parted just enough to let them pass through to the platform rising ahead. Taking in the sight of it put his heart in his throat. He believed what Aelos had said, but so many people had died here. It left him cold.

They neared the base of the platform, and Jace looked up. Standing between several guards was the emperor. Davira stood there as well, with whom appeared to be her mother and brother. The emperor must have something big planned to include the royal family. Jace couldn't stop the twisting in his gut.

Aelos and Riyel remained at his side as Jace climbed the platform, where Daican gave him an evilly satisfied look. Jace shivered at the intensity of it and the chilling sense that the emperor was merely a pawn maneuvered by a supremely evil force. He looked away, unable to hold the unnerving gaze.

One of the guards took hold of his arm now, drawing him to the front and center of the platform to face the many thousands of staring eyes. He swallowed, his mouth going dry, and glanced over his shoulder. Aelos and Riyel stood only a couple of feet behind him, their faces hard-set. Though they possessed no visible weapons, Jace had the distinct feeling that they wouldn't need any if they had reason to step in and defend him.

His gaze swung around as Daican stepped past him, his focus on the crowd.

"Citizens of Arcacia."

The square went quiet—so quiet that Jace could hear his heart.

"Do you know what we have here?" The emperor gestured to Jace, his voice loud and carrying. "A half ryrik."

Gasps and exclamations of revulsion trickled through the crowd, followed by hisses and hateful jeers.

"A half-blood monster of the vilest descent," Daican continued hatefully.

Jace breathed steadily. How incredible to find how such words had lost their sting now that he was fully shielded by the truth. Elôm loved him, and that was all that mattered now. Whatever people said meant nothing.

"Not only that, but a rebel, bent on destroying our way of life!"

Daican had the crowd fired up now, their faces scowling and grumbling.

"Is not death a fitting punishment for such a pitiless, loathsome creature?"

The crowd responded with a resounding, "Yes!" that vibrated in the wood under Jace's feet.

"And who here would come forward to save him?"

This question drew a chorus of sharp, grating laughter. Somewhere nearby, a man shouted, "No one! Kill him!" and the others echoed the words.

Jace was nothing to them. Worse than nothing. This had once cut so deeply but, with Elôm's help, it never would again if he made it off this platform.

"Yet, there is One who has chosen to ransom his life," Daican announced, causing a reaction of confusion and disbelief among the people. "Behold, the so-called Savior of Ilyon."

Daican swept his arm back, and Jace's gaze followed, locking on Elon as two guards led Him forward. The sight socked the air from Jace's lungs and left him weak. Elon's badly bruised and bloodied face blurred as tears poured into Jace's eyes. How could Daican have done this to Him? Why had He let them?

The guards dragged Elon to the front with Jace and Daican. Jace clearly heard His heavy, difficult breathing, but the reaction from the crowd then drowned it out. Vicious, mocking jeers and insults rose up around them, starting a fire in Jace's blood.

Shaking, he glared out at them. How dare they? They should be on their knees in reverence, yet they stood in mockery. Could they not see? Jace wanted to scream at them, but his voice locked in his throat. How could they be such fools?

"It is said He came to overthrow us and rule Himself," Daican said. Boos and shouts of opposition rose from the people, and Jace ground his teeth at such lies. "But look at Him now! Does He look like a conqueror?"

A tear slipped down Jace's cheek as a raucous wave of laughter filled his ears. He couldn't take it. Why didn't Elon do something? But He just stood there, taking it all without a word.

"No," Daican said. "Instead, He has traded His life for this *animal's.*"

His finger pointed at Jace, and ice shot through Jace's heart. It was exactly what he had feared.

"No," he gasped. Elon couldn't die in his place. He wasn't worthy of such a sacrifice.

But Elon looked him in the eyes, and Jace saw the love—love so great and powerful it took his breath away as it filled him. Then Elon looked out at the crowd, facing their ridicule. Instead of a look that condemned their mockery and disbelief, the love remained; saddened, but strong and constant.

The glint of metal jerked Jace's gaze to the long, thin dagger Daican had just pulled from its sheath. Only now did it register that the crowd chanted for death. The emperor faced Elon, murder in his eyes. Elon stood silently, His battered face never once hinting at hatred or anger. As the emperor drew near, Jace stepped forward. He had to stop this. But Aelos and Riyel's strong hands gripped him by the arms and held him back.

Jace's heart screamed in protest, but it never made it to his lips. His eyes locked on Elon, and his breaths came shallow and fast. Surely, Elon would stop this. He had forced Richard back with a mere word. Jace had heard the power and authority in His voice. He could heal Himself, break the chains that bound Him, demand the worship of every person standing here—

Daican's blade sank into Elon's chest, turning every thought into a numbing haze. Pain of disbelief erupted in Jace's own heart. He couldn't feel anything but the horror of the scene that seemed frozen before him. This couldn't be.

Daican's dagger slid back out, dripping scarlet. Elon sank slowly to His knees, and Jace watched deep red blood seep down the front of His white shirt just like the blood of the sacrificial lambs.

JACE STOOD PARALYZED. He couldn't draw his eyes away from Elon's still body and the pool of blood seeping across the platform. Blood so fresh, so vivid, reflecting the clear sky overhead. Blood that moments ago sustained life now spilled out in front of him. How could this be?

Like waking from a dream, the murmur of the crowd registered slowly. Jace looked up, first seeing Daican and the still-dripping dagger. When his gaze rose farther, it met with the amber-eyed Prince Daniel across from him. They stared at each other, eyes wide, faces slack, sharing the shock of what they had just witnessed.

Aelos and Riyel still held Jace's arms. He took a halting step as they guided him away from the scene, and then followed numbly. No coherent thoughts would form. He only kept seeing the same things in his mind—the dagger, the blood, Elon's last breath.

At the bottom of the steps, they met the crowd. All the people who had not only stood and watched Elon die, but had screamed for it. Even now, their hatred wasn't quenched. They glared and sneered at him. Some even reached out to grab him, but as Aelos and Riyel led him through their midst it was as if an invisible shield surrounded them. A crowd this size would have

345

overwhelmed them in a moment, yet no one could get close enough. Many of them tried though. Like feral animals, they reached and shouted, but there was no mistaking the love in Elon's eyes when He had looked out at them. How were they so blind? But then, how long had it taken Jace to see? Only on the verge of death and hearing it straight from Elon's lips had he finally understood.

He hung his head, his eyes burning as regret stung his heart. "I'm sorry."

When at last they broke free of the crowd, Aelos and Riyel hurried him northward through the city. The buildings passed in a blur, and before he knew it they'd arrived outside the city wall, where they stopped. Jace bent over panting, and braced himself against his knees. Sweat rolled down his back, but a chill encased him. Away from the crowd now, it all sank in. Dizziness and nausea overwhelmed him, and his stomach retched and emptied. Taking a few wobbly steps, he sank down by the side of the road and held his throbbing head in his hands.

All was silent but for his heavy breaths that slowly regulated. Finally, he looked up at Aelos and Riyel's tense and solemn faces. Aelos reached down and helped him up.

"Your friends are waiting for you just up the mountain. Go to them now, but do not let them remain here tonight. Find a safer place and then journey quickly back to Samara."

Jace nodded numbly, incapable of any other response. Turning, he stared into the forest that led up the mountainside. He'd been this way before. He started walking, but then looked back. Aelos and Riyel had vanished.

Trudging on, Jace made his way steadily upward, both longing and reluctant. This was the second time he had made this trek carrying news of a loved one's death. The memories of having to take such news back to Kyrin made him cold again. But the thought of her also drew him forward. At each step, his heart beat a little faster. Then came the faint murmur of voices ahead, and his anticipation heightened.

Breaking through the obstruction of trees, he stopped, his eyes drinking in the sight of them. Though they had been parted for only a few days, the intensity of his feelings made it seem more like a lifetime. Love filled him, deeper and more yearning than he had ever experienced. The walls were gone. Walls that had held him back, even from Kyrin and Rayad.

"Jace!"

Kyrin's voice soothed his heart. She jumped up and ran to him. Already his throat thickened. She slowed as she came near, her eyes wide. He hadn't thought until now how much blood covered him. By all appearances, he should be dead. He drew her into his arms, needing the connection to her. She held him lightly at first, but then her embrace tightened. Overcome, tears worked their way again to Jace's eyes and rolled down his face. He shouldn't be here right now—shouldn't be alive—but he was, thanks to Elon's sacrifice that was beyond understanding. He breathed hard, his chest aching with the emotion of it.

Kyrin stepped back and looked up into his face. "You're crying," she gasped. Her gaze dropped to the blood on his shirt and her voice trembled. "You're hurt."

"No." She met his gaze again, and Jace said, "He healed me."

The tears continued to fall, because those words meant so much more than physical healing. Kyrin's eyes registered understanding, and filled with her own tears.

"He told you," she whispered.

Jace nodded, and they hugged again, both crying silently. When they parted, Jace's gaze rested on Rayad and the nearly-overflowing moisture in the man's eyes. Only now did he fully realize just how much this man meant to him. He stepped away from Kyrin and into Rayad's arms, embracing him.

"Oh, Jace, thank the King you're safe," Rayad said hoarsely.

Jace breathed out hard. Only because of Elôm and His Son was he standing here.

The others—Holden, Timothy, and Aaron—gathered around them, all expressing their joy to have Jace back. Holden took his arm firmly, but then pulled him into an embrace. Jace smiled. What joy to fully know and feel the bond of true friendship.

Before anything more was said, Gem forced her way through the gathering with a high trill. The dragon pressed her head against his chest so enthusiastically that she almost knocked him to the ground. A laugh escaped him, and he rubbed her neck.

"I know, I'm sorry," he murmured. He never should have left her behind when he had gone into that forest. Things would have turned out far differently if he hadn't. And yet . . . would things have been better that way? Deep inside, he understood that this was just as it needed to be.

The group drew him into the middle of camp, all with curious expressions. Stopping near their small fire, Timothy asked, "Where is Elon?"

Jace sobered, his throat tightening again. How did he tell them? How did he explain what he had witnessed? It replayed in his mind, bringing fresh tears, and he surely had an abundance of them after all these years. He tried to speak, but his voice failed him. Everyone's faces paled as understanding dawned, but no one said a word until Jace murmured, "He traded His life for mine."

No one seemed to breathe for a long moment.

"You mean He's . . ." Timothy swallowed. "The emperor already . . ."

Jace nodded, wiping at the tear streaks down his face. "Less than an hour ago."

Everyone looked at each other in stunned silence, and tears streamed down Kyrin's cheeks.

"But He said everything would be all right," she said. "He told us to wait here. We could have stopped it."

"It doesn't make sense." Timothy shook his head, a look of devastation in his eyes.

"It does," Jace murmured, and they looked at him. Though it was more than he could hope to understand, he had felt something on that platform. Something life-altering, history-altering. Elon had died for Jace personally, but Jace sensed something greater and farther reaching. He had stood beside Him, his life bought by Elon's, but when Elon had looked out at the crowd, it was as if every one of them could be standing there, not only Jace.

He cleared his throat, but his voice still came out rough. "He was the ultimate Lamb sacrifice."

The magnitude of this truth left them all in silence. Slowly, Timothy sank down, overcome by it. After a minute or two, he nodded.

"You're right," he breathed.

And again, they were quiet, processing the fact that the final sacrifice they had looked ahead to was not some animal, but the life and blood of Elôm's Son. He had sacrificed *Himself* for them. Not one of them had a dry eye as this sank in.

Her voice wavering, Kyrin asked, "Now what will we do without Him?"

No one had an answer, but it left a heavy feeling hovering over them. What of Samara and all the people who had looked to Elon to save them from Arcacia's invasion?

For several minutes no one moved, but then Rayad put his hand on Jace's shoulder. In a husky voice, he said, "Let's get you cleaned up."

They walked over to the supplies, where Jace's pack lay amidst the others. He grabbed it and stepped behind the dragons to change. Rayad stayed to assist him, and though Jace didn't need it he did not turn him away.

Pulling off his bloodied shirt, Jace looked over his shoulder. The arrow wound was only a faint scar. He took a deep breath.

The struggle to breathe at all still hung vividly in his mind, the phantom taste of blood stinging his throat. However, comforting warmth grew in his chest where Elon had touched and healed him. Tears stung his nose.

Once cleaned of blood and freshly clothed, Jace followed Rayad back to the fire, where everyone looked at him with the desire to know what had happened. Starting with the night in Feldmor Forest, he recounted the journey to Valcré and the night in the dungeon. Kyrin cried, and he cried. It felt so strange, yet cleansing and freeing. He even caught Rayad brushing away a tear, and knew how much they all loved him despite any enemy's claims.

Jace awoke to the breaking of dawn at their new mountain campsite several miles from Valcré. Lying still in his bedroll, he stared up at the clear sky. He didn't believe he had ever experienced such a deep and restful sleep. He breathed in a long, fresh breath, his lungs freer than they had been his whole life. It was as if everything about him had changed. He felt . . . new.

But at such a great price. A price someone else had paid.

"Help me never to waste it, Elôm," he prayed into the stillness.

The others stirred around him and soon rose to prepare breakfast and pack camp. As he saddled Gem, her contented purr rumbling in his ears, he looked off to the north and thought of Aelos's urge to hasten back to Samara. He thought of the future they faced there. His personal fight had been won, but a battle still loomed. One they had hoped Elon would fight for them.

-Part Four-

Battle

EVERYTHING HAD CHANGED as they approached Samara for the second time. The anxiousness Jace experienced now was nothing like the despair that had so heavily weighed him down. At last, he could see a purpose to his life that fear and lies had once hidden. That purpose now involved trying to save Samara. After all, the fate of everyone he cared so deeply for was tied to it.

Flying over the walls of Stonehelm, they beheld an impressive sight. Dozens of dragons dotted the fields outside the fortress, chirping and trilling as they glided down near the gate.

Jace was barely out of the saddle before he heard Kaden's voice. He smiled as the young man rushed toward them. Directly behind Kaden came Marcus and Liam. Kyrin met each of her brothers with a crushing hug. The men then gathered around Jace to make sure he was all right. Talas appeared, along with Captain Darq and Leetra, all relieved to see them.

"When did you and the militia get here?" Kyrin asked her older brothers.

"Just after you left," Marcus said. "If you'd been around for another couple of hours, we could have joined you."

"We managed," Kyrin replied.

The group around her grew quiet. They still had grave news to share. So many had counted on Elon's intervention in this fight. Would they stand strong in the face of what seemed like a devastating defeat?

Rayad stepped up. "Is the king inside?"

Talas nodded. "In the keep with General Mason."

"We must speak with him."

Leaving the dragons, the entire group entered the fortress. In the war room, Balen stood with General Mason and his officers. Trask and the rest of their group were also present. All eyes turned to them, their expressions lighting when they saw Jace. Those from Landale hurried to meet them. Jace greeted each one, smiling at their enthusiasm. He found it incredible how much he would miss them if they were no longer part of his life. People had never meant so much to him. Only those few he had allowed into the deepest place of his heart.

The joy of the reunion, however, had to end. They had no time to dally with the rest of the news they carried.

"As you all can see, Jace is alive and well, thank Elôm," Rayad said. He hesitated. "But we also bring grave news as well."

He motioned to Timothy, who was the most knowledgeable and capable of explaining what had happened to Elon and why. Complete silence engulfed the hall as he spoke. He started out strong, but his voice wavered at the end. Even now, Jace experienced the pain of watching Elon die. Stunned faces turned to expressions of deep sadness as everyone took the news in their own way. The soldiers were more stoic than most, though their eyes expressed their emotions. Balen braced himself against the table, his head bowed. A quiet moment passed before Rayad spoke reluctantly.

"I'm afraid there's more."

Balen looked up, and then straightened to receive the rest of their news.

"Late yesterday, we caught sight of Daican's army. At the pace they were traveling, they should arrive around midday tomorrow."

The king cleared his throat, though his voice still came out a little hoarse. "How large a force?"

Rayad shook his head. "We couldn't get close enough to know for sure."

"And firedrakes?"

Rayad nodded. "We saw quite a number, but that is why we kept our distance." He looked at Darq. "How many riders were you able to gather?"

"About eighty." The crete captain crossed his muscular arms, his brows furrowing. "Not as many as I hoped. My people aren't as willing to join this fight as I thought they would be."

"They should be," Leetra grumbled, her eyes fiery, "after what Falcor did."

"At least some came," Rayad said.

Darq gave a brief nod. "I've sent half the riders to the capital with Glynn. Including Kaden's men, that leaves us with just over fifty here. This is where we expect to face the greatest number of firedrakes."

Rayad agreed and looked at the king. "So we are prepared to face them?"

"As prepared as we can be."

The moons rose into the dark sky and spilled soft light across the wall. Resting against the parapet, Jace gazed out at the Arcacian plains. Normally, he wouldn't have chosen such a spot to go and think, but the open air and fresh breeze soothed him as he considered what had happened and what was to come. The horizon gave up no sign of Daican's army, but it would in just hours. They would come and make their attack. What then? Even if they defeated Daican this time, how long could they hold their ground? How many would die in the effort?

Jace bowed his head and forced himself to remember that Elôm was in control of this. The outcome was already decided. However, uncertainty was an old habit and not easy to break. Raising his eyes back to the stars, Jace reached out to his King for reassurance. He was no longer afraid to die, knowing with full confidence where he would go, but it came with an intense desire to live. To make up for the years he had wasted in doubt. To experience a life of fullness. Maybe it was too late for that, but at least he wouldn't go out in despair.

With lookouts and many of the cretes on the wall nearby, Jace gave little notice to the approach of footsteps until they stopped alongside him. He looked over, right into Kyrin's face. Her moonlit eyes stared up at him, her lips curved with a hint of a smile.

"Are you all right?" she asked.

"I was just thinking about . . . everything." He smiled and shook his head. "When Rayad first rescued me, there was so much I had to get used to. It was a completely different way of life. I kind of feel that way now. Still getting used to it."

"A lot of things changed for you in Valcré."

"Yes." Jace paused, wrestling with some of the emotions inside. "I'm tempted to feel guilty. Not so much about my past anymore, but how I've handled it."

"You've suffered enough guilt. I think Elôm wants you to be free of that."

Jace nodded and stared at her, taking note of the sparkle in her eyes and the way the breeze fluttered her hair about her shoulders. It looked soft. He let out his breath slowly. "I'm sorry."

Her forehead wrinkled. "For what?"

"For all the times I've been so difficult. I never made it easy for you to help me."

Smiling, she shook her head. "Maybe not, but I never wanted to give up."

"Why?" What was it that drove her so strongly to help?

"I care about you . . . a lot." She shrugged and glanced down at her hands. "Something about the first time I saw you. I just didn't want you to suffer so much. It was Elôm, I guess."

"You're good at imitating His love."

Kyrin's smile widened, but she looked away shyly. "Thanks."

He watched her stare out past the wall. Her smile faded and left him wishing he could say something to bring it back. Finally, she looked at him. Something had changed in her eyes. Their soft glow had lost their brightness, and her expression tensed. She was afraid. Who wouldn't be on a night like this?

"I'll let you go back to your thinking," she said, her voice low.

He turned to watch her walk away. He didn't want her to go and almost called her back, but what would he say if he did? One thing that hadn't changed in Valcré was his feelings for her. If anything, they had only deepened at the possibility of never seeing her again. Certain barriers had lifted now, but what did that mean for them? He shook his head as he turned back to the parapet. The verge of war was not a good time to sort through such things.

Jace watched the sunrise lift over the hilly horizon from his comfortable perch on Gem's back. Aside from the cretes, he was alone. They had regarded him curiously when he'd first arrived at the break of dawn, but for the first time he gave no notice to the reactions of others. He had his own thoughts and things to ponder in the last bit of calm before the storm.

He breathed in the cool air of the new day, so fresh and yet untainted by the threat marching their way. Strange how he could feel such peace, yet be anxious. So much unknown lay ahead. With this in mind, he prayed. Looking toward the fortress, he thought of everyone inside. Some of them would die. Maybe even him.

He dropped his gaze to the writing supplies and folded parchment in his lap, bearing his simple script on the front. *To my mother, Rachel, from Jace.* This was the first time since Rayad had taught him to read and write that he'd had the opportunity to appreciate it. Satisfied, he packed away the supplies he'd borrowed, tucked the letter safely in his pocket, and slid down from Gem. Patting the dragon on the shoulder, he headed back to the keep.

Soldiers were up and about now, preparing, their faces set and determined. Still, Jace sensed their unease. None knew what to expect, or had experience to draw courage from. No one had attacked Samara in centuries. Not like this. War was new to all of them.

Inside the keep, Jace walked into the mess hall, where he found his friends gathered at one of the long tables. Rayad met him first. The familiar creases in his brow showed concern. Perhaps, if they both survived the coming days, that look would no longer be so familiar.

"Sleep all right?"

Jace nodded to reassure him. "I was just up early and went out to see Gem."

Rayad gripped his shoulder, and they took seats at the table across from Kyrin and her brothers. She smiled at him, though it lacked its usual brilliance. The weariness in it suggested that she hadn't slept nearly as well as he had. She stood to lose so much in this fight. She had already lost so much. Jace hated to see her suffer any further grief. *Spare her.*

As everyone ate their breakfast, they shared stories and moments of reminiscing—memories from camp and before that. They had all come from such different walks of life. Jace looked down the table at them—a baron's son, a one-time enemy spy, a former captain in Daican's army, and him, a former slave and gladiator with both noble and ryrik blood. All so different, but so important to each other. Only Elôm could bring together such a mix of backgrounds and personalities.

Near the end of the meal, General Mason approached their table. "King Balen wanted me to let you know that you have full access to the armory. Whatever you need to arm yourselves, you're free to use."

"Thank you, General," Trask replied.

When the general walked away, Trask looked around the table. "I guess we'd better see to that. If they do arrive by midday, we only have a few hours."

Everyone rose.

Across from Jace, Kyrin said, "I think I'll go see if Josef needs help with anything."

Her unease showed even more clearly now. If only Jace could convey reassurance to her, but it was all so much bigger than that.

Everyone from Landale, including Marcus's militia and Kaden's riders, gathered in the large, well-stocked armory, and spread out around the tables and displays of extra armor and weaponry. Before seeking any for himself, Marcus worked his way through the men to make sure that each was properly equipped. It wasn't quite the same as preparing his unit at Fort Rivor. The armor was mismatched, for the most part, and predominately chainmail and leather. Not the plate mail he had grown used to, but it would do. He stopped along the way to help any of the men who weren't familiar with the process. He assisted Jeremy, one of the youngest men in his force, and gave him an encouraging clap on the shoulder in response to the nervousness in the young man's eyes. No amount of training or sparring back at camp would take that away.

Finally, he reached Liam. His brother nodded to a well-crafted chainmail shirt lying on the table.

"Thought that would fit you."

"Thank you." Marcus gave him a quick smile. His brother was always thinking of him.

He swapped out his jerkin for a padded gambeson to wear under the chainmail. Satisfied with the fit, he reached for the armor, and Liam helped him slip the weighty chainmail over his head and adjust it. It had been some time since he had worn armor, but he hadn't forgotten how heavy and hot it was, especially in such warm temperatures. Over the chainmail shirt, Liam assisted him in buckling on a tooled leather breastplate, and then a matching pair of bracers and greaves.

Marcus thanked him again and gave everything one final inspection. From the corner of his eye, he saw Liam slip off his jerkin and reach for a second gambeson. Marcus stopped him, and looked into his brother's eyes.

"You don't have to do this."

Their grandfather had forced Liam to be a soldier and learn to fight against his will. Marcus would never hold him to that.

"You've been a great help to me in training the men, but you don't have to take it any farther than this."

Liam held his gaze steadily. "I know."

He then looked down at the gambeson in silence for a few moments. When he looked back up, the conviction in his eyes matched the time he had refused the General's direct order to whip Jace.

"I've never wanted to fight, but I never had a reason to before. Now there's something to fight for and people I want to protect." He shrugged. "I don't know if I *can* do it, but I have to try."

Marcus's eyes burned, and he gripped Liam's shoulder with a nod. It went against every desire to protect him and keep him away from the struggle, but he couldn't be more proud of his brother. Of all the men here, he considered Liam the bravest for what he had to overcome to join them.

"You're a good man, Liam," he said, his voice thick.

Liam smiled.

Clearing his throat, Marcus reached for the gambeson and helped his younger brother suit up.

Following his older brother's example, Kaden made sure his men were well-prepared before seeking his own equipment with Talas. The two of them picked through the pieces and each chose a leather breastplate and matching pauldrons, bracers, and greaves. They skipped the chainmail. It was too heavy and restricting to maneuver properly in the air. Besides, it wouldn't do much good against a direct blast of fire or the powerful jaws of a firedrake anyway. Their best defense was their ability to outmaneuver their opponents.

As he worked on the side buckles of the breastplate, Kaden drew a hard breath. His heart raced, and he had trouble keeping his breakfast down. He and his men had trained for months for just such an occasion as this. Where was that preparation now? It all seemed to have vanished, and here he was supposed to be their leader. He should have all the answers and project confidence to his men. He wasn't supposed to have this half-panicked urge to look to someone else for guidance. It all came down to the undeniable truth. He was afraid. Maybe the most he had ever been, even over facing the emperor. Something about the unknown stripped away all confidence. How was he supposed to lead when he was afraid?

Gritting his teeth, Kaden scowled as he tried to adjust the pauldron strap at his shoulder, but his fingers slipped.

"Let me help you with that."

He looked up to find Marcus. Talas had moved off, leaving just the two of them at the table. Marcus stepped to his side and worked the buckle easily. Kaden let out another pent-up breath. He had to get a grip on his emotions. The only reason he'd struggled with the buckle in the first place was how unsteady his hands were. He clenched them, but they still trembled.

Marcus moved on to the other strap, and Kaden watched him, awed by his calm, collected expression. He acted effortlessly, as if he'd been through this a dozen times, yet he had little more experience in actually facing down an enemy than Kaden did. So how did Marcus take it so well when Kaden thought he might be sick?

Swallowing hard, Kaden cleared his voice and tried to speak casually. "Are you nervous at all?"

Marcus's brown eyes rose to meet his. An understanding light shone in them. "Terrified."

Kaden raised his brows, not sure he could believe it, but his brother sounded completely serious. "Really?"

Marcus nodded, picking up one of Kaden's arm bracers. Kaden held out his arm.

"I think you'd have to have something awfully hard inside of you not to be, deep down."

Kaden let his breath out slowly and drew it in a bit more easily.

Marcus helped him finish with his armor. Stepping back, his brother nodded in approval.

"Looks like you're ready."

Kaden checked his weapons—his sword and two daggers from Talas—and made certain the armor wasn't too restricting. "I think so."

The work done, his brother turned.

"Marcus, thanks."

He looked back and, with a fortifying smile, gave a nod. In that brief moment, Kaden saw their father in him.

KYRIN SPREAD OUT clean blankets on the last cot she and Josef had set up in the great hall, now an extension of the infirmary. Straightening, she took in the sight of all the others sitting in neat rows, but even this large number surely wouldn't be enough for all the wounded. She pressed her hand to her aching stomach. Ever since the men had left for the armory, it had churned fitfully. Who would fill these cots in the next few days? Such a question numbed her.

"Are you all right, my dear?"

Kyrin shifted her attention to Josef's compassionate gaze.

"It's just overwhelming to think of so many getting injured or . . ." she swallowed hard, "killed."

Josef touched a gentle, wrinkled hand to her shoulder. "It is indeed."

Kyrin's voice trembled. "How do you prepare yourself to lose people you love?"

"Prayer. That is the only thing I know."

Kyrin nodded and bit her lip to hold back tears. Even with prayer, how could she ever really be prepared? The pain would never be any less great.

When someone entered the room, she didn't know if it helped or hurt to see Jace walking towards them. He wore a chainmail shirt under his jerkin, and a pair of dark bracers. Never had he looked like such a warrior, but it wasn't so much the armor as the way he carried himself and the confidence in his eyes. It took her breath away, considering where he had come from and his transformation. He probably didn't even realize the extent of the change she saw in him.

He nodded to Josef, but his eyes rested on Kyrin, so blue and clear without the constant warring of doubts. "The others are heading up to the wall to watch and wait. We thought you would like to go with us."

Kyrin looked over at Josef, and the physician said, "Go on. You've done a great deal here, and I am very thankful for your help."

Kyrin smiled and joined Jace as he turned to leave the hall. Along the way, she said, "You look different."

Jace shrugged. "I haven't worn armor since the arenas."

She looked up at him. How different to hear him speaking so openly about his past. If only there were time to talk and enjoy it. Tears pricked her eyes again, desperation suddenly welling inside her. *Please don't take him from me, Elôm.* She worked quickly to compose herself before he noticed.

Just as they stepped out of the keep and into the courtyard, an upraised female voice drew their attention.

"What do you mean I can't fight?"

Captain Darq strode into view, Leetra on his heels. He turned to face her flashing expression.

"I mean I've given you an order."

Leetra's mouth hung open for a moment before her voice came. She struggled visibly to keep it controlled, but it was clipped. "With respect, Captain, I am among the best at aerial combat."

"I'm not arguing your combat skills, but you also have medical knowledge. Josef is the only trained physician here and will need all the help he can get. I have therefore decided your skills are best utilized on the ground caring for the wounded."

Leetra stood rigidly, breathing hard, and balled her fists, but her jaw clamped tight.

"Leetra," Darq said, now speaking more as a friend than a captain, "I know you wish to fight, but you are needed here in the keep."

Still, she did not speak, only gave a stiff nod. Darq turned away from her. When he caught sight of Kyrin and Jace, he raised his brows before moving on. With one more glance at Leetra, they hurried on as well, leaving the crete to come to grips with being ordered out of the fight.

At the base of the wall, most of their Landale group was waiting, including Kyrin's brothers. What a sight they made. Like Jace, they had never looked like such warriors. She had to be proud of them, for their courage and dedication to standing and fighting for what was right. Each had to overcome something to be here—Kaden with his doubts about leading, Liam who had always struggled to be a soldier, and Marcus who, only months ago, had captained the emperor's men.

This struck her especially. If things had happened differently last winter, they could be facing Marcus as an opponent. The thought broke her heart.

When she reached him, she murmured, "I'm glad you're here with us."

He frowned at first, but then appeared to understand. "So am I."

Together, the group ascended the wall. Many of Samara's soldiers had already gathered. Kyrin looked around and spotted King Balen with his general and several other officers. The king had donned leather armor and chainmail similar to what Mason wore. It appeared that Balen intended to fight alongside his men, while Emperor Daican sat safe and comfortable back in Auréa.

At the parapet, they looked out toward Arcacia, but the sky and plains were deceptively empty. Still, Kyrin had already seen what marched their way. If only they were going in the opposite direction.

Silence fell over them—an anxious, heavy silence that made Kyrin fidgety. At last, Kaden spoke.

"Remember that tree we used to climb by the pond?"

Kyrin and their older brothers looked at him.

"The one you fell out of?" Marcus asked.

Kaden laughed. "That's right, I did, didn't I?"

Marcus nodded. "I told you not to climb that high."

"Which is exactly why I did."

They shared a grin.

It was good for Kyrin to see them getting along so well. They all needed each other for strength.

"And you still like heights?" Jace joined in, sending Kaden an incredulous look.

He shrugged. "I guess so."

Jace shook his head. "You four remind me of what Kalli used to tell me about her nine siblings."

"Nine?" Marcus raised his brows.

"Six boys and four girls, including Kalli."

"And I thought five was a lot," Kaden said.

Another moment of silence followed before Liam spoke up. "Didn't we hide some old glass and a bottle with a note in one of the holes in that tree?"

"Oh, yeah," Kaden replied. "I wonder if it's still there."

"We'll have to go back and see," Marcus said.

He, Kyrin, Kaden, and Liam looked at each other and a silent pact was made. Now they just needed to survive.

The sun arced higher, bright and hot. Kyrin pitied the men in all their heavy layers, but no one said a word about it. She kept glancing up to see how close the sun came to its pinnacle.

Just before noon, Jace straightened, staring out to the south. Everyone looked at him.

"See something?" Marcus asked.

Jace squinted. "I think so."

On the other side of Kaden, Talas hopped up onto the parapet for a better view. After a moment, he said, "Yeah, it's them." He turned and gave a shrill whistle, signaling to Captain Darq farther down the wall.

Restless murmurs and energy swept through the men. Balen and General Mason joined their group.

"They're coming?" Balen asked.

Jace nodded.

Mason looked at Marcus. "You believe they will offer terms of surrender before attacking?"

"That is what I would expect. They'll make a show of force and then offer us a chance to surrender peacefully."

General Mason nodded and moved on down the line to give encouragement and make sure the soldiers were prepared for whatever may happen.

Over the next hour, Daican's army marched steadily over the grasslands. Dozens of firedrakes and their riders circled overhead, appearing like giant black vultures in the distance. Kyrin swallowed and looked up at Kaden. It was up to him, his men, and the cretes to fight the beasts. She worried for him, but he looked determined. Despite his fears, she knew he would give his new role everything he had.

It happened just as Marcus said it would. When the army finally reached the river that marked the border of Samara, they spread out, forming their neat ranks to display the full might of their gold and black force. Here, the firedrakes landed amongst the units. One by one, they unleashed a series of wailing, shattering roars, all joining together and rising to a pitch and volume that nearly vibrated the stones. Kyrin trembled and had to cover her ears at the spine-chilling sound. She had hated firedrakes ever since the one that had nearly killed her in Valcré.

Even with her ears covered, the sound seemed to consume her and threatened to drive her to her knees. At a gentle touch on her arm, she looked up into Jace's eyes and held them until the beasts grew quiet and she uncovered her ears.

Silence reigned for a moment, but then Mason strode along behind his men, speaking in a steady voice. "Stand firm. Don't let their overconfidence and show of strength get the best of you. Yes, they are strong, but so are we. We are neither helpless nor defenseless, and they are not invincible."

His words didn't just bolster the soldiers, but Kyrin too. Only Elôm was invincible, and He was on their side.

Nothing much seemed to happen now that the firedrakes were silent, but then three horses broke from the ranks and crossed the river. Even from here, Kyrin recognized the big gray warhorse in the lead and its rider.

"It's the General." She swallowed, her throat suddenly dry. She glanced at Marcus. His expression was stony.

One of the three riders held a black and white parley flag aloft. The third rider looked completely out of place. He didn't wear the gold and black uniforms of the other two and had long dark hair.

"Falcor," Jace murmured.

He touched his neck, and Kyrin thought of the cruel things the crete had done to him. Not only that, she thought of her father, and a hard thumping hammer took the place of her heart.

Balen, Mason, and Darq gathered behind them and spoke to Trask.

"We think there should be someone down there to represent your force," Mason said.

Both Trask and Marcus stepped forward.

"You don't have to go down there," Trask told him.

Marcus stood up tall. "I'm your military leader. I should be there."

Trask nodded, and they turned for the stairs, but Kyrin stopped her brother for a moment.

"Are you sure you'll be all right . . . with him?" She glanced over the parapet to the approaching riders.

"I'll be fine."

He moved on, but Kyrin worried for him. Their grandfather's words had a way of cutting deep and destroying confidence. *Be with him, Elôm.*

Kaden suddenly turned from glaring at the approaching group, and headed for the stairs as well.

"Where are you going?" Kyrin asked. She would definitely not let him go down there. That would turn ugly far too quickly.

"To get Exsis," he said over his shoulder, "just in case they don't play fair."

Marcus pulled his shoulders back and walked steadily beside Trask, but his stomach did somersaults. He hadn't come face to face with the General since they had cut ties back home and chosen two different sides. It was more difficult than he wanted to admit to walk out and face him again. He had dedicated nearly his entire life to following the man. This reminded him too painfully of how blind he had been.

"Captain!"

They all turned as Leetra rushed toward them to Captain Darq.

"I want to go with you." Her eyes churned a deep, stormy purple.

Darq shook his head. "No."

"Please." She glanced at the other men and lowered her voice to a hard murmur. "I need to see him."

Marcus watched the crete captain. He couldn't imagine it would be a good idea to let Leetra go out with them when her hostile feelings were so evident. Still, Darq did not refuse her.

"You will take no action. None," he said.

Leetra gave a curt nod. "Yes, Captain."

"And you will not speak to them. Do you understand?"

Leetra hesitated and glanced at the others again, but answered just as firmly. "Yes, Captain."

Darq nodded and they continued toward the gate. Marcus still questioned the wisdom of the crete girl joining them, but maybe she had to face Falcor the same way he felt he had to face his grandfather to be able to move on. That he could understand.

He drew a fortifying breath as the sentries opened the gate for them. Striding out, he caught his first sight of the General just down the hill. He glanced up at the wall and, though he couldn't see anyone, he knew all were watching.

After a couple of yards, his grandfather recognized him, and their eyes locked. Marcus fought to keep his confidence strong under that crippling, razor-edged stare. It was not how the General used to look at him. Such looks he had reserved for Liam. Anger built over these memories and strengthened Marcus's resolve. His grandfather was a cruel tyrant who had brought great pain to the family, and Marcus would not be cowed.

His gaze drifted to the crete standing at the General's side. This was the first time he had ever seen Falcor, the man responsible for turning in his father and treating Jace so barbarically. Marcus clenched his fists but, like Leetra, he must not let emotion take over. There would be plenty of opportunity for action and fighting later.

On the sloping, rocky ground between the river and the walls of Stonehelm, the two parties met. Mason stepped forward first.

"I am General Mason. You speak to Lord Balen, King of Samara." He motioned to Balen, who came to his side.

The General took stock of the king, appearing unimpressed. "I am General Marcus Veshiron, commander of the emperor's armies, and I am here to offer you terms of surrender."

Balen took another step forward, facing the General down. For once, Marcus's grandfather didn't look so massive in front of the Samaran king.

"Samara is a sovereign country," Balen said. "We have been since the early days of Ilyon. You have no right to make war on my people."

The General snorted. "Emperor Daican needs no right. He has power. Power you do not have."

"No?" Balen raised his brows. "I think you underestimate the might of Samara's warriors."

"Even the mightiest warriors cannot stand forever against a superior force, which is why I am offering you a chance you'd best heed." The General glanced up at the wall. "Surrender to me and your men will be allowed to live. Emperor Daican is not looking to destroy your country, otherwise he would have sent the firedrakes to the villages beyond your walls, but he will accept nothing less than your full surrender."

Balen stood for a long moment. "And what if the answer is no?"

In all his years under his grandfather's command, Marcus had never seen any man stand up to the General the way Balen did.

The General's gray eyes narrowed. "Then we fight and you die. Look around you. Do you see the force I command? It is but a fraction of the power the emperor has at his disposal." His gaze shifted. "Marcus—"

"Captain Altair of the Landale Militia," he cut in coldly.

As far as he was concerned, his grandfather had lost the privilege of addressing him with the familiarity of family. Now, as regrettable as it was, they were enemy commanders—one against the other.

The General scoffed, peering down at him. "A captain of the traitors now, are we? Well, *Captain*, you can tell them that I'm right. Arcacia has far greater military power than what you see here."

It was true. This force was only a small part of the army—smaller even than Marcus had expected—but since this was all a ruse to distract them from the true target, it didn't surprise him. He said nothing, holding his grandfather's iron gaze.

The General scowled and turned back to Balen. "You can be sure the emperor won't stop until Samara is in his power. Save your men from slaughter and surrender now."

Standing tall, Balen responded, "You may have your numbers, but no army has ever breached Stonehelm. And though outnumbered, my men have greater purpose for fighting, and we have forces on our side that you do not."

A smirk grew on the General's face. "Falcor tells me the emperor killed your so-called God in Valcré. If He can't even save Himself, how can He save you?"

Balen's jaw went taut. "You do not understand what you speak of."

"No? We shall see."

"And we will take our chances," Balen said decidedly.

Marcus breathed in deeply. Nothing had changed, but the king's declaration seemed to mark the beginning of the battle.

"If it is your will to do so." The General turned. "Falcor."

The crete stepped forward, his intense eyes only on Darq. "Captain, the same offer is extended to you and our people. Any crete who leaves now and returns to Dorland will not be considered an enemy. Let the humans fight amongst themselves. It is not your fight."

Darq raised his brows, glancing past Falcor to the army across the river. "No? What about Josan? And what about your attempt to murder Talas? What of the beasts out there you helped train? It seems to me that it is our fight. Will it not be when the emperor marches next on Dorland to destroy our people?"

"He won't," Falcor said with odd certainty. "As long as we cooperate and do not hinder him, he will leave the cretes out of this. And, in the end, I will restore our race to its former glory."

Darq glared at him. "You?" He shook his head incredulously. "By allying yourself with a murderer and committing such atrocities yourself? That is not the way of the cretes, and you know it. What about honor?"

Falcor did not answer, and his gaze switched to Leetra. It was the first Marcus saw of any softening, but Leetra's face was hard as ice. Falcor said her name quietly, almost as if hoping for reconciliation, but she would have none of it.

"You're not worthy of those markings you bear," she spat. "Not worthy of your family name." She shook her head. "They've already cut you off. You're dead to them."

Falcor's jaw shifted and real pain flashed in his eyes. "That is unfortunate. I could have done much for them."

Leetra nearly shook, her breaths loud, even to Marcus.

"Like this? Are you mad? Good people are dying while tyrants like him are gaining power." She gestured at the General, who only scowled at her.

"They wouldn't have to die. They should know when they are beaten." Falcor glanced at Balen, and then at the men on the walls before returning his gaze to Leetra. "You should know."

Leetra balled her fists and drew herself up, but tears glittered in her eyes. "You are no crete. You are a traitor, and you will always be remembered as such."

Again, pain pinched Falcor's face, but he hardened himself. Darq's voice drew his attention away from Leetra.

"The cretcs are part of this fight now, and we will not back away from it."

"Suit yourself," the General cut in. "You can all die together."

He lifted his eyes to scan the wall and their defenses. After a cursory look, he released a harsh laugh and dropped his gaze to Marcus. "I imagine your brothers are up there, aren't they? Or is Liam hiding back at home?"

Indignation flared inside Marcus. "Liam has chosen to fight by my side of his own will, not through any use of force or cruelty."

The General dismissed him and looked once more at King Balen. "You have until dawn to reconsider. Maybe some of your men actually want to live."

He turned, and he and Marcus traded a scathing look before he strode back to his horse. The flag carrier followed, but Falcor lingered a moment with a dour look at Darq.

"Someday you'll see I was right . . . if you survive."

Darq just shook his head. "Whatever the emperor has promised you, he will not deliver. You cannot trust him. No good will come to the cretes or anyone in Ilyon for granting him this power."

Dismissing his words, Falcor took a final look at Leetra and walked away.

Marcus watched the three men mount and turn toward the river. At the bank, the General glanced back, and it struck Marcus—the horror of going to battle against family. Looking heavenward, he thanked Elôm that he was not riding beside his grandfather. Win or lose, he knew he fought for what was right.

THAT NIGHT, WHEN Arcacia's force was no more than hundreds of campfires twinkling in the distance, Jace followed the others back to the keep for supper. They sat down to eat as they had that morning, though they talked less, weighed down with weariness and anxiety about the future. Only hours remained before they would find themselves in battle, and Jace guessed the night would pass more quickly than the day had. The closer it came, the more he wished he could slow time.

If only Elon were here. Jace still had to wonder why He had sacrificed Himself just before a battle that would shape Ilyon's future. Yes, Jace would be dead now if He hadn't, but surely this fight was more important. Jace shook his head to himself. Elon knew what He was doing. Jace could not doubt that.

Silence dragged on as everyone seemed intent on their food until Marcus looked up and cleared his throat.

"I think we should have a plan in place in case something goes wrong." He looked over at Kyrin. "If we are somehow overrun or can't hold them back, you need to escape with Ivoris."

Kyrin's face tensed in a struggle to accept her brother's words. Before she could say anything, Marcus continued, "Gather provisions either tonight or first thing tomorrow. Enough to get you back to Landale. You'll probably have to go east first, out of sight of the firedrakes, and then head south to camp."

Kyrin's throat moved as she swallowed. "Alone?"

She glanced at Leetra. Jace looked too, but the crete's expression said she would stay to fight and die before she would retreat.

"Those of us who are able would join you there as soon as we could," Marcus tried to reassure her.

Kyrin drew a slow breath, barely nodding, but Jace saw that it did little good. She didn't touch the rest of the food on her plate. His own stomach was in a knot, but he ate for the sake of strength.

When most plates were empty, Trask broke the silence next. "It is important we all try to sleep tonight. Sitting up and waiting won't win the battle if we're exhausted before it even begins."

The others agreed, and they all headed for their sleeping quarters. At the door of the mess hall, Jace stopped Kyrin and let the others go ahead. Peering down into her upturned face, he said, "Can you keep something safe for me?"

He reached into his pocket and withdrew the letter he had written earlier. "If something were to happen to me, I want to make sure this letter gets to my mother."

She took it with a trembling hand, and her eyes welled.

"Kyrin," he spoke gently, and she looked back up at him. "I'm not saying anything will happen, it's just . . . I want to make sure she knows how things have changed and what happened with Elon."

He couldn't take the chance of her never knowing. He didn't want her to have to worry about him like that anymore.

Kyrin nodded. "Of course." Her voice barely rose above a whisper. She made a valiant attempt not to cry, but tears threatened to overflow.

Jace's own eyes stung. If only he could prevent her from ever hurting again. He hated to see her cry when he could do nothing to stop it. He hesitated for an uncertain moment, but then pulled her closer. She wrapped her arms around him, hugging him tightly. Even through the chainmail, he could feel her silent crying.

"Things will be all right . . . somehow," he murmured.

He had to believe it. Somewhere this had to fit into Elôm's plans.

She nodded against his shoulder, and he just held her. His thoughts drifted to the first time he had ever done so, when Sir Richard had held Kaden prisoner. Their struggle had turned into something so much bigger since then.

After a few moments, Kyrin slipped from his arms and reached up to wipe her cheeks. She looked up at him, strength lurking in her eyes where there had only been fear.

"Thank you." She looked down at the letter in her hand, studying it. A little smile touched her lips.

"What?" Jace asked.

She raised the smile to him. "I've never seen your hand-writing before."

Jace shrugged. "I don't practice much. It's not very good."

"It's just fine."

Spirits lifted, they followed the others. Down the hall, they found Kyrin's brothers waiting.

"Are you all right?" Kaden asked as they neared.

She nodded slowly. "For now, yes."

Satisfied, Marcus said, "We'll see you in the morning."

They traded goodnights, and Kyrin's gaze rested on Jace before she went off to the small room she shared with Leetra. Jace let out a sigh, turning to follow Kaden and the others. He would rather just sit with Kyrin all night. If these were his final hours, he would like to spend them with her, but Trask was right.

He couldn't fight a battle, at least not to his greatest capacity, on no sleep.

In the sleeping quarters, Rayad helped him out of his chainmail and he sat on his cot, only now realizing how weary he was. As he sat there, contemplating what the next short few hours would bring, a growing dread gnawed his stomach with uncomfortable familiarity. It felt the same as it had on his nights before entering an arena as a gladiator. However, unlike then, he now had the reassuring knowledge of Elôm. Bowing his head, he reached out to his God, stilling the voice of uncertainty.

"Jace."

Coming to consciousness, he first thought it was Elon's voice. He longed for it to be, but recognition told him it was Rayad. With it came remembrance. He pushed himself up quickly, his heart pounding.

"It will soon be dawn," Rayad said.

Jace let out a long breath. He hadn't expected to sleep much, but he had, deeply, and he thanked Elôm for it. It would certainly benefit him in the hours to come.

Jace rose to his feet as Holden got up from the cot next to him. The three of them helped each other into their armor. All around them, men were preparing. Jace glanced to where Kaden, Marcus, and Liam helped each other suit up. It brought a wistful smile to his face as he thought of his own siblings. He couldn't wait to see Elanor again now that things had changed, if he got that chance. Part of him would have even liked to see James again and have a good talk with his younger brother. Had anything he'd said had an effect on him?

As they followed the steady stream of men out of their sleeping quarters, Holden gave a quiet chuckle.

Jace looked over at him. "What?"

"It's odd how things change. A year ago, I was afraid you would kill us all in our sleep. Now I trust you more than anyone to watch my back."

He clapped him on the shoulder, and Jace smiled. He trusted Holden to watch his back too. He already had in multiple ways lately.

In the mess hall, the soldiers gathered to grab a quick bite to eat. Kyrin met them there. She looked tired, but stronger than the night before. She even managed a smile for her brothers and Jace—a smile that made him contemplate all kinds of what-ifs. Again, he lamented the lack of time.

They ate quickly, compelled by the urgency to be ready and in place by the first light of dawn. This left little time for talk, but they could only hope they had said everything they needed to say by now.

Once fed, they all gathered in the torch-lit courtyard. Jace looked up at the dim sky. A scattering of stars still twinkled faintly but would soon disappear. The sounds of footsteps and armor filled the enclosure as soldiers hurried to their positions. From what Jace knew of General Veshiron, he would attack right at dawn. That left them less than half an hour.

Jace focused on Kyrin. She consumed his thoughts in these final minutes. With clear difficulty, she went around to trade parting words and embraces with everyone. Her emotion was especially evident when she came to Timothy and he told her, no matter what happened, to keep reading and copying the Scrolls. She nodded, tears filling her eyes, before giving him a hug.

The worst for her was her brothers. She lingered longer with them, and a few tears did fall, but Jace admired how bravely she faced it. She could have broken down completely—no one would blame her—but she somehow held herself together. After giving each of her brothers a long, tight hug, she stepped back to encompass all of them.

"Be careful," she said, her voice a little shaky. "Don't do anything foolish or take risks, all right? Just . . . be careful."

They gave her their solemn promise.

A mischievous grin came to Kaden's face, lightening the mood. "We're always careful."

It drew a breathy chuckle laced with skepticism from Kyrin. "Right."

Kaden's face grew more serious again, though a faint smile remained. "We'll see you later."

Kyrin nodded.

Her three brothers turned to join up with the rest of the men, who slowly moved toward the wall. Kyrin stared after them for a long moment, and Jace almost wondered if he had been forgotten, but then she turned to him. He was the last of the group and thankful to have a private moment with her.

She drew closer, and he looked down at her. Determination hardened her expression, but fear flickered in the captivating misty blue of her eyes. Again, he admired the strength she projected in spite of it, but his own fear that coiled around his chest overshadowed the admiration. What if something happened to her? As safe as the keep may be, she was still right in the middle of the battle. Anything could happen. His throat barely functioned when he tried to swallow the horror of losing her.

"Well, here we are," she said. All the unspoken fear and uncertainties passed between them. She glanced around at the men, torchlight casting wavering shadows on her face that somehow made her look more vulnerable. "In all the preparation, I never really considered what it would be like to reach this point."

She looked up at him, her eyes seeking.

"I know," he murmured. He didn't believe any of them had.

They just stared at each other, neither one wanting to bring this to a close. With a shaky breath, Kyrin looked up at the sky. Jace glanced up too. The stars had faded now.

"I suppose you should join the others." Her eyes dropped back to his, glittering with moisture.

Jace's voice seemed to abandon him, and he could only nod. She took another step closer, and they embraced, but for Jace it was intensely painful. This could be their last. He held her a little tighter as if it could somehow change the future.

"You are my best friend, Jace," her voice came to his ears a little muffled, but earnest. "I don't want to lose you."

He swallowed hard, his voice breaking. "I don't want to lose you either."

Sniffing, she nodded against his shoulder. A moment later, she stepped away, though it tortured him to let her go. Her cheeks were damp, but she didn't cry. Instead, she forced a weak smile.

"I'll be praying for you."

Jace nodded, once again unable to find his voice. With reluctance written all over her face, Kyrin turned and started toward the keep. All at once, Jace's heart plowed into his ribs as a rush of regret and panic jolted through his entire body. *What are you doing, you fool?* The question rang out like an alarm bell in his mind. They could lose each other today. Was this really how he wanted them to part for the last time? He had always known how much she meant to him, but right now it was so clear it took his breath away. Did he want it to end without her ever truly knowing what his intentions were?

"Kyrin!"

His heart rate spiked when she turned back to him. Confusion and fears scrambled through his mind, but he wouldn't let this moment just slip away. He closed the distance between them and reached out to cup her face in his hands, pressing his lips to hers.

She gasped, but didn't try to pull away. For a few fleeting seconds, he lost himself in the engulfing sweetness of the kiss and connection to her. When he pulled back, his pulse thundering, he stared into her wide eyes and witnessed the twinkle of shock, wonder, and a swirling of other emotions he couldn't identify. Whatever they were, they had eclipsed the fear he'd seen moments ago.

Again, his voice stuck in his throat, but words didn't seem so necessary at this point. Finally, he managed, "Stay safe."

Kyrin nodded and said breathlessly, "You too."

Taking a deep breath, he rubbed his thumbs over the softness of her cheeks. "I'll see you when this is over."

It was as close to a promise as he could make. Reluctantly, he pulled away from her. She was just as reluctant to relinquish her light grasp on his forearms. But time wouldn't allow for anything more. Turning toward the wall, he pulled his shoulders back, a sudden rush of confidence and determination coursing through him. His mindset began to shift back to the struggle at hand, but he couldn't resist another look back. Kyrin still stood where he had left her. Despite the circumstances, a smile grew on his face. The one she returned he would carry with him long into whatever the day brought.

Near the stairs, he caught up with his group, coming alongside Rayad. After a moment, he sensed Rayad watching him. Jace glanced at him. Rayad's lips were upturned in a barely perceptible smile, his eyes crinkled.

"What?"

The smile grew, but Rayad shook his head. "Nothing."

However, they both knew exactly what it was. His heart thrumming with the memory of the kiss, Jace couldn't hold back a smile of his own, though he did his best to hide it. A moment later, a low rumble of a chuckle came from Rayad, and Jace gave up pretending or trying to hide anything.

"I've been waiting a long time for this," Rayad said.

Jace lifted his brows.

Stepping closer, Rayad grasped his shoulder and spoke quietly.

"I'm no matchmaker, but if any woman was capable of winning your heart, I knew it was Kyrin. I suspected you had developed feelings for her. I just wasn't sure when or if you would act on them."

"That makes two of us."

Kyrin's feet pounded up the stairs inside the keep at the same rhythm as her heart. At one of the top floors, she reached a set of windows overlooking the wall and soon-to-be battlefield. Leetra already stood there, but Kyrin barely noticed her. Stopping, she worked to catch her breath, but it wasn't just from the run. Jace had kissed her! She put her hand to her chest. Goodness, how her heart raced at the memory. After all this time of struggling to temper her feelings toward him to avoid disappointment, *he* had kissed her. It made her giddy and terrified at the same time. *Oh, Lord, protect him!*

A questioning voice invaded her thoughts, and her gaze snapped to Leetra. The crete girl gave her an odd look.

"Are you all right?"

"Yes," Kyrin gasped. She cleared her throat. "I'm fine."

Leetra just stared at her, not at all convinced. Warmth flushed Kyrin's face, and she ducked her head. Clearing her throat again, she moved to the window to look out at the wall. Out of the corner of her eye, she saw Leetra shaking her head before focusing outside too. No longer under her scrutiny, Kyrin allowed herself a small, private smile as she relived the moment in the courtyard once more.

Kaden's heart pounded against his breastbone with disturbing ferocity. Could it be possible to break a rib this way? He forced himself to draw in a steady breath. The time had come to step up, to act, to lead. The time to banish all outward fear and project confidence to his men, even if it wasn't so plentiful deep down. There was no more wondering *how* he would lead these men; he just had to do it.

Near the wall, he stopped with his two brothers, and they faced each other. A moment of silence fell between them as they shifted, searching for the right words.

"We'd better join our men," Marcus said finally.

He faced Kaden, holding out his hand. Kaden grasped his arm, but Marcus pulled him in for a hug, slapping him on the back.

"Trask made a good choice in appointing you captain," he said. They parted to look each other in the eye. "You have a natural instinct when it comes to dragons. You'll lead your men well."

Kaden's nose stung and he fought to tamp down the emotion. "Thanks."

Marcus smiled and nodded.

Kaden turned to Liam next, and they traded a crushing embrace. Right as they parted, a sound echoed in the distance, rising into the dawn sky. War horns.

"That's the attack signal." Marcus's alert eyes fell on Kaden. "Take care."

"You too."

Kaden watched for only a moment as his brothers hurried for the stairs. Then he spun around and sprinted to where Talas and the rest of his riders waited for him, the sound of war horns still resonating against the fortress. He scrambled onto Exsis and faced the men as the noise died away. Swallowing, he willed moisture into his throat. He could imagine Marcus boldly giving his men a rallying speech before going out to battle, but with all eyes on him, he struggled. He swallowed again.

"This is it, men. This is what we've all trained for. Over that wall, Daican's men believe they've already won because of their numbers." His heart crashed, adrenaline, fear, and determination all lighting a fire inside him. "Well, I say let's show them what we're made of."

Shouts broke out around him, and at last came the confidence to lead them. He glanced at Talas, who gave an affirming nod. Kaden gripped Exsis's guide bar and raised his voice.

"Everyone, with me!"

At only a slight signal, his dragon spread his wings and shot upward, climbing above the walls. The rest of the dragon riders followed right behind him.

KADEN HELD HIS breath. Exsis's pumping wings matched the pounding beat of his heart. They soared up, past the walls and into the dim sky. The glowing eastern horizon greeted them first. The other dragons ascended all around him, both his force and Captain Darq's. A thrill raced through him to see them airborne. Surely, between them, they could hold back the firedrakes.

With these thoughts, he swung his gaze to the south. Though it was still too dim to see much more than smoldering campfires and torches, his eyes slowly adjusted and locked on something dark materializing in the deep blue of the horizon straight ahead. His heart jolted, lodging in his throat. Monstrous dark forms dotted the sky. Despite seeing the size of the firedrake force the day before, the sheer number facing them down in the air momentarily paralyzed him. There were so many.

"Elôm, help us," he gasped.

It was as if he were frozen in place as the beasts fast approached, but then something clicked inside him. Instinct and training took over. Adrenaline bursting through his veins, he gripped Exsis's guide bar and leaned forward, homing in on the first firedrake that barreled straight for them. The drake's jaws hung open, an orange glow growing at the back of its throat. Two heartbeats later, Kaden signaled his dragon to pull up. Fire jetted from the firedrake's mouth, but Exsis shot upward, the flames passing just beneath them.

"*Roven!*" Kaden shouted.

Streaking mere feet above the firedrake and its rider, Exsis poured out a cascade of his own flames as they passed over. The firedrake released a thunderous roar. But satisfaction for Kaden was only fleeting. Another firedrake followed just behind the first. Kaden pushed Exsis into a sharp dive. He grabbed the saddle bar to keep from being separated from the dragon and ducked just out of reach of the firedrake's sharp claws. The air from the beast's wings buffeted him as it flew over.

Kaden took a quick breath as they leveled out. At least he hadn't been killed right off. He looked back. Bursts of fire flashed across the sky, accompanied by roars and ear-piercing shrieks. Curving sharply, Kaden focused in on his next target.

Jace stared upward, riveted to the sky battle above him. Such dangerous maneuvering left him short of breath. Thank Elôm he did not have to be up there. He had enormous respect for Kaden and the other men who had taken up their air defenses.

"Archers, at the ready!" General Mason shouted from just down the wall.

Jace tore his gaze from the dragons and fit an arrow to the longbow he had taken from the armory. He looked out at Daican's army. It was quite a distance to the other side of the river. They would have to fire high and hope the majority of their arrows found targets.

"Take aim!"

Using his shoulders, Jace drew back his bowstring as far as he could and aimed into the horizon. A heartbeat of a second passed.

"Fire!"

With the release, Jace watched the cloud of arrows streak into the sky, arching above the river, and then descend in a deadly rain. Despite the distance, most reached the opposite bank. Men in the front rows toppled over. Jace's heart gave a slight stutter. The bloodshed had started.

They repeated several volleys with fair success. Each one brought down numerous enemies, but a loud mechanical clank in the distance interrupted their attack. A boulder flew toward them. It seemed to come slowly at first, but all at once it was there, smashing into the wall about fifteen feet below with a deafening crash. The stones trembled, but the wall stood solid. Samara's defenders quickly answered with a volley from their own trebuchets.

"Keep alert!" General Mason called out.

Jace continued firing, but he kept a close watch for flying projectiles. The first rocks hurled at them impacted low or didn't reach the wall at all but, with a few adjustments, they would likely find their mark. While it might not cause significant damage to the wall itself, it would to human lives.

But the greatest threat to the soldiers did not come only in the form of siege weaponry. A gust of wind tugged Jace's hair and drew his eyes upward to a firedrake just overhead. The beast headed straight for them, but a sudden blast of dragon fire deterred and drove it away. Jace breathed out. A burst of flames from a firedrake would likely kill even more men than a well-aimed boulder.

He looked out over the wall again. His stomach lurched. A growing blur hurtled towards the parapet.

"Look out!"

He grabbed Holden, who stood closest, and threw them both to the side.

The boulder shattered against the parapet, spraying jagged stones into the air. Jace covered his head, pelted by debris. When it settled, he looked up and met Holden's eyes.

"See?" Holden said. "What did I tell you about watching my back?"

Jace brushed the pebbles and dust from his armor and turned back to assess the damage. The boulder had torn a large section of the parapet off, but no one appeared seriously injured, thank Elôm. It was a grim reminder to remain alert as the bombardment continued and would only gain accuracy.

Kyrin flinched at another tremendous shattering of rock. Between the siege attack and the dragons battling above, she didn't know where to look. It all left her stomach in knots. So many of the people she loved most in this world were out there, right in the middle of the violent chaos. How could anyone come out of it alive?

She then glanced at Leetra, who stood at the other end of the window. The crete didn't look so much afraid as angry. Everything from her rigid posture to her fiery expression said she wanted to be out there, but she followed her captain's orders and remained inside the keep.

Kyrin gazed back out at the wall and tried to catch a glimpse of Jace. It proved impossible in the midst of all the men. She looked for Kaden as well, and perhaps caught sight of Exsis, but all the male dragons looked alike and moved too fast for her to be able to distinguish the rider.

A few minutes later, Leetra leaned over the sill to look down into the courtyard. "Looks like they're bringing in some of the wounded."

She backed away and turned for the stairs. Kyrin watched the battle for a moment more. She hated to leave her spot, but she couldn't stand here all day. It would not give either side an advantage. Helping with the wounded would keep her busy, though the thought of her task left her apprehensive. Her experience in assisting Lenae back at camp consisted mainly of accidental cuts and scrapes. Certainly not battle wounds.

Hardening herself, she hurried after Leetra. Down in the great hall, Josef directed soldiers where to sit and gave instructions to Leetra, who acted promptly. At least most of the men walked on their own. A couple needed the aid of fellow soldiers. When Josef saw Kyrin, he motioned her closer.

"Most of these are only flesh wounds," he said. "Leetra and I will tend the more serious ones. If you could work your way through the others, I'd appreciate it."

Kyrin nodded. She would do her best.

"Just clean the wounds and apply bandages if necessary," Josef told her. "If you are unsure, do what you can, and I'll finish."

With another nod, Kyrin moved determinedly to gather supplies and approached the first soldier. The Samaran man had a collection of cuts to his face from flying debris. While they bled heavily, they were minor, and he quickly returned to the wall once the bleeding ceased.

The fourth soldier she tended turned out to be a familiar face.

"Jeremy!"

He held a hand to his forehead, blood rolling down the side of his face and dripping slowly from his chin.

"Hey, Kyrin." He flashed a smile, but it didn't quite reach his eyes.

Shakiness overwhelmed Kyrin's insides to tend to someone she knew. It was so much more personal, especially since he was Lenae's son, but she quickly calmed herself.

"Let's see your wound."

He pulled his hand away. A large gash ran just above his brow and still oozed blood. Kyrin's stomach pinched, and she grabbed a cloth to press to the wound. Waiting for the blood to stop, she licked her lips.

"How is it out there?"

Jeremy winced. "Not like anything I've ever seen."

He let out a weak laugh, but Kyrin caught the fear that flickered in his eyes. He kept good control over it, though.

"Are a lot of men getting wounded?" Kyrin asked.

He shrugged. "We're trying to avoid the attacks, but it's not always easy. They come fast."

Kyrin nodded, drawing a deep breath. Any one of those attacks could obliterate her friends. If only it could all just be over. She reached for a wet cloth to clean Jeremy's face.

"I saw Jace just before I came in."

Kyrin met his eyes.

"He was doing all right."

A look of understanding and acceptance settled in Jeremy's expression, and Kyrin had a suspicion that he had seen what had happened in the courtyard.

"Thank you," she said, "for letting me know."

He nodded, and a little disappointment lurked in his eyes, but not animosity.

Kyrin finished cleaning the blood from his face and wrapped a bandage around his head. As soon as she finished, he stood.

"I better get back out there."

"Be careful."

It would devastate Lenae to lose her only surviving son. Kyrin didn't want her to have to go through such heartache again.

"I will."

He walked out, and Kyrin focused on the next soldier, praying earnestly for the safety, strength, and courage of their army.

Time blurred during the battle, but by the angle of the sun and the empty feeling in his stomach, Kaden knew it neared midday. However, the only thing that mattered right now was to keep focused and keep fighting. Anything like hunger, thirst, or weariness could not distract him.

A firedrake in his periphery gained his full attention. The beast headed straight for the men on the wall. Kaden ground his teeth. Not if he could help it. He swung Exsis around and urged him to intercept. Bracing himself, they crashed claws first into the firedrake's head. The monster roared and snapped at them, but Exsis flapped hard, rising just out of reach. At Kaden's command, his dragon spewed fire right down into the drake's face and routed it away from the wall. Kaden traded a glare with the other rider.

They battled each other for a minute or two—teeth, claws, and fire—but then the firedrake broke away, retreating. Typical of what Kaden had faced all morning. The firedrakes would fight until things got desperate, then pull back to regroup before attacking their next targets. Kaden sensed a lack of confidence and skill on the part of the riders. They may have an advantage in size and numbers, but the dragon riders had more experience and agility. Or maybe the emperor's force didn't intend to fight to the death. It was only supposed to be a diversion after all.

Yeah, well, Samara's forces weren't playing games.

He pursued the firedrake. Below him, another boulder exploded against the wall. He winced. Hopefully the bombardment wasn't decimating their ground force.

"Kaden!"

He caught the voice in the wind and turned as Talas and Storm came up alongside him.

"Let's try to take the catapults!"

Kaden nodded. He should have thought of that sooner. If they were going to win this fight, he needed to be more aware of the situation outside of their battle with the firedrakes.

He looked around and let out a shrill whistle. A couple nearby riders heard him, and he motioned to them. Together, they turned to follow. As a group, the six of them flew out over Daican's force at the river.

Talas dove down first, Storm's claws outstretched to tear into the wood of the tall trebuchet. An upward hail of arrows met them, but they managed to damage the war machine and added a spurt of fire for good measure. Kaden followed suit, leading the rest of the riders. Arrows met them as well, and Kaden ducked low over Exsis's neck. They managed to take out three more trebuchets and catapults before a blasting roar signaled the approach of firedrakes.

Kaden looked back toward the wall. About twenty-five firedrakes were on their way. He straightened, preparing to meet the onslaught.

KADEN HAD EXPERIENCED some long, exhausting days in his life, and this one was right up near the top. The battle seemed to stretch out for days, not just hours. Never was he so happy to be on the ground as when he and Exsis landed in the deepening gloom of the courtyard that evening. Soldiers hurried around to light torches as night descended.

For a long moment, he just sat still. His whole body ached, and his throat felt as if he had gone a week without water—not to mention how empty his stomach was. He winced at the pain radiating from his throbbing right shoulder and glanced at it. His leather pauldron was blackened and the fabric underneath it charred. The last hour had been brutal. The firedrakes and their riders finally seemed to have found their confidence. Still, Samara's forces had held them back. For now, at least. Once the sun came up and they could see well enough to fight again, that might change.

Biting back a groan, Kaden lifted his leg over the saddle and slid down. Even this simple move was a chore. His adrenaline reserve had run dry, leaving his body stiff and heavy. He rested his hand against Exsis's shoulder. The dragon panted loud, gusting breaths, stirring up dust, and his wings drooped to the ground. They had been in the air all day. Exsis needed this nighttime reprieve even more than Kaden did. He rubbed the dragon's scales.

"Good boy."

Kaden's hand traveled along the dragon's body. He spotted a few cuts and burns he would have to tend to, but first he needed to check on the rest of the men. Forcing his wobbly legs to cooperate, he walked around to where they had all landed. He had lost four men today. He couldn't help wondering if he could have done something to prevent it, but at least he hadn't lost the whole group. Actually, if he looked at it objectively, it was a miracle they were not all dead.

He worked his way to each of them, checking them and their dragons. None of the survivors had more than minor wounds. He reached Talas last. His friend appeared to have fared the best, and asked him how he was.

Kaden sighed. "Could be worse. Ready to get something in my stomach."

Talas grinned at him. "Let's get these dragons taken care of and go find some food."

Kyrin focused half on her work bandaging a soldier's hand and half on the door of the great hall as men trickled in. Her stomach wouldn't stop turning with the desperation to see her brothers and friends come through that door. She had wanted to run out to the courtyard to look for them the moment the fighting had ceased, but she couldn't abandon Josef, Leetra, and the other women. So she waited, praying and tending injuries. Most now were men with minor wounds who had waited until nightfall to leave the wall and have them tended.

Finishing with her current patient, Kyrin crossed the room to refill her basin with fresh water. That's when she caught sight of her brothers and Jace. She set the sloshing bowl down hurriedly and rushed to meet them. She reached Kaden first, embracing him tightly.

"Thank Elôm you're all right!"

She looked up into his face. He looked drained. Well, she would see that he received proper care to restore his strength.

She hugged Marcus next, and then Liam. Finally, she came to Jace. Looking up into his eyes, seeing the tenderness in them that was so clear now, her heart gave a little flutter and memories of the morning already left her breathless. She felt a little shy and uncertain, unused to allowing such feelings for Jace. She had held them in check for so long.

When he opened his arms in invitation, she accepted his embrace eagerly. All day she had fought to be strong, but for just these few moments, she let herself completely sink into the security his arms brought her. She blinked away the smarting in her eyes and listened to his steady breathing. How nice it would be just to stay here for a while, but that didn't seem quite appropriate, standing here in the middle of the infirmary for all to see.

They shared a brief smile when they parted, and Kyrin refocused on what needed to be done next. She turned to her brothers.

"Are any of you hurt?"

Marcus nodded at Kaden. "He ought to have his shoulder looked after."

Kyrin spied the burnt armor and winced. It was the second time he had been burnt fighting firedrakes.

Kaden, however, wasn't concerned and said, "Food first," sounding more like himself.

Kyrin shook her head, but smiled. "War hasn't changed your priorities, has it?"

He gave a little grin back.

"The refugee women made stew and fresh rolls in the mess hall. They wanted to make sure you men had a good meal tonight."

Kaden rubbed his stomach. "Thank Elôm for the refugee women."

Kyrin chuckled. "You go on and eat and then come back here to take care of your shoulder."

As the four of them headed for the mess hall, Kyrin traded another quick glance with Jace. He looked like he wanted to talk. So did she, and she prayed for a little time to do so. They only had a couple short hours until the men would try to get the sleep they so desperately needed before dawn threw them right back into the fight.

Turning back to her work, Kyrin nursed the wounded and directed soldiers to the mess hall. Before long, and to her immense joy, all her friends made an appearance, and she praised Elôm for each one. They had survived their first day of battle with minimal loss. If they could continue like this, and their forces at Amberin could turn back Daican's surprise attack, perhaps they would win the battle strong. Kyrin was afraid to hope, but certainly prayed for such an outcome. Maybe it would deter Daican from trying again.

When her brothers and Jace returned, Kaden carried an extra dinner roll he had no doubt sweet-talked from one of the women. Food seemed to have done wonders in reviving him. He temporarily set it aside as Marcus and Liam helped him out of his armor. The pauldron had taken the most damage, thankfully, but when he pulled off his shirt it revealed a patch of red, blistered skin.

"Well, it doesn't look as bad as your last burn," Kyrin said, cleaning it gently as he munched on his roll.

He swallowed. "At least you don't have any of that stuff Leetra put on it."

"That *stuff* kept it from getting infected and helped it heal." Leetra's unamused voice came from just behind Kyrin.

Looking over her shoulder, she caught the crete giving her brother her infamous raised eyebrow.

Kaden shrugged. "It still didn't feel good."

"Leetra, will I have to do anything more than apply the burn salve and bandage it?" Kyrin asked.

The crete took a quick look at the burn and shook her head. "No, he'll live."

She moved on, and Kyrin finished, wrapping Kaden's shoulder lightly. He pulled his shirt back on, and Marcus helped him into his armor once more. Kyrin imagined that it would have been nice to go without it, but the men had to remain prepared in case of a nighttime surprise attack. Not likely, though, as crete dragon riders would have a significant advantage in the dark over the human firedrake riders.

"We'd better go," Marcus said when they finished. "King Balen and General Mason have called a meeting with all the commanders."

The three Altair brothers walked out of the infirmary, which left Jace alone with Kyrin. She turned and looked up at him, a weary smile lifting her lips. She looked exhausted, a little pale even. From what he had seen in just this short time back in the keep, she had worked very hard to assist Josef and Leetra with the wounded—an admirable job. Still, her wellbeing concerned him.

"Have you eaten yet?" he asked. Had she even thought of herself while she was so busy caring for others?

She shook her head. "Not yet. My stomach was too agitated worrying about all of you."

"You should eat something."

Kyrin looked around the infirmary. The wounded seemed to be resting comfortably and no new patients were coming in.

"I guess it looks like Josef and Leetra have things under control."

They turned for the mess hall, and she fell into step beside him. Silence followed them, but Jace's mind was far from quiet. There hadn't been time to ponder much on the wall, but now thoughts rushed in of things he needed to say and discuss with her, and it had to be tonight. He had already risked losing the chance.

When Kyrin received a bowl of stew and a roll from one of the women, Jace gently guided her toward an empty table in one corner. Though the others from Landale sat nearby, Jace needed a little privacy to talk, and Kyrin went right along with him. To be certain she didn't mind, he asked, "Is it all right if we sit here?"

"Yes, this is fine."

Jace waited until she sat down before taking the seat across from her. He didn't say anything at first, letting her take a few bites of her stew first. Clearly, her hunger had returned. Finally she looked up at him, her expression receptive and waiting.

He licked his lips, his heart suddenly pounding. "I think we should talk about this morning."

She nodded, her eyes holding a little sparkle, yet nervousness twisted his gut. Emotions and feelings, especially such unfamiliar ones, were sometimes harder to face and understand than the enemy outside.

"I feel like I should apologize."

She looked at him in surprise, but he pressed on.

"I shouldn't have done that. It was foolish and reckless. I'm sorry."

Now that he'd had time to think it over, he realized he could have caused all sorts of unwanted complications. Still, she just gave him a quizzical look.

"Why?"

He shifted uncomfortably. "I should have talked to you first. I don't want to have made things awkward or . . . ruined anything between . . ."

He let his voice trail off. Would she confirm what he expected? Her brow wrinkled a bit more as she waited for him to finish.

"Between you and Timothy," he spat it out, cringing a little. He berated himself for not considering this earlier, before he had kissed her. It wasn't as if he couldn't see how close they were.

Kyrin's brows lifted now, but a little smile peeked out. "Jace, the only thing between me and Timothy is friendship."

Jace let out the breath he was holding. So it wasn't more?

Her smile widened. "Besides, I'm not the one he's interested in."

Now it was Jace's turn to be surprised. Timothy was interested in someone other than Kyrin? Who? But she didn't get into that.

Blushing, she murmured, "You did surprise me this morning."

Jace almost laughed as a little of his stress released. "I surprised myself."

"I didn't think you felt that way about me."

"I never thought I could feel this way . . . about anyone." He held her eyes earnestly. "But I do." Uncertainty hit him again. "But if you don't want it to be like that, I don't want to ruin . . ."

"Jace," she stopped him, mirth in her voice. She stared at him, her eyes getting a little watery. "You don't know how I've hoped you would feel this way."

"You have?" He sat back. All this time he had pined over her, she was just waiting for him.

Kyrin gave a little chuckle and nodded. "Honestly, I'm quite shocked I never realized how you felt. I mean, there were times I did wonder, but I guess I never dared to let myself hope. I didn't want to be disappointed."

Jace shook his head. He could have avoided so much heartache if he had just told her the truth in the beginning. "It would probably be a good thing from now on to be completely honest about how we feel." That had never been easy for him, but he was determined to change it going forward, especially with her.

"I agree."

Jace cleared his throat. Now that they had determined to be honest, he needed to confess, though he hated the feeling of inadequacy.

"I don't really know how to go about any of this." He paused, glancing at his hands. "I never thought it would have any place in my life."

"Don't worry," Kyrin told him. "I don't really know either, but after all we've been through I think we can figure it out."

They shared a warm smile, and Jace's anxiety melted away. How could it not, staring into her lovely face and knowing she returned his feelings? But then he noticed moisture building in her eyes again, and she looked down.

"What's wrong?"

She tried to give him a smile, but the attempt wobbled. "I was just thinking about my father."

A couple of tears slipped down her cheeks, and she swiped at them. Had he been sitting closer, Jace would have been tempted to wipe them away himself.

"He saw something between us before we did, I think. The first night we camped on the way to Valcré, he asked if we were just friends. I don't think he believed me when I said we were. I guess he was right. Somehow, he knew."

Wishing so much he could take some of the sorrow she would always carry, Jace reached his hand across the table. Kyrin took it and rested her soft fingers in his as he gently rubbed his thumb over her knuckles. They had never held hands like this before. He could still hardly believe she had stuck by him after how difficult he'd been. He shouldn't even have this life at all after where he had come from. How good Elôm was to someone so undeserving. He almost felt hesitant to ask for more, but he had to pray that both he and Kyrin would survive past this struggle. He wanted so much to see what the future could bring them.

Jace's attention drifted past Kyrin when her brothers walked in from their meeting. He did not know much about how to proceed with relationships, but he did know one thing. "I suppose I should talk to Kaden and the rest of your brothers." The timing couldn't be worse, but he didn't want to hide how he felt anymore. They would see it, and it seemed more appropriate to tell them outright. Then, at least, he would know exactly where they stood on the matter.

Kyrin's smile resurfaced and chased away any remaining tears. "You probably should."

He pushed up from the table, reluctantly releasing her hand. "I'll let you finish your supper while I talk to them."

She nodded, and he crossed the room to where her brothers stood talking with the other Landale men. No one seemed aware that he and Kyrin had sat alone, except for Rayad, who wore a knowing look.

Jace waited for Marcus to finish speaking with Trask and then said, "Can I speak to you three?"

The brothers looked at him curiously.

"Sure," Marcus answered.

Jace led them away from the table where they could talk in relative privacy. Most men had to face a girl's father, not her three adult brothers. Jace didn't know which would be more intimidating. And what if they turned him down? His stomach clenched, but he wouldn't let fear deter him. They were his friends, after all.

He set his gaze on Kyrin's twin and cleared his throat. "Kaden, you said once that anyone interested in Kyrin would have to meet with your approval."

Kaden nodded slowly. "Yeah." His brows lowered suspiciously. "Who's asking?"

Jace drew a breath. Here went everything. "I am."

Suspicion vanished, replaced swiftly by a look of surprise from Kaden. "You?"

"Yes."

Kaden glanced at his brothers. Marcus and Liam had the beginnings of smiles on their faces. Even so, Jace held his breath, waiting.

"Well," Kaden said, focusing once more on Jace, "I guess I don't see anything wrong with that."

"I suppose this would be the time to warn you that if she gets hurt, you answer to us," Marcus added in, "but you're always the first one to jump in to protect her."

Jace detected a hint of teasing and mock severity from both of them, but he took it seriously. "Still, you have my word. I could never hurt her."

"Does she know yet?" Kaden asked.

"Yes, it sort of came out this morning." He paused, but couldn't come right out and say that he had kissed her. "I realized it might be the only chance to let her know."

"Well, then, you have our approval."

Marcus and Liam nodded in confirmation.

Jace breathed out, undeniably relieved. "Thanks. I wish I could have talked to your father too."

The three of them sobered.

"He would have approved," Marcus said.

Kaden agreed. "Yeah, he liked you."

Jace's eyes stung. He had only known him for a couple of days, but William Altair was one of the most honorable men he had ever met. He would never forget the one time they had talked. Kyrin was so much like him.

Clearing his throat, Jace thanked them again, and they turned back toward the table. Along the way, Kaden gave him a half-hearted slug to the shoulder that lost most of its effect through his armor.

"Took you long enough." The mischievous look had returned to his expression.

Jace laughed. "Trust me, I know."

Kyrin had joined the men at their table. She glanced at Jace, and then questioned her brothers with a look. At their smiles and nods, a grin lit her face. The others at the table caught the exchange.

"What's going on here?" Trask asked, his eyes holding a distinct twinkle.

A little blush rose to Kyrin's cheeks, and she looked down shyly. Jace couldn't hold back a grin, half in light of his joy, and half in light of her cute face.

"Oh, I know what's going on," Holden said.

By now, it would have been hard to miss. There were some lighthearted jests, and everyone insisted that they knew this would happen. Jace was beginning to think he and Kyrin were the only two who hadn't thought so. Words of encouragement followed the good-hearted teasing, and conversation slowly drifted back to the events of the day.

Sitting beside Kyrin, Jace didn't hear much of it. He was too intent on her. Now that he had accepted and declared his feelings, he realized they were even deeper than he'd first thought. Every fiber of his being wanted to be with her, to protect her, to do whatever it took to make her happy always. Once in a while, she looked over and caught him staring. She smiled her gentle, innocent smile, laughter in her eyes.

It grew late fast. The cretes offered to take the night watch in case Daican's army tried a surprise attack. Most men had already sought sleep when the Landale group left their table. In the hall, they paused. Jace took particular notice of Kyrin's brothers lingering at the other end. As much as he would have liked a moment alone with Kyrin, he commended them for taking their roles seriously. It was a little odd, though, to have them now watching so closely. He had always feared that his feelings would change their friendship. Things had changed today, but he certainly couldn't say it was for the worse.

Turning to Kyrin, he smiled, something he probably hadn't done so much in his entire life. She smiled back at him, and he glanced at her upturned lips. After the kiss this morning, another was incredibly tempting, but he thought it wise to take things slowly and not get carried away. They may have declared their feelings for each other, but that didn't mean she was his.

"Good night," Jace murmured.

She echoed him softly, and he was happy to see her like this instead of so worried.

Moving reluctantly, they parted. In the sleeping quarters, Jace walked quietly to his cot and lay down. With everything on his mind, he barely noticed the chainmail he still wore. He closed his eyes, and sleep claimed his body quickly as he drifted into a slumber of calm and peace.

"I DON'T KNOW if I'm ready for this again." Kyrin looked up, her wide eyes displaying the deep internal struggle to fight fear.

Jace understood just how she felt. The night had passed much too fast. Now they stood in the courtyard once more just before dawn, trading goodbyes that could be their last. The fact that they had already experienced one day of battle didn't make this new one any less uncertain or difficult to face. So much could change in the next hours.

He stared down at her. These moments were too fleeting. They needed more than the few minutes they had. It was hard to see her scared and not be able to fix it. He took her gently into his arms, and she curled into his chest, her head tucked under his chin. She breathed out a heavy sigh, and he held her tightly. He wanted to will some of his own strength into her to help her endure the day. What would she do if she lost all of them? It made him sick inside.

Her voice came to him, small and quiet, but achingly desperate. "Please don't die."

The tremor at the end told him she was crying. He ached to console her and tell her he wouldn't, but he didn't have control over the future. He couldn't make such promises under the very real threat of breaking them. It left him at a loss, but then he spoke what was beating so clearly in his heart.

"I love you." He never imagined such words could be so easy to speak, but he meant it with everything inside him.

She pulled away from him just enough to look up, her eyes a watery, earnest blue. "You do?"

He nodded and began wiping away the tear streaks from her face, as he had wanted to the night before. Her cheeks were so soft under his fingers, and he savored it.

A smile flickered across her lips, but her voice was still a little choked. "I love you too."

And Jace couldn't think of anything more satisfying to hear than those words. Elôm had blessed him beyond anything he could imagine by placing her in his life. If only she could know exactly how much it meant to him.

He dropped his hands to cup her shoulders. "Thank you for everything you've done for me. I don't know if I'll ever understand exactly why, but from the moment we met, you've been fighting to help me." No one besides Rayad had fought for him the way she had. "You've always brought out the best in me, and I am grateful for that."

Her eyes grew teary again. "And thank you for being there for me when I've needed it. I think you always underestimate your worth to me."

Jace sighed. That was true, but he would try to work on it.

By now, the courtyard stretched around them, almost emptied of soldiers save for the dragon riders. Arcacia's first attack would surely come at any minute.

"You should go inside now," Jace said gently.

Kyrin nodded, but didn't move to pull away just yet.

Jace gave her shoulders a gentle squeeze. "Remember, while you're taking care of everyone else, take care of yourself too. Make sure to eat and rest when you can."

Another strained smile peeked out. That was just the sort of thing she would normally tell him.

"I will."

Jace put his hand to her cheek again, memorizing every detail of her face, and peered into her eyes. From the beginning, they seemed to see right into him, but always looked past the darkness to see the good. He placed a quick kiss on the top of her head, inhaling the scent of her, and then motioned to the keep. She turned toward it, her face set bravely. Her hand brushed his, linking for a moment as she moved past. When the connection was broken, Jace sighed and watched until she entered the keep. She paused to look back in the doorway, and Jace prayed once again that they wouldn't die.

The moment she was out of sight, Jace hurried to the wall and climbed the stairs to locate the others. Taking his place between Holden and Rayad, he looked to the south. Things appeared quiet across the river so far. Surely it would be only minutes before the attack began, but Jace had so much on his heart. He turned to Rayad.

"I'm sorry."

Rayad gave him a questioning look, and Jace continued, "For how I shut you out when I was struggling. After what happened in Ashwood, I felt like I was losing the only family I had and lost sight of how you, Kyrin, and others have been my family. And in thinking of what could have been if Elian had been my father, I forgot all you've done for me. I'm sorry. No matter what has happened or what will happen, I will always consider *you* my father."

Rayad's eyes turned a little misty in the dimness. He gripped Jace's shoulder, his voice thick. "It's an honor to consider you my son, Jace. You've made me very proud."

Jace flashed a smile, but couldn't hold it as his throat swelled too. Kyrin wasn't the only incredible blessing Elôm had placed in his life. He took a deep breath, glad he had spoken because, a moment later, the now familiar mechanical sound echoed in the distance. His gaze jerked to it and locked on a rapidly growing dark projectile on its way.

Kaden settled in on Exsis's back and faced his men. His body still hurt from yesterday and he didn't feel like he'd had nearly enough hours of sleep, but he pushed it away. Today they all had to be strong. He thought of General Mason's meeting last night and their discussion of the enemy's tactics. He gathered his voice.

"Yesterday we got our first taste of what we're up against. We believe the first attack was to test us. Test our strength and find our weakness. Today they will surely attack harder. We saw a little of that last night. Watch your backs. And more than that, watch each other's backs. We have a greater chance of survival if we stick together as much as we can. Is everyone with me?"

The men voiced their assent.

A resounding crash shattered the air at the wall behind Kaden. The bombardment had begun, and no doubt firedrakes were on their way. Grabbing the saddle bar, Kaden gave the command to fly.

Once again, they took to the early morning sky. Just as Kaden suspected, the firedrakes had nearly reached the wall, but the dragons formed a line to meet them. There was no hesitation today on Kaden's part. Despite his weariness, a fire burned inside him. Today would be an ugly fight, but he was ready for it.

The firedrakes met them with a barrage of fire. Kaden barely touched the guide bar, and Exsis banked to avoid the danger. Even so, the heat rose around them as they soared over the first drake. The monsters didn't hesitate to press their attack. Though clumsy in their maneuvers, the black beasts were fast in a straight flight path. As soon as they turned around, they raced after the dragon riders.

Using Exsis's agility to his advantage, Kaden curved around so sharply that it snatched his breath away. They soared diagonally across the top of a firedrake, blasting its rider with fire. It was a direct hit, though too fast to know if he had incapacitated the man. Even if he had, they'd learned the day before that firedrakes fought with or without their riders. They were fierce, brutish beasts compared to the dragons, and their wild instincts drove them to fight.

Flaming a couple more in his path, Kaden looked toward the wall and glimpsed a few firedrakes hovering near it. Kaden motioned to some of the other dragon riders and dove toward them. Claws outstretched, Exsis descended on one of the firedrakes, smashing into its side. The beast roared as the dragon latched on. In a flurry of wings and snapping teeth, they both fought to stay airborne and mortally wound their opponent.

Kaden yanked out his sword. Pushing himself as far forward as possible, he thrust the blade into the firedrake's neck. It took nearly all his strength to pierce the scales, but the blade sank in halfway to the hilt. With a shattering roar, the firedrake broke away, dripping dark blood, and flew off to recover.

Exsis quickly regained altitude, and Kaden looked for any other threats to his comrades on the wall. Finding none in the immediate vicinity, he tried to locate his men. Most battled nearby. The sun was nearly above the horizon now, giving them plenty of light to see by.

Kaden caught sight of one of the younger riders engaged in battle with a huge firedrake, and urged Exsis to attack from the opposite side. The firedrake went wild in an attempt to dislodge the two dragons, and its rider flailed his sword around, but didn't have quite enough reach. Kaden gripped his own sword again and slashed at the firedrake's vulnerable wings. Between him and the other rider, they dealt the beast serious injury. As a final measure, Exsis shot a scorching stream of fire toward the drake's head, engulfing the rider and searing the scales of the monster's neck. The beast at last broke away, but its shredded wings faltered and it plummeted to the ground in a twitching, tangled black heap just outside the wall. One less to worry about.

When he surveyed the area again, Kaden found the firedrake force surprisingly thinned. He frowned. They couldn't have killed so many so quickly. It was impossible. He turned in the saddle and found the missing beasts amassing to the west. But why? A tiny flash of light caught his eye like sunlight on metal. It came from the wall a couple of miles off.

He pushed Exsis in that direction, avoiding the firedrakes along the way, but he didn't have to go far for his answer. He scowled. Just what they needed. He curved Exsis around, back toward the fortress. That's when he spotted other firedrakes gathered to the east as well. Not good.

Kaden dove down and glided just above the wall as he searched for Marcus among the men. When he spotted the Landale group, he brought Exsis down toward the parapet. Digging his feet into the stirrups, Kaden held on tightly as his dragon scrambled for a hold and clung to the edge of the parapet in front of the men.

"Marcus!"

In a moment, his brother appeared at the front.

"There are men on the wall. Coming from the west and east." As far as he could tell, the firedrakes had ferried them up there under the cover of darkness. They would probably transport even more units of men as the day went on.

Marcus glanced to the right. "How many?"

"A few hundred to the west, and I'm sure just as many east. They were about two miles off and moving fast. I'll see if we can stop them, but warn everyone."

Marcus nodded and hurried off.

With a couple hard flaps, Exsis separated from the wall, and Kaden guided him up to where the others fought overhead. He had to gather some of the riders and try to head off the approaching force, or his brothers and friends would soon be engaged in a fight of their own.

Despite the dragon riders' attempt to stop Daican's force on the wall, the firedrakes kept the soldiers well-protected. The first line of Samara's defenses farther down the wall held strong for a while, keeping the Arcacians at bay, but eventually began to falter. Arcacia pressed in, more and more men slipping through the ranks.

Jace stood with those of Landale, gripping his sword tightly as the first of Daican's men reached them. All around him, the sounds of battle rose up—swords clashing, men screaming. He forced away the old memories that resurfaced and focused on the threat.

When a black and gold figure appeared in front of him, he raised his sword to block the advancing blade. He'd never had to fight in such close quarters before. He would have to take care not to harm any of his allies, or get too close to the edge of the wall where he could topple to his death. His legs weakened at the thought.

Parrying one more attack, Jace pressed forward for a counter-strike. His blood flowed hot now, fueling his reflexes, driving him on. For one of the first times in his life, it brought no shame. It was merely an advantage to help keep him alive.

The soldier fell before him. He regretted having to take another life, but had no time to dwell on it. More soldiers were on their way. Marcus's men were about to be put to the test.

Shouting orders, Marcus kept his militia in tight ranks, holding back the Arcacians. The rest of the men from Landale stood behind to face those who slipped past. The struggle turned into a frenzied mass with as much pushing and shoving as blade wielding. Once spacious, the wall didn't seem so wide now. Jace would rather they had an open plain with freedom to move. Attacking would be so much more effective without the fear of hurting one of his comrades.

A soldier turned up just to Jace's right and engaged him. Their swords crashed together in a violent ringing. The man was big and strong. The force of the impact tingled in Jace's fingers. They traded a couple of back and forth blows, testing each other.

Jace had just finished a counterattack when something smashed into his back, forcing the air from his lungs. He recovered just in time to block his original foe's next attack and glance back. A second soldier loomed behind him, his sword rising for a second attack. Jace's chainmail had stopped the cutting power of the sword, but his shoulder blade ached fiercely. The next blow would surely kill him, but if he turned to engage the man, his original foe would take him out from behind. With room, he could take on both, but not here in these cramped conditions. His only choice was to try to block the second man's attack with his arm. He would probably lose it, but what was worse? Instant death or losing his arm?

He had no time to debate. The first man swung, and Jace batted the attack away with his sword while raising his arm to stop the second attack aimed for his head.

Just before it would have connected, another blade caught it and forced the soldier back. Jace gasped as Holden came to stand at his back, freeing him to focus solely on the man in front of him. They both dropped their opponents in a few moments and turned to face each other.

"Thanks," Jace breathed.

Holden flashed a smile. "You're still one up on me."

Before he could reply, a flash of gold caught Jace's eye down in the courtyard. It was only a glimpse, but several men disappeared around the corner of the keep, straight toward the entrance. If the doors had been left unlocked to allow wounded soldiers access, Daican's men might overpower the guards and slip right in. Jace's heart stumbled.

Kyrin!

Even from within the thick stone walls, Kyrin could hear the dull, distant ringing of swords. She and Leetra had seen the beginning of the attack, but it was too hard for Kyrin to watch. Both of them had shortly returned to the infirmary. Casualties had been light the day before, but Kyrin didn't believe they could hope for such today. Would her stomach take it? Already it twisted sickeningly inside her.

A crash came from the front of the keep, and a woman's scream made Kyrin jump. One of the refugee women rushed into the room.

"They've broken in!"

Kyrin's blood went cold. There were soldiers inside the keep? How?

Leetra sprang to action first, whipping out a pair of twin swords she had strapped to her back. The not-so-seriously-injured soldiers pushed up from their cots, ignoring their wounds, and Josef reached for a sword he had propped against the wall.

Only a moment later, five black and gold clad men burst into the room. A couple held torches they had grabbed from the wall. Kyrin could just imagine what they meant to do with them. Without a second's hesitation, Leetra rushed to meet them. How could a girl so small be so fearless?

Her action broke Kyrin from shock. The clashing of swords echoed behind her as she turned and sprinted across the room for her staff. One of the soldiers pursued her. Snatching the carved oaken branch, Kyrin turned to face him. She quivered inside, but training took over, and she raised the staff to shield herself from the downward stroke of the soldier's sword. The blade put a deep notch in the staff. It would only withstand so many of these attacks. Kyrin would have to disarm him quickly.

The sword still pressing down, Kyrin pushed sharply with her right hand, slamming the end of the staff into the man's vulnerable ribs. Thank Elôm he wore chainmail instead of plate mail. The blow was solid, forcing his breath out in a gust. He jumped back, grabbing for his side, and swore.

Kyrin came after him. With a well-placed blow, she could take him down, but he recovered quickly, batting her staff away and forcing her back. Enraged, he pursued her, no mercy in his eyes.

"Elôm, help me!"

Holding the staff in both hands, she blocked again. Each hacking blow drove her back a step and sent bits of wood into the air. The man didn't let up, knowing as well as she did that the staff could only withstand so much. Finally, it cracked, and the next blow rent it in two. Still holding one half, she tried to use it as a makeshift sword, but he battered it out of her hands.

Kyrin turned to run, but he caught her arm and threw her into the wall. The back of her head thumped against it. Stars burst before her eyes, and her knees almost buckled. She blinked and fumbled for the dagger Jace had given her. The soldier raised his sword to finish her off, and her heart paused in gut-turning dread. Just as he swung, he froze, his eyes going wide and his mouth opening with a gasp and soundless cry. A moment later, he crumpled. Jace stood behind him. He pulled his sword free, the point glistening red, and their eyes locked.

Fear and concern filled Jace's expression. "Are you all right?"

Kyrin nodded, her voice still fear-locked.

Jace stepped over the dead soldier and put his hand gently on her upper arm, his eyes searching her face. "Are you sure?"

Again, she nodded, and then collapsed into his chest, weakened by the trauma of near death. He enveloped her in his arms, his fingers sinking into her hair, gently caressing the back of her head and soothing the dull ache there.

"I'm all right," she finally managed, for both him and herself. Then she remembered. "My staff." Her beautiful gift from Jace, ruined. Tears filled her eyes. It would be ridiculous to cry over a simple staff, but . . .

He pulled away slightly to look into her eyes. "I'll make you a new one."

She sniffed back the tears, but if anything, his words only made them more relentless. He would have to survive to do that, and she cried inside that he would.

Grabbing hold of her emotions, she looked around. Holden, Rayad, Timothy, Aaron, Trev, and King Balen were all there. Seven soldiers lay dead on the floor. Tragically, three Samarans also lay still, crimson pools growing around them. Kyrin's stomach lurched, especially at the scent of blood and charred cloth. Two cots lay blackened and still smoking. If Jace and the others had not shown up, the soldiers surely would have burnt out the inside of the keep.

Faintness swirled inside Kyrin's head, but she leaned into Jace and took another moment to collect herself.

Balen stepped forward, grimacing at the bodies. "We'll take them out, and I'll double the guard at the door." He looked first at Josef and then Kyrin. "This won't happen again."

419

As he and the other men carried out the dead, Kyrin watched Leetra wipe her blood-slicked swords on one of the soldier's uniforms and slide them back into place. She had obviously fared all right. Better than Kyrin had. She looked up at Jace.

"Thank you."

Jace shook his head. "Thank Elôm I was here in time."

She stared at him. A desperate longing rushed up inside her to ask him to stay with her. He probably would at her request, but she kept her mouth clamped on these words because they would be selfish of her.

"I have to go," he said quietly, his expression reluctant, as if he somehow knew what she was thinking.

Kyrin just nodded, fighting the urge to cry. It was hard to see him and immediately let him go again.

Squeezing her arm, he turned and hurried away, perhaps before he could change his mind.

Gaining a brief respite, Marcus brushed beads of sweat from his face that rolled down from his forehead and stung his eyes. The warmth of the afternoon sun was oppressive. His saturated clothing encased him underneath his armor, and his throat burned as if it hadn't tasted water in a month. It was enough to make a man lightheaded, but the Arcacian forces wouldn't let up, so neither could he.

Tuning out the ache of thirst and the pain screaming in his weary limbs, he looked around for Liam. Now that it had come down to hand-to-hand combat, he questioned letting his brother be out here. He'd watched him in training and took time to spar with him. He could hold his own, but facing an enemy out to kill you was something else entirely. It took focus and decisiveness to stay alive. He didn't doubt his brother, but war was never his calling. Could he handle it? Marcus wanted to trust Elôm to protect his brother, but his instinct to do it himself as the oldest Altair sibling warred with his faith.

When he spotted his brother among the men, relief coursed through him. He appeared to be faring well enough.

An Arcacian soldier broke out in front of Marcus, commanding his full attention. After dropping him and coming to the aid of a Samaran, Marcus caught another glimpse of Liam, but this time was not comforted. Unknown to his brother, who focused on another opponent, a group of spearmen were forcing their way amidst the ranks. With their long range, they had brought the most casualties so far to Samara's army.

"Liam!" he tried to warn his brother, but his voice didn't carry above the din of battle. "Liam!"

Desperate now as the spearmen drew closer, Marcus pushed his way toward his brother. He had to reach him before they did. They were close now. Just about close enough to use their spears, and one was on a direct path toward Liam. Marcus's heart stuttered.

"Liam!"

His brother's opponent fell, and he turned to Marcus's voice, but the spearmen had reached him. The man drew back his spear. Marcus lunged toward his brother, throwing them out of the spear's path.

But a hard impact and fire spread through his right side, taking his breath away as sharp metal ripped through his flesh.

RECOVERING HIS BALANCE, Liam turned just in time to see the spear jerk free of Marcus, dripping blood onto the stones. He froze, his thoughts numbing to a slow-moving blur. Nothing seemed to move until Marcus fell to one knee and grabbed at his side. One of Liam's deepest fears played out in front of him, leaving him paralyzed.

But then, Marcus pushed back to his feet and grabbed the spear. He yanked the man closer and brought him down. The world rushed back into motion. Marcus went after the remaining spearmen, and Liam followed. Chaos ensued. Liam's body thankfully seemed to work on its own, because his mind had trouble keeping up. This was harder and more brutal than anything he had ever imagined. He should be dead by now, but somehow he kept going.

Once they dealt with the spearmen, they received a brief moment to breathe. Liam rushed to his brother and grabbed his shoulder. A large split in the bottom of Marcus's leather breastplate drew Liam's attention. The chainmail below it glimmered red, and a growing dark stain spattered his pants. It was a lot of blood to have lost already. Liam looked up into his brother's eyes. They were strong, as always, but pain lurked in them. His face had grown pale. That spear had more than just clipped him. Liam fought panic.

"We have to get you inside."

Marcus grimaced, his expression reluctant, but he nodded. This scared Liam even more than the blood. His brother would never leave the battlefield without real cause. Liam begged Elôm to let him be all right.

Taking his brother by the arm, he guided him toward the nearest stairs. The going was slow, adding to the desperation. When they made it to the courtyard, Marcus was breathing hard, but at least he was still walking.

At the door, guards let them inside the keep. The moment they entered the infirmary, Kyrin gasped their names and rushed toward them. At the sight of blood oozing down the front of Marcus's armor, her face turned the same pale shade as his.

"What happened?"

"A spear," Liam answered.

Josef was right behind Kyrin and led Marcus to a cot, where he sank down with a groan.

"Help me get his armor off," Josef said.

Liam nodded and worked at the breastplate's buckles. Here, something took over inside him, a calm determination. While it didn't replace his fear, it did override it, allowing him to work without hesitation. After they pulled off the breastplate, he and Josef grabbed the edges of the chainmail and lifted the heavy armor over Marcus's head. The bloodstained gambeson came off next, and finally Marcus's shirt, giving them the first look at the wound.

His skin was split open in a deep laceration along his side. Blood welled in it and spilled over. Josef grabbed a cloth from Leetra and pressed it to the wound. Marcus sucked in his breath.

"Can you lie down on your left side?" Josef said.

Marcus moved slowly, easing himself down, and exhaled loudly.

"Is there anything I can do?" Liam needed to do something for his brother. He couldn't just stand there.

"You and Kyrin get a couple candles," Josef told him. "I need more light."

Liam followed Kyrin to the nearby table, and they each grabbed a candlestick. He glanced at his sister. Her face was still drawn and pale. His probably matched. War and injury were always a part of the life he had grown up in, but he had never actually anticipated seeing Marcus go down like this.

Back around their brother's cot, they held the candles close for Josef to work. He pulled the bloodied cloth away from the wound with care. It wasn't bleeding so heavily now, and he inspected it closely.

"It doesn't appear any organs were hit, praise the King."

"He'll be all right?" Liam asked.

Josef glanced at him, his weathered and wise face compassionate. "If I am correct and the wound doesn't fester, he should be."

Liam let out a long breath and looked at Kyrin, sharing the relief. He couldn't imagine losing Marcus. He had always been there.

Scrubbing his hands, Josef went to work on cleaning and stitching the wound. When he had finished, Marcus sat up again to make it easier for Josef to bandage him. He still looked pale after the blood he had lost. He sat for a moment and then held a hand out for his shirt.

"Help me get dressed."

Liam frowned down at him. "What?"

Marcus glanced up, his face determined. "I need to get back out there."

"I wouldn't advise that," Josef said. "I don't believe you have any serious internal damage, but that doesn't mean you won't if you put stress on the wound."

"I need to be out with the men," Marcus insisted. "I need to make sure they're all right."

Liam agreed with Josef. He understood Marcus's sense of duty, but he wasn't about to let his brother risk his life unnecessarily when they had nearly lost him already.

"I'll be there." The words were out of his mouth before he could reconsider. "I'll make sure they're all right."

He swallowed, his gut twisting. He had no idea what he was doing. It had never occurred to him that he might have to take over command for his brother. It was the last thing he felt capable of, but if it would keep Marcus safe, he had to do it.

Marcus gave him a hesitant look, and Liam tried to project courage into his voice. "I am your lieutenant, after all."

Marcus had never come out and named Liam his lieutenant, but Liam had performed all the duties in the last months. Liam never would have sought the position, but it had fallen to him now.

A slow smile came to Marcus's face. "Yes, you are."

Liam took a deep breath, feeling a rush of confidence. "I'll take care the men." And he would, to the very best of whatever ability he possessed. He licked his lips, still unable to shake his concern for Marcus. "But don't you dare die on us. The men still need their captain."

Marcus gave a short chuckle that broke off with a wince, but a smile still hinted on his lips. "I won't."

Liam nodded and looked at Kyrin. She was worried about him. Even he could see that. The last thing in Ilyon he wanted to do was go back out to that fight, but it had to be done. Determinedly, he turned for the door, but Marcus grabbed his arm. Liam looked down into his serious eyes.

"I'm holding you to the same promise, you know."

Liam swallowed and gave a brief nod, though there wasn't much confidence behind it. He strode for the door without looking back. If he did, it would destroy his resolve.

Outside the fortress, the sounds of battle raged. His heart faltered and his footsteps grew heavy. Following Marcus into battle was one thing. Heading into it alone was quite another. Underneath his sweat-drenched clothes, a chill raced through him. He wasn't made for this. He didn't have the skills or smarts his brothers had. Back at Fort Rivor, he'd been the fool. Everyone would have laughed to see him in this position. He should have taken the spear instead of Marcus.

He glanced at the sky. "I don't understand, Elôm."

But it didn't change the fact that he had a job to do. An important one. On the way up the steps, he brushed his clammy hands against his pants and pulled out his sword. He hoped he wouldn't choke on his heart as it worked up into his throat.

Moving down the wall, Liam reached the Landale men. The Samarans were successfully fending off the Arcacians for the moment, giving the militia a chance to question Liam.

"Is the captain all right?"

"What happened?"

Liam looked around at all the questioning eyes boring into him. He fought the fuzziness in his head. "He took a spear to the side, but Josef thinks he will be all right."

Relief swept through the men. Marcus may not have commanded them for very long, but he inspired a lot of respect. Because of this, Liam saw what a blow it was to lose him in the middle of battle. Such a hit to their morale wouldn't help them fight. He had to fix it, somehow, but he shook inside, his mouth like dry clay. He cleared his throat.

"He may be injured, but he still expects us to keep up the fight." Liam winced at the lack of strength in his voice, but pressed on. "We must stand firm and hold our ground." His heartbeat drummed in his head. "Let's send Daican's army back to Valcré with a message that he can't just walk in and take Samara for himself." Around him, heads nodded, bolstering his courage. "And if they do succeed in taking it, then I say we make them pay for it."

Now the men gave hearty agreement, the fight back in their eyes. Some of the nearest men thumped Liam on the back. Though his innards were a jumble, Liam didn't remember a time he had felt so strong. Taking Marcus's place at the head of the men, he turned with them to face the next wave to break through.

Kaden ducked under a blast of fire and swung Exsis around to take the firedrake from the side. Fire jetted from Exsis's mouth, but it only scorched the beast's tail. Kaden growled in frustration. This firedrake was more agile and dragon-like than most. Banking again, Kaden pursued it, focusing on the wings. He had a particular grudge against this one. The beast had left him with a painful burn to his left knee and hand.

He was almost on top of it when movement flickered at his side. Glancing left, his mind registered the form of a dragon with a crete rider flying right at him. He ducked, but the dragon's wing crashed into him. Pain exploded in his head and through his shoulder, and his hands yanked away from the saddle bar. He scrambled for a grip as he lurched sideways, but his left arm wouldn't work. He slipped from Exsis's back, open air meeting him. The plains below rushed upward.

He was going to die.

In the brief milliseconds, he accepted this. He wanted to close his eyes, but couldn't. The ground was there in the next heartbeat, so close he could have touched it right as claws wrapped around him, snatching him up from instant death.

A yell tore free at the pain that ripped through his shoulder. His dragon's wings stirred up dust and dry grass as he slowed and set Kaden gently on the ground. Kaden stumbled forward and hit his knees, gasping. He'd fallen from Exsis before, but death had never been so close. He could still see the ground only feet from impact.

"Thank You, Elôm," he murmured, hanging his head.

Blood dripped into his lap, and he reached up to his face, the oozing warmth of his blood coating his fingers. His left cheekbone stung, but it was the pain that shot through his left arm that consumed him. Biting back a groan, he reached for his dislocated shoulder and squeezed his eyes shut. Exsis grumbled fretfully behind him.

At the approach of dragon wings, Kaden looked up. Talas landed nearby and jumped off Storm.

"Kaden!" He rushed over and knelt in front of him.

"My shoulder," Kaden said through his teeth. "Put it back in."

Talas eyed his injured face, and then moved to his side. His strong fingers wrapped around his arm. "Ready?"

Kaden dragged in a couple deep breaths and nodded. He bit down hard, and Talas carefully maneuvered his arm. It burned like fire inside him, but then popped back into place. He let out a groan and exhaled. Letting the pain subside to a dull throb, he pushed to his feet and wiped the sleeve of his good arm across his face.

"What happened?" Talas asked.

Kaden's jaw went taut as he looked to the battle overhead. "A dragon rammed me."

"A dragon?"

Kaden nodded, dropping his gaze back to Talas. "Must have been one of Falcor's men."

He shook his head. They blended in completely with the other cretes from Dorland. No one would realize they were enemies until it was too late. Who knew how many riders they had killed already?

"We have to find him and any others. And warn everyone we can to be on alert." He turned for Exsis.

"I think you should go back to the keep," Talas said. "That arm won't be much use to you."

Kaden glanced back. "It'll be fine."

There was no way he would leave the battle and his men for a dislocated shoulder. He'd have to be bleeding out before that happened. He climbed back onto Exsis, ignoring all the pain signals his brain was sending. The firedrake he had been after was forgotten. Now he was on a hunt for traitors.

Talas rushed back to Storm and followed Kaden into the air. Kaden scanned the fighting above. If only he'd had a better look at the attacking dragon. It was female, so it couldn't be Falcor, but the thought of the crete somewhere nearby burned inside him.

There! A female dragon attacking another rider—one of Kaden's men. Leaning forward, he urged Exsis toward the battle. As hard as they had trained, Kaden's riders didn't have the experience of a crete rider. The man struggled and would be dead if Kaden didn't intervene quickly. Exsis let out a thunderous roar. The traitor crete looked back, and swooped around to meet them. The two dragons came together in a shrieking frenzy. All Kaden could do for the moment was hang on.

The other dragon snapped at Exsis's throat.

"*Roven!*" Kaden shouted.

With a burst of flames, they broke apart. Kaden prepared for another assault, but the dragon had disappeared. He looked all around, but in a sky full of dragons, it was nearly impossible to tell one from another. He scowled, but then caught the swoosh of wings over Exsis's. He whipped his head around. The dragon soared up right behind him, its mouth already open to pour out fire. Kaden pushed Exsis into a sharp dive, but heat blasted his back.

He glanced over his shoulder. The dragon and crete were right on his tail. He banked and dove, climbed, and dove again—any maneuver he could think of—but he couldn't shake the dragon. With every minute, it got ever closer to doing serious harm.

Kaden ground his teeth together. He had only one idea left—the very maneuver that had thrown him from Exsis in training. It was the only time he had ever tried it. Did he feel like getting thrown and risking death again? Not really, but what other choice did he have? The traitor crete would roast him if he didn't act now.

Taking a gulping breath, potentially one of his last, Kaden dug his feet deep into the stirrups and gripped the saddle bar with both hands. Before he had a chance to question his sanity, he gave Exsis the command. In a blink, the dragon curled his head down and did a somersault in the air, Kaden dangling upside down from his back. He tried not to yell at the fiery pain streaking through his shoulder as he held on for dear life. The female dragon shot over them, and Exsis flamed her underside.

Just as they began to fall, Exsis flapped and righted himself. Kaden breathed hard, dizzied, and shook his head to clear it before urging Exsis to follow the other dragon. Now he was the pursuer.

The traitor crete attempted to evade him, but that last attack had slowed the female dragon. Her right wing was blackened and tattered. Kaden hated harming such a fine creature, but this was war. If he didn't stop the crete, others would die.

Closing the distance, Kaden commanded another burst of fire aimed right at the crete's back. The man slumped forward. With one more lengthy blast, the dragon and rider plummeted. A moment of regret stung Kaden, but a sky still full of battling dragons and firedrakes commanded his attention.

WAS HE STILL alive? Kaden didn't know how it was possible after a day like this, but here he was in the courtyard again as darkness descended. Thinking of how sore he thought he was the night before, he would have laughed if it didn't hurt so much. That was nothing. Tonight, he didn't even know if he could move. He cast his fatigue-blurred eyes about as others landed around him.

Six.

Only six of his men had survived, including Talas. He hung his head. Most of his force was decimated, and those left looked half-dead—exhausted, miserable, and sporting a large array of wounds.

Wanting to just lie back and stay right where he was, Kaden forced himself up and almost fell out of the saddle. From the ground, he glanced toward the cretes gathering. Their ranks were disturbingly thinned as well. He was glad to spot Captain Darq among them. The crete captain's right arm looked badly burned, but he walked amongst his men as if unaware of it. Where did he get that kind of energy?

Kaden turned to Exsis to unbuckle his saddle, though with only the use of his right arm. To try to raise his left was agony.

Talas walked over to him as he struggled with a buckle. "Go inside. I'll look after Exsis."

Kaden shook his head. Even injured, he wouldn't shirk his duties. Talas sighed.

Glancing to the steady stream of men coming from the wall, Kaden caught sight of several familiar faces. To see them alive soothed some of the weariness. Jace and Liam broke from the group and came toward him. Neither appeared seriously injured, though Jace had blood dripping down one side of his face.

Kaden's heart thudded. Someone was missing.

"Where's Marcus?" he asked the moment they reached him.

"He was injured by a spear," Liam answered, "but last time I saw him, Josef thought he'd be all right."

Kaden breathed out hard. He'd worried there for a moment. He swallowed, his parched throat raw. In reluctance, he asked, "Did we lose anyone?"

"We lost quite a few from the militia." Liam winced. "But Trask and the others are safe."

Kaden was too tired to do more than nod and whisper thanks in his heart.

Stepping up, Talas said to Jace and Liam, "Would you two take him inside? He's being stubborn about it."

Kaden sent him a dark look, but couldn't resist them. Cradling his aching arm, he walked with them to the keep.

"What happened to you?"

Kaden looked at Liam and recounted how he had received his injuries, but they were the last things on his mind when they entered the keep. In the nearly full infirmary, he sought one person.

"This way," Liam said.

Kaden followed him toward a nearby cot, where Marcus was lying propped up but clearly alert. A smile stretched across his face when he saw Kaden and Liam. They walked over to him.

Kaden dropped to his knees beside him, his burnt skin stinging. Now that he was down, he didn't know how he would get back up.

"How are you feeling?" he asked his brother.

Marcus eyed his condition. "Better than you, I expect."

Kaden laughed dryly. "Probably." He winced, pain shooting down his arm.

"You should get those injuries looked at."

Kaden glanced around the room. So many were wounded, and more coming in. Many were worse than him.

"I will when things quiet down." He eased back against the wall. He could easily fall asleep here.

Marcus looked up at Liam. "How are the men?"

Liam grimaced. "We lost about a third of them. Quite a few are wounded."

Marcus breathed out slowly.

Liam looked around the room. "I'm going to see what I can do to help."

He left Kaden and Marcus, quickly pitching in to tend the wounded. It surprised Kaden. He wasn't usually so outgoing.

"He commanded the militia today after I was wounded," Marcus said.

Kaden raised his brows. That didn't sound like Liam at all, but he must have done a perfectly fine job.

"Honestly, I wasn't sure he could survive the day," Marcus said quietly. He shook his head. "But look at him. Barely has a scratch."

Kaden peered at his brother. Marcus was right. Elôm must have put a shield of protection around him.

A moment later, General Mason walked over to them. He asked after their health and then focused on Marcus.

"I wanted to let you know that your men were vital today. From all the reports I've received, we couldn't have done it without you. Make sure your men know that, and how grateful we are for your assistance."

"I will," Marcus replied.

Liam certainly had done a fine job.

The general's attention shifted to Kaden. "And we'd be lost entirely without your men and the cretes."

"Glad to help, General," Kaden said.

Mason nodded at both of them, moving on and stopping at each of the cots bearing the wounded soldiers. Things were quiet between Kaden and Marcus for a minute or two before Marcus looked over at him.

"So, what happened to you out there?"

Kaden sighed, and they traded their battle stories. Kaden could sense his older brother's frustration over being taken out of the fight so early. After a time, they grew silent again, and Kaden did doze off, though he didn't realize it until Kyrin woke him sometime later. Kneeling in front of him, she smiled gently.

"Let's get your wounds looked after so you can get some food and go to bed."

Taking his right hand, she helped him up. For once in his life, Kaden was too tired to think about food . . . not that he would refuse it.

Beside him, Marcus pushed himself into a sitting position, hissing out a breath.

"What are you doing?" Kyrin asked him.

"I should go to the sleeping quarters so someone else can have this cot."

"Not without help, you're not," Kyrin said, sounding amusingly like their mother.

Jace came up behind her. "I'll help him."

She smiled and nodded, and Jace helped Marcus stand. As the two left the infirmary, Kyrin led Kaden to a table, where Leetra waited. He sat down in a chair, and they helped him get his armor and shirt off, which he would have been more than happy to leave on considering the pain it caused to remove them. Looking at his bare shoulder, he found it had turned an interesting shade of blue and purple.

"I'll make sure it's not broken," Leetra said.

Before he could protest, she took his arm in her hands. For someone so petite, one would have expected a light and gentle touch, but no. Her fingers practically dug into his arm and the bruising. He clamped his teeth together, fighting a groan, but it forced its way out.

Finally, he pulled away from her, clutching his throbbing arm to his chest.

"It's fine. Just bruised and was dislocated."

She gave him an irritable look, but he wasn't about to let her continue her painful probing.

They moved on to his burns next, which wasn't much more pleasant, and then helped him slip into a fresh shirt. When Kyrin lifted a sling for his arm, he stopped her.

"Help me get my armor back on first."

"You shouldn't do any more fighting with that arm."

"It's fine," Kaden insisted.

"Well, at least get some rest first. You can put it on in the morning."

He wanted to argue, but Talas appeared, cutting him off.

"Being stubborn with you too, is he?"

A little hint of a smile came to Kyrin's face. "Yes. Would you please see that he eats and gets to bed?"

Talas grinned. "My turn to babysit again."

Kaden rolled his eyes. He had to admit, though, that it would be nice to go without the armor for a while.

Kyrin tied his arm up in the sling, which helped immensely, and then he rose to follow Talas. Before he left, Kyrin touched his arm.

"Rest well." She smiled, but her face grew more serious and her eyes a little teary. "I'm glad you're all right."

Any irritation with his situation melted. "Me too," he murmured.

Jace helped Marcus to his cot next to Kaden and Liam's empty ones, supporting his weight as he sat down slowly.

"Need anything else?" he asked once Marcus was settled.

Marcus breathed out a long breath and shook his head. "No, thank you."

Jace backed away, but Marcus stopped him, "We haven't had a chance to say much since the other night, but I'm glad you feel the way you do about Kyrin."

"Really?" It was one thing to have Kyrin's brothers be happy for them, but that Marcus was actually glad about their relationship meant a lot.

Marcus nodded. "I wouldn't trust many men with her, but I trust you."

Jace took this with a deep sense of gratitude. He would do everything in his power never to violate that trust. "Thank you."

Marcus smiled, and Jace left him feeling remarkably content.

When he returned to the infirmary, things had quieted down. Kyrin waited there to look at the cut to his head, courtesy of a knee to the forehead when a soldier had knocked him down at one point. Thankfully, he'd had enough allies around to help him back up.

He sat down near a table, and Kyrin wet a cloth, dabbing the blood from his face. Her fingers were gentle as she brushed back his hair and cleaned the wound near his hairline. It hardly even hurt. A little smile came to his lips.

"What?" she asked.

"You've done this before, back in Mernin."

Opposite of his, Kyrin's face grew somber. He'd been in much worse condition then.

"That was horrible."

Clearly the memory was difficult for her, but not so much for him.

"It wasn't so bad."

She stopped and stared at him, her brows raised. "You could barely stand up, let alone breathe. It *was* horrible."

Jace shrugged as she focused back on his wound. He wouldn't make light of it. Still, that moment had changed things for him.

"That's when I first noticed you as more than a friend."

She looked down into his eyes again. "You felt that way all this time?"

Jace nodded, and now he sobered. "I should have told you." Prolonging it had only made him miserable, and perhaps her as well at times.

But Kyrin shook her head with a gentle smile. "Everything has its time. You needed to figure out your relationship with Elôm before thinking about one with me."

His gaze glued to her face, he marveled over her. Blushing under his intent staring, she went back to work. Still, Jace watched her, thinking her lovely in every way.

When she finished, she asked, "Do you have any more injuries that need to be tended?"

He shook his head, not mentioning the sore bruises to his shoulder and back from the sword blow. "None that won't heal themselves."

"You should get some rest then."

Jace stood. As always, it was hard to leave her, but he wasn't sure how much longer he could keep himself awake. Taking her hand, he squeezed it gently before leaving the infirmary.

Timothy smiled at Kyrin and Jace's interaction. He couldn't think of a better match after all they had been through together. Jace was smart for making his feelings known before he lost his chance.

Timothy sighed.

"Do you want me to look at your arm?"

He jumped at the voice, meeting Leetra's gaze. His thoughts scattered like shattering glass. She stared up at him, her eyes so large and bright. Such a beautiful, unique shade of lavender, and, at the moment, snapping with impatience as he slowly processed her words.

"Oh, yes." He glanced down at his bloodstained sleeve. "Thank you."

He followed her. If only he could blame his poor response time on exhaustion, but it was more than that. He scolded himself.

She went to work, removing his bracer and rolling his sleeve up to reveal a deep cut to his left arm. "Looks like I'll have to stitch it."

She worked efficiently and was focused, not speaking. She offered nothing in the way of encouragement for his internal struggle. He watched her slender brown hands expertly clean and stitch the wound. As she finished tying off the bandage, Timothy moved almost without thinking and rested his hand over hers. Her skin was so soft and warm under his rough palm. She stilled.

Slowly, he looked up and met her eyes. Her steely external shell was gone, revealing her innermost shock and confusion. She stared at him, completely disarmed. Timothy's heart pounded, yearning for some small signal that his feelings, whatever they were, would be welcome.

Leetra jerked her eyes away, breaking the trance, and pulled her hand from his. The shield was back in place—hard and emotionless. Without looking at him, she gathered her supplies and strode away.

Timothy sighed again and rubbed his forehead. He shouldn't be so disappointed. What had he expected? All he knew was that something had happened to him when he'd come upon her crying last winter. He'd seen something in her—something soft, vulnerable, wounded—that most people probably didn't know existed. She had her pride and stubbornness for sure, but underneath it was more. He thought it was only compassion he felt, but when he had left for Dorland last winter, she came to his mind strangely often, especially after meeting her family. After returning to Landale, she caught his attention more than anyone he had ever met, confusing him. A frustrating predicament when he was used to being so sure of things. He shook his head to himself. *Lord, it's Your will and Your desires I seek, not my own. Confusion is not from You. Give me clarity, wisdom, and direction. Whatever it is You want of me, that is what I desire.*

A hand clasped Timothy's shoulder, and Aaron stepped around in front of him, his expression sympathetic. "You gonna be all right?"

Timothy looked at him, understanding that his brother didn't refer to his arm. "I'll be fine."

"I think it's about time we got some rest."

Timothy agreed. He hadn't been this tired since he had worked for Harold back in Dunlow. Rising, he followed Aaron out of the infirmary. At the door, he glanced back, catching eyes with Leetra. She held them for only a moment before turning her back to him.

Kyrin rubbed her sore, sleep-deprived eyes and filled a fresh basin of water. Only a few more soldiers waited for someone to tend them.

"Kyrin."

She turned to Josef's kindly smile.

"Why don't you take your brother and you both get some sleep?" He nodded to Liam, who hadn't ceased working with them since he had come in.

"Are you sure you don't need me?"

Josef gave her a firm nod. "Leetra will be here for a while. We'll manage. You go on."

Kyrin turned to take off the bloodstained apron she wore, relief settling. She had seen so much pain and so many injuries throughout the day.

"Your brother impresses me," Josef said when Kyrin turned back to him. He was watching Liam across the room. "He's been a big help. I'd say he has a knack for this."

Kyrin stared at Liam. He had never displayed a talent for any unique skill set before. "Really?"

"Yes. When he's working with the wounded, you can see the shared pain and compassion, but it doesn't paralyze him as it might some. He works very calmly. I'd like to work with him more if there is ever the opportunity."

Kyrin continued to stare at Liam. He had been brought up and trained as a soldier, against his nature. What if healing people was what he had been called to do all along?

Morning. Dread settled inside Jace, weighing down his already heavy limbs. Soldiers filed out into the inky predawn, their expressions determined and hard, but not quite hiding the bone-deep weariness in their bloodshot eyes. Every morning Jace and the others gathered in the courtyard felt more and more as if it would be their last day. Parting grew harder too, the emotions difficult to contain when one was so tired.

The hardest part for Jace was Kyrin's struggle. She fought so hard to be brave, but this morning she looked fragile enough to crumble at the slightest touch. Even so, when she was near, she gripped his hand tightly as if meaning to keep him here with her. How deeply he wanted to stay, but Elôm controlled their destiny, and if it was his to die in battle, he had to face it. So, with a whispered, "I love you," they parted again.

Up on the wall, the men took their places on the blood-spattered stones, half their force focused to the left, and half to the right. Jace studied their ranks. They were thinner today. He could only hope and pray that Arcacia's would be too, but in all likelihood, fresh soldiers had filled the ranks on the wall overnight.

Though still in its scabbard, Jace rested his hand on his sword, waiting. The eastern sky hinted of sunlight, and the dragons already circled overhead. He flexed his fingers anxiously and looked over at Rayad. Where would he be if the man had never found him? Probably still a gladiator if he hadn't gone through with his plan to die in the arena or just killed himself. How hard would he have been by now?

"I never think enough of how incredible it was for you to see me fighting in the arena and then come upon me when you did. Or what it took for you to free me, knowing I could kill you."

Rayad turned a little to face him. "Did you consider it? Killing me?"

Jace shook his head, thinking back to that first night alone with Rayad and those that followed. "No. I thought about stealing Niton, but I never would have killed you."

Rayad smiled. "I didn't think so."

In a short time, the first sliver of the sun peeked over the horizon. Where was Arcacia's attack? Not even the firedrakes had made an appearance yet. The men were growing antsy, but the Arcacian camp seemed still. What were they up to now? What new and unpleasant surprise would they bring today? A warning of danger crawled along Jace's skin. He didn't dare hope that the army had given up.

Oppressive silence reigned. The sun grew higher until it was a full, golden globe above the distant mountains. The men murmured, some hopeful while others shared Jace's suspicion of something sinister at work.

Just when their confusion was at its height, a dragon glided down toward the wall.

"My lord!"

Jace recognized Captain Darq's voice. King Balen came forward to meet the crete as he landed in an open spot nearby. Trask and the others drew closer to hear the news.

"My lord, a large force is coming from the northwest," Darq reported, his face grave. "They march under the banners of Arcacia."

Like the ominous rumbling of thunder, dread rolled through them as they absorbed the implications of this news. It could only mean their forces in Amberin had failed. Their chance of victory was destroyed. Jace's heart sank. They had fought too hard for this. Surely Elôm intended them to have victory . . . didn't He? Jace reached out to Him, but it didn't change the fact that they now had enemy forces on both sides.

"There was another banner at the front," Darq said, "not of Arcacia. I couldn't get close because they are escorted by fire-drakes, but it appeared to be the colors of Samara with a white lily."

Balen's eyes grew wide, and he looked at General Mason. "That's the queen's banner."

BALEN STRODE TOWARD his waiting horse with General Mason at his side. What was Queen Rhosin doing at the head of the Arcacian invaders? None of the answers that presented themselves were good ones. If she had done what he was afraid she had . . .

He gritted his teeth and mounted his tall, bay gelding. The guards at the gate opened it just enough to let him and his general ride through. A couple hundred yards ahead, a group of Arcacian riders awaited under the parley flag. He glanced up. Most of the dragons had landed, lined up on the walls surrounding the keep, but a couple—Captain Darq, Talas, and Kaden—circled overhead as a precaution.

Drawing closer to the gathering, Balen recognized General Veshiron's daunting form. He must have taken a firedrake to Amberin after their meeting with him three days ago. And next to him, on a roan mare, sat the queen, her burgundy, gold, and white banner fluttering over her head. As they closed the distance, he could more clearly make out her features—dark, reddish hair with wisps of gray, and a hard, lined face. The very essence of a strong, capable woman. He couldn't recall a single memory of her smiling. She sat astride her horse, clothed in rich linen of deep blue and burgundy hues, a golden circlet holding back her long, loose hair. She didn't look like a prisoner, adding to Balen's suspicions.

He reined his horse a few feet away from the other riders.

"King Balen," General Veshiron said, his face smug with a lack of respect.

Balen ignored him, locking eyes with Rhosin. "What is the meaning of this?"

In the cold, unfeeling tone she always used with him, she answered, "I've surrendered Samara."

Balen's eyes slid closed. She had. They popped open again as his anger rose to the surface. "How could you do that?"

"For the people," Rhosin snapped. "I will not see them slaughtered needlessly."

Balen looked out at the force that had come from Amberin. It was large, yes, but nothing his men couldn't have handled, prepared as they were.

"We could have held them back."

Rhosin gave him a look of disgust, as if he had no knowledge of what he spoke. She had never viewed him as a competent leader. "For how long? Do you not think the emperor would have struck at us again, only harder? How many men are you willing to sacrifice?"

"We could have trusted Elôm to protect us and give us victory as He has in the past."

"And you think He would have spared the lives of our soldiers?"

Balen dug his fingers into the leather of the reins at her mocking tone. No wonder Samara had fallen so far if even she was so quick to dismiss the hand of Elôm. "If it was His will, yes."

The queen scoffed. "You are a fool and have no business leading our people."

Such venom stunned Balen, rendering him speechless. He wanted nothing but the best for their people. Couldn't she see that? He had never asked to be king. He had never even wanted it, but he had bowed to King Alton's wishes and accepted the position as a way to serve and protect his country. Now, because of the queen undermining him at every turn, he had failed.

The moment of silence gave General Veshiron the chance to speak. "Surrender the fortress and I will allow your people, including your soldiers, to live. If you refuse, the siege will continue until you are either annihilated or starved out. It's your choice. I suggest you choose wisely."

The gravity of the decision seemed to suck away all the air around Balen. His country's capital was now under enemy control while he, half his army, and their allies found themselves trapped inside their own keep. What choice did he have?

"The emperor promised us peaceful lives if we cooperate and submit to his rule," Rhosin told him.

For a woman of such pride, he couldn't believe she was going along with this. "You've been in contact with Daican?"

"Yes."

A horrible realization suddenly struck Balen. "Did you tell him of our plans?"

Rhosin stiffened as if caught, but tipped her chin up. "I did what I had to in order to save the lives of my people."

Balen breathed hard, fighting to control his raging thoughts. How could she have done this? Did she have any idea of the misery this would bring them? His voice shook. "You've brought down our country and handed it over to a tyrant. You betrayed our people."

Rhosin's lips pinched, her eyes ice cold. "I saved them."

They glared at each other before General Veshiron broke in again.

"As before, you have until dawn to make your final decision. Come first light, you'll see the true might of Arcacia."

It was done then. Samara had fallen.

447

Stiffly, Balen backed his horse up a few steps, shooting a hard look at the man before he locked his gaze once more on Rhosin.

"I am not the fool if you believe Daican will honor any of his promises."

Spinning his horse around, he rode back to the keep.

Deafening silence hung in the war room as King Balen and General Mason relayed the information from their meeting with Daican's force. Heat stirred Jace's blood. After how hard they had fought, after how many had *died*, the queen had simply let Daican's men march in? All the preparation, all the risks they had taken were for nothing. He glanced at Kyrin. She could have died. Her brothers could have died. He drew a deep breath to calm himself and focused again on Balen.

"I don't see that we have much choice but to surrender." The king grimaced, as if the words pained him. "We can't fight them. We were doomed from the start if the queen did indeed inform the emperor of our plans."

"What about Glynn and the others?" Leetra asked, the look of fury in her eyes matching what Jace felt inside. "Why didn't they warn us of this?"

Darq looked grimly at her, but didn't speak. He didn't have to. There could only be one answer. They were all dead.

Leetra's face went pale as this sank in, but then flushed in anger, her fist balling. Jace could imagine how Darq felt inside, even if he did a remarkable job of holding it in. Glynn had been like a brother to him. If he didn't have to hold everything together as a leader, his fury probably would have topped Leetra's. Hints of it flashed in his eyes.

Darq faced Balen again. "Unfortunately, I believe you're right. Surrender seems to be the only option."

"The problem is that General Veshiron made no mention of those of us from Landale in his offer of mercy," Trask said. "We're all fugitives, and the moment the emperor gets his hands on us, he'll no doubt execute us. There was no mention of the cretes either."

Balen nodded, grimacing. "You must all leave here."

"I don't know if that would be possible, even by dragon," Darq said. "They have us surrounded. Firedrakes patrol the skies and are posted along the wall. Some may get by, but not everyone."

Another silence followed. Jace looked over at Kyrin. If they didn't get out of here, they would all die. They would be paraded in front of the citizens of Valcré and be put to death on the platform both he and Kyrin had already stood on once before. He might even have to watch her die.

No.

He would find some way to get her out of here, no matter what. She must have sensed his gaze and looked at him, her eyes troubled. He tried to project calm to her. He would die before he let any of Daican's men lay a hand on her.

Before he could attempt to figure out how, Balen spoke.

"There is another way out." He glanced at Mason, who gave him a confirming nod. "It is a closely-guarded secret, known only by the kings and their closest advisors. A secret for just such a time as this."

Jace let out a heavy breath, hope returning.

"Underneath the fortress there is a hidden door to a tunnel that the giants built along the base of the wall. It connects to a series of caves in the mountains, which lead into a hidden valley. This would allow you to bypass Daican's forces without them ever knowing you left until it was too late."

"What about the dragons?" Darq asked.

"One at a time, the passage should be large enough for them."

Everyone seemed to breathe easier at this news.

"Thank you, my lord, for sharing this secret with us," Trask said.

"It's the least we can do after the aid you've provided us. I only regret that we can't make up for the men you lost needlessly."

True regret shadowed Balen's face, but Trask reassured him.

"We did what we had to do."

"You can be certain that those who fought here will not forget it. I will show you where the tunnel will lead you." He reached for a map of the area, but Mason stepped in.

"My lord, I believe you should go with them."

They looked at him.

"What?" Balen asked.

"General Veshiron offered mercy to the men, but not to you. You are the king of Samara and the biggest threat to the emperor. The simplest way to eliminate that threat is to kill you."

"I can't just leave Samara. How could I abandon the people while Daican takes over?"

"He may have control now, but are we just going to let him keep it?" Mason's gaze swept everyone in the room. "Are we just accepting that Daican has conquered us? Or are we going to do something about it? I say this fight doesn't end here."

Jace didn't think any of them had taken time yet to look beyond this moment of defeat, but the idea of overturning what had taken place here seemed to light a fire in everyone. They had lost this battle, yes, but that didn't have to mean the war was over.

Mason looked back at Balen. "I am asking you as both the general of your army and as your friend to leave now so that you can one day, Elôm willing, return as our king."

Balen responded with silence as he allowed this to sink in. From what Jace had seen of him since they had arrived in Samara, this would be an intensely difficult decision for him to make. One that surely needed more time than they had.

450

Before he could speak, a dragon roar thundered outside. Jace jerked, grabbing his sword. Had the General changed his mind? Would they descend upon the fortress and just slaughter everyone?

They bolted for the door as another roar rumbled through the corridors. Heat flushed through Jace's body as they rushed outside. Dragons and their riders streaked across the sky over the keep.

"What's going on?" Darq asked a nearby crete.

Before the man could answer, three panting dragons landed in the courtyard, their wings ripped and singed, and their scales streaked with both dried and fresh blood.

"Glynn!"

Darq rushed to the nearest dragon as its rider slid down. The moment Glynn's feet touched the ground, he nearly collapsed, but Darq caught him. Blood stained the crete lieutenant's breastplate, and his arm hung uselessly. Jace winced at the awkward angle. It was a wonder he had made it here in this condition. The two other cretes jumped down, sporting their own injuries, but none as serious as their commander's. Glynn grabbed Darq's jerkin with his good hand and tried to speak, but didn't have the strength. Darq and Talas picked him up.

They carried him straight to the infirmary, the rest of the group following. Leetra rushed ahead to prepare a cot. Laying Glynn down, Darq helped Josef remove his armor, and then stepped back to allow room for Leetra and Liam to help. When they cut off Glynn's shirt, they found several deep wounds near his neck and around his shoulder. Claw wounds. A couple of inches closer to his throat, and he wouldn't have made it here alive.

While Josef worked on cleaning the ragged lacerations, Leetra grabbed a waterskin and helped Glynn drink. This seemed to help revive him.

"Leetra," Josef said, "Liam can help me. Why don't you see to the others?"

She nodded, but remained close. Everyone did.

Glynn motioned for Darq. The captain knelt down near the cot.

"What happened?"

"They took us by surprise," Glynn gasped. "They came from all directions. There were more than we expected. It looked like the capital was surrendered without a fight, and the firedrakes tried to take us all out. It's like they knew what we were planning."

Darq's jaw went taut, the fury in his eyes much more noticeable than before. "They did." Glynn frowned, but Darq didn't go into an explanation. "Did anyone else make it out?"

Glynn shook his head, groaning. "We fought until there were only a few of us left. We tried to make it to the forest. We hid there as long as we could. We three are the only ones who made it here. We wanted to warn you."

Darq grasped his good shoulder. "I'm just glad you made it." His voice was even deeper than normal and a bit husky.

Josef looked at Darq and some of the other men. "His arm is broken. I need to set it and will need help holding him still."

A couple of the men moved closer, but Jace noticed Kyrin turn away. She looked deeply disturbed and tears pooled in her eyes. He put his arm around her, and she turned into him, burying her face in his chest. Wrapping his other arm around her, he held her tightly. Were it possible, he would not let her go until they reached the safety of camp.

Once the men were no longer needed, Trask assembled everyone from Landale, except for Liam, who stayed to help Josef.

"Let's gather our things and provisions for the trip back to Landale. I'll let the militia know, but I want to keep our means of escape between us for now so it's not spread to more people than necessary."

Everyone agreed.

"Will we have enough dragons to fly everyone back to camp?" Rayad asked.

"Most of us will have to ride double, but we'll manage," Trask answered.

Following this, the group dispersed to prepare. In the hall on the way to their rooms, Jace saw Kyrin wiping her eyes as she walked next to him.

"Will you be all right?"

She nodded. "It's just hard seeing Glynn injured so badly and thinking of all the riders they lost."

"I know," Jace murmured. Half of those Darq had brought from Dorland had been slaughtered. Did the queen realize how many people had died fighting for a country that wasn't even their own?

Kyrin shook her head, a hopeless look in her eyes. "You know, I almost believed we might win this."

Jace sighed. So had he.

He turned with the others into the men's sleeping quarters. Here, Holden helped him slip his chainmail off. It slid to the floor with a metallic thud, and Jace's straightened, but his shoulders sagged. Every muscle in his body seemed to ache at once. If he didn't keep moving, they would quickly stiffen up.

He stepped to a shelf along the wall, where a basin of clean water sat, and pulled off his sweat and blood-stained shirt. For a moment, discomfort gripped him. He had always avoided changing in front of strangers who would see his multitude of scars, but he let the sensation fade. The markings of his past might always remain, but Elon had erased the shame of it.

Elon.

Jace's heart thumped heavily. The battle had demanded everyone's full attention, but the memories he carried from Valcré now descended. Moisture bit his eyes before he could stop it, and he braced his hands on either side of the basin as he hung his head. First they had lost Elon, and now they had lost Samara. Where was Elôm in such crushing defeat?

Jace closed his eyes tightly against the onslaught of tears as the memories from Valcré and the last couple days of battle all melded into a frenzy of death, blood, and violence. He pulled in a hard breath, grasping for the peace of Elôm's presence. It did not come immediately, but his heart rate settled slowly, and he breathed more easily.

He still could not understand their defeat. Perhaps no answer would ever be forthcoming, but if he had learned one thing in the last couple of weeks, it was that they must move on. Dwelling in the past would accomplish nothing. The only thing left to them in this moment was to pray for a safe escape.

Balen stood at the top of the keep and looked out at Samara. It appeared from here that Daican's men had taken over Westing Castle and occupied the village—his home. Was it a peaceful takeover or were the soldiers wreaking havoc among his friends and neighbors? Would they harm his aunt and uncle or Baron Thomas? If he left, he wouldn't even get to say goodbye to them. His heart ached with the powerlessness to stop Daican's men or even offer comfort to his people. He tried to pray, but it hurt so much. He begged for the people's safety and for his own wisdom.

In the courtyard below, the cretes and Landale men were loading up their dragons. Even some of his own soldiers were packing supplies for themselves. While there weren't enough dragons to transport them all to Landale, Mason had encouraged them to leave and make their way to their home villages or hide out in the mountains. General Veshiron had said they would be shown mercy, but it held no guarantee. Best to get as many out as possible. They would all leave soon. It left him little time to make his decision.

At the sound of footsteps, he looked over his shoulder. Mason joined him, standing at his side and sharing the view. All was quiet for several moments, but for the banners snapping in the breeze.

"So you believe I should choose exile to Arcacia as opposed to surrendering myself to Daican?" He looked over at his general.

"I do only because I know Daican will kill you if you don't." Mason faced him. "If Samara is to rise again and throw off Daican's rule, she will need a strong king. She will need *you*. The people will eagerly rally around you when the time comes."

"*If* that time comes, and even then, who knows?"

"You doubt your influence over them?"

Balen sighed, and didn't answer. Was he truly the leader they believed he was? So far he had failed to bring any worthwhile change.

"You are the best king this country has seen in the last hundred years, and the people know it," Mason told him.

Balen almost laughed. It was hard to believe that when Samara had fallen for the first time in her history during his rule. "I'm not even of noble birth."

"Perhaps that's what makes you a great king. The people have always been eager to follow one of their own." Mason put his hand on Balen's shoulder. "When you saved King Alton from the wildcat, it was no accident or mere chance. Elôm put you there. He made you king, and I don't believe it was just so you could watch your country crumble into nothing."

Slowly, Balen nodded. "I only wish I knew what the right answer truly is. It seems right to stay and face this with my people, but if leaving could help them in the end . . ." He grimaced. "I don't want to go to save myself."

"I don't believe anyone could ever accuse you of that."

Balen thought it over once more and, though it went against everything inside him, he said, "All right, I'll go."

Mason smiled a sad, but relieved smile. "Good."

"But what of you? Daican could just as easily kill you."

"I know, but someone has to keep the men ready and keep hope alive. I'm willing to risk it."

The turmoil inside him would not cease, but Balen prayed he was doing the right thing as he looked once more out at his beloved Samara. *Please, save her.*

JUST AFTER SUNDOWN, Balen, dressed in simple leather and linen, led the entire group down into the storage rooms under the fortress. Jace looked around amongst the extra supplies and provisions, but didn't spot anything out of the ordinary. Though the solid stone walls didn't look capable of hiding a secret passage, Balen walked straight to the south wall and pressed one of the stones. A loud click echoed behind it. He and Mason then pushed together, and a large section opened inward, dust swirling, to reveal a pitch black hole. Holding a torch aloft, he illuminated stone stairs and a dark tunnel. Without prior knowledge, no one would have ever been able to find it.

Balen turned back into the room. Though he had chosen to go with them, his face revealed the struggle he still fought inside. No doubt he constantly second-guessed the decision.

He looked at his general. "Are you sure you won't need Josef here?"

Mason shook his head. "It will be difficult for the wounded to travel so far. They might need him. Besides, we have to send someone to look after you."

Despite the hardship of the moment, Balen smiled. They gripped each other's arms tightly.

"I'll be praying for your safety," Balen said.

Mason returned the smile. "And I'll be praying for your return."

With a deep breath, Balen turned to the secret door again, as if every moment spent here threatened to change his mind. "I'll go first. I know the way through the caves."

As he descended the stairs, Mason approached Trask.

"I wanted to give this to you. I think you and your people ought to have it."

Trask took the cloth bundle from the general and unfolded it to reveal a cerulean blue flag with gold trim and a gold sunburst appliqued in the center. Jace had never seen a flag of that sort before.

"It's the flag of Arcacia before Daican's grandfather changed the blue to black and incorporated Aertus and Vilai," Mason explained.

Everyone stared at it with new interest. The sun shining in the middle was the exact opposite of the moons that so many people in Arcacia worshipped. Just one old piece of history told the whole story of their downfall.

"I thought it looked familiar," Trask said. "I saw a drawing of it once in one of my father's books. I didn't think any of them existed anymore."

Mason brushed his fingers along the thick, rich colored cloth. "I found it at a market once and felt compelled to buy it. I see it as a symbol of all that was once good in Arcacia. I want you to take it with the prayer that, one day, that good will be restored."

"Thank you very much." Trask refolded it almost reverently, and Jace caught a look in his eyes that said he had an idea forming.

Trading their final goodbyes, Trask followed Balen into the murky darkness of the tunnel, his dragon coming along behind. As Balen had said, the tunnel was just wide and tall enough for the animals to go single file. When it came time, Jace motioned to Kyrin, but she remained rooted in place, ill-concealed fear breaking through her expression. Her throat moved as she swallowed.

"Caves," she murmured.

At once Jace remembered when he had nearly refused to ride Gem over his fear of heights. Kyrin had admitted her fear of caves to make him feel better.

"Come on, Kyrin," Marcus coaxed. He stood nearby with Kaden and Liam, insisting on walking part of the way. "You know you have to go in."

Kyrin eyed her brothers. "I know." She shook her head. "It's just . . . hard. No thanks to you three."

They traded confused looks.

She raised her brows at them. "You don't remember that time in the cave back home?"

They shook their heads.

"Well, I do," Kyrin muttered. She took a deep breath.

"It's no different from the dungeon in Auréa," Kaden offered.

Kyrin stared at him. "That's not exactly a pleasant memory either."

Jace certainly agreed with her on that. He stepped forward, offering his hand. She looked at it, and then up into his eyes.

"Come on," he said gently. "No one or nothing will scare you in these caves. Not with me here. I promise."

A hint of a smile came to her lips, and she took his hand.

To the two female dragons waiting on the stairs, Jace commanded, "Gem, Ivy, réma."

Then, holding Kyrin close, he started for the tunnel. He paused with her when she looked back.

"Marcus, you make sure you stop and get on one of the dragons if you need to. Liam, you keep an eye on him."

They both chuckled, and Jace smiled.

Lighting a torch from the one Mason held, he led Kyrin down toward the glow of the other torches ahead. Cool, damp air enveloped them with the strong scent of earth. The tunnel walls were roughhewn for the first fifty yards, but then they took a sharp left turn, where huge blocks of precisely-fitted stones surrounded them. This must be the base of the wall. Thick cobwebs hung down from the ceiling, but everyone ahead had already cleared most of them.

Jace noticed Kyrin's hand relaxing in his. "Doing all right?"

She nodded and smiled up at him.

The dragons shuffled along behind them, their loud snuffles blending with their footsteps as they took in the scents. Thank Elôm they were all so well behaved or this trek could quickly turn dangerous. He could just imagine the fire-engulfed panic that could ensue, but he kept it to himself. Kyrin didn't need anything to worry about.

On and on they went. It was difficult to tell how long or how far when everything looked the same. He imagined walking the path on top of the wall, but this seemed longer. After a while, Kyrin's grip tightened again, her expression pensive. She glanced at him.

"Just a little claustrophobic," she said, a bit breathless. "I'll manage."

"I'm sure it's not too much farther." He hoped not, for her sake.

Jace estimated that about two hours had passed when, at last, the tunnel opened up into a vast cavern. At least here they wouldn't feel quite so closed in. He raised his torch, illuminating the impressive natural structures all around them. Just to their right, water dripped loudly into a clear underground lake. He looked again at Kyrin. This time she peered around in interest.

"Caves aren't so bad," he said.

She shook her head. "Not really."

They pushed on, their caravan of people and dragons winding along an unseen path, torches bobbing in the darkness. Good thing Balen knew the way or they would all become hopelessly lost.

Another hour passed before, finally, Jace spotted the subtle glow of moonlight ahead. Beside him, Kyrin let out a sigh. Several minutes later, they emerged from the cave system into a small valley lit up by Aertus and Vilai hovering over the eastern mountain peaks.

Gathering in the center of the valley, they waited as, one by one, their entire group joined them—men, cretes, and dragons. As soon as everyone was present, Balen spoke.

"We'll have a good few hours of darkness before the Arcacians know we're gone. I suggest we head a little further east and then south to be safe."

Trask and the others agreed, and all turned for their dragons. Before letting her go, Jace gave Kyrin's hand a slight squeeze.

"Thank you," she said.

She walked over to Ivoris and mounted up with Liam. Beside her, Kaden mounted Exsis where Marcus already sat. Taking one of the militiamen with him, Jace turned for Gem. Once everyone without a dragon had found someone to ride with and Balen had bid a difficult farewell to his remaining men, the entire company took to the air, flying low over the mountains until Stonehelm was far behind them.

The sun peeked above the horizon as they gathered on the Arcacian plains for breakfast and a short rest. Jace rubbed his sore eyes. After the days of battle and flying throughout the night, everyone could have used several hours of sleep, but General Veshiron would discover their escape any time now. They didn't have the luxury of more than a brief pause to let the dragons catch their breaths.

With a hard roll and fruit in hand, Jace sank down next to Kyrin and her brothers. They ate in relative silence. The shock of their defeat still hovered like a cold shadow. He wasn't sure what they were thinking, but for him it was strange to be in Arcacia again. It felt different somehow—bleaker, darker. Half of their continent now lay under Daican's power. How could they ever stop him? Any hopes to do so seemed dashed now, despite General Mason's enthusiasm yesterday. What could they ever do after a defeat like this?

He sighed. He shouldn't think such bleak thoughts, but it was hard when he looked around at everyone, so tired and defeated.

This was all that stood of their effort in Samara.

Swallowing his breakfast down hard, Jace glanced to the east. A man walked toward them. Jace's heart nearly punched a hole through his ribs. He pushed to his feet, unsure if he could believe his own weary eyes.

"Elon!" he gasped.

The commotion of movement and astonished murmurs surrounded him, but he could not take his gaze away from the familiar figure. No matter how many times he blinked, expecting to see a stranger, the face never changed. It *was* Him. As He drew near, Elon smiled, and tears filled Jace's eyes. Trembling, this time from awe and joy, Jace dropped to his knees.

"My Lord."

Quiet thuds sounded around him as all went to their knees. He was here. He was *alive*!

After a moment, Elon reached down for Jace, drawing him to his feet. "Rise, all of you."

Jace looked into His eyes, the incredible, consuming love washing through him, filling up his soul.

"How?" he breathed. "You died."

Elon nodded in confirmation of this truth. "But death has no hold or victory over Me, and neither does it on any who trust in My name."

He moved past Jace, His attention shifting between the others of the group.

"I know you mourn your defeat in Samara."

Slowly, Balen nodded. "It is a difficult loss to understand. We prepared as much as we could and trusted Elôm for victory."

"You, yes, but so many others did not. Samara must learn and remember the faith she once had. Arcacia as well. Sometimes adversity is what's needed to produce that faith. Samara's defeat may yet be her victory if it turns her people's hearts back towards My Father."

Balen bowed his head, nodding again. When he looked up, the reluctance that had been so present since yesterday revealed itself strongly. "Did I make the right choice in leaving?"

"Yes," Elon told him in a tone of comforting reassurance. "General Veshiron would have had you executed in front of your men, along with the cretes and anyone with ties to Landale."

Balen released a long breath, and everyone looked at each other. The entire group would have been killed. Jace moved closer to Kyrin, his heartbeat shallow as he considered it.

Elon moved deeper into their temporary camp. "You have wounded who need tending."

He reached Marcus first and touched his side. By the look of awe on Marcus's face, Jace knew he was immediately healed of his wound.

One at a time, Elon healed each of their wounded soldiers and even their battle-scarred dragons. Despite what they had experienced and seen in Samara, everyone wore radiant smiles. With Him in their midst, even their defeat didn't seem quite so dark.

When He finished, He came to the center of the group again. "Your fight is not finished. You have much yet to do. You must continue to share the knowledge of Me and My Father and of salvation. You will be My witnesses to Ilyon."

"Can You stay with us?" Jace asked, longing in his heart transferring to his voice.

Elon smiled gently at him. "I must return to My Father, but don't fear. I am giving you My Spirit as a helper in the days ahead. You are never alone. You can call to Me wherever you are, and I will hear you. I will be with you always, until the end of time."

With these words, He rose heavenward and bright light engulfed them. When it had faded, He was gone. For a long moment, they all just stared into the sky, but a sudden breeze rippled through their camp. When it touched Jace, cool and soft, it seemed to seep into him and fill him with a strength and power he had never known before. He looked at the others. The awe on their faces said that everyone else felt it too.

Jace looked to the sky again. To come from such darkness to this moment was something he knew he would never fully comprehend, but he praised Elôm for how his life had been transformed.

A moment later, Kyrin's hand slipped into his. He dropped his gaze to her face. With Elon's Spirit inside him and Kyrin at his side, he was ready to face whatever lay ahead of them. As Elon had said, their fight was not yet finished.

CHARACTERS & INFORMATION

RETURNING CHARACTERS

Aaron—A half-crete and former miner from Dunlow. Timothy's older brother.

Aertus (AYR - tuhs)—Arcacia's male moon god.

Altair (AL - tayr)—Kyrin's family name.

Anne—The daughter of Sir John Wyland.

Aric (AHR - ick)—Emperor Daican's head of security.

Daican (DYE - can)—The emperor of Arcacia.

Davira (Duh - VEER - uh)—Daican's daughter, the princess of Arcacia.

Elôm (EE - lohm)—The one true God of Ilyon.

Falcor Tarn—A crete traitor and Leetra's former fiancé.

Glynn (GLIN)—A crete from Dorland. Captain Darq's lieutenant.

Goler—An Arcacian army captain and bitter rival of Trask.

Grey—The baron of Landale.

Holden (HOHL - den)—A former informant for Daican but now part of the resistance.

Jace—A half-ryrik former slave and gladiator.

Jeremy—Lenae's son.

John Wyland—A retired knight.

Kaden (KAY - den)—Kyrin's twin brother.

Kyrin (KYE - rin)—A young Arcacian woman with the ability to remember everything.

Leetra Almere (LEE - truh AL - meer)—A female crete from Dorland. Talas's cousin.

Lenae (LEH - nay)—A widowed Landale woman.

Liam—Kyrin's older brother.

Lydia—Kyrin's mother and the General's daughter.

Maera (MAYR - uh)—Kyrin's dappled buckskin horse.

Marcus—Kyrin's eldest brother and captain of the Landale militia.

Marcus Veshiron (Veh - SHEER - on)—Kyrin's grandfather and an Arcacian general.

Meredith—Lenae's adoptive daughter.

Mick—A resistance member from a wealthy mining family.

Michael—Kyrin's younger brother.

Niton (NYE - tuhn)—Jace's black horse.

Rayad (RAY - ad)—One of Jace's close friends and mentor.

Richard Blaine—A knight and old family friend of Daican.

Ronan "Ronny"—Kyrin's youngest brother.

Sam "Endathlorsam"—A talcrin man and former scholar from Tarvin Hall.

Talas Folkan (TAL - as FAHL - kan)—A friendly crete from Dorland. Leetra's cousin.

Tane "Imhonriltane"—Sam's nephew.

Timothy—A half-crete young man from Dunlow. Aaron's younger brother.

Trask—Resistance leader and son of Baron Grey.

Trev—A former member of Daican's security force. Now part of the resistance.

Tyra—Jace's black wolf.

Verus Darq (VAYR - uhs DARK)—A crete captain from Dorland.

Vilai (VI - lye)—Arcacia's female moon god.

Warin (WOHR - in)—An Arcacian man active in the resistance. Lifelong friend of Rayad.

New Characters

Aelos (AY - lohs)—One of Elon's mysterious companions.
Alice—A refugee at camp.
Baron Thomas—The Baron of Westing.
Charles Ilvaran (Ill - VAHR - an)—Henry and Evelyn's son, the Viscount Ilvaran.
Elanor—Rothas and Rachel's daughter.
Elian (EL - ee - an)—Head of security at Ashwood.
Elon (EE - lahn)—Rumored Savior.
Evelyn Ilvaran—Henry's wife, the Countess of Dunrick.
General Mason—Samaran general.
Henry Ilvaran—The Earl of Dunrick.
Hyde (HIDE)—One of Daican's men working with Falcor.
James—Rothas and Rachel's son.
King Balen (BAY - len)—The king of Samara.
Mister Hagen—Alice's father.
Rachel Cantan—Rothas's wife and the daughter of Henry Ilvaran.
Riyel (RYE - ell)— One of Elon's mysterious companions.
Rothas Cantan (ROTH - uhs CAN - tan)—Emperor Daican's war strategist.
Tina—A maid at Ashwood.
Walton—The butler at Ashwood.

DRAGONS

Brayle (BRAYL)—Holden's dragon.
Exsis (EX - sis)—Kaden's dragon.
Gem—Jace's dragon.
Ivoris "Ivy" (EYE - vohr - is)—Kyrin's dragon.
Shalmar (SHAL - mahr)—Warin's dragon.
Storm—Talas's dragon.

LOCATIONS

Arcacia (Ahr - CAY - shee - uh)—The largest country of the Ilyon mainland.

Ashwood—Home of Rothas Cantan.

Auréa (Awr - RAY - uh)—Daican's palace in Valcré.

Dorland—Ilyon's easternmost country. Inhabited by cretes and giants.

Fort Rivor (RYE - vohr)—Arcacia's largest military fort located southeast of Valcré.

Ilyon (IL - yahn)—The known world.

Landale—A prosperous province in Arcacia ruled over by Baron Grey.

Marlton Hall—Home of Sir John Wyland.

Samara (Sa - MAHR - uh)—A small country north of Arcacia.

Stonehelm—Samara's greatest stronghold along its southern border.

Valcré (VAL - cray)—Arcacia's capital city.

Westing Castle—Home of Baron Thomas.

Race Profiles

RYRIKS

HOMELAND: Wildmor

PHYSICAL APPEARANCE: Ryriks tend to be large-bodied, muscular, and very athletic. They average between six, to six and a half feet tall. They have thick black hair that is usually worn long. All have aqua-blue colored eyes that appear almost luminescent, especially during intense or emotional situations. Their ears are pointed, which makes them very distinct from the other races. They have strong, striking features, though they can pass as humans by letting their hair hide their ears and avoiding eye contact. Ryriks typically dress in rough, sturdy clothing—whatever they find by stealing.

PHYSICAL CHARACTERISTICS: Ryriks are a very hardy race and incredibly resistant to physical abuse and sickness; however, they have one great weakness. Their lungs are highly sensitive to harsh air conditions, pollutants, and respiratory illness. Under these conditions, their lungs bleed. Short exposure causes great discomfort, but is not life-threatening. More severe, prolonged exposure, however, could cause their lungs to fill with blood and suffocate them. It is said to be a curse from choosing to follow the path of evil. Ryriks' eyes are very sensitive, able to pick out the slightest movement, and they can see well in the dark. Both their sense of hearing and smell are very keen—much higher than that of humans. In times of great distress or anger, ryriks can react with devastating bursts of speed and strength.

RACE CHARACTERISTICS: Ryriks are the center of fireside tales all across Ilyon. They are seen as a savage people, very fierce and cunning. To other races, they seem to have almost animal-like instincts; therefore, it is commonly believed they don't have souls. They are a hot-blooded people and quick to action, especially when roused. They have quick tempers and are easily driven to blind rage. They prefer decisive action over conversation. Most have a barbaric thirst for bloodshed and inflicting pain. They view fear and pain as weaknesses and like to see them in others. They are typically forest dwellers and feel most comfortable in cover they can use to their advantage.

SKILLS: Ryriks are highly skilled in the woods and living off the land. They are excellent hunters and especially proficient in setting ambushes. They're experts in taming and raising almost any type of animal. They make the fiercest of any warriors. A ryrik's favorite weapons are a heavy broadsword and a large dagger. Ryriks aren't masters of any type of craft or art. Most of their possessions come from stealing. What they can't gain by thieving, they make for themselves, but not anything of quality. They think art, music, or any such thing to be frivolous. Most ryriks can't read or write and have no desire to.

SOCIAL: Ryriks are not a very social race. Settlements are scattered and usually small. They have no major cities. Families often live on small farms in the forest and consist of no more than four to six people. Children are typically on their own by the time they are sixteen or seventeen—even younger for some males. Ryriks have a poor view of women. They see them as a necessity and more of a possession than a partner. Once claimed, a ryrik woman almost never leaves her home. She is required to care for the farm while the men are away. Most ryrik men group together in raiding parties, pillaging and destroying unprotected villages and preying on unsuspecting travelers. Ryriks have an intense hatred of other races, particularly humans.

GOVERNMENT: Ryriks have no acting government. Raiding parties and settlements are dictated by the strongest or fiercest ryrik, so the position can be challenged by anyone and changes often.

PREFERRED OCCUPATIONS: The vast majority of ryriks are thieves. A few hold positions as blacksmiths and other necessary professions.

FAITH: Ryriks disdain religion of any kind. They were the first to rebel against King Elôm and led others to do so as well.

TALCRINS

HOMELAND: Arda

PHYSICAL APPEARANCE: Talcrins are a tall, powerful people. Talcrin men are seldom less than six feet tall. They have rich, dark skin and black hair of various lengths and styles. Their most unique feature besides their dark skin is their metallic-looking eyes. They have a very regal, graceful appearance. Men often dress in long, expertly crafted jerkins, while women wear simple but elegant flowing gowns of rich colors, particularly deep purple.

RACE CHARACTERISTICS: Talcrins are considered the wisest of all Ilyon's peoples. Some of their greatest pleasures are learning and teaching. Reading is one of their favorite pastimes. They have excellent memories and intellects. Talcrins are a calm people, adept at hiding and controlling strong emotion. They are peace-loving and prefer to solve problems with diplomacy, but if all else fails, they can fight fiercely. They have a deep sense of morality, justice, loyalty, and above all, honesty. They are an astute people and don't miss much, particularly when it comes to others. Besides learning, they are also fond of art and music. Most talcrins are city dwellers, preferring large cities where libraries and universities can be found. Of all the races, they live the longest and reach ages of one hundred fifty, though many live even longer. Because of this, they age slower than the other races. Talcrin names are known to be very long, though they use shortened versions outside of Arda.

SKILLS: Talcrins excel in everything pertaining to books, languages, legal matters, and history, and are excellent at passing on their wisdom. They are often sought as advisors for their ability to easily think through situations and assess different outcomes. They are master storytellers and delight in entertaining people in this way. Though they strive for peace, most talcrin men train as warriors when they are young. They make incredible fighters who are highly skilled with long swords, high-power longbows, and spears. When not reading, many talcrin women enjoy painting and weaving. Their tapestries are among the most sought after. Both men and women enjoy music and dancing. They are expert harpists. Beautiful two-person dances are very popular in talcrin culture and are considered an art form. Metal-working is another skill in which talcrins are considered experts. Their gold and silver jewelry and armor are some of the finest in Ilyon.

SOCIAL: Talcrins are a family-oriented people and fiercely loyal to both family and friends alike. Families are average in size, with between three to seven children. Men are very protective of their families and believe their well-being is of utmost importance. Their island country of Arda is almost exclusively populated with talcrins. Scholars from the Ilyon mainland often come to visit their famous libraries, but other races rarely settle there. Many talcrins inhabit the mainland as well, but are widely scattered. The highest population is found in Valcré, the capital of Arcacia. They get along well with all races, except for ryriks. Though generally kindhearted, they can hold themselves at a distance and consider others ignorant.

GOVERNMENT: The governing lord in Arda is voted into authority by the talcrin people and serves for a period of two years at a time, but may be elected an unlimited number of times. His word is seen as final, but he is surrounded by a large number of advisors, who are also chosen by the people, and is expected to include them in all decisions. Those living on the mainland are under the authority of the king or lord of whichever country they inhabit.

PREFERRED OCCUPATIONS: Scholars, lawyers, and positions in government are the talcrins' choice occupations, as well as positions in artistry.

FAITH: Talcrins are the most faithful of all races in following King Elôm. The majority of those living in Arda are firm believers, but this has become less so among those living on the mainland.

CRETES

HOMELAND: Arcacia and Dorland

PHYSICAL APPEARANCE: Cretes are a slim people, yet very agile and strong. They are the shortest of Ilyon's races, and stand between five foot and five foot ten inches tall. It is rare for one to reach six feet. They are brown-skinned and have straight, dark hair. Black is most common. It is never lighter than dark brown unless they are of mixed blood. Both men and women let it grow long. They like to decorate their hair with braids, beads, leather, and feathers. Crete men do not grow facial hair. A crete's eyes are a bit larger than a human's, and very bright and colorful. A full-blood crete will never have brown eyes. They dress in earthy colors and lots of leather. All cretes have intricate brown tattoos depicting family symbols and genealogy.

PHYSICAL CHARACTERISTICS: The crete's body is far more resilient to the elements and sickness than other races. They are very tolerant of the cold and other harsh conditions. Their larger eyes give them excellent vision and enable them to see well in the dark. They don't need as much sleep as other races and sleep only for a couple of hours before dawn. Their bodies heal and recuperate quickly.

RACE CHARACTERISTICS: Cretes are tree dwellers and never build on the ground except when absolutely necessary. They love heights and flying and have a superb sense of balance. They are very daring and enjoy a thrilling adventure. They mature a bit more quickly than other races. A crete is considered nearly an adult by fifteen or sixteen and a mature adult by eighteen. They are a high-energy race and prone to taking quick action. Cretes are straightforward and blunt, coming across as rather abrupt at times. They are not the most patient, nor understanding, and they have high expectations for themselves and others. They are a stubborn, proud, and independent people, and don't like to conform to the laws and standards of other races.

SKILLS: Cretes are excellent climbers, even from a very young age, able to race up trees effortlessly and scale the most impassible cliffs and obstacles. Because of this fearlessness and love for heights, they are renowned dragon trainers. They are masters at blending in with their surroundings and moving silently, which makes them excellent hunters. All crete males, as well as many females, are trained as skilled warriors. Their choice weapons are bows and throwing knives, though they can be equally skilled with lightweight swords. Cretes are also a musical race, their favorite instruments being small flutes and hand drums.

SOCIAL: Cretes live in close communities and often have very large families, maintaining close connections with extended family. They are very proud of their family line and make sure each generation is well-educated in their particular traditions and histories. They consider it a tragedy when a family line is broken. Still, all children are cherished, both sons and daughters. Every crete is part of one of twelve clans named after various animals. Men are always part of whichever clan they are born into. When a woman marries, she becomes part of her husband's clan. Though cretes are proud of their clans, they show no discrimination, and their cities always have a mixed-clan population. Cretes are hospitable to their own people and well-known acquaintances, but suspicious and aloof when it comes to strangers. It takes time to earn one's trust, and even longer to earn their respect.

GOVERNMENT: The highest governing official is the crete lord. He is essentially a king, but directly below him are twelve men who serve as representatives of each of the twelve clans. The lord is unable to make any drastic decisions without the cooperation of the majority of the twelve clan leaders. Each crete city has a governing official who answers to the twelve representatives. Directly below him is a council of men consisting of the elders of each major family in the city. In the past, the cretes ultimately fell under the authority of the king of Arcacia, but with the deterioration of the Arcacian government, they've pulled away from its rule.

PREFERRED OCCUPATIONS: Hunters, dragon trainers, and warriors are the favored occupations of the cretes. But leather-working is another desirable occupation. This is typically done by the women of a household.

FAITH: Most cretes have remained faithful to King Elôm, or at least are aware of Him.

GIANTS

(Also known as **Dorlanders**)

HOMELAND: Dorland

PHYSICAL APPEARANCE: Giants are the largest race in Ilyon. Standing between seven to nine feet tall, they tower above most other peoples. They are heavily built and powerful, but can be surprisingly quick and agile when the occasion calls for it. They are fair-skinned, and their hair and eye color varies greatly like humans. They dress simply and practically in sturdy, homespun clothing.

RACE CHARACTERISTICS: Despite their great size and power, giants are a very quiet and gentle people. They dislike confrontation and will avoid it at all cost. They are naturally good-natured and honest, and enjoy simple lives and hard work. To those who don't take the time to get to know them, they can seem slow and ignorant, but they are very methodical thinkers, thinking things over carefully and thoroughly. While not quick-witted, they are very knowledgeable in their fields of interest. They are generally a humble race and easy to get along with. They tend to see the best in everyone. Their biggest failing is that, in their methodical manner, it often takes too long for them to decide to take action when it is needed.

SKILLS: Giants are very skilled in anything to do with the land. Much of the gold, silver, and jewels in Ilyon come from the giants' mines in the mountains of northern Dorland. They are also excellent builders. While lacking in style or decoration, the architecture of their structures is strong and durable, built to last for centuries. They have often been hired to build fortifications and strongholds. Unlike other races, it is not common for giants to train as warriors. Only the king's men are required to be able to fight. While not a musical or artistic race, giants do love a good story, and they've been said to have, beautiful, powerful singing voices.

SOCIAL: Giants typically live in tight farming or mining communities. Family and friends are important. Families usually consist of two to three children who remain in the household for as long as they wish. Many children remain on their parents' farm after they are married, and the farm expands. Giants are known throughout Ilyon for their hospitality. They'll invite almost anyone into their homes. Some people even find them too hospitable and generous. They are very averse to cruelty, dishonesty, and seeing their own hurt. Despite moving slowly in most other areas, justice is swift and decisive.

GOVERNMENT: Giants are ruled over by a king who comes to power through succession. However, most communities more or less govern themselves. The only time the king's rule is evident is when large numbers of giants are required to gather for a certain purpose.

PREFERRED OCCUPATIONS: The majority of giants are farmers, miners, or builders.

FAITH: Almost all giants agree King Elôm is real, but in their simplistic and practical mindset, fewer giants have actually come to a true trusting faith.

AUTHOR NOTES

Thank you so much for reading *Samara's Peril!* These are a sampling of the notes I wrote when first planning the book. I hope you will enjoy this little peek into how my stories come together.

- July 17, 2011 -

At some point in the story, I think Jace should meet his mother. It would be fascinating. Now I'm thinking the man she ended up marrying is not a good man and is really cruel to Jace. Maybe he even gets him arrested for something, perhaps a false accusation. I'm also thinking Jace will have half-siblings. Perhaps he has a brother who is cruel like his father, but maybe his sister is kind. Now I have to figure out when this reunion takes place.

- October 2, 2011 -

I was just thinking it would be really cool to have Jace's mother come from a noble family. I'm thinking her father could be a prominent noble. That would give Jace noble blood. That's definitely an interesting thought.

- November 18, 2011 -

It's funny how many random people are turning up in this series. My latest actor casting is for the king of Samara. I've mentioned his existence briefly in Resistance, but since he doesn't come in until book three, I didn't give much thought to him other than he is fairly young and a good king. So, this morning, I saw a poster of Christ Hemsworth from Snow White and the Huntsman and my brain was instantly like, "That is so the king of Samara." LOL I had sort of been considering it before, but this confirmed it. It also got me thinking about his character. He's a pretty cool king. Pretty much the exact opposite of Daican. He's the kind of king who will help out around the castle or go till the fields. Yeah, he's cool.

– December 3, 2011 –

I thought of a good idea why they would go see Jace's family. What if his mother's husband is a strategist and he's working with the emperor? Perhaps they go so Kyrin can sneak into his office to memorize all his maps and strategies. The thing is, they can't steal them because he will know and simply change the plans and no one else can be in there long enough to replicate them. Kyrin only has to look at them to remember all the details.

– December 18, 2011 –

I have this idea. I've been thinking about Kyrin and Jace's relationship. Obviously, there's a point where it becomes common knowledge they love each other. I keep imagining this scene right before battle after they've said goodbye and Jace turns back around and kisses Kyrin and that's the turning point in their relationship. It's such a cute scene.

- December 23, 2011 -

I was thinking about Liam the other night. What if his gift is healing? I think that would be neat. They could meet a healer at some point who he can learn from.

- March 20, 2012 -

I was thinking about Jace in book three and why he's so down on himself. What if he accidentally kills someone?

- Maye 22, 2012 -

What if Timothy falls in love with Leetra? I have no idea how I feel about that. They do not seem to go together...and yet...I don't know. Leetra would have to grow quite a bit, but that would be interesting. She'd have to deal with her pride issues first. It might be cool. We shall see.

- January 1, 2013 -

I think this is the book where Kaden becomes captain of the dragon riders. They've gotten more dragons over the winter and Kaden's been helping to train the riders. Trask and Darq see how well the men respond to him and decide to make him the captain. I was thinking it would be cool to have a scene where Kaden asks Marcus for his advice in leading. I think it would be sweet since they tend to clash.

- February 16, 2013 -

I was just thinking about Rachel. I always pictured her as an only child, but I just realized that's the same with Lydia. I don't want them both to be only children, so what if Rachel has an older brother? And I think he should be a believer too, and Rachel is really close to him. He probably tried to help her find Jace when he was taken away. He could also help in Jace's escape. Yeah, I'm liking him. Now he needs a name.

- March 8, 2013 -

I had some thoughts about Jace and how badly he wants to know if he truly has a soul. So, why doesn't he just go to Elon and ask? Well, he's afraid. Now that he has the chance to actually find out, he's too scared.

- March 29, 2013 -

I was thinking about Elon appearing to them. I think, after His sacrifice, things will be pretty solemn. And then, of course, after their defeat, they'll really be wondering what to do since everything seems to have gone wrong. Their journey back to Landale will look pretty bleak, so it's the perfect time to have Elon appear to them and give them hope. I think it would be perfect for the end scene of the book, giving hope for the rest of the series.

- April 3, 2013 -

I've been contemplating how Timothy and Leetra's relationship progresses. I had an idea last night. What if Timothy gets a minor wound during the battle and she tends to him? It could be a cute moment. I can see her working on him and then they end up just looking at each other. Maybe Timothy touches her hand. Then she sort of freaks out and walks away. I'm thinking Aaron will see it and try to encourage Timothy afterward. That would be a good way to get Timothy's feelings out in the open and show that Leetra isn't falling as quickly.

- April 24, 2013 -

I think Marcus should get wounded—stabbed or something. Not life-threatening, but not just a scratch either. And I think it should happen while defending Liam. It would be a good moment and will probably happen during their second day of battle.

- April 25, 2013 -

I think, as he's getting ready to fight, Kaden feels sick and really unsure, but that also makes him feel weak. He'll ask Marcus if he's afraid. After all, this is the first time Marcus has been in battle too. Marcus tells him that he is afraid and there'd be something wrong if he wasn't.

About the Author

JAYE L. KNIGHT is an award-winning author and shameless tea addict with a passion for Christian fantasy. Armed with an active imagination and love for adventure, Jaye weaves stories of truth, faith, and courage with a message that, even in the deepest darkness, God's love shines as a light to offer hope. When not writing fantasy, she dabbles in contemporary romance under the name Jaye Elliot.

To learn more about Jaye and her work, visit:
www.jayelknight.com

Milton Keynes UK
Ingram Content Group UK Ltd.
UKHW010215010524
442030UK00014B/177/J